A ROOM FULL OF
NAKED MEN

Hope you enjoy!

Leslie Whitson

Oliver

A ROOM FULL OF NAKED MEN

LESLIE WHITSON

TATE PUBLISHING
AND ENTERPRISES, LLC

Published by Tate Publishing & Enterprises, LLC
127 E. Trade Center Terrace | Mustang, Oklahoma 73064 USA
1.888.361.9473 | www.tatepublishing.com

Tate Publishing is committed to excellence in the publishing industry. The company reflects the philosophy established by the founders, based on Psalm 68:11,
"The Lord gave the word and great was the company of those who published it."

Book design copyright © 2016 by Tate Publishing, LLC. All rights reserved.
Cover design by Joshua Rafols
Interior design by Mary Jean Archival

Published in the United States of America

ISBN: 978-1-68207-074-1
1. Fiction / Humorous
2. Fiction / Satire
15.11.12

PROLOGUE

Lucinda Hardin-Powell pulled open the drawer to her bathroom vanity and peered into an abyss of eyeliner, rouge, and fifty-three shades of nail polish. Her pursed lips showed she was giving those fifty-three shades some serious consideration.

She pulled one, then two, and only stopped when she had seven shades of pinky red on the vanity's top. Picking each one up, one at a time, she pressed them beside a blouse, with a profusion of red flowers on a black background, that she held in her other hand.

"Hon?"

She was interrupted by the voice of her husband, BJ, coming from down the hall. She didn't answer him.

He called her again, "Hon, something in the kitchen is making a beeping sound!"

"The timer on the oven," she mumbled to herself. She pushed six of the bottles of nail polish back into the abyss and shut the drawer. Picking up the remaining bottle, she turned it in the light from the bathroom sconce.

"Yes," she said half out loud, "fuchsia!"

Tomorrow, when she showed up for her volunteer job at the Art Guild, she would be as color coordinated as anyone else there, maybe even more color coordinated. That would be nice. Lucinda liked being better than others.

———✦———

Across town, Clara Dorphman was going through the closet of her bedroom. She had opened the double doors to the closet to get her old walking shoes. The ones that were painfully out of fashion and ugly were most comfortable on her feet.

Clara, the only occupant of her large old home, wanted to take a little walk around the house and look at the spring flowers. But easily distracted, she began to straighten up the pile of other shoes on the floor of the closet; and when that was done, she started on the collection of expensive scarves that hung on the back of one door.

The late-afternoon walk was no longer on her mind. Instead, she was admiring her scarves. Each one had a story—gifts from her sons, daughters-in-law, grandchildren, purchases on shopping trips to exclusive stores in Nashville or Bowling Green.

One after another, she tried to remember occasions, people, holidays—then she pulled one from the door.

Clutching it to her, she remembered the first Sulphur Springs Art Guild's Spring Fling Art Show and Antique Auction. That was nine, no...ten years ago. Her late husband had given it to her for the occasion.

She turned the shiny silk over in her hands. *Such a pretty shade of fuchsia*, she thought.

But then a classic black-and-white by Vera Wang caught her eye, and she took another trip into her memory.

———✦———

Huey Eugene Pugh pulled his substantial weight up the steps to his back door and crossed the threshold into the small room that doubled as a pantry, toolroom, coat closet, and laundry room. There, on the wall, hung his favorite garden clippers. He pulled them from their hook and turned his hefty self around to face his backyard.

In a few minutes, he was busy pruning branches from one of his many rose bushes. He had, of course, done his major pruning before the first warm winds of spring, but there were always a few bushes that needed additional shaping.

Huey was a master gardener, a wine connoisseur, an interior decorator, an artist, and Sulphur Spring's most easily recognizable bon vivant. It wasn't just his flashy clothes or witty remarks that caught people's attention. It was all those pounds in a five-foot-two-inch body.

Huey snipped a few inches from the long stem of a tea rose. He stood back to see if that gave him the right proportion he needed. "No, Princess Eugenie, you need a little off the left if you want to make the other girls jealous!"

He snipped again.

The Princess Eugenie rose was his favorite. He spent so much time with it. Perhaps it was that lovely name. Every rose has a name, and only his Maria Callas got equal attention. But maybe it was that lovely color, a light fuchsia.

Pleased with his sculpturing, Huey turned to admire his Barbara Streisand and his Marilyn Monroe, the latter one a brazen red.

He had to hurry, though; he still had the steak to cut up and stir-fry. Then he had to eat his supper, clean up the kitchen, do the dishes, catch up on his Facebook and Twitter, and then sit down with the list of last year's entrants in the annual art show. He had to divide them up into shorter lists for tomorrow, when he and the other volunteers would begin making phone calls.

There was so much to do—but first, a few snips off Marilyn's hips.

In her studio apartment, Sarah Louise Upshaw dipped her paintbrush into a small glass of water and then back into the dab of paint on her palette. The water made the paint flow from her brush easier.

She made a few strokes on the large canvas that perched on her easel. The strokes were helping define the contour of a vase that held a profusion of flowers. Another dip into the water, and then she touched the pointed brush to a dab of black paint and added two more brushstrokes to the vase.

On the table beside her was the vase she was trying so hard to copy. She always painted from life.

Everything on the canvas could be found in her studio—the couch, the table, the window, the vase and flowers, and even the penciled-in outline of her cat, Buford, whom lay stretched out on the couch, his feet in the air and his backbone bent to match the lumps on the cushions.

Hurriedly, Sarah Louise dipped the brush back into the water; only this time, she swished it around, trying to get all the color out. She pulled it from the water and looked about for a piece of cloth to wipe it on to make sure it was clean.

Spotting a T-shirt on the back of her couch, she grabbed it and pulled the brush through the folded cloth. It was a bad habit she had, using whatever piece of rag or cloth or clothing that was handy to clean her brush.

Yet it was clean, and she quickly stuck the brush into some white paint, also on the palette, and put a highlight on the side of the vase. The painting was only partially done, but she had another week or so before the annual Spring Fling Art Show and Antique Auction. That is, if she decided to enter it again this year.

She had given the matter a lot of thought. She had good reasons not to enter.

Still, the flowers had turned out nice, and now the vase was almost done. The spot of white she had added to the vase had really made the flowers stand out. They were fuchsia, and the shade of fuchsia she had chosen was particularly enticing, she felt.

"Fuchsia," she murmured to herself, "such an interesting color."

Fuchsia—it seemed to be everywhere this spring evening in the sleepy little town of Sulphur Springs, but the town wouldn't be sleepy for long, and fuchsia flowers were just the beginning!

1

"Sarah Louise, you've done it again," Claudette said out loud. She shook her head and repeated the statement, "Sarah Louise, you've done it again!" She shook her head slightly from side to side. Then she held the white blouse up to the light coming through the laundry-room window.

The enhanced view only confirmed what she knew. Sarah Louise had ruined another white blouse with paint—this time, a trendy shade of fuchsia.

Knowing full well that Sarah Louise hadn't heard a word she had said but determined she would, Claudette headed out of the laundry room, up the four steps to the kitchen, across that room, and down the hall. She passed the old spare bedroom, but now a den, then backed up a few steps.

"'Sarah Louise has done it again!"

Claudette stood there waiting for a comment from the lone occupant of the room. There was just the drone of the TV. It was the Cajun accent of a TV chef as he was declaring his jambalaya the best in the state of Louisiana.

She repeated herself, "I said…Sarah Louise has done it again!"

Two eyes turned in her direction and peered over a pair of bifocals perched precariously on the tip of a stubby little sixty-eight-year-old nose. The eyes took in the disgruntled look of the speaker and the wet blouse in her hands.

"She's your daughter. She doesn't claim me unless she needs money!"

Not content to let it go, Claudette held the blouse out in front of her for her husband to see. "This time, it's fuchsia!"

"What, may I ask, is a fuchsia?"

"It's a color, Winslow...a color! The curtains of this room are fuchsia!"

Winslow cast an eye at the curtains then looked at his wife. Her once-blonde hair was giving its way to grey just as her once-svelte body had given way to gravity and extra pounds over the years. He pursed his lips, as if considering a solution to the problem.

"Well, at least she'll match the curtains."

"Think you're funny, don't you, Winslow! This is the third blouse in three weeks...I'm tired of telling her!"

Winslow turned back to the TV. He wasn't sure what it was Claudette was tired of telling Sarah Louise, but he didn't care. Claudette might go into Sarah Louise's studio to fuss at her, but he knew his wife well enough to know that Claudette never got mad at anyone for very long. In fact, that was one reason they had been married so long—forty-five years. He never messed up too bad, and Claudette never got too mad. Besides, he really wanted to know what was in that jambalaya that made it taste go good, even though he had never eaten jambalaya and had no intention of ever having any.

Claudette could read her husband's body language. She turned and headed back down the hallway of the rambling 1960s ranch house and turned a corner. She walked down another shorter hallway and, without knocking, opened the door to the former-garage-turned-into-a-studio apartment. As she did, a large gray cat jumped off a small sofa and scurried toward the open door.

Entering the room, Claudette began, "You're painting fuchsia flowers, aren't you!"

A pert face peered from behind a large wooden easel. Blonde hair was pulled into a bun, which made her facial features even more noticeable. Combined with a bright twinkle in her eyes, it was a face any mother could love.

"Why, yes, I am."

"I guess you'd like to know how I suddenly became so psychic."

"Mmmmm, from the tone of your voice, Mother, I don't think I need to ask that. I have a feeling you're going to tell me."

Claudette held out the white blouse with the offending stain. "Does this look familiar?"

"The blouse? Certainly, Mother. That's my blouse!"

"I know it's your blouse! I'm talking about the stain on the sleeve here!"

She held the sleeve up for Sarah Louise to see.

"This stain is fuchsia, Sarah Louise—fuchsia!"

Sarah Louise's face disappeared behind the large canvas, making her reply a little muted. "I know what you're going to say, Mother. You're going to say, 'Sarah Louise, this is the second blouse you've ruined in as many weeks. Do you think new clothes grow on trees? When are you—'"

Before she could finish, Claudette interrupted, "No, Sarah Louise…it's the third blouse you've ruined in as many weeks… well, at least the third in the last month. Really now, can't you be a little careful?"

Claudette waited for a reply, but there was none. Sarah Louise knew her mother was already running out of steam.

"Well?"

"Well, Mother…come look at these flowers. I think I've done a tolerable job. Tell me what you think."

Claudette stood her ground for a moment, but when Sarah Louise said nothing else, she caved in and walked around to the other side of the easel. There she looked at the colorful canvas.

"Oh, Sarah Louise Upshaw…they look so real…I just don't understand…I just don't understand."

"Understand what, Mother? How I can ruin so many blouses in so little time? I guess I'm a woman of many talents."

"Oh, forget about the blouse. I only paid five ninety-five for it at Biederman's…it was marked half price and on the sale table for an additional 30 percent off…let me see…just how much it was really worth…well, math's not my strong suit. I didn't pay much for it…I guess you could still wear it to teach in."

"Why? Because all high school art teachers wear stained clothes?"

"No, Sarah Louise, I meant you could wear it under a sweater…or under one of those horrible black-and-orange sweatshirts they make you wear on Fridays."

"Ah yes, the school colors…orange and black. That's why every football game reminds me of Halloween. Now, what was it that you don't understand?"

"I don't understand?"

"Yes, you were looking at my flowers, the fuchsia flowers, and saying you didn't understand something."

"Oh yes…I remember now. I just don't understand how you can make such beautiful paintings, and yet you can't sell any of them…just look around this room…it's full of lovely paintings…flowers, cats, gardens of flowers, cats, and flowers…"

"Mother, I've told you before. I can sell them. It's just that people won't pay me what they're worth. I could sell every one of them in the parking lot of the Super Walmart for ten dollars apiece. If, that included the frame!"

"I know…I know…people in Sulphur Springs don't appreciate art. But…somewhere out there…there must be someone who would pay you what they are worth."

"Somewhere out there! Isn't that the name of a song?"

"Oh, take me serious, Sarah Louise…maybe you could try the Internet…don't they sell things on the Internet?"

"Yes, they sell time-shares, vitamins, weekends in Orlando, and male-potency pills!"

"Do they?"

"Mother, you've never been on the Internet! What makes you think you can sell paintings on the Internet?"

"Well, Hannah Bugleman said her nephew sold his collection of *Superman* comics on the Internet…she makes it sound like everyone goes to this b-bay place, and you can buy and sell anything!"

"That's eBay, Mother, and Hannah Bugleman's nephew spends his life in front of a computer. He's the original computer geek!"

"Oh, I know her nephew's a geek…but he buys and sells things on…what did you say it was again?"

"eBay!"

"Yes, eBay…what kind of a name is that anyway…eBay?"

Their conversation was suddenly interrupted by a loud sneeze. "Achoo!"

"Uh oh…that's your father…where's the cat?"

Sarah Louise and Claudette both made a quick glance around the room.

"Achoo! Who let the cat in here?"

Sarah Louise raised her voice so that it would carry down the hall. "Sorry, Pop! Mother left the door open. She was on a tangent about fuchsia paint, and—"

Winslow was now standing at the door, a piece of Kleenex stuffed up each of his nostrils. His hands were on his hips, and he had a scowl on his face.

Sarah Louise stopped in the middle of her explanation to take in the full picture of her father and then burst into laughter.

"It's not funny, young lady. You know I'm allergic to cats! Somebody better find that gray-haired vermin before I do, or I'll—"

"You'll do nothing, Winslow…you don't have the heart to set a mousetrap…I can't imagine you doing harm to a cat!"

"Mice don't make me sneeze, Claudette. If they did, I could get brutal. I could!"

"Yes, Pop. I'm sorry. But it was Mother's fault this time. I've been better about keeping the door shut. I promise it won't happen again!"

"That's what you said about getting paint on your blouse," Claudette interrupted. "But don't get me started on that…let's go cat hunting, Sarah Louise!"

The mother and daughter left the room and made their way down the hall of the rambling house.

"Women," Winslow muttered, except that with the Kleenex stuffed up his nose, it sounded more like, *weemean!*

2

By suppertime, the effects of cat hair had diminished enough that Winslow could remove the Kleenex from his nostrils. His anger, never very strong in the first place, had diminished as well; but he didn't mind playing the martyr as he sat at the small kitchen table, reminding his wife and daughter of his suffering.

"I knew as soon as my eyes started to water that that cat was in the house. It's amazing how that stuck-up, overgrown hair ball can simply enter the room, and I start to tear up. Then I start sneezing, then—"

"Yes, yes, Winslow…we know. If you were to touch the cat, you would break out in hives and, heaven forbid…you might even drop dead!"

"Don't make light of it, Claudette. People do die from allergies, you know!"

"Actually, Winslow, I don't know a soul who has ever died from breathing cat fur!"

"Well, I'm sure if you were to do a little research, you'd find out that a lot of people have died from undue exposure to cat's fur."

By this time, Sarah Louise felt the need to say something. "Actually, Pop, I've read that it's not cat fur that makes people sneeze. It's cat dander."

"Dander?" Winslow and Claudette both said at the same time.

"Dander is the residue in their fur left over from when they lick themselves," Sarah Louise said.

"Great!" Winslow reacted. "It's not bad enough that they're covered with hair, but they're also covered with cat spit!"

"Oh, Pop, don't be so paranoid. I promise I won't let Buford into the house again."

"When we turned the garage into a studio and bedroom for you, Lou [his pet name for his daughter], we did it with the understanding that it was to be your world. We would live in our world, and any animals would stay in your world, not stray over into our world!" Winslow said.

"You sound like the opening lines of a soap opera, Winslow— *As Our World Turns*," Claudette offered.

To which, Winslow retorted, "How about, *When Our Worlds Collide?*" They were interrupted by the ringing of the telephone.

Riiiiing!

The three of them looked at the slightly orange plastic phone hanging on the wall. None of them made any move to answer it.

Riiiiing, it went again.

Winslow was the first to say something. "It won't be for me. I'm retired and uninvolved!"

"I never get any calls unless it's the same day report cards come out. That was two weeks ago. So, Mother, I guess it's for you," Sarah Louise said.

"Just because it's for me doesn't mean someone else can't answer it," Claudette mumbled as she got up from her chair. "Hello…Yes, it is…No, I'm not interested…Yes, I'm quite sure… Our house is fully insured…Oh no, I'm sure…My husband works for an insurance company…Nice talking to you too."

As she sat back down, Claudette asserted, "Insurance salesmen! I wish we had caller ID. I could tell before I answer the phone who I'm going to talk to."

"You mean, who you are going to lie to. I didn't know I was an insurance salesman. Before I retired, I sold car parts down at the dealership," Winslow said, giving his wife a sly look.

"Put a dollar in the jar, Mother. You told a lie."

"Now see, you two, if we had caller ID, then I wouldn't have to lie…I would have handed the phone to one of you…you can both hang up on people…I can't!"

"I've told you, Claudette. I can't get caller ID on a tangerine phone made in the '70s."

"Get a new phone, Pop!"

"He won't do that, Sarah Louise…he's afraid I'd want to redo the whole kitchen to match…but while we're on the subject of phone calls, the Art Guild called for you today, Sarah Louise. It's time for the annual Spring Fling Art Show and Antique Auction to Benefit the Art Guild's Town-Beautification Project."

Sarah Louise made a face. "Oh boy!"

"What's wrong with that, Lou? I thought you liked to enter the Spring Fling and whatever else it is," Winslow said.

"Oh, I do, Pop. I guess. But I don't know why I bother. I never win anything higher than third place, much less Best of Show. I never get written up in the paper. I never sell my entry."

"Don't feel bad, Lou. I never get my name in the paper either. Now, if the two of you will excuse me, it's time for *Emeril.*" Winslow stood up, took another piece of corn bread from the plate at the center of the table, and headed for the den.

"Winslow, if you get crumbs all over the carpet… I'm not getting them up…do you hear me, Winslow?" Claudette called after him.

He didn't answer, but they heard him ramble down the hall, and then they heard the *clunk, clunk* of the recliner mechanism.

Claudette turned to her daughter, the two of them still picking at the last of their meal. "Oh, honey…don't be that way…you do beautiful work…and you have sold some of your paintings!"

"Family doesn't count, Mother, or close friends!"

"Maybe you should paint something different, Sarah Louise. All you paint are flowers and cats...and cats and flowers...maybe you should paint a nice lighthouse...people like lighthouses."

"I paint what I see, Mother. If I lived next to a lighthouse, I'd paint one."

"Can't you look at a picture of a lighthouse...or make one up?"

"I don't work that way, Mother. I paint what I see...and what I like. I don't like lighthouses or unicorns or angels or rainbows over snowcapped mountains or..."

Claudette could tell that her daughter was frustrated. Frustrated that, at age thirty, she was still living at home with her parents. Frustrated that the only male in her life was a fifteen-pound cat named Buford. Frustrated that as talented as she was, she never sold her paintings. When Sarah Louise hurt, her mother hurt. It's one of those little laws of parenthood, so Claudette tried to help.

"That nice painting you're working on, the one with the fuchsia flowers...you should be finished with that in time for the Spring Fling. Why don't you just enter that? We'll give it a fancy name, like *Study in Fuchsia #19*."

"Mother, that sounds like something Picasso would do!"

"Well, maybe catchy names are what your paintings need...what are you going to call it?"

"You won't like it."

"Of course, I will! I like anything you do."

"Okay, but I know you're not going to like it...*A Room Full of Cats*."

"*A Room Full of Cats?*"

There was something in Claudette's voice. "I knew you wouldn't like it!" Sarah Louise exclaimed.

"Oh no...it's not that...it's just that...well, it's so much like what you entered last year. Now, what was it...*Cat with...*"

"Irises!"

"Yes, that was it...*Cat With Irises*."

"And the year before that, it was *Cat With A Ming Vase*. And the year before that, it was *Red Poppies and Cat*. Can't you paint something besides cats, Sarah Louise?"

"Well, Mother, if you find me a lighthouse to sit in my studio for a few hours, I'd paint that. But we live in Sulphur Springs, Tennessee, just five miles from the border with Kentucky and a hundred miles from…from anything interesting. The only things I can see out the window are hills, trees, and grass…and mowers in the backyard and my cats!"

"I know, I know." Then repeating the mantra she heard so regularly that she knew it by heart, Claudette said, "You…can't paint from your imagination or from a photo…you only paint from life…like all the great painters of the past." Claudette finished with a dramatic flair like a tired Shakespearean actor giving their final lines of a soliloquy.

"But it's true, Mother. I teach my students to draw and paint what they see. I can always tell when they make something up. It lacks realism! And I think it lacks feeling too!"

"Okay…paint cats and flowers…but at least be more creative with the name of the painting!"

Sarah Louise pondered this last bit of advice for a moment. "Actually, Mother, you may be on to something."

"I may?"

"Yes, the Art Guild wants to know if I'm going to enter the show, and then they will ask if I'm entering a painting or a drawing or a sculpture or something else…and then they'll want to know the name of the work. So if we come up with a clever title, at least it will give them something to talk about!"

"Oh, I see…create a little buzz!"

"You're so with it, Mother. Yes, a buzz!"

Claudette thought for a moment, absentmindedly pushing together the empty plates on the table then stacking them one on top of another. "How about *Buford with Flowers*?"

"Mmmmmm, that's not crazy enough, Mother. We need something really wild." Sarah Louise searched her memory for an example from the art world she had studied and then taught with such devotion. "You know, Mother, something like what Rembrandt Peale did."

"Rembrandt who?"

"Rembrandt Peale. He was from a famous family of painters. His uncle painted George Washington."

"Well, I've never heard of him…what is it that he did that was so special?"

"He wanted people to come to an exhibit of his work, so he told them he was going to show his painting of *A Young Lady Exiting Her Bath*. This was back when America was still pretty puritanical. You didn't paint nude women. The public was simply scandalized by the thought. But when the exhibit opened, it was full of people…all those high-minded people wanted to see the naughty painting!"

"And was the painting naughty?"

"Hardly! He played a joke on them with *trompe-l'oeil*. That's French for 'fool the eye.'"

Claudette was trying to see where this story was going and leaned closer to her daughter, as if that would help.

Sarah Louise continued, "He painted what looked like a large piece of cloth, clothes pinned in front of a naked girl stepping out of her bath. All you can see are her feet, the top of her head, and a little bit of her backside. The cloth looked so real that people walked up to it to peek behind it!"

"So his painting was really just a painting of a large piece of cloth?"

"Yes, but so real that it fooled their eyes, and it was a clear example of his ability, which is what he really wanted people to see. He got the crowd, and—to quote my own mother—he created quite a buzz!"

Claudette took the story in as she picked up the silverware from the table to add to the stack of dishes she was about to take to the sink. She was trying to take this new bit of information and use it to some advantage in her goal to make Sarah Louise's painting more with it.

She turned to face her daughter, her face satisfied with what she had just come up with. "Maybe we could tell the Art Guild that the painting you are going to show is called *Naked Buford with Fuchsia Flowers*!"

Sarah Louise looked oddly at her mother then slowly started to giggle, and then the giggle became a laugh. Her mother began to laugh too, and soon they were both laughing hysterically.

"Be quiet in there, you two! I'm trying to watch TV!" Winslow's voice suddenly bellowed.

To which the two females of the family only laughed louder.

3

"I thought spades were trumps!"

"They are, Hannah."

"Then why did you just lay a two of diamonds down, Claudette?"

"Because I'm out of spades, Hannah!"

"You bid six, and you only had four spades?" said the obviously contrite Hannah.

"I thought there would be a spade or two in the widow!"

"Well, I guess you thought wrong!"

Claudette turned to Bonnie and then to Annie, the other pair in this hotly contested card game.

"Ladies, now that you know I'm out of trumps, thanks to Hannah's inquisition, I hope you take mercy on us!"

"Ha!" laughed Bonnie, whose turn was next, as she laid down an eight of spades. "Not on your life!"

Hannah made one of those faces that seemed to say, *Why do I suffer fools?* She looked at her hand. "Now, I've got to play a king of diamonds, and Bonnie gets the trick with just a measly eight of spades!"

Annie looked at Claudette and then at Hannah and then at Bonnie and then back at Hannah as she played a seven of diamonds. She spoke carefully, "Looks like you're going to lose another one, Hannah. That's the way the cookie crumbles!"

"Oh, stop it with the homilies, Annie. If Claudette had her mind on the game, we'd be ahead!"

Claudette laid her cards down, took off her reading glasses, and used the edge of the cross-stitched tablecloth to clean them. It was a nervous habit when she was at a loss for words.

"Fess up, Claudette. What's bothering you?" Hannah put her cards down too and stared at Claudette, waiting for an answer to her question.

"I believe it's my play, girls," said Bonnie, just as curious to know what was bothering Claudette as the others but knowing she had a chance to ruin Claudette's bid. She laid down a jack of spades.

Hannah looked at the jack. "That's it. We're sunk!" She pushed her cards across the table and scowled.

Annie pushed her cards to the center too and picked up the small pad of paper by her side and pulled a stub of a pencil from behind her ear. She spoke out loud as she wrote, "Let's see now. That makes us six, and Hannah and Claudette are…" She dragged out the obvious as if she really had to do some serious deducing of the score. "Ah yes, Hannah and Claudette are three. Yep, the score is six to three!"

Hannah turned her famous scowl from the direction of Claudette, who was still fiddling with her glasses, to the direction of Annie. "Rub it in, why don't you, Annie!"

Bonnie patted Hannah on the arm and, barely concealing her laughter, said, "Oh, it's just a game, Hannah. You and Claudette skunked us last week!"

Hannah let the scowl leave her face since it wasn't achieving the desired effect from Claudette anyway. She picked up the cards from the mahogany dining-room table and began shuffling them.

The weekly card game took place in what Claudette considered the nicest room in the house, the one reserved for entertaining guests, her dining room. In this case, the guests were her dearest friends and confidants and, if truth be told, her weekly sources of local news and gossip.

Claudette finished adjusting her glasses on her face and rejoined the conversation. "Sorry, Hannah...I should have let you have the bid! I just can't seem to concentrate today."

"So what's up, Claudette? Problems?" asked a triumphant but sincere Annie. "Anything wrong?"

"Oh, nothing major, girls. I'm trying to get Sarah Louise to enter the Spring Fling Art Show again this year, but she doesn't want to."

"Why not?" Hannah was always curious, if not always tactful.

"She never wins, and she thinks it's a waste of time."

Bonnie reacted quickly, "Don't let the girls down at the Art Guild hear you say that. The Spring Fling is their baby. They think it's the greatest thing to ever happen to Sulphur Springs. It's like the annual Swan Ball and Junior League Antiques and Garden Extravaganza in Belle Meade in Nashville only on a much smaller scale."

"The greatest thing to ever happen in Sulphur Springs was when they put a bypass around town, and Walmart finally had a place to build!" said Hannah.

She always saw the practical side of things.

So Sarah Louise is not impressed with our annual Spring Fling," questioned Bonnie, who didn't agree with Hannah's declaration because her husband's tire-recapping shop had seen a 25 percent drop in business since Walmart had opened.

"If she would just win something besides a third-place ribbon, like first place or even Best of Show...or get some kind of attention...she's so talented...even if she is my own daughter...I can't even draw a stick figure!" Claudette said.

"But you do such nice cross-stitch. That's talent, isn't it?" said a meek Annie, trying to cheer Claudette up.

It was Hannah who put things out in the open. "Of course, she's talented—Sarah Louise, that is. But all she ever paints are cats and flowers. Now, I like pictures of flowers, and I guess cats are okay, but give me a tropical sunset any day. I asked Sarah Louise to paint me a tropical sunset. Two years ago, I asked her to. Do I have it yet? No, I don't! She doesn't do tropical sunsets, she says. Something about painting 'what you see.' If you ask me, a really good artist can paint anything!"

Claudette was so used to Hannah's blunt way of putting things that the snide remark didn't faze her, but she did try to clarify things for Annie and Bonnie. "Sarah Louise is stubborn about what she paints. She paints what she likes and doesn't care what the judges like. It's like talking to a brick wall."

"All children are like that, Claudette. My Robert Jr. hasn't heard a word I've said to him since he turned sixteen. And now Robert the Third is about to become a teenager, and I hope it all comes back to haunt him!" Annie offered.

"You're right, Annie." Claudette sighed. "I don't think Sarah Louise has really listened to me since she was a teenager either." Although she didn't mention it, that was when her youngest daughter stopped calling her *mom* and replaced it with *mother*, which sounded so impersonal to Claudette.

Bonnie commiserated with them, "Jeff and Elizabeth listen to me, all the time. Then they go right ahead and do as they please!"

Hannah put her two cents in. "And people say they feel sorry for me because I never married and had children. Why, I told my nephew just last week, 'Get married and have a house full of kids, and you'll regret it!'"

"Kids aren't that bad, Hannah, but they can be an aggravation. I just want Sarah Louise to be happy."

Hannah laid the cards down and cut them once. Then she let them lie there, not sure if it was worth the effort to play another hand. She looked at Claudette and decided to continue saying what was on her mind.

"Tell Sarah Louise that a tropical sunset with a boat on the horizon would take Best of Show, or at least a first-place ribbon—I'm sure of it!"

"Oh, I don't know, Hannah," Annie said. "The judges are a bunch of people they bring in here from out of town. They always have at least one professor from the state college, and those college professors today are all hippies!"

"Oh, Annie, they haven't had hippies since the '70s. Today they're all potheads and liberals!" Hannah spoke with authority.

"Whatever." Claudette sighed again. She then changed the subject. "How about dessert?"

"Nothing too fattening, I hope," spoke up a suddenly enthusiastic Annie, who always had the delusion that a "little fat" was okay.

"I got the recipe from *Southern Living*. It has chocolate, cashews, and cherries in it," said Claudette as she got up from the table.

"Does it have cream cheese in it?" asked Bonnie. "Everything they have in *Southern Living* has either cream cheese or sour cream in it!"

Before Claudette could answer, the phone rang.

"Get that, Winslow. I'm busy!" yelled Claudette as she left the dining room for the kitchen. If she had only known what that phone call would lead to, Claudette would have cut the phone line in two and left town in a hurry!

4

It wasn't until the three members of her weekly card group left that Claudette bothered to ask Winslow about the phone call. He was in the kitchen cleaning up—not cleaning up the kitchen but cleaning up the last of the dessert bowl.

"I hope you don't go into a diabetic coma from all the sugar you've just eaten!" she said to her husband, reaching for the empty bowl so she could wash it.

"I don't have diabetes!"

"Yet!"

"Oh, hush. A little sugar is good for you."

"Where did you hear that? On the Food Channel?"

"No, on CNN!"

"I find that hard to believe. Who called?"

"Called what?"

"Who called on the phone, Winslow? About an hour ago…I yelled for you to get it…remember?"

"Oh, that! It was somebody named Lucinda Something-or-other with the Art Guild. She wanted to know if Lou was going to enter the Spring Fling this year."

"What did you tell her?"

"I said yes."

"Oh, Winslow…I wish you had called me to the phone…I'm not sure Sarah Louise wants to enter it this year!"

"Really? I thought you two talked about it after supper last night."

"We did, but…she never really said for sure."

"Well, you'll get a chance to talk to her yourself. She's going to call back." Winslow said this as he got up from the table and started down the hall to the den and the TV. It was time for *Sara's Secrets* on the Food Channel.

"Why is she going to call back?"

"I told her Lou was going to enter a painting, and she wanted to know what the name of the painting was, so I told her to call back in an hour."

"An hour!"

"You heard me!"

By now, his voice was a distant echo coming from the hallway.

"Oh dear," Claudette mumbled to herself. She sat down and began to think. Unfortunately, she didn't get very far in her thoughts when the tangerine plastic telephone on the kitchen wall started to ring.

"I'll get that," Claudette said half out loud, even though there was no one around to hear. "Hello!"

The voice on the other end of the line was very professional. "Is this Sarah Louise Upshaw? I'm Lucinda Hardin-Powell with the Art Guild, and I need to speak to her."

"This is her mother…she's not here right now…she teaches, you know…can I help you?"

"I believe I spoke to Mr. Upshaw earlier. He told me that Sarah Louise was going to enter the Spring Fling Art Show and Antiques Auction to benefit the Art Guild's town-beautification program. This year, we hope to raise enough money to tear down the old Shell station next to the City Park. It's an eyesore, you know."

"Yes, I know…I often say to Winslow, 'What an eyesore.' Who does it belong to?"

"The city took it for back taxes two years ago, but they claim they don't have the money to clean it up. But they have kept it weed eaten since they got the deed."

"Oh, how nice," Claudette muttered, trying to stall while her overtaxed brain fumbled with what to say when this Lucinda person asked the big question.

"Your husband stated that Sarah Louise plans to enter a painting. I need to know the title of the painting so I can enter it into my computer."

There was a long pause. A very long pause.

"Mrs. Upshaw? Are you still there?"

"Oh yes…I'm still here."

"The title of the painting?"

Claudette tried to stall some more. She never did think clearly under pressure. "I believe that last year, she entered *Cat with Irises.*"

"Yes, I remember that painting, Mrs. Upshaw, but I need to know what she plans to enter this year."

"Two years ago, she had one titled *Cat with a Ming Vase.*"

"*Cat with a Mean Face?*"

"No, no…*Cat with a Ming Vase.*"

"Oh, sorry. I thought you said *mean face.* Well?"

"Well, what?"

"What is the title of this year's painting?"

"This year's painting! I think she told me that it was going to be called…A Room Full of…,yes, that's it…A Room Full of…"

"Full of what, Mrs. Upshaw?"

Words were rushing through Claudette's head, works like *cat, flowers, fuchsia, Rembrandt Peal, naked Buford,* creating a buzz, and rooms full of something. Then Claudette took the plunge. She leaped off the ledge. She waded in it up to her chin. She let her mouth speak without consulting her brain. She spoke right into the receiver clearly and loudly, "*A Room Full of Naked Men!*"

Lucinda Hardin-Powell was suddenly quiet. Speechless in fact. She cleared her throat then asked Claudette to repeat herself. "What did you say, Mrs. Upshaw? *A Room Full of Naked Men?*"

"Yes...that's right. *A Room Full of Naked Men!*"

Lucinda was very professional. "Let me see if I got this right. I don't want to make any mistakes. That's n-a-k-e-d, *naked*...and m-e-n, *men*...am I right?"

Claudette nodded, which did Lucinda Hardin-Powell no good.

"Am I right, Mrs. Upshaw? *A Room Full of Naked Men?*"

Claudette finally got up the energy to speak instead of just nodding. "Yes, that's correct." Then she quickly hung up.

She sat there a long time, cleaning the lens of her reading glasses. She kept telling herself that she was creating a little buzz, and as Martha Stewart would say, "That's a good thing." Besides, Sarah Louise would have some clever way to fix this—or maybe she wouldn't. Claudette let the thoughts and consequences of each thought run amok in her brain till her brain hurt. After at least fifteen minutes, she cleared her throat and hollered to Winslow.

"Winslow, I need you to do me a favor. Please, dear!"

Winslow hated it when she called him *dear*. It always meant something was dead under the kitchen sink. "What now?"

"I need you to come in here and shoot me!"

5

"Now, let me get this straight. You told the lady at the Art Guild the name of Lou's painting, correct?"

"Yes, Winslow…that's correct."

"You told her the picture was called *A Room Full* of something, but you won't tell me what that something is…am I still correct?"

"Yes, Winslow…you're still correct."

"But whatever it is that you told the lady that something was is not what the something is, am I correct?"

"Yes, Winslow…do you have to make it sound so much like a police interrogation? I'm your wife, not a mass murderer!"

"Don't interrupt me, Claudette. You want me to shoot you. I at least need to know why before I pull the trigger!"

"Pull the trigger—Winslow!"

"I'm not going to shoot you, Claudette. But I need to get to the bottom of this. Whatever you told the lady at the Art Guild is going to get you in trouble with Lou when she finds out, am I correct?"

Claudette begrudgingly accepted his interrogation technique. "Yes, Winslow, that's correct."

"And whatever this something is, you won't tell me, am I—"

There was the noise of a car entering the driveway and pulling up behind the house. Winslow stopped in midsentence, and Claudette caught her breath. They both listened as the car engine stopped, a car door was opened and shut, and footsteps came up the outside kitchen steps. When Sarah Louise entered the kitchen door, both her parents were staring at her wide-eyed and with gaping mouths.

Sarah Louise entered the room, setting down a small stack of papers to be graded and her purse, and turned to face her parents. "What's wrong with you two? You both look like you've just seen a ghost."

Winslow suddenly stood up and dramatically announced, "Your mother needs to talk to you, Lou. I'll be in the den."

Winslow decided to leave the dilemma to those who were part of it since he really didn't have any real clue to what the dilemma was.

Claudette turned to watch her husband disappear down the hall then muttered to herself, "Coward!" She then turned to face Sarah Louise, but her daughter had crossed the room and was reaching for the door of the tangerine refrigerator.

"I'm thirsty, Mother. What do we have that's cold? Anything left over from your card party?"

"Just some lemonade...your father finished the dessert...he didn't leave a crumb."

"Since he became addicted to the Food Channel, he's become quite a connoisseur," Sarah Louise said as she looked in the fridge, pulling out the pitcher of lemonade and searching for something to go with it.

She finally found some Cheese Whiz and placed it on the kitchen table. Then she opened up a cabinet door and pulled out a box of Ritz Crackers. Claudette got up and took a clean glass from the drainer by the sink then returned to the small kitchen table as her daughter pulled out a slat-back chair and sat down.

"So, Mother, what is it that you need to talk to me about?"

"Sarah Louise, you know that story about that Rembrandt fellow...the story about his naked-lady painting that wasn't a painting of a naked lady?"

"Sure," Sarah Louise said, stuffing two Cheese Whiz crackers into her mouth.

"Well..."

Winslow had just gotten deeply involved in a recipe for clam chowder when he heard his daughter scream. He wasn't sure if it was a scream or a yell or maybe a combination of the two. He was sure, however, that he heard the words, "Naked what?"

He toyed with the idea of staying to hear how long the chowder had to cook to be what the host of the cooking show called "the epitome of New England" but decided anything that his wife wanted killing for was probably more important. Besides, who could listen to TV with all that yelling?

When he got to the door of the kitchen, Sarah Louise was sitting down at the kitchen table with her head in her hands, and Claudette was standing over her, patting her on the back.

"It's not that bad, Sarah Louise. I just wanted to create a little buzz for you, that's all...a little bitty buzz, like that Rembrandt fellow."

"Ohhhhh, I should have never told you that story, Mother!"

Winslow stood in the doorway a little longer then went to sit beside his daughter. "I don't know what this is all about, Lou, but I know your mother felt so bad about what she's done that she practically begged me to shoot her before you got home."

Sarah Louise sat up straight and turned to look at Claudette straight in the face. Claudette looked hopefully into her daughter's eyes for a ray of forgiveness. It wasn't there.

"Just give me the gun, Pop. I'll do it for you!"

Claudette was overwhelmed. She sat down at the table, and half out loud and half to herself, she mumbled, "It seemed like a good idea at the time."

"Mother, that's how Napoleon explained the invasion of Russia to the French people. It seemed like a good idea at the time!"

"Oh, Sarah Louise, it's not funny …you've got to think of some way to make this all work out, like that story you told me!"

"Will somebody explain to me what's going on here!" Winslow demanded.

Both women turned to face the perplexed Winslow.

"Mother told the lady at the Art Guild that my painting was titled *A Room Full of Naked Men!*"

"NAKED WHAT?"

"You heard me, Pop, *A Room Full of Naked Men!*"

Winslow repeated the words, only at a much higher decibel than his daughter had, "A ROOM FULL OF NAKED MEN!"

Claudette looked panicky at her husband and said, "Not so loud, Winslow…do you want the neighbors to hear you?"

"Why not, Mother? They'll probably read about it in the paper!"

Winslow and Claudette looked at each other from across the table. "The paper!" they both said simultaneously.

"Of course, the paper. They publish the names of all the artwork to get people interested in the show. Boy, are they going to be interested now!"

It took a full hour of explaining before Winslow finally got a grasp on what had happened and why. Sarah Louise had to find a picture of Rembrandt Peale's painting *A Young Lady Exiting Her Bath* in an art book from her studio, and Claudette had to repeat for the umpteenth time that she was just trying to create a little buzz.

"Maybe we can call the Art Guild back and explain that it's all been a big mistake," Claudette said hopefully.

"It will have to wait until tomorrow. I'm sure they've gone home by now. Those volunteers don't work long hours, you know," Winslow reminded her.

Sarah Louise turned to her mother. "Who was the lady you spoke to on the phone?"

"Oh, good, Sarah Louise, we can call her at home. It was Lucinda Something-Something. She had two last names…like one of those celebrities."

"Was it Lucinda Hardin-Powell?"

"Yes, Sarah Louise, that's it!"

"Oh, great!"

"What do you mean 'oh, great'?" her father asked.

"It's just that Lucinda is both a gossip and a busybody. We went to school together, and we never got along…I know her all too well. I bet she has told everyone in the guild by now, and it will probably be on the six-o'clock news! She is the very last person I would call and try to explain this to."

The three of them sat there stunned for a long while. Then Sarah Louise pushed her chair back from the table and spoke up loudly, "There's just one thing to do!"

Her parents looked at her questioningly.

Sarah stood up, and she had a strange smile on her face.

"What, Sarah Louise?" Claudette asked.

"Yes, what, Lou?" Winslow echoed.

"I guess I'll just have to paint a room full of naked men!"

The moan from both parents was audible all the way down the hall as Sarah Louise strode toward her studio with the strange smile still on her face.

6

Abraham Lincoln once said that if you wanted to test a person's character, give them power. Lucinda Hardin-Powell would have been a good example of what he was speaking of. When Lucinda had power, everyone around her knew it.

Just now, she was no longer in shock from Claudette's conversation; rather, she was considering all the ways she could use this bit of information to her advantage. You see, Lucinda Hardin-Powell really wanted to run the Sulphur Springs Art Guild, although she was technically only the membership secretary. To be honest, Lucinda Hardin-Powell wanted to be president of the State Art Guild, maybe even president of the National Art Guild. It was within her grasp if things would just work out the way she dreamed them. For now, she would settle for membership secretary, but the future beckoned to her with a leering smile, not unlike the smile on her own face as she absorbed her new knowledge.

Lucinda Hardin-Powell walked from the tiny office that was reserved for the membership secretary and down the hall. She passed the much larger office of the chairman of exhibitions. They all had offices larger than hers, but that would all change one day. She paused there but decided to give her news to the volunteers supervisor instead. They usually thought alike anyway.

The Sulphur Springs Art Guild occupied what had once been the Sulphur Springs High School; only, most of the building had been torn down. The old ninth-grade wing, six rooms and two restrooms, were all that remained, except for the gym, of course—that was where the Art Guild held their exhibits. The board of education had unloaded the property on the city, which is why two of the old classrooms were on loan to the Chamber of Commerce.

The city was too cheap to rent them their own place when the school could be used for free. Three rooms were reserved for teaching community-wide art classes, and the remaining room was used for storage. That left the old coaches' offices and gym-equipment-storage rooms for use as offices.

When push came to shove, the smallest room was given to the membership secretary, but that was before Lucinda got the job. Now that she had gone from being just a member of the guild to an elected officer, she coveted the larger office of the chairman of exhibitions. It didn't smell like old gym socks!

It was a roundabout course she was taking, but Lucinda knew how the gossip mill worked. Yes, she went to Malvenna Botts first, walking right in with a contrived worried look on her face. She found Malvenna sitting at her desk, looking at the newest issue of *Southern Accents*. Malvenna felt that if she had the money, her house could look like one of the richly ornate yet sublimely decorated mansions the magazine featured.

"Oh, Malvenna, I'm so glad I found you still here. I just don't know what to do!"

Malvenna pulled the little bubble she had made with her chewing gum back into her mouth with a little popping noise. She folded down the corner of the page she was looking at then closed the magazine. From the tone of Lucinda's voice, it might be a while before she could get back to the living room decorated in pink and black.

"What's the matter, Lucinda? You look upset."

"Oh, maybe it's nothing. But I just don't know what to think of this." She waved a piece of paper in front of Malvenna, careful not to let Malvenna read a word of it. She then pulled the piece of paper to her bosom and sighed. "No, maybe it's best if I don't say anything." And she started to leave the room.

Lucinda knew how to make people beg for gossip. Somehow it never seemed so bad if people forced the information out of you.

"Oh, tell me, tell me. What is it?"

Lucinda turned to face Malvenna and shook her head sadly. "I guess it's for the best if I just keep this to myself…I just hope it's not what I think it is!" She turned to leave.

Before she could get two steps, Malvenna was by her side, keeping her from leaving the room. "Now, Lucinda, you don't dare leave here until you tell me what's on that piece of paper that's got you so upset!"

Malvenna then grabbed Lucinda by the shoulders and pulled her back into the room, looking both ways down the hall to make sure no one else was aware of what was going on. The only thing Malvenna loved more than good gossip was being the first to know!

She pushed Lucinda down into the only other chair in the cramped little room and tried to see what was on the paper, but Lucinda carefully kept it clutched close to her size-double-d bosom, which amply hid anything that she clutched to it.

"Now, what's all this about, Lucinda?"

"Malvenna, you know I want what's best for the Art Guild. I mean, I would be the last one to make us a laughingstock to… to…to the nation!"

"The nation! What is it, Lucinda?" Malvenna was so excited she was almost doing a dance.

"Well, now, promise you won't tell anyone until I speak to Mrs. Dorphman. But she won't be here until tomorrow…and I just need to tell someone!"

Mrs. Dorphman was the ninety-year-old president of the Art Guild. In fact, she was the only president the guild had ever had. She founded the group with a substantial donation from her family's huge trust fund ten years earlier. It was always a token of the guild's esteem to keep her as president, although she did little more than show up once a month and make a large annual donation, which made the Art Guild possible.

The fact that this would need Mrs. Dorphman's attention made Malvenna salivate. "Is it that bad?"

"It could be." Lucinda gasped, loosening her grip on the piece of paper. "The annual Spring Fling is such a good thing for our community. It puts us right up there with Bowling Green and Nashville. No other town our size has an art guild. But to see someone cheapen our efforts with a tawdry piece of artwork—it's more that I can bear!"

"What do you mean, Lucinda? What piece of artwork?"

"It's that Sarah Louise Upshaw. She always has this attitude that her artwork is more meaningful because she only paints what she sees—"

Malvenna interrupted, "Oh, I know what you mean. When she teaches the beginners' class in the summer art program, she constantly tells the children, 'Draw what you see, draw what you see.' But what's wrong with that?"

"You've never noticed her condescending air when she looks at other people's work?"

"Uh…no, I haven't."

"Well, I have. She looks at my tole party trays like they're something you'd get from the Lillian Vernon catalogue."

"Ohhhh…and I order from Lillian Vernon myself! But what's that got to do with the Spring Fling?"

"She is trying to destroy the dignity of the show! I just spoke to her mother and asked what was the title of Sarah Louise's entry…and you won't believe what she told me. Why, I think the poor woman was in shock herself!"

"What was it? I bet it had something to do with cats…or flowers. She paints them rather well, you know."

"That may be, but she's never won first prize! So I guess this is just her way of getting back at us." Lucinda paused dramatically. "Look at this!"

Lucinda turned the piece of paper, which she had held to her chest so long that it now smelled like Eau de Midnight Walk, her favorite bath powder. Malvenna peered closely at the perfumed paper. She focused on the name: "Sarah Louise Upshaw…*A Room Full…*" Malvenna let out a gasp. Her face turned red. She had to sit down. As she sat, she began to make a mental list of all the people she would have to call tonight.

Yes, Lucinda Hardin-Powell had told the right person!

7

While Lucinda Hardin-Powell and Malvenna Botts were having their tête-à-tête, Sarah Louise was busy in her studio. She was looking at the canvas she had been working on for the last two weeks. She had one hand to her chin, and her eyelids were drawn close together as she tried to envision the changes she would have to make—all the while, the phrase *create a little buzz* echoed through her brain.

The canvas was large; in fact, much larger than her usual work. She had earlier, when considering what she would do for the Spring Fling, felt that maybe a larger canvas would strike the judges' fancy. So she had gone down town to the only place in Sulphur Springs that carried art supplies, Dorphman's Hardware and Appliances. The Dorphmans owned half of Sulphur Springs. They were the founding fathers, and what businesses they didn't start, they bought out. The hardware store, the old hotel, the bank, the lumberyard, the feed mill. They were all Dorphman properties.

Michael Dorphman ran the hardware store, the deed still in his grandmother's name. He carried art supplies because his grandmother asked him to. She occasionally dabbled in art herself. She had a large macramé something or other behind the cash register at the hardware store that someone had pinned the annual bank calendar to. Her fingers weren't as agile as they had once been, so she didn't do macramé anymore, although the back of the hardware store still kept a display of yarns and exotic beads in stock at her request.

Michael had ordered the large canvas for Sarah Louise since it wasn't a size he normally carried. He was always good about carrying things that she wanted her art students to have. She always had to explain what she needed in detail since Michael had absolutely no inclination toward art himself.

When he carried the canvas out to her car, parked in front of the store in its small parking lot, he had insisted, he commented on its size and accused her of doing another *Mona Lisa*. She didn't tell him that the famous painting was really quite small, but did tell him that she planned to do something dramatic. And now, thanks to her own mother, *dramatic* was actually an understatement.

So she stared at the partially painted canvas. In the foreground was a couch with a fern stand at one end and a coffee table in front. A pot of fuchsia flowers sat on the stand. A window with colorful curtains took up some of the background.

Sarah had tentatively roughed out five cats—that was the idea, a room full of cats. She had also roughed out a person sitting on one end of the couch, a person that was beginning to look a lot like Sarah.

As she had envisioned the picture, she had made a couple of rough sketches on paper, it would show her on one end of the couch, Buford on the other, with four other cats scattered about the room: one draped on the back of the couch, one under the coffee table, one on the fern stand, and one looking out the window—a room full of cats!

All that had to change now. She had to replace the cats with naked men. One could take Buford's place. One could stand behind the fern stand. One could look out the window. The one draped on the back of the couch and the one under the coffee table might present a problem.

The gears in her head were turning. Fortunately, she thought best under pressure, unlike her mother, whose common sense went out the window when things got hectic. There was the time Sarah and her sister, Cornelia, fell off the swing in the backyard. They were trying to share it. Sarah cut her knee bad, and Cornelia rushed into the house to tell her mother. It wasn't until she was in the car and halfway to the emergency room that Claudette realized that Sarah Louise was still sitting on the ground in the backyard, waiting for someone to come to her aid.

If she turned the men this way or that way or placed them just right, the painting wouldn't be too revealing. That is, each man's "manhood" would not be on display for public scrutiny. Sarah pulled a pencil from a cup on her cluttered worktable and picked up a sketchpad. She began to sketch several ideas, each a variation of what she had in mind.

"It can be done!" she told herself out loud. She nodded her head in tacit triumph. She had met the beast, and she had tamed it. It was only when Buford meowed and rubbed himself against her legs that Sarah Louise was brought back down to earth.

As she picked the hefty cat up and placed him on the desk so she could scratch his back easier, it dawned on her. She couldn't paint a naked or even a half-naked man unless she had one to look at! It was her mantra—draw what you see!

Her face flushed. She felt a drop of moisture come to each temple. She was beginning to sweat at the thought. What was she to do? Where would she get five naked men to pose for her?

Lost in her thoughts, she didn't hear the soft tapping at the door to the studio. It was only after Claudette tapped a third time and spoke up that Sarah heard anything.

"Sarah Louise, honey, supper's ready. I hope you'll come and eat with your father and me. We're worried about you."

Sarah Louise turned her face to the door, and she spun the gears in her brain. Just like that, she knew what to do. "Sure, Mother. Let me give Buford his supper, and I'll be right there."

Claudette was afraid to say anything else—after all, she had said enough today already. So she made her way back to the kitchen, stopping long enough in the den to pull Winslow from reruns of *Iron Chef America*.

In the studio, her daughter walked across the room. There, a small stove, sink, and refrigerator were lined up on the far wall, although Sarah Louise ate all her meals with her parents. Behind the kitchen wall, a small bathroom separated the rest of the studio from a tiny bedroom. What had once been a two-car garage had been cleverly converted into a studio and apartment for her and whatever number of cats she had at any given time.

Sarah Louise, meanwhile, was actually singing to herself as she put a small bowl of Fancy Feast in front of Buford. Yes, she had the solution. Since her mother had gotten her into this situation, her mother could find five naked men for her—yes, that should keep Claudette busy.

Sarah would tell her mother this new development just as soon as she was finished with supper.

8

"Huey" Eugene Pugh had the finest rose garden in Sulphur Springs, or in the whole county, for that matter. Since Sulphur Springs was the largest town in the county and the county seat, it was pretty much one and the same. If you were the best in Sulphur Springs, you were the best in Franklin County. It was because he was pruning in his rose garden that Malvenna Botts wasn't able to get him on the phone until the fifth try.

Huey had just gotten inside the house when he heard the phone ring. He hurried his three-hundred-pound-plus body across the kitchen floor to the ornate French boudoir phone, which sat on the small Louis XIV desk he had next to his refrigerator. Huey was into decorating in the French style, despite the fact his home was a 1920s bungalow.

As soon as he picked up the phone, he caught Malvenna's excited voice, "Oh, Huey, I've been trying to get you for an hour. Where have you been? Oh, it doesn't matter. Sit down! I need to talk to you about the exhibit!"

As all the volunteers at the Art Guild knew, *the exhibit* meant the Spring Fling art show, and Huey was the curator of all the exhibits.

"Why, what's happened? The floor in the gym doesn't have termites again, does it?"

"No, Huey, it's more serious than that!"

"More serious than termites, Malvenna? Tell me!"

"Have you seen the list of paintings to go in the exhibit?"

"I think so…at least I saw the preliminary list this morning. We all were taking names to call and verify the entries. Why?"

"Did you know that Sarah Louise was going to enter a painting?"

"Sarah Louise Upshaw?"

"She's the only Sarah Louise in town, Huey! Yes! Did you know she was going to enter a painting?"

"She wasn't on the list of people I had to call. I believe she was on Lucinda's list…but she always enters the Spring Fling. So what's so sensational about that? You sound like a woman with diarrhea and no quarter for the pay toilet!" Huey always had the most unique way of saying things. His wit was legendary.

"Don't be silly with me, Huey. This is serious. Do you know what Sarah Louise is going to enter in the show?"

"A painting of flowers, I'm sure. The girl has a one-track mind!"

"Well, her mind is on a different track this time! Lucinda spoke to her mother today and asked her what the title of Sarah's painting was going to be…and do you want to try and guess what it is? No, don't even try! You'll never guess! I may as well tell you!" She paused for dramatic effect.

"Go on, Malvenna. Tell me before you bust a gusset."

"*A Room Full of Naked Men!*"

"Come again?"

"You heard me, Huey Eugene! *A Room Full of Naked Men!* She's going to show a painting called *A Room Full of Naked Men!* You do know what that means, don't you, Huey! It means her painting will have naked men in it—a roomful!"

The thought raced through Huey's mind. This would be a first for the Spring Fling, a picture of a naked anything! The only thing slightly close to that was when Lucy Pendergrass painted the Venus de Milo as she thought she would have looked if she had arms, which to Lucy's thinking would have been draped across her bare bosom. It was hardly controversial since her belly button was about the only thing that was uncovered; and the belly button, on close inspection, looked a little like a cross-eyed Winston Churchill. Lucy painted everyone with eyes that looked slightly crossed. The Venus de Milo had slightly crossed eyes as well, but it was the belly button that was the highlight of her painting.

"Well, Huey, what are you going to do about this?"

"Me?"

"You're the curator of the exhibits! It's up to you to tell her she can't do this! We can't have paintings of naked men when children and old ladies may see them! What will Mrs. Dorphman think?"

Huey used his sardonic wit again. "Malvenna, Clara Dorphman had a husband and four sons! I expect she's seen a few naked men in her day!"

"Huey, don't be smart with me! You've got to do something!"

"Okay, Malvenna, I'll do something. Just don't you worry that gum-chewing little head of yours! I'll take care of it."

Malvenna and Huey talked longer, but it was just to rehash everything so Malvenna could emphasize the seriousness of the affair and to quote Lucinda that the Art Guild would be responsible for corrupting the morals of Sulphur Springs.

After Malvenna hung up and after he had finished two glasses of Pinot Noir, Huey gave serious thought to what was the best course of action. The Pinot Noir had been on sale at Pat's Highway Liquors, and the crystal cut glass he had gotten at a tag sale in Atlanta.

It wasn't that the idea of a painting of naked men bothered Huey. He had his own little collection of pictures of naked men in his closet, but no one was aware of them except Huey. He also had a nice collection of ladies' shoes there. He just couldn't pass up a pair of pumps at a yard sale or flea market. One day, he intended to do a painting of them in all their gaudy colors and shapes. There were other interesting things in Huey's closet, which was why he always kept it locked.

For now, he considered all the implications of Sarah Louise's painting: the newspaper getting a hold of this, the shock to the public, the uproar, the crowds of people—yes, the crowds!

You see, the Art Guild's annual Spring Fling was drawing smaller crowds every year. The displays of paintings, photographs, needlecrafts, poor attempts at sculpture, and folk art might fill the gym, but the public was largely absent. The first year, there were big crowds. The gym was full of people. They had refreshments that first year! Huey was convinced that refreshments get the people out. There were people in Sulphur Springs who would go anywhere if there was free food. Huey was one of them!

But the cost of refreshments was considered too high, and there was always the extra cleanup involved—cookie crumbs everywhere, napkins and empty Styrofoam cups stuck behind displays, and somebody always spilling the peppermint punch in the most awkward places.

The public was getting tired of seeing canvases of cross-eyed people, tole platters, photographs of someone's grandchild in overalls with a contrived smile; and Psalm 23 can only be cross-stitched so many ways.

Huey was tired of people copying Thomas Kinkade's work or students who thought they could do Jackson Pollock one better with splatters of paint on canvas. Sarah Louise Upshaw was actually one of the best painters in town. She painted realistically, and she had feeling in her flowers and cats. The judges always went for the Thomas Kinkade knockoffs, though. Huey was sick of lighthouse beacons and Victorian cottages in the snow.

The more Huey thought about it, the more he liked the idea of a little controversy, a little real public reaction. At least they would know there was an art show! They might even come! Besides, he knew Sarah Louise Upshaw. She wouldn't do anything to disgrace the Art Guild…or would she?

Yes, the next week and a half might prove to be very interesting!

9

Supper had gone remarkably well. Conversation had been kept to trivial subjects. Neither Claudette nor Winslow wanted to bring up the subject of naked men, individually or by the roomful. They were both secretly hoping that Sarah Louise had been kidding when she said she was going to actually paint a room full of naked men.

"How do you like the chicken, Sarah Louise?"

"This really is very good, Mother. Now, what did you call it again?"

"Singapore chicken and noodles! I'm glad you like it."

"Don't forget the mandarin-orange sauce, Claudette," Winslow added.

"Oh yes, with mandarin-orange sauce—how could I forget?"

"I got the recipe from Rachel and gave it to your mother, Lou. It's one of those four-ingredients-and-less-than-thirty-minutes meals."

"Who's Rachel?" Sarah asked.

"Rachel Ray! She's one of your father's new girlfriends!"

"Girlfriends?"

"Yes, your father thinks all the cooks on the Food Channel are talking to him, especially the women. He calls them all by their first name, and he's started bringing me all these wild recipes to try!" Claudia answered for her husband.

"A little something different in the kitchen! There's nothing wrong with that!"

"Yes, dear, as long as you keep the recipes simple. Last week, you wanted me to stuff a pork chop with pickled cow's tongue. I don't do cow tongues!"

"Pops, that was a little extreme!"

"It looked good when Bobby did it on the barbeque. I thought I'd get your mother to try it," Winslow explained.

"Bobby?"

"Bobby Flay. He has a show on the Food Channel. I told you, your father calls all the chefs by their first name!"

After this pronouncement, the conversation took a momentary lull. It is a fact well documented by behavioral scientists that conversation has naturally occurring lulls about every three minutes, something to do with primitive man needing to constantly stop and look over his shoulder to make sure a saber-toothed tiger wasn't about to lunge.

However, these normally occurring lulls scared both Claudette and Winslow, who were trying to avoid any topic that included the words *naked* and *men*. They had kept the conversation rather lively all evening and done a good job so far. This new lull sent both of them into a panic, and at the same time, they both blurted out, "How are things at school?"

Sarah Louise, who had already figured out their ploy, politely smiled and tried not to laugh. "So nice of you both to ask. About the same." She deliberately stopped there with no further comment, just to see what new topic her parents would experiment with.

Claudette grabbed the platter of Singapore chicken and noodles with mandarin-orange sauce and pushed it into Sarah Louise's face. "More, dear?"

"No thanks, Mother. I've had plenty."

Another lull. This time, Winslow came to the rescue. "Why don't you finish your last few bites, Lou, and then come with me into the den. It's about time for *The Barefoot Contessa*."

"Thanks, but no thanks, Pop. I need to get back to the studio." Then carefully measuring her words, she dropped the bomb they had successfully avoided all evening. "I have a painting to work on, you know!"

Sarah looked up from her plate to see the panicked expression on both her parents' faces. Then, as both Claudette and Winslow tried to look away—as if studying the kitchen ceiling was suddenly of the greatest importance—Sarah began to laugh. First, a giggle, then a chuckle, then a good hearty ha-ha.

The more she laughed, the more confused her parents looked. And the more confounded their expressions, the more she laughed, until her mother broke her silence. But she wasn't in a jovial mood.

"Sarah Louise Upshaw, stop that laughing right now! I don't know what you think is so funny! I've made a mess of things, and I don't know what to do about it, and all you can do is laugh!" Tears came to Claudette's eyes, big tears. "I was just trying to help. I just wanted the people at the Art Guild to know who Sarah Louise Upshaw is and to know that she is going to paint something special…I just wanted to…"

"I know, Mother, you just wanted to create a *little* buzz. And now you've probably got the whole Art Guild on the phone to each other."

Sarah paused for a second and then began to laugh again. "I wish I could be there"—Sarah laughed—"to see the look on Malvenna Bott's face…or Baby Huey's…"

Confused by all this crying and laughing, Winslow grabbed on to something he could talk about. "Who, pray God, is Baby Huey?"

The new bit of insight offered by Sarah had stopped, briefly, Claudette's tears. She too was trying to picture the look on Malvenna and Huey's faces, and now she was trying not to laugh.

"Oh, Pop, you know Huey Eugene Pugh! He is Robert Lee's son, and he looks just like him too. You can't miss him. He weighs…God only knows how much. The gym floor shakes when he walks across the room."

Winslow screwed up his face, and then the light of recognition showed up. "Yes, I remember him…big like his father. All the Pughs are big. Isn't he the one who always wears those loud Hawaiian shirts and white pants?"

Sarah stopped laughing long enough to nod in the affirmative.

"So you call him *Baby Huey*?"

"Not to his face! We call him that behind his back. There's a comic-book character who goes by the same name. Huey Eugene would be mortified if he knew that half the people in the county call him that." Sarah was wiping tears from her eyes from having laughed so hard.

Claudette shook her head. "Poor Baby Huey…I can only imagine what he's thinking."

Winslow now realized he knew who Baby Huey was, but he still had no idea what Huey did or why he would be important in this situation. "Does it matter what Huey Eugene thinks?"

Sarah looked at her father. "Huey is the curator of all the Art Guild exhibits. He'll be the one to hang every painting in the gym. Sooner or later, he'll have to be told I'm doing a painting called *A Room Full of Naked Men*, and it will be up to him to hang it where everybody can see it or to hang it in the janitor's closet. I'm sure Lucinda or Malvenna have called him by now. They've probably called everyone in the Art Guild by now, at least all the officers."

Claudette got serious again and forced the question to her lips, "Sarah Louise, are you really going to paint a room full of naked men?"

Winslow and Claudette looked at Sarah, both hoping the answer would be in the negative, but they were about to be disappointed.

"Yes, Mother, I am." Then seeing the woeful look on their faces, she began to explain, "Oh, relax, you two! I'm not going to paint some pornographic spectacle. The school board would have me up on charges of lewd and lascivious behavior in a skinny minute!"

"But what are you going to do, Sarah Louise?"

"Mother, I'm going to replace the cats in the painting with naked men, but I'm going to put them behind furniture or behind the pot of fuchsia flowers so that nothing is too revealing. It won't be any different than seeing someone like Pop cutting grass with his shirt off."

"Oh." Claudette placed one hand over her heart. "I'm so relieved."

"I knew you could do it, Lou!" her father said with a little forced gusto.

Then Claudette made sure she understood correctly. "So when you look at the painting, you won't see any…any…" She reached for the right euphemism.

Winslow came to the rescue. "You won't see any private parts, right, Lou?"

"Right, Pop, no 'private parts.' The whole painting will, I'm afraid, be rather tame. But in the meantime, people are free to think anything they want to think. And that's the buzz you wanted to create. Right, Mother?"

"Oh, I don't want to ever hear that word again!"

Winslow took his finger and stuck it into the remaining pool of mandarin-orange sauce on the platter and then, dripping it all the way, placed it into his mouth. "Yep, that was a pretty good sauce, Claudette!"

He stood up and turned to leave the room. "As always, I'll leave you girls to the dishes!"

As the sound of his footsteps echoed down the hallway, Claudette picked up the empty platter to take it to the sink. When she did, Sarah Louise reached over and, grabbing Claudette's hand, said, "Just a second, Mother. I need to tell you something else."

Sarah sounded so serious that Claudette's eyes got big again.

Sarah had to force herself not to start laughing again, but the best part was about to take place. If Claudette was sorry she had even opened her mouth to Lucinda Hardin-Powell, she was really going to regret it when she found out that it would be up to her to procure five naked men.

Sarah cleared her voice. "Now, Mother, there's just one little problem that I expect you to help me with…"

10

The doorbell to the Upshaw house works perfectly. The large red front door even has a knocker. But none of this mattered to Hannah Bugleman. She simply walked right in. Hannah was the oldest of Claudette's weekly card foursome and the boldest. It wasn't her age that made her so forward; it was just her natural inclination to be loud and domineering.

"Claudette! Claudette!"

"In here, Hannah, in the kitchen!"

Hannah passed through the hallway, into the dining room, and then through a Dutch door to the kitchen.

"Well, Claudette, this better be important. I had to call my nephew and tell him not to come by. He was going to put some boxes in the attic for me. I've been waiting a week for him to come do that, and now I've got to reschedule!"

Hannah liked to help her friends, but she didn't do it without making them realize she was having to put herself out to do it.

"Oh, Hannah…I'm sorry. I'll get Winslow to go by and do it!"

"No, no, that's okay. Herman knows where to put things in my attic. I have a system, you know. Winslow would just mess things up!"

Claudette didn't know why she bothered. She knew Hannah, and she knew there was never any way to mitigate the trouble Hannah had to go through for whatever the situation was. Still, Claudette always tried, and Hannah always brushed her efforts aside.

"I'm sorry I've messed your plans up. It's just that something has come up, and I need your help. I don't think I got an hour's sleep last night fretting about it."

"Well, Claudette, what is it? Winslow's not leaving you for a younger woman, is he?"

Claudette gave Hannah a look of incredulity. "Winslow leave me for a younger woman? Don't make me laugh. A richer woman, maybe—but not a younger woman!"

"Well, what then?"

Claudette didn't want to have to tell this story more than once, and since she had also called Bonnie and Annie, she decided to stall Hannah until they could both get there. "What were you going to put in the attic, anyway?"

"Forget the attic, Claudette! I want to know why you called me so early this morning and told me to get here as soon as I could. You had an emergency."

"Oh, it's an emergency."

"What then?"

"Can you wait a minute? It's just that I was hoping I could tell you all at the same time. Bonnie and Annie, I called them to come over."

"You called Bonnie and Annie too? This is a triple-alarm problem?"

"Oh yes, I'm afraid it is."

Before Hannah could get Claudette to divulge more, there was a soft tapping at the kitchen door. Then Annie, ever so slowly, stuck her head into the room. "Anybody home?" Annie shyly asked, her voice barely carrying across the room.

Hannah answered the question before Claudette had the chance to say anything. "Of course, somebody's home, Annie. Didn't you see Claudette's car? It's right there in the driveway!"

Annie poked her head farther into the room, relieved that somebody had answered her question. Annie was the meekest of the card group. She had married right out of high school and had always been a housewife, which made her a little shy around women who had careers or outside interests. She was easily intimidated by the others. She quietly said, "Well, you never know!"

"Anyone with any sense would know, Annie! Now come on in here so Claudette can tell us what's bothering her!"

Annie looked at Claudette, ignoring Hannah's assumption regarding her intellect. "Oh, Claudette, you look so worn out!"

"She didn't get any sleep last night!" Hannah's voice again rang out.

Annie replied, "It must be something dreadful!"

"It is! She called me at seven o'clock this morning!"

Claudette was listening as the two of them spoke about her, as if she were incapable of speaking for herself. She was just about to open her mouth and say something when Bonnie came to the door. "Yoo hoo, Claudette!"

"She's in here, Bonnie. Come on in and hurry up. Annie and I are already here," Hannah's voice boomed out again.

Bonnie was the most sensible of the girls. She had helped her husband for years down at his recapping business, doing his bookkeeping and answering the phone, even placing orders. She was dependable and easygoing.

As Bonnie entered the room, Hannah continued, "Hurry over and sit down. Claudette has a problem, and she wouldn't tell us what it is until you got here, and the poor thing didn't get any sleep last night. Look at her. You can tell by the bags under her eyes. They're bigger than they usually are—that's how you can tell!"

Claudette was suddenly speechless at the suggestion that her eyes usually had bags under them. She gave Hannah a wide-eyed stare and was about to comment on Hannah's crow's-feet when Winslow walked in.

"What's all the commotion?" he said as he stepped into the kitchen. Then looking at the four women gathered at the kitchen table, he added, "Oh, I might have known. The hens have all sprung the chicken coop and landed here!"

"Very funny, Winslow," Hannah threw back at him. "But if we're hens, that makes you an old rooster!"

Hannah enjoyed putting men in their places, and she smiled big as the other three at the table laughed at her comment.

Winslow, never too partial to Hannah in the best of times, decided to just grab the pot of coffee and take it with him back to the den. But he was determined not to let her have the last word. "Old? You graduated from Sulphur Springs High with my older sister!"

He smiled to himself as he took the pot of coffee and sashayed back down the hall, but Hannah wasn't through with him yet. She hollered after him, "I was the youngest in my class, Winslow! sixteen when I graduated!"

Winslow shut the door to the den—rather hard.

"I didn't know you were the youngest in your class, Hannah," Annie said, suddenly interested in this new bit of knowledge.

"I knew that," Bonnie said. "Her mother started her in school when she was barely five. I've heard the story before. Her mother taught first grade at the old Beech Grove school, and…"

By now, Claudette was furious. They were there to help her find naked men, and they were discussing Hannah's education. "Excuse me! I thought you girls were here to help me!"

"Oh dear, Claudette, you look like you're about to have a stroke. What is it that's bothering you?"

This came from Bonnie, the most sensible of the three. Claudette could have used three Bonnies, but she was stuck with one Bonnie, one light-headed Annie, and one cantankerous Hannah.

Claudette had rehearsed what she was going to say many times. That was one reason she hadn't gotten any sleep. Trying to picture naked men in her daughter's studio, which doubled as her bedroom, was the other reason.

"Let me start at the beginning. I got this phone call from the Art Guild…"

For the next hour, Claudette recounted—word for word, action for action—the events of the last two days, trying to make light of it but occasionally letting go with a deep sigh, always echoed by the others, and then continuing. She had just finished the part where Sarah Louise had told her she had to find the five naked men to pose for the painting when she stopped to catch her breath.

The three had mostly been speechless while she talked, occasionally letting out an "I declare" or "you don't say." Now, given a moment of quiet, it was Hannah who spoke, "None of this would have happened if she had listened to me. Lighthouses, I told her. You can't go wrong with lighthouses!"

"But I love the flowers Sarah Louise does," Bonnie countered. "I have one in my living room. Don't you remember? She gave it to Dewey and me for our anniversary one year!"

Annie agreed, "I remember. Pink peonies!"

"Yes, pink peonies," Bonnie repeated. "I've always loved peonies."

It was Hannah, however, who was on top of the situation. "So, Claudette, Sarah Louise expects you to find her five naked men!"

Bonnie quickly corrected her, "She's not going to find five naked men, Hannah. She has to find five men who will get naked! There's a difference. Right, Claudette?"

Claudette nodded a reluctant agreement.

"Oh, Claudette," Annie's voice sounded sympathetic, "no wonder you seem so upset. Where are you going to find those five naked men? I mean, men who will get naked?"

Under her breath, Hannah muttered, "What man won't get naked?"

Claudette swallowed hard again and tried to explain, "Actually, girls, that's why I called you all here. You see…I hate to do this, but then you are my best friends…we've all been through a lot together…what's that saying, 'All for one and one for all'…I wanted you to help me."

The three girls' jaws dropped.

"I figured that if each of you were to help…that is, if each of you were to find one man…"

The blood drained from the three girls' faces.

"It will be so much easier if we make this a group effort…if each of you could just find one naked man—"

Claudette had to stop right there. There was a loud thump. Hannah Bugleman had just fainted and slid off her chair and onto the floor, landing squarely under the kitchen table!

11

A shiny black '78 Lincoln Continental made its way up a long pea gravel driveway. The driver was barely visible behind the steering wheel, despite the fact that between her rear end and the seat was a small pillow embroidered with the words, "Souvenir of Niagara Falls."

It pulled up to the old Dorphman homeplace, a rambling two-story brick home, painted white in the 1950s but slowly turning pink as the red brick began to reemerge. The house dated back to 1850 but had been added on to over the years till it was twice its original size, considerably more impressive, but looked nothing like its simple federal-style origin. Ester Mae Washington stopped right in front of the house and parked.

Since Dr. King's "I Have a Dream" speech, she had stopped parking behind the house she cleaned two days a week.

Ester Mae reached into her purse and pulled her gold-plated bridgework out and pushed it into place in her mouth. Mrs. Dorphman liked for all of Ester Mae's teeth to be in place, although Ester Mae was more comfortable without her two bicuspids.

Satisfied that she was presentable, she got out of the huge car and pulled her big black purse after her. She then reached across the seat and grabbed a folded-up old brown paper bag and stuck it under her arm. She never went to work without her brown paper bag. It was what she used to carry home the days' treasures—whatever Mrs. Dorphman gave her or she retrieved from the Dorphman trash cans. As she often told her family, "Those fool white folks throw away enough to keep half the county outta the poorhouse!"

Ester Mae entered the house through the front door and walked back to the kitchen.

There, Clara Dorphman was sitting at a small round oak breakfast table, drinking a cup of tea and nibbling a piece of toast. The toast had enough butter on it to float a battleship, but that was the way Clara Dorphman had eaten her morning toast since she was a child; and the family couldn't convince her that real butter had bad cholesterol, though they had tried repeatedly. It wasn't that Clara didn't believe them; it was that five minutes after they told her anything, she forgot it. This is why she turned to face Ester Mae and spoke in a surprised tone, "Ester Mae, is this your day to clean?"

"Yes, Miss Clara. Today is Thursday. I come two days a week, every Tuesday and every Thursday!" Then, under her breath, Ester Mae mumbled, "Been doing it for fifty years!"

"Is today Thursday? I guess it is. Where does time go? Well, I'm glad you're here, Ester Mae. I need you to help me clean out the hall closet."

Ester Mae looked at Clara Dorphman and gave her a puzzled look. "What you wanna go and do that for, Miss Clara? We cleaned the hall closet out two months ago!"

"We did?"

"Yes, Miss Clara. You were looking for your long winter coat."

"Oh, that's right. I remember now."

But she didn't really remember. Ninety years had come and gone in Clara Dorphman's mind, and sometimes all the things she had done just kind of got mixed up. She had learned to accept what people told her. It was no longer worth the trouble of trying to remember. If Ester Mae, or anyone else for that matter, told her she had forgotten something, she believed them.

"What you need outta that hall closet, Miss Clara?"

Actually, Clara wanted her long winter coat to add to a pile of clothes she wanted to take to the cleaners, but now she was too embarrassed to ask Ester Mae if they had found the long winter coat and, if they had found it, where was it now.

Clara hadn't totally lost her facilities, which was the sad part. She was painfully aware of her forgetfulness and did her best to hide her shame. "I need to take something to the cleaners, Ester Mae. I'm sure there is something in there that needs cleaning!"

"Yes, Miss Clara, I'm sure there is."

Ester Mae knew one of the things in the hall closet wouldn't be the long winter coat. It was hanging in Ester Mae's closet at her own home. Clara Dorphman had given it to her two months ago. They were the same size, which is one reason Ester Mae kept working for Miss Clara. Miss Clara kept Ester Mae in clothes. But the real reason was Ester Mae fretted over what would happen to Miss Clara if she didn't come in and look after her two days a week. The only family member who checked on her regularly was grandson Michael.

Michael joined his grandmother for breakfast every morning. He would be arriving any moment now.

Ester Mae got two eggs out of the old Coldspot refrigerator and set them beside the stove. She and Clara made small talk while she got a small cast-iron skillet out and turned the burner on low.

Then, right on schedule, Michael popped in the back door. "Morning, Gramma," he said as he leaned over and gave his grandmother a kiss. He turned to Ester Mae. "Morning Ester Mae." And he planted a big kiss on her cheek as well.

Ester Mae blushed, although her dark skin kept it from being noticed.

"Over easy, Ester Mae," Michael said while getting a gallon container of milk out of the fridge and pouring himself a glass. Michael sat down opposite his grandmother and pulled a folded-up piece of paper from his pocket.

"Here's that paper you wanted me to bring you, Gramma." Then—before Clara Dorphman could ask, "What piece of paper?"—he added, "This year's flyer for the Spring Fling. You wanted me to get a sample from the printers."

"Oh yes, thank you, Michael."

She took it from him and unfolded it, looking it over as she read it out loud, "The Tenth Annual Spring Fling Art Show and Antique Auction to Benefit the Art Guild's Town-Beautification Project!" She nodded in approval then read some more, "April 2nd and 3rd at the old Sulphur Springs High School."

"Here you go, Michael, two over easy. The toast is in the toaster," Ester Mae said.

"Thanks, Ester Mae! Gramma, hand me the butter!"

Michael waited for the toast to pop up and then slathered almost as much butter on the two slices as his grandmother had. "So you expecting a big show this year, Gramma?"

"Oh, I hope so. I've got to go by the school today and check on how things are going. Did you take that piece of plywood by like I told you?"

"Yes, ma'am, one piece of plywood, two feet by three feet, exterior grade, painted white on both sides!"

"Who did you give it to?"

"The first person I saw...Lucinda, I think she said her name was."

"Lucinda, that name sounds familiar...oh yes, she called me last night. Now, what was it she called for? There was something she wanted to tell me...but she wanted to tell me in person. I think that's what she said."

"I bet you have a big show this year! I've sold a bunch of canvases at the store. I even had to order a large canvas for one customer."

"Really? Who wanted a large canvas?"

"The teacher at the high school. You know her, Sarah Louise Upshaw."

"Oh yes, she's the one who always paints such nice flowers."

"Well, I guess she's going to paint some really big flowers this year because it was a huge canvas." Then Michael took one last gulp of milk and jumped up from the table. "Gotta go, Gramma. Keep her outta trouble, Ester Mae!"

With that, he was gone.

Ester Mae sat down at the table where Michael had been sitting and stacked up his plate, glass, and silverware to take to the sink. "Hand me your plate, Miss Clara. I might as well take it too."

Clara passed it across to Ester Mae.

"He shore is a fine boy, that Michael. It's a shame the way that girl done him," Ester Mae commented.

Clara nodded in agreement. Michael's wife had left him to pursue a career in interior decorating. Sulphur Springs didn't have the type of clientele that Sophie, his ex-wife, felt were deserving of her talents. She had felt that Boca Raton was calling her, although there was a rumor that a man she had met at a conference in Louisville may also have been calling. But Clara didn't pay attention to such rumors, even when she could remember them.

Right now, she was exited about the annual Spring Fling. She would take the flyer with her to the school today. And she had a bit of news to share with them. Sarah Louise Upshaw was going to enter a huge canvas. Wouldn't they all be glad to hear that!

12

When the bell rang that marked the start of third period at Sulphur Springs High School, Dotie Fisher walked to the door of her classroom. The room was empty. This was Dotie's planning period, although she rarely did any planning. To Dotie, this was a chance to go to the teacher's lounge and catch up on the latest gossip, compare problem students, and check her school mailbox.

It wasn't that Dotie didn't need to do some occasional planning, but Dotie was of the school of thought that if it was important enough, it would come to her. Besides, she had been teaching eight years, and the plans she made that first year were still good enough for her.

She looked back at her deserted classroom to make sure all the stoves were off, the food processors clean and lined up, and all the measuring cups hanging above each sink. She was the home economics teacher. Satisfied, Dotie started down the hall.

As was her usual routine, she stopped by the art room first. This was also Sarah Louise's planning period. Dotie felt a special bond with Sarah Louise since they had both been relegated to the end of the east hallway. Everything exciting seemed to happen at the end of the west hallway, where the gym was located.

Dotie and Sarah Louise had other reasons to bond. They had gone to high school together and graduated together, and both had attended the state college for teachers, just an hour down the highway.

After that, the similarities ended. Dotie was a talker. Sarah Louise tended to be quiet and introspective. Dotie tended to—well, to talk! It didn't matter what you were talking about, Dotie could enter the conversation at full speed and never drop behind.

Another difference between them was their respective sizes. Dotie was slightly pudgy. She had been from birth. Her mother was an outstanding cook, and so was Dotie. Dotie loved to cook even more than she liked to eat, although she was no slacker there.

The biggest difference between the two girls was their marital status. Dotie was married. She had married her high school sweetheart, Moose Fisher. Moose had been captain of the school wrestling team and never hesitated to tell people it was Dotie's double-fudge brownies that made him fall in love with her. Sarah Louise thought Moose looked like a lumberjack would look: short and stout, with more muscle than brain.

Dotie was short too and not nearly as petite as she had been in high school—two kids and time spent in the kitchen adding a few pounds. Nevertheless, Dotie was married, and Sarah Louise wasn't. Dotie had watched Sarah Louise go through boyfriends, significant others, and one "almost." Together, they could commiserate about romance, and they often did.

Dotie always stuck her head into Sarah Louise's door to gab a little. She rarely stayed long because Sarah Louise seemed to always be busy cleaning up the mess in her room from her class's last art project or getting art materials ready for the next class. All that activity was distressing to Dotie, so she usually visited for a few minutes and then continued down the hall—unless, of course, Sarah Louise had something she needed to talk about. Today, to Dotie's surprise, was one of those days.

"Making mud pies again?" Dotie said as she entered the room. Sarah Louise looked up from a table of red clay pots.

"Oh, hi, Dotie. Yes, they just finished their first pinch pots."

Dotie could have asked Sarah Louise what a *pinch pot* was, but to be honest, she really didn't care to know. Dotie could talk about food for hours or about her own children or teacher gossip, which was always there; but art held little interest.

"I see you're busy, like always." Then turning to go, she added, "Do you need something from the office?"

Sarah Louise wiped her hands on the artist's smock she was wearing over her clothes and walked toward the door of the room where Dotie stood poised to leave. "I don't need anything from the office, but I would like to talk to you for a minute."

Dotie's eyes lit up. It was always nice when someone wanted to talk to her. "Sure, Sarah Louise. What's up?"

Sarah Louise passed Dotie and stepped into the hallway to pull the door shut.

This action took Dotie back. It had been ages since the two had talked with the door closed, not since Sarah Louise had broken up with the investment banker from Atlanta. He had been the "almost." Now, Dotie's mind churned with all the things that Sarah Louise might need to discuss in private.

"Oooooh, this must be serious, Sarah Louise. You're closing the door!"

"Maybe a little serious, but certainly interesting, Dotie!"

"You're engaged! Oh, I should have seen it coming! You haven't mentioned men in a year or more—that's always a giveaway! When a woman doesn't talk about her relationships, it's serious! I've seen it happen a dozen times. Who is it?"

That was the way Dotie talked. She would say ten things to any one thing you said.

Sarah Louise looked at Dotie in shock. "Engaged? I'm not even dating anyone!"

"Oh!" Dotie was let down.

Before Dotie could launch further with another barrage, Sarah Louise began, "It's my mother, Dotie. She's got me in hot water!" Sarah Louise pulled up two chairs. "You may want to sit down. This is going to take a second."

Dotie sat down, not squarely, but right on the edge of the chair, leaning forward, so as not to miss a word.

As Sarah Louise revealed her problem, Dotie took it all in, nodding in agreement with every opinion that Sarah Louise had on the situation. When Sarah Louise finished, Dotie was primed and ready to express herself.

"Oh, Sarah Louise, I think this is the funniest thing I've ever heard! You, doing a painting of naked men! It's a hoot! No, it's two hoots!"

"I'm glad somebody finds it funny."

"It is, Sarah Louise, it is! I can just imagine your mother asking some stranger in Walmart if he'll pose naked for her daughter. That's three hoots!"

Suddenly the image hit Sarah Louise. She hadn't gotten that far in her thinking to visualize how her mother would find a model. Now it all seemed beyond her imagination.

"Oh my gosh! You don't think she'd do that, do you, Dotie?"

"Claudette? I wouldn't put anything past your mother. This is the woman who decorated her kitchen in tangerine after seeing one on the cover of *Better Homes and Gardens* magazine! What about the time she got on a skateboard so you would think she was cool and hip with our generation! Remember her broken leg! And don't forget the time she marched on city hall to protest the conditions down at the animal shelter!"

"Oh, Dotie, if you only knew all the things my mother has done! Poor Pop, Mother is always doing something to embarrass him—"

Dotie was inspired with the idea of Claudette and her search for naked men. She didn't let Sarah Louise finish, but butted right in, "Maybe Winslow could go with your mother to keep her from being arrested for solicitation!"

"Solicitation?"

Sarah Louise realized there might be some truth in what Dotie was saying. What if, at this very moment, her mother was at some store grabbing strange men by the arm and asking them to undress. Sarah Louise suddenly felt faint.

Dotie, however, was laughing at the mental image of Claudette in handcuffs.

"Oh, Dotie! Stop laughing. This could be serious…what if my mother is somewhere going up to perfect strangers and…and… she could really be arrested!"

Dotie, by now, had tears in her eyes from laughing so hard, but she saw how serious Sarah Louise had gotten, so she bit her lip and got quiet, with just occasional gasps of stifled laughter.

"Now, Sarah Louise. I'm sure Claudette wouldn't do anything that crazy. I know she's a little wacky sometimes, but she is usually rational in the long run." Dottie paused to stifle another laugh then continued, "I'm sorry I said anything about her grabbing men and—" She had to stop again and regain her composure. "Well, anyway, you look terrified. Relax, girl! Take a deep breath!"

Sarah Louise tried to get her panicky feeling under control. She took a deep breath. What was she thinking when she told Claudette she had to find five naked men? If she was trying to teach her mother a lesson for opening her big mouth, it might end up being a lesson they would all regret. She took another deep breath.

"That's better! Your color's coming back. Now, take another deep breath!" Dotie paused, but not for long. "Tell me, Sarah Louise, did you tell your mother what kind of men to get, where to get them? Is she going to pay them?"

For the first time, Sarah Louise realized she hadn't given her mother any specifics—who, what, when, where, or how. But

Claudette hadn't asked for any directions. Maybe it was the shock, Sarah Louise reasoned. Still, the possibilities of what her mother might try were overwhelming. Sarah Louise felt faint again. Dotie was no help whatsoever!

Dotie was starting to laugh out loud again. She tried biting her lip, but it wasn't working, so Dotie did what she did best. She talked.

"You don't even know for sure that your mother is looking for someone. She may be home right now watching *The Price is Right* or fixing Winslow's lunch. If she is at Walmart or at the grocery, she's probably not even thinking about finding you a model. Then again, I can just see her asking some man, 'Will you get undressed in front of my daughter?'" Dotie had the gift of gab, but not the gift of tact.

Sarah Louise gave Dotie another look of amazement.

"I'm sorry, Sarah Louise, but you have to admit it. This is a funny situation!"

Sarah Louise looked at the woman who was probably her best friend and had to agree. It was all pretty silly. Her mother was a little goofy at times, but even Claudette wouldn't go up to a stranger and ask them to do something crazy.

"Dotie, if only this were happening to someone else—"

Just then, the door to the art room opened. A student stuck their head in the door. "Ms. Upshaw, you're wanted in the office." The student sounded serious.

Sarah Louise was still a little light-headed, and the surprise of this request and the student's tone of voice made her speechless.

Dotie quickly spoke up, "She'll be right there, thank you."

The student left, and the two women looked at each other.

"Oh, Dotie, what could they want me in the office for?"

"Relax, Sarah Louise. I'm sure it has nothing to do with your mother or strange men in Walmart. I bet it's some paperwork you have to fill out or should have filled out…or it could be some salesman. I'm always getting called to the office because some salesman wants to sell the school new sewing machines. I can't tell you how many times I've been called to the office to find some obnoxious salesman there. Why, I…"

So as Dotie talked away, she and Sarah Louise made their way to the office. Nothing Dotie said took away the uneasy feeling that Sarah Louise had.

13

As Lucinda Hardin-Powell walked across the old Sulphur Springs High School gym, now the exhibition room for the Art Guild, her heels made a tapping noise that echoed through the empty room. Lucinda was in one of those moods where she wanted people to know she was coming.

Otherwise, she would have worn her SAS, which were infinitely more comfortable. A smart-looking black outfit with a yellow blouse and matching black jacket completed her look. She topped it off with a rather large Dooney & Bourke purse.

Lucinda had a serious, almost grim expression on her face—but it was only skin-deep. Inside, she was beaming. Yesterday she had been the membership chairman of the Art Guild, probably the lowest man on the totem pole of power. Today she was wielding power like the prima donna of a third-rate Italian opera company. In the last twenty-four hours, she had been the bearer of the best gossip to hit Sulphur Springs since the First Baptist Church's minister ran off with the wife of the First Methodist Church's choir director. That had been a really good scandal because neither congregation could gloat over the other. The shadow of sin had been cast on both churches, and it was painful to the core. Only the Church of Christ got any real pleasure from the affair.

Lucinda had been careful about whom she called, enjoying each second in the spotlight. She had told Malvenna first. Malvenna traveled in a different circle than Lucinda, so there wouldn't be any overlapping of calls. She knew Malvenna would call Huey Eugene because they were such good friends, and Lucinda personally found Huey Eugene offensive, not only for his loud Hawaiian shirts but for his bon-vivant attitude.

After Malvenna, she called Isadora Biederman. Isadora was the vice president of the Art Guild, but she really ran the guild. The president, Mrs. Dorphman (as we all know), was merely a figurehead. As she had done with Malvenna, Lucinda dropped clues and innuendos until Isadora pleaded with her to spill the beans on what she knew that "threatened to destroy the reputation of the Sulphur Springs Art Guild."

Even before she called Isadora, Lucinda had made a mental list of people who would be indebted to her for being "the first one" she had called and told the potentially explosive news. Of course, she told each person she called that they were "the very first" person she had called, and she then had them each swear they wouldn't tell another soul. Lucinda knew that just as soon as she hung up, each person she called would be speed-dialing their best friend with the news. The age-old mantra of "don't tell anyone I told you this" or "you didn't hear it from me" was as effective as it had been since the first caveman cheated on his wife and the neighbors began to talk.

Lucinda's husband, BJ Powell, worked at the Merchants and Farmers Bank, which put her in the upper crust of Sulphur Springs society. BJ's given name was Bubba Joe, but Lucinda had insisted that he use his initials professionally. Lucinda and BJ belonged to the La Vista Country Club and 18 Hole Golf Course, where they swam, golfed, and partied with the town's elite: the doctors, druggists, lawyers, leading merchants, and (most recently) real estate developers.

With each little tap of her heels, Lucinda Hardin-Powell thought of all the "best friends" she now had and drooled with the knowledge that they all *owed* her one.

There had only been one clinker. When she had called Wanda Hudson, she was dismayed to find that Wanda already knew; and Wanda, whom Lucinda only called because her husband had the GM dealership, refused to tell Lucinda where she had heard the news. It didn't matter. Lucinda was *somebody* today, and that made up for all the years she had run for—but never been elected to—class favorite or cheerleader or Beta Club president.

Lucinda always lost to perky, cute people like Sarah Louise Upshaw. In fact, it was Sarah Louise Upshaw who had beaten her out for Most Versatile in the Sulphur Springs High School yearbook, all of which made this whole affair all the more pleasurable. Yes, it was very hard for Lucinda to keep the scowl on her face, for she was enjoying every minute of this.

"Oh, Lucinda, is that you? I thought that sounded like you walking across the gym!"

Lucinda looked up to see Malvenna Botts standing by the door to the old coaches' office.

"You're late, Lucinda," Malvenna added. "Everyone's here but you and Mrs. Dorphman."

"I had to drop by the bank and give BJ his banana. He forgot it again."

Huey Eugene appeared at the door. "Good Lord, Lucinda! What does a banker need with a banana, and don't tell me it has anything to do with interest rates."

"BJ has to get his cholesterol down, Dr. Oakley said, so I pack his lunch every day, but this is the second time this week he's gone off and forgotten it!"

"Well, forget BJ's banana and get your bootie in here. We've been waiting for you!"

Lucinda walked into the old coaches' office, the largest of the offices, the very one Lucinda coveted the most. Huey and Malvenna had stepped in ahead of her and taken seats. Isadora was there, and so was Louise Smith, the chairman of exhibitions. And to Lucinda's surprise, there was Calpurnia Pendergrass, the director of the Chamber of Commerce.

After token "how do you dos" and "fine, thank-yous," Isadora turned to face Lucinda. "Now, Lucinda, I hope you realize the seriousness of this, and so I'm going to ask you again, just to make sure. What is the title of Ms. Upshaw's painting?"

Lucinda looked dutifully serious. "*A Room Full of Naked Men.*" Then as she took in the faces of everyone in the room, she continued, "I heard it clearly from her mother. I even asked her to repeat herself." She made another pause. "And I checked the spelling to make triple sure!"

Isadora turned to Calpurnia Pendergrass. "Just like I told you, Calpurnia. I told you it was something shocking!"

Calpurnia Pendergrass was the director of the Chamber of Commerce for two reasons. One, she worked cheap. Two, she was a crafty old bitty! If it was good for Sulphur Springs, Calpurnia pursued it with zeal. Her thick horn-rimmed glasses and clothes, unchanged from the 1950s, were no indication of her intellect or cunning, which were considerable. Her small stature and thin build might make her look demure, but she could stare down a charging bull.

Without blinking an eye, Calpurnia took the disclosure and swallowed it and then blurted out, "I love it! It's just what this town needs—a little controversy! This is great, great, great! I bet I can get the Louisville, Nashville, Hopkinsville, and Bowling Green TV stations here! This is beyond great. This is fantastic, fantastic, fantastic."

Calpurnia had a tendency to repeat herself in threes.

Lucinda's mouth dropped open. Malvenna popped the bubble of gum she had in her mouth. Louise's eyes got big. Isadora put her hand to her bosom. They all four were speechless.

Huey Eugene, however, was anything but. "Oh, Calpurnia, that's what I've been trying to tell Malvenna all morning, before you all arrived. It's the best thing that could happen to the Spring Fling—controversy!"

"You're right, Huey Eugene, right, right, right! There's no such thing as bad press. All press is good! It puts Sulphur Springs in the spotlight. It lets people know we are here! I've been trying to tell the mayor and the alderman for years. We need to do something big to put Sulphur Springs on the map!" Then she repeated herself, "I love it, I love it, I love it!"

For the next thirty minutes, the six of them argued and discussed, discussed and argued. Eventually it came to this: Lucinda, Malvenna, and Isadora were sure it was the end of the Art Guild. It would be a disaster. Huey Eugene and Calpurnia were excited. This would indeed put Sulphur Springs on the map and the Art Guild on the tongues of everyone within two hundred miles. Louise had been swayed by Huey Eugene and Calpurnia and had somewhat timidly agreed with them.

Isadora looked at her watch. "Clara will be here any moment now."

They always met for an hour or so before Clara Dorphman arrived. This way, they took care of all business, and Clara just came in to make things official. Since she had gotten so forgetful, it just worked best that way. Isadora continued, "I don't know what she will say when we tell her, but I think—and, folks, we have to be honest here, we wouldn't have any Art Guild without Clara Dorphman's money...I think we should leave any decision this big up to her!"

They each one mulled this over, nodding in agreement with what Isadora had said. Lucinda and Malvenna were sure the old lady would be mortified and refuse to let the painting be in the show. Huey, who secretly wanted to see the painting regardless, and Clapurnia, who had to leave soon to get to the ribbon cutting for the grand opening of Poppa Joey's Pizza and Sub Parlor, were positive Clara would see it their way.

In the distance, the group heard a door shut, and tiny footsteps began to echo across the gym floor. In a minute, Clara Dorphman entered the room.

Clara looked around at the assembled people, each with a look of concern on their face. Clara knew that look. It was the same look people gave her when she had forgotten something. It was slightly patronizing. Clara couldn't stand that look, yet it had become a part of her life.

Everyone exchanged greetings, and Clara Dorphman sat down, thinking, *Am I late? Is this the wrong day? What have I forgotten?* It was always an embarrassment to show up for a meeting late or to show up on the wrong day, but Clara knew she had the right day and time because Ester Mae had reminded her twice. Still, there was something she had been trying to remember all the way into town.

"After you drop them clothes off at the cleaners, Miss Clara, you go by the old school. This is the day you meet with them folks at the Art Guild. Now, don't you forget!" Clara could still hear Ester Mae's voice, but the people in the room were all looking so funny at her. *Oh dear*, thought Clara, *oh dear*. And she nervously moved her purse from her lap to the floor and then back to her lap.

Isadora spoke first, "Miss Clara, we have something we need to discuss with you…a little bit of news."

"News?" Clara repeated, all the while trying to recall what it was she had forgotten.

Lucinda saw an opening, "Yes, Ms. Dorphman, it's about a painting for the Spring Fling. I told you about it last night when I called you, that we had something come up, and you needed to know about it."

Clara vaguely remembered the phone call. She nodded politely at Lucinda, who looked ever more serious.

Lucinda continued, "It's about a painting by that Sarah Louise Upshaw."

Then it came to Clara. That was what she had been trying to remember all morning. Michael had told her about Sarah Louise Upshaw's big painting! Yes, that was it! She was going to tell the group that Sarah Louise was going to enter a huge painting, and now they already knew it. So Clara did her best to make things look normal, like she hadn't forgotten anything.

Clara spoke up loudly, smiling and excited, "Oh yes, I know all about it! And I think it's wonderful! Don't you? Michael told me all about it. He ordered the canvas for her himself. That's how he came to know. Yes, I know all about it. We need more artists to do what Sarah Louise is doing!"

Lucinda's jaw dropped so far that Huey Eugene was tempted to push it back in place for her. But instead, he spoke up, "I agree, Miss Clara, and I know just the place to hang it! Right in the center of the exhibition…so you don't see it when you walk right in but when you turn past the old scoreboard and go left—the very center of the exhibition!"

Clara was so glad that she had remembered something. She smiled triumphantly to herself then told Huey, "Oh, that would be a wonderful place! I'm so glad you thought of that, Huey Eugene!"

"But, Mrs. Dorphman," Lucinda almost yelled, "this painting is not going to be like all the others. It's going to be—"

"Something big, yes. Isn't that grand!" Clara said, almost ecstatic.

Calpurnia ramped up. "I have to get to a ribbon cutting, but don't worry. I'll put the word out. This is going to be the best Spring Fling ever! It's going to be fantastic, fantastic, fantastic!"

With that, she left.

The meeting then seemed to dissolve quietly as Huey gloated, Lucinda and Malvenna made some excuse to go to their offices, and Louise and Isadora made small talk with Clara about unimportant details of the show.

When Clara left, smiling in her absentminded way, the decision had been made. Sarah Louise's *A Room Full of Naked Men* was going to be in the Tenth Annual Spring Fling Art Show and Antique Auction to Benefit the Art Guild's Town-Beautification Project.

14

When Winslow grabbed the prostrate body of Hannah Bugleman by the arms and pulled her out from under the kitchen table, he pulled a muscle in his back. With Hannah revived and sipping tea with the others, he had returned to the den and was stretched out on the sofa. He had pulled this muscle before—anytime he tried to pick up something heavier than himself—and he always suffered for it.

Now, when he wasn't suppressing expletives, he was moaning out loud. Claudette entered the room, "Here, Winslow, I've got the hot pad. It was at the bottom of the cedar chest. I knew it was in there somewhere. I'm sorry I took so long."

"Ohhhhh," Winslow moaned.

"Don't carry on so, Winslow. You sound like you're on your deathbed."

"I may be...ohhhhhhh!"

"This should help some...I'll get some Advil from the bathroom."

"Get two!"

As Claudette plugged the hot pad in and placed it on his lower back, Winslow stopped moaning long enough to interrogate her. "Now, will you just tell me, what you did, or said, to cause Hannah to faint."

"Ohhhh, Winslow…I'll have to tell you later…I need to get back to the girls. There, now, want me to put an afghan on top of the pad? It will help hold the heat in."

"Use the plaid one. The knitted one is too heavy."

"Yes, Winslow…now, you rest, and I'll get the Advil."

Winslow moaned one more time for dramatic effect as Claudette left the room. Then he thought, *Something fishy is going on here.* It was not card-playing day, yet the gang of four (as he referred to them) were here. And another thing. It was early. Too early to be playing cards. Maybe they were all going shopping. That would make sense, but it still didn't explain why Hannah had fainted or why Claudette wouldn't tell him more.

"Here, Winslow. Two Advil and a glass of water," Claudette offered up as she reentered the room.

"Ohhhhhh," Winslow responded, as if on cue.

She handed him the two pills and the water and checked to see if the heating pad was working.

"I wish you'd tell me what is going on, Claudette! Are you four girls about to go out on some kind of a shopping trip?"

Claudette thought for a moment. "You might say that, Winslow…yes, I guess you could call it that…" Then she left him to his misery, closing the door to keep from hearing his sporadic gasps of pain.

As she returned to the tangerine-and-orange kitchen, Claudette tried to get her mind off Winslow's pulled back muscle and back to the problem at hand: how to procure five naked men. Maybe, *procure* wasn't such a good choice of words.

Before Claudette could pull her chair out and sit down, Hannah sat her cup of tea down and began a tirade. "Claudette, if you think I'm going to help you find a passel of naked men, you're off you rocker!"

"Not a passel, Hannah, only five. That's not a passel, is it?" This was said by Annie, a little sheepishly.

"Passel, caboodle, tribe! It doesn't matter! I'm not going to leave here and go searching for men to pose for Sarah Louise. If she painted lighthouses like I told her, we wouldn't have this problem!"

Bonnie spoke up, "Hannah, Claudette needs us. If she can't turn to her best friends, who can she turn to?"

"Besides, Hannah, we don't have to really find naked men, just men who will take their shirts off...I think. Am I right, Claudette?" Annie timidly asked.

Hannah, Bonnie, and Annie all looked at Claudette for her response.

"Now that you think about it, you're right, Annie. Sarah Louise said she wasn't going to really show the men naked, only partly. Like I told you, one behind the sofa, one looking out the window..."

"So if we can find a man who will agree to pose with his shirt off, that would do? Right, Claudette?" Annie said, her voice hopeful.

"Yes, Annie, I think that would work...at least for the man behind the sofa..."

Bonnie took this as good news. "That's not so bad. I think we can all find a man who will take his shirt off."

Hannah, always the contrary one, spoke up, "Just hope that's all they take off. I know enough about men to know they would take advantage of a situation like that! Sarah Louise better keep a loaded gun by her easel."

Claudette grimaced at the thought of a loaded gun in the house. "I suppose I could put Winslow in there while Sarah Louise is painting. I bet that would work. I don't think anybody would try anything funny with him there."

Hannah smiled. "Let Winslow have the loaded gun! That would make them keep their hands to themselves!"

"So you see, Hannah, if each of us helps Claudette by finding one man who will take his shirt off and pose for Sarah Louise, and Winslow stands there with a loaded gun—I think it will work out fine!" Bonnie smiled as she spoke.

Annie pursed her lips, a sure sign she was in deep thought. "Now, let me make sure I have this right. We each need to find a man who will agree to pose for Sarah Louise, but they just have to take off their shirt, and it should be somebody we can trust... but Winslow will be standing there with a loaded gun...just in case." She paused then added, "Am I right?"

Claudette nodded in agreement.

Annie continued, "I guess my next question is, What kind of men does Sarah Louise want to paint?"

Hannah looked surprised. "What do you mean, what kind of men?"

"Well, there are all kinds of men...young, old, fat, skinny," Annie said.

"Or what about hair?" Bonnie blurted out.

"Hair?" Hannah and Claudette both said at the same time.

"Yes, hair! Some men have hairy chests! My brother has a hairy back. Why, we used to tell him he would make a good bearskin rug. He didn't think it was as funny as we did," Bonnie explained.

"And to see your brother now, he has more hair on his back than he does on his head!" Hannah said.

"You're right, Hannah. And that's something else. Does she want a bald-headed man?"

Claudette looked at Bonnie and answered, "Oh, I don't think so."

Then Annie spoke up, "Shaved heads are very trendy today. A lot of actors have them, and those rap people. I think they all shave their heads."

Claudette put her hand to her forehead. "This is getting to be complicated. I didn't think about those things."

"Well, you should have, Claudette! You expect us to go out and find naked men, and you can't even tell us what kind of men to get," Hannah announced in her usual condescending way.

"Maybe Sarah Louise could give you a shopping list, Claudette," Annie suggested.

"A shopping list?" Hannah repeated in shock. "That's great! Why don't the four of us just head out to Walmart right now with our shopping lists in hand and go shopping for naked men? I'll go to hardware, and, Annie, you can go to produce. And, Bonnie, why don't you take housewares—"

Claudette had heard enough. She raised her voice, "Stop right there, Hannah. We get the idea. I need to talk to Sarah Louise again. She just said *men*, and I never thought to ask her what type. Tall, dark, and handsome or blond and muscular...I just don't know."

Bonnie patted Claudette on the arm. "She may have to take whatever we can find. I mean, it may not be so easy to find someone. If she wants a sixty-two-year-old man with a beer belly, I guess I could talk my husband, Dewey, into taking his shirt off—"

"Dewey?" Hannah said in shock. "I'm sure she doesn't want to paint an old geezer like Dewey!"

Bonnie was already getting a little aggravated with Hannah's uncooperative attitude, but that was too much. "And I guess you think she would rather paint that computer-geek nephew of yours!"

"And what's wrong with my nephew? He doesn't have a beer belly!"

"He doesn't have any common sense either! The boy doesn't know enough to come in out of the rain..."

Claudette looked in dismay at Bonnie and Hannah as they continued to berate each other. Annie was trying to separate them before they came to blows. Claudette put her hands on both sides of her head and shook her head in confusion. If the day was starting off this bad, what would the next week and a half bring?

15

By the time Dotie and Sarah Louise got to the office area of the high school, Sarah Louise had gotten her breathing back to normal. When they made their way behind the long counter that separated the students from the office workers' area, Miss Jean, the school secretary and the real brains behind the school, looked Sarah Louise square in the eye and pointed to the principal's office. Her tone of voice, when she spoke, was serious. "Coach Hatton's expecting you, Sarah Louise. Go right in."

Sarah Louise turned to Dotie. The panicked look came to both their faces. Coach Hatton was Mr. Hatton to the students but Coach to everyone else who remembered when he was a member of the faculty like them. A couple of state championships in football had catapulted him to the principal's office, but his brain was still on the forty-yard line. Even so, to be called into his office meant you were in trouble.

Coach ran the school like he did the football field. He went out on the field and talked to his players in person. If he wanted to talk to a teacher, he just popped up in their room. When he called you to the locker room or the office, it meant something serious.

Sarah Louise turned to face Dotie. "Wish me luck, Dotie," she said.

"Oh, I do, I do," Dotie whispered as Sarah Louise turned back around and headed across the office area.

As Sarah Louise walked past the secretary's desk, she took a deep breath; then she suddenly let it back out. Looking ahead, she saw that someone else was sitting in Coach Hatton's office, and she recognized his profile. It was William Simpson, the chairman of the school board!

She stopped at the entrance to the office, took another breath, and knocked feebly on the door facing. Coach Hatton looked up from his desk. "Come in, Upshaw, and close the door behind you."

Sarah Louise did just as he requested. As she pushed the door, she looked back into the office and saw Dotie, standing there with fingers crossed on both hands and holding them up so Sarah Louise could see. Her lips were mouthing the words *good luck*.

The door shut, she turned to face the coach turned principal.

"Sit down, Upshaw. I'm sure you've met Simpson, chairman of the school board!"

"Yes, Coach, Mr. Simpson and his wife go to the same church I do. I've known him all my life."

Simpson smiled at her and nodded slightly. "Nice to see you, Sarah Louise." He then turned to face Coach Hatton, as if expecting him to be the next one to say something.

"Upshaw, Simpson here has brought something to my attention, something that...uh...uh..."

Coach never was good with words. Give him a football or a weight bench, and he could stay busy for hours, but paperwork and mental work were beyond him. In fact, his desk was immaculate. Not because he was tidy but because anything that needed doing and required thought, he gave to Miss Jean.

Coach could discipline students well; his own personal bulk kept even the most belligerent of students respectful. But other than a good pep talk now and then, he was tongue-tied when something complicated came up, and this evidently was beyond his grasp.

"Uh...something that needs clearing up. Have you...uh... that is...are you...uh..."

Simpson took over. "Sarah Louise, my wife got a phone call last night from..." He stopped there, and Sarah Louise could see he was considering the consequences of naming someone. "A friend...and she had some shocking accusations concerning you."

Simpson turned to face Coach Hatton, but again, the coach was at a loss for words. So Simpson continued, "Sarah Louise, are you going to enter the Spring Fling Art Show?"

That was it, Sarah Louise thought. That had to be it. She hadn't murdered any students, or even harmed one. She hadn't been arrested for any heinous crimes, hadn't even written a bad check. She was on the carpet because of a silly title for a painting!

Sarah Louise was riled, and more than just a little. She eyed Simpson, who had been patronizing each time he used her name. She knew enough of him to be on the other side of this interrogation. There was that brief scandal about back taxes, and the words *tax evasion* came to mind, but she decided to play it cool. She would see if she could make him say the words that Coach was already hesitant to utter.

She smiled big and answered loud and confidently, "Yes, I am!"

Both men looked at her, but she didn't offer any more information. They looked at each other.

"Are you entering a painting, Upshaw?" Coach was now back in the conversation.

"Oh yes, I always do a painting for the Spring Fling...every year since I was in high school."

Again she stopped short of giving them what they wanted to hear. Simpson spoke again, "Sarah Louise, I have heard that your painting is...uh...is of something...something we think is a little...shall we say, unbefitting a teacher in the public school system!"

She was almost enjoying this. "Oh, really? What have you heard?" Again she put the pressure back on them. She could see Simpson squirm in his chair.

"Well, we've heard that you…uh, that you are going to do a painting of…uh…"

"Of what, Mr. Simpson?"

Simpson swallowed.

"Of naked men, Upshaw!" Coach Hatton suddenly blurted out. "Of naked men!"

Where was the candid camera crew when you needed them? Sarah Louise would like to have captured the look on both their faces. Coach's face was contorted, and Simpson's face had turned a bright red.

"Oh, is that what you've heard?"

She said it so easy and calmly that Simpson was confused. Again he turned to look at the Coach, but Coach was once again speechless. Simpson turned back to face Sarah Louise and almost shouted, "Are you doing a painting called *A Room Full of Naked Men?*"

"Oh yes!" she replied. Sarah Louise smiled at both men, wondering what was going on in the not-so-deep recesses of their brains.

"Would you please do some explaining, Upshaw! Just what kind of painting is this? Tell Simpson and me what's going on!" Coach demanded.

Sarah Louise was on a roll. She had been intimidated when she had walked into the room, but now she had both men nervous and confused. And while sitting there, she had come up with an ingenious ploy.

"Coach, would you look behind you, on the bookshelf there."

Coach Hatton turned slightly and seemed to notice for the first time that there were shelves of books in the room.

"If you'll look on the second shelf, right there next to your elbow, those are copies of all the textbooks used in this school. You keep a copy of each and every one, in case some parent complains about what we are teaching their impressionable children."

"Oh, really. Is that what these are?"

Sarah Louise almost shook her head in disbelief. He had been principal for two years and didn't know what the shelves of books behind his desk were for. "The big book, the spine says *A Student's History of Art* in gold letters, do you see it?"

Simpson spoke up, "Next to the yellow books on accounting, Coach."

Coach squinted his eyes and located the requested book. He pulled it off the shelf and started to hand it to Sarah Louise. She refused it, however.

"Oh, I don't need it. You keep it. Open it up to the index."

It took Coach a moment. He couldn't remember if the index came at the front of a book or at the back. They didn't use textbooks on the football field. When he found it, with Simpson's help, he looked at Sarah Louise for further instructions.

"Now, look up Marcel Duchamp. That's d-u-c-h-a-m-p."

Coach squinted again.

"When you find it, look under his name for the painting *Nude Descending a Staircase.*"

Coach and Simpson both looked at Sarah Louise in dismay.

"You mean there is a painting in this book of a naked woman walking down a staircase?"

Sarah Louise thought, *And paintings of cavemen and fertility symbols and naked Greek gods and goddesses and Renaissance Venuses. If they only knew.* But she kept those to herself. "Just turn to whatever page it gives there. I believe it's toward the end of the book, 'The Modern Art Years.'"

"What's that say, Simpson? I don't have my reading glasses!"

Simpson leaned a little farther over the desk. "It's 398, page 398!"

Coach's big thumbs turned to the page. He opened the book widely, and both men stared at the page. Their eyes ran down the page, but the naked woman evaded them.

"Let me see that index again, Coach. There's no picture of a naked woman there!"

But Sarah Louise interrupted the search. "You're on the right page. At the bottom of the page! The picture in shades of brown. Look closely at what the title of that picture is."

Simpson looked. He placed his forefinger on the caption below the picture and read it out loud, "*Nude Descending a Staircase* by French cubist artist Marcel Duchamp."

Sarah Louise knew this cubist masterpiece by heart. She had a large reproduction of it in her room. Every year, when she had her students study shapes, she would announce that they were going to look at the famous painting *Nude Descending a Staircase*. And every year, the students all giggled, particularly the boys, their hormones betraying their excitement at the thought of looking at a picture of a naked woman. And every year, she got a big laugh when she held up the reproduction. It was a confused mass of shapes and forms. The naked lady had been reduced by the artist into a series of brown and yellow shapes that bore little resemblance to a flesh-and-blood naked woman.

"Upshaw, I don't see a naked lady. This here picture is just a bunch of triangles and squares!"

"You see, Coach—and you too, Mr. Simpson—you can't tell what a painting is going to look like by its title. I think you are both worried over nothing."

At that moment, the bell rang, and Sarah Louise got up from her seat. "That's the bell for fourth period, and I need to get to my classroom. Any thing else?"

The two men were still looking at Duchamp's picture. Coach looked up from the mass of cubist shapes. "You mean your painting is going to look like this, Upshaw?"

"I mean, Coach, that you shouldn't judge a picture by its title. May I go now?"

"Uh…sure, Upshaw."

As she left, Coach and Simpson turned the book upside down, still determined to find the naked woman in the painting.

16

Lucinda Hardin-Powell strained to attach the end of her seat belt to its latch. She had to take a deep breath and suck in her stomach to get it to reach. It wasn't that she was fat. But she wasn't skinny either. The problem was that BJ was fat, except his fat was all in his belly while Lucinda's was more evenly distributed with perhaps a second helping on top.

For them both to be able to use the family car and not have to readjust the seat belt each time, they had come to a compromise position. This worked for both of them, but only if Lucinda took a deep breath and sucked her stomach in. BJ just let the belt slide under his belly and let his fat lap over it.

It was one of life's little imponderables. We can put a man on the moon, but we can't make seat belts that automatically adjust to the person who's using them.

Lucinda had once clasped the belt with a twist in the latch so that when she reached over to push the release, it was turned backward. She spent fifteen minutes straining to find the release so she could reach over the back of the seat and smack BJ Junior for fighting with his little sister, Princess.

That had been a very frustrating fifteen minutes, much like the meeting she had just left.

Lucinda had been so sure Clara Dorphman would be shocked over Sarah Louise Upshaw's painting that she would have placed money on it down at the pool hall where all the county's illegal gambling went on. As it was, she was wrong. The old lady had been enthusiastic about the picture.

"Old dingbat," Lucinda muttered half out loud as the seat belt finally closed with a click. She turned the ignition and then gunned the engine. As the eight cylinders spun around, she slid the gearshift into reverse and backed out of her parking spot.

After the meeting, Malvenna and Lucinda had gone back to their smelly old offices and rehashed everything. Malvenna wanted to spare the Art Guild the humiliation she knew they would have when people saw the scandalous painting. Lucinda felt the same way, but she also wanted to put perky little Sarah Louise "Most Versatile" Upshaw in her place. No one—not even Malvenna or even her husband, BJ—realized the double motive behind everything she had done in the past twenty-four hours.

When they had both left the old school building turned Art Guild—Malvenna to get home in time for *The Young and the Restless* and Lucinda to double-check on BJ's ability to stick to his diet—they had both felt up against a stone wall. They couldn't argue with Clara Dorphman. Not only did she control the Art Guild, but her oldest son, Jefferson Davis Dorphman, was the president of the bank and BJ's boss.

Malvenna's husband, "Booger," operated a backhoe. His specialty was sewer drain lines. Malvenna didn't feel quite as obligated to not argue with Clara Dorphman, but Booger would need a new backhoe one day, and they would go to Jefferson Davis Dorphman for the loan.

Lucinda turned out of the parking lot and started to the bank. She drove down the main street of town. Everything was on this one street or just off it, except the new Walmart and a couple of new fast-food restaurants that had located on the bypass. Rumor had it that a bowling alley was going to be built next to the megastore. Calpurnia Pendergrass would have a ribbon cutting for that too. Lucinda could visualize the front page of the *Sulphur Springs Sentinel* with a picture of Calpurnia in her 1950s fashions, holding a giant cardboard pair of scissors, cutting a bold red ribbon, and—

The brakes on the car squealed!

Lucinda had just gotten an idea. She slammed her foot on the brake and jerked the steering wheel to the left, making a U-turn right at the center of town. If she had looked to see if there was anyone behind her, or even on the other lane, you wouldn't have been able to tell by any outward actions such as using a turn signal!

No, she made the U-turn and sped down the street to Sputnik Boulevard. There, she took a sharp right and headed to a small black-and-orange cinder-block building with the words, also in orange and black, "Sulphur Springs Sentinel." In smaller orange letters, it said, "Your weekly source of all the news that's fit to print."

Sputnik Boulevard had been Peeler Road but was renamed in the 1950s when the former alley was widened and paved and the newspaper moved to new offices. The Peelers were some of the town's first residents, but they were all gone or deceased, so no one complained when the trendy new name was placed on the old dirt road that had once led to their simple two-room shack. The city fathers had touted the new road as a sign of progress and the new newspaper office as a sign of new development. Sixty years later, and the only other buildings on the street were a wishy-washy and Paw Paw's Year-Round Flea Market and Junque Store. So much for development!

Lucinda pulled up in front of the garish building. The paper took pride in reporting all the high school sports news, and the orange and black were to remind people of their devotion to the hometown team, the Warriors. A fiberglass Indian brave with a tomahawk, the team's mascot, had once stood outside the building, but it had become an annual senior prank to either steal it or cover it with toilet paper. The statue was now kept safely inside.

As she turned the ignition key off, Lucinda looked around and saw a small green two-seater sports car parked in the side Employees Only parking lot. Yes, it was there. That was good. That meant that Avis was there, and Avis was just who Lucinda wanted to see.

Avis Lipowitz was the only child of the paper's owners, George Thomas and Elizabeth Ann Stump. As such, she had inherited the paper and—along with her husband, Clarence C. Lipowitz— ran the town's weekly. Avis had been "too good" to go to the state college down the road. At least her parents felt that way so they had sent her back east to an exclusive all-girl's college. It was there that she met her husband. He attended a prominent university in the same town. That explains how a Stump became a Lipowitz, and it also explains how a Yankee was now the editor of the town's newspaper, whose roots went back to the Civil War and when it was called *The Confederate Patriot.*

With luck, Lucinda thought as she got out of the car, Clarence C. wouldn't be there. He wasn't as easy to manipulate as Avis was. Avis, never a pretty girl in the first place, had few friends growing up; and since her marriage to out-of-towner Clarence, the couple had even fewer. This made Avis even lonelier, and when someone made an effort to speak to her, she took it as a sign of genuine friendship.

Lucinda didn't mind taking advantage of Avis this way. Lucinda was always one to see another person's weaknesses and could quickly conceive of a way to exploit them, even if she was unaware of her own weaknesses.

As she walked in the door of the newspaper and passed the fiberglass brave, Lucinda could see that Avis was sitting at a desk in the back office. Lucinda went straight there, not giving so much as a howdy to any of the three employees up front.

"Oh, hi, Avis, so glad I caught you in!"

Avis looked up from a stack of AP news releases. "Lucinda… how are you? I haven't seen you since the New Year's party at the country club!"

"Yes, wasn't that fun! You know, BJ and I have been meaning to have you two over to our house for a cookout, as soon as the weather gets good and warm!"

"Oh, that sounds like so much fun. It's so hard for me to get Clarence out of the house. Between the paper and his golf game, I swear I sometimes feel like a widow. What can I do for you?"

Lucinda could tell by the naive look on Avis's face that she hadn't heard about the painting yet. But then, who would have called her? Avis had no life other than Clarence and the paper. She had no close friends. This was good for Lucinda, though; it would let her be the first to tell her and allow her to put her own spin on the story.

"It's time for the annual Spring Fling Art Show and Antique Auction!" Lucinda began.

"Is it that time again? Where does time go?" Avis had never developed conversation skills. She tended to use a lot of common expressions.

"We always have it around the last week of March or first weekend of April. We have to be careful to not have it too close to Easter, you know. This year, it is April 2 and 3."

"If you have your press release, I'll see that one of the girls writes it up."

"Oh no, I need you to take care of this personally!"

"Personally…" Avis liked the sound of that. She leaned forward. Lucinda continued, "I guess you know Sarah Louise Upshaw?"

"The art teacher at the high school?"

"Yes, her."

"I know her like I know the back of my own hand."

"Well, then you know how hard she can be to work with…"

Actually, Avis didn't know that. Actually, she didn't know Sarah Louise Upshaw like the back of her own hand. She had just said that because it seemed like a good thing to say, but if her good friend Lucinda said so…

"Oh yes, she is, isn't she!" Avis agreed.

"She's going to enter a painting in the show this year." Lucinda paused dramatically. "And I'm afraid that it's going to create a little problem"—another pause—"and that's why I wanted to talk to you. You're such a good friend."

Avis was smiling at the word *friend*, and she hardly noticed when Lucinda got up from her seat, shut the door to the office, and sat back down. "And I thought you should be the first to know…"

17

Ruby Stafford dropped four coins into the old red Coke machine at Pearl's Beauty Shoppe, spelled with two *p*'s, like the one Pearl had seen on the window of a shop in the movie *Down and Out in Beverly Hills*. Pearl thought it brought a little class to the establishment she had run for most of her life.

Just now, Pearl looked over at Ruby, who was waiting patiently for her Coke to pop out. "It's on the blink again, Ruby. You'll have to hit it broadside with your rear end!"

Ruby, who had been coming to Pearl's every Thursday for twenty-plus years to get her hair done, looked up at Pearl, confused.

Pearl made a swinging motion with her hip to show Ruby how it was done then added, "Just slam it once good on the side with your hip—works every time!"

All the eyes in the beauty shop were now looking at Ruby to see if she could swing her hip just right and make the old machine cough up its sugary potion. Ruby sucked her gut in and gave her hip a twist, but she didn't have enough oomph to produce any results.

"Hold on, Miss Ruby, I'll show you," hollered Charlene, the other beautician. She laid her scissors down and scurried across the black linoleum floor to the machine. There, she pulled Ruby to the side and swung her own ample hip against the metal box.

Clunk, the machine sounded; and a second later, the cold drink popped down into the vacant slot in front.

"Oh, thank you, Charlene. I don't think I could have ever got up the strength to hit it like you did."

Before Ruby could grab her drink, Charlene reached down and pulled it out. Then she placed the bottle into the built-in bottle opener and, with a nice fizzy *pop*, opened it for Ruby. As Charlene handed it to Ruby, she reached over and felt Ruby's hair. "You need to get back under the hair dryer, Miss Ruby. Your hair ain't half dry!"

As the two walked back across the room, Ruby spoke, "Well, let me finish this first, and I'll get back under the dryer. You're not ready for me now, are you?"

Charlene put an arm around the old woman. "No, sweetie, not yet. You go ahead and swallow that drink, and I'll get to you in a bit, okay?"

As she sat down on the red Naugahyde sofa that set opposite the beauty-shop chairs, Ruby turned to face Pearl. "Pearl, I guess that old Coke machine is as old as you and I are. How long have you had it?"

"It was here when I bought the shop back in '68, so I don't rightly know. But the Coke man has to order the bottles special for me 'cause it's so old."

"And they taste so much better in the bottles!"

"Don't they!"

Pearl turned her attention back to her customer, Thelma Montgomery. "So, Thelma, before I put this rinse on, what was it you said you wanted to tell me about Fred Macon over at the feed store?"

"Well, it's just that I heard that he and Mavis were getting a new carport from some guy they saw advertising on channel 30, and it was supposed to cost them four hundred dollars. That's the price they advertised."

Ruby, ever attentive to any conversations going on in the shop, quickly put her own two cents worth in, "Oh, I've seen those ads myself. My late husband Harold and I were thinking of getting one."

"Then you need to listen good, Ruby, 'cause when that man got finished, he gave Fred and Mavis a bill for nearly double that—seven hundred and fifty dollars!"

There was a collective sigh that went across the shop as each woman pulled in her breath in shock.

Pearl put it into words, "Well, I declare!"

Ruby quickly added, "I bet that gave Fred a heart attack. He's so tight with his money Mavis had to hang her laundry on the line the first ten years they were married. He was too cheap to buy her a dryer!"

Betty Jean Hopper, who was sitting in Charlene's chair, turned to face Pearl and Thelma.

"Why did the man charge Fred double?" Thelma continued with her story.

"Oh, he said that the TV special was for their basic model and that Fred and Mavis got the deluxe model. Of course, Fred wouldn't order a deluxe anything, but the man had a piece of paper that they had both signed, and on the top of the paper, in big letters, it said, 'Deluxe'!"

"Sounds like a flimflam to me," Pearl said, pulling a bobby pin from Thelma's hair.

Ruby took another swallow from her drink and decided to offer up a tidbit of her own. "Does anybody know anything about Theresa Smith and her husband? I heard that they're separated again!"

"If so, it makes about the umpteenth time. I don't know why she keeps letting that two-timer back in the house. I tell you, if a man cheats once, he'll cheat twice—and so on and so on!" Pearl spoke this as if she knew from experience.

As the rest of the women tacitly nodded in agreement with Pearl's bit of philosophy, the door to the shop opened, and in walked Mable Turner.

"You're an hour early, Mable! Your clock not on daylight savings time yet?"

Mable laughed at Pearl's comment and rushed over and sat next to Ruby on the Naugahyde couch, acknowledging Ruby's presence by reaching over and grabbing her hand and giving it a squeeze.

"Oh, Pearl, we weren't busy down at the store, so I told Elmer he could run things by himself, and I just drove myself on down here to be with all my Thursday friends…besides, I've got some really good gossip," Mable said.

Mable didn't mind calling gossip just that—gossip! The others might say they had a "bit of news" or that they had "overheard something," or they might ask if anyone "knew the whole story," but they rarely admitted to *gossip*. Not Mable. She would, as the old saying goes, call a spade a spade.

Ruby Stafford put the Coke bottle down and sat closer to Mable. "If it's about Theresa Smith and that no-count husband of hers, we've heard that!"

"Oh no, Ruby, that's two days' old—it's already stale! I heard this last night and straight from the horse's mouth. It has to do with the Annual Spring Fling Art Show down at the old high school gym and a certain unmarried school teacher, and…"

And so it spread. The phone line was the first level of communication. Then it hit the beauty shops around town. The next level would be the soccer games and Little League games on Saturday. The final and ultimate step in spreading the "have you heard the latest?" would be the church crowd on Sunday. By Sunday evening, everyone in town would know the story—or at least a variation of it.

In fact, news spread faster this way than if it was on the front page of the paper, but that too was right around the corner.

18

When the bell sounded to end sixth period, Sarah Louise was at wit's end. Already in a tizzy because she had to change her painting from *A Room Full of Cats* to *A Room Full of Naked Men*, she only got more uptight when her best friend, Dotie, tried to picture Claudette getting arrested for asking men in Walmart to "get naked for my daughter." But the incident that got her even tizzier was when she got called into Coach Hatton's office and had to tell him and Mr. Simpson of the school board that, indeed, she was doing a painting of naked men for the Annual Spring Fling and Antique Auction to Benefit the Art Guild's Town-Beautification Project!

Spring Fling! Sarah Louise wished she had never heard those words. The only bright spot was that there was no school Friday because the Sulphur Springs High School band was hosting the Midstate Annual Regional Invitational Band Competition. There would be bands competing from a ten-county region, and they would all be descending on Sulphur Springs High School tomorrow. So the school board had decided to give the students and teachers the day off so that the entire school could be given over to the competition.

Students blowing tubas, clanging on cymbals, and beating drums would be in every room—in the cafeteria, in the gym, and in the auditorium.

Sarah Louise gave her room a quick once-over to make sure that it was prepared for tomorrow's onslaught. The drying clay pinch pots were on shelves in the closet. All tables were clear and all supplies locked away in cabinets or drawers.

As she was about to grab her purse and jacket, two burly football boys entered the room.

"Coach Hatton told us to get a table from you for the front hall," the larger of the two boys said in a voice that was two octaves deeper than most boys his age but went along with his stout body.

The second boy was staring at Sarah Louise but didn't say anything. It wasn't unusual for other teachers to borrow tables from her room since she didn't use desks in her classroom like the others. People were always needing a table for something or other; in this case, it would probably be used in the front hall for registration during the band competition.

"Take this one right here," Sarah Louise said, pointing to the one closest to the door. "Just be careful not to hit the doorway as you go out. You'll have to turn it sideways!"

She helped the boys pull the chairs away from the table. She didn't know the boys by name, but their faces were familiar, as were most of the faces of the students. The school held grades seven to twelve, and that gave her plenty of time to see pretty much all the students by the time they graduated.

Even so, one of the two continued to stare at her every chance he got. *Peculiar*, she thought. *Maybe I've got a smudge of clay on my face. I've certainly done that before.*

As the two boys left the room with the table, Sarah Louise flipped the light switch and, grabbing her purse and jacket, shut the door and locked it. She looked up the hall, where the boys were carrying the table, and going slow because one of them, the "starer," was walking backward. Oblivious to her presence, he was saying, "That's her. She's the one I told you about!" It wasn't until she was leaving the building and starting across the parking lot that she realized what was going on.

He knew!

He knew that she was painting a picture of five naked men for the Annual Spring Fling Art Show and Antique Auction to Benefit the Art Guild's Town-Beautification Project! That's why he was staring!

Just like Coach Hatton and Mr. Simpson with the school board, he had heard all about the painting she was going to do. Sarah Louise stopped in her tracks. "Who else knows?" she asked herself. "Why, half the people in the county know!" she said out loud.

Startled by the sound of her own voice, she looked around her to see if anyone had heard her. Students were still getting in cars and leaving school. Other teachers were leaving the building. Noises were drifting across the parking lot from the band room. They were getting in one more practice before tomorrow's competition.

No one was looking at her in particular, so no one must have heard. She started walking again.

A car drove by, and a seventh-grade girl with wire-rimmed glasses and freckles looked at Sarah Louise from the rear window. As the car drove off, the girl continued to glare. "Ohhhh," Sarah said, half out loud again, "she knows! She's probably saying to the others in the car, 'There's that teacher that paints pictures of naked men!'"

When she got to her car, Sarah Louise jumped in and shut the door. She took a deep breath and tried to calm down. She took another breath. It wasn't helping any. She took a third deep breath—no good!

Sarah reached into the side-door pocket and grabbed a pair of sunglasses and hastily put them on her face. That helped a little. She wasn't so recognizable. An idea hit her. She opened the glove compartment and dug through its contents, pulling maps, pencils, store receipts, and such from its depths. "Aha!" she said, again out loud.

She pulled a rubber band from the compartment and then pulled her hair back and pulled the band around it, giving herself a ponytail. She looked into her rearview mirror. "I haven't looked like this since high school!"

She put her key into the ignition and started the engine. As she pulled out of her parking spot, Ms. Atwood, the French teacher, was getting into her car, two spaces down. She looked at Sarah Louise and waved big, yelling, "Bonjour, Ms. Upshaw! See you Monday week!"

Sarah waved back. "So much for trying to be incognito!" she mumbled to herself. Then she repeated Ms. Atwood's last two words, "Monday week." That was good. Next week was spring break. She wouldn't be back at school till the Spring Fling was over and forgotten. Forgotten…if only!

As she drove home, Sarah thought over the previous two days and all that had transpired. After going over it several times, she concluded that what was done was done, and there was no use trying to hide. Eventually everyone would know, so she might as well hold her head up high. After all, she wasn't going to really paint a picture of five naked men—just partially naked men!

Having the day off tomorrow and all of next week would give her the extra painting time she needed. That was a plus. She visualized herself at her canvas, painting away.

Then it hit her.

She didn't have enough flesh-colored paint—not if she was going to substitute five cats with five naked men. No, she was going to need a lot of flesh-colored paint.

Sarah Louise pulled into the parking lot of the Piggly Wiggly and made a U-turn. She then got back on the road and headed toward Dorphman's Hardware and Appliance. She hoped

Michael Dorphman wouldn't ask her why she was buying so much flesh-colored paint. What would she say if he did?

Just then, the light turned yellow thirty feet in front of her, and she came to a stop. Across the intersection, facing her, was a car full of people. They were looking in her direction—in fact, they were looking right at her.

Sarah Louise sunk a little lower in her car seat so that her head barely peered over the dashboard.

19

Clarence Lipowitz parked his big SUV next to his wife's green sports car and took one last sip from his Nehi grape soda. It did the best job of hiding the smell of martinis on his breath. Today had been a three-martini day.

Usually he stopped at two martinis, but his golf game hadn't gone as well as he liked. It wasn't that he was a bad golfer. He was one of the best at the La Vista Country Club and 18 Hole Golf Course. It was just that today he actually played with someone better than himself, Joe Silverman with State Farm Insurance. Joe didn't live here, but he was a regional manager and passed through here quarterly. Joe had come as a guest of Steven, who ran the local office—Steven Butts, that is. Around here he was just Steven B. Steven B had brought Joe along with him.

Clarence could beat Steven B any day of the week. But today Joe Silverman was with him, and Joe had the low score by a good five strokes. Clarence hated that. There was a lot Clarence hated. He hated his job, his wife, his house, his kids, his neighbors, his lot in life. There were things he liked of course: money, big cars, prestige, loose women, beating people at golf, beating people at anything.

Clarence sighed and climbed out of the SUV. It was big and ebony black and had a shine that was the envy of every car in Sulphur Springs—if cars could show envy. It was the most expensive SUV on the car lot. That was the main reason he talked Avis, his wife, into buying it. He told her that the bigger the SUV, the safer he would be in case of an accident.

Avis!

What would he tell Avis when he walked into the *Sulphur Springs Sentinel*, and she asked him where he had been? He was supposed to be back by 1:00 p.m., and here it was, almost 3:00 p.m. He wouldn't tell her that three martinis took a while, at least if you wanted to relish every drop. Well, he would have to think of something to say, or perhaps say nothing. That sometimes worked as well.

Avis was short, with mouse-colored hair and a plain face to match. She had no personality, which was why she had been attracted to Clarence. He had a bold personality. He was tall, dark, and handsome—except for his nose. There was no way to describe his nose other than to say that it entered the room two minutes before he did. The attraction had been mutual. She had been emotionally needy, and he had been financially needy.

When Avis looked up from the counter in the front office of the *Sentinel*, where she was going over accounts with Rebecca, the bookkeeper, she anxiously looked into her husband's brooding eyes. She could gauge his moods that way and adjust her tone of voice to fit whatever mood he was in. If he was in a bad mood, she tried to soothe him over. If he was in a good mood, she tried to keep him that way. In fact, she pretty much did everything she could to keep him happy—with varying degrees of success.

Right now he looked strangely moodless. He wasn't mad. That was good. Yet he wasn't particularly happy either. Poor Avis. To play it safe, she took the cheerful route. "Oh, there you are, Clarence. How was your golf game? I was starting to get a little worried."

Clarence didn't answer. He walked past her and Rebecca and into the back office and sat down at the desk where he then pretended to go through the stack of memos that lay there.

Avis, embarrassed by his lack of response to her question, turned to her bookkeeper. "He's had so much on him lately. That's why I sent him off to play a little golf. It relaxes him, you know."

Rebecca nodded as if she understood.

"You can finish this, Rebecca. I need to go over some things with Clarence."

Avis turned and walked into the back office, carefully closing the door behind her. She so hated it when Clarence was moody or yelled at her, and the employees could hear.

Rebecca, meanwhile, turned to face Julie and Edward, the other employees of the paper. Julie was a staff writer, specializing in obituaries; and Edward was the sports writer but, like all of them, could do anything as the need arose.

"Poor Clarence, he has it so tough," Rebecca said.

"I'll say," answered Edward. "It's not easy being the lapdog of a poor little rich girl. I should have it so tough."

Julie joined the discussion, keeping her voice down, lest Avis overheard. "I feel sorry for Avis. She does everything she can to make him happy, and he treats her like dirt."

"I don't feel too sorry for her. She bought him and paid for him. She can have him!" Rebecca, as the bookkeeper, knew just how expensive it was to keep Clarence happy.

Edward made one more comment before getting back to his writing, "Besides, he knows he can't be too mean to her. She does sign all the checks!"

"I guess you're right." Julie sighed, and she too got back to work. If people only knew how hard it was to write an obituary for someone who had a boring life, like the one she was working on now.

Back in the office, Avis leaned over her husband and gave him a peck on the cheek. "Don't worry about the memos, dear. I'll take care of them." She took them and walked over to her side of the double desk. "You look tired, Clarence." Then, before he could answer, she added, "Who did you play with today?"

Clarence realized he would have to say something eventually. "Just some guys."

That was a clear signal not to ask anymore about the golf game, so Avis changed the subject. She actually had something to talk about that Clarence might enjoy hearing. "Guess who came by to see me today?"

Clarence shrugged. "Let me guess, Avis. The queen of England!"

That was good; Clarence was being funny. Avis breathed a sigh of relief. "Oh, silly, no! Lucinda Hardin-Powell."

Clarence thought for a moment. "The snobby fat lady with the two brats and redneck husband?" To Clarence, everyone in Sulphur Springs was a redneck. Actually, to Clarence, everyone this side of the Mason-Dixon line was a redneck.

"Oh, Clarence, she's one of my best friends!"

That was news to Clarence.

"Anyway, she had some really good gossip about the Annual Spring Fling and Antique Auction."

"Oh yes, the annual Let's Try to Have a Little Class and Impress Our Neighbors with Our Fingerpainting affair!"

Avis laughed as his acid comment. She had no idea that it was his third martini doing the talking. "They mean well, Clarence."

"So what's the gossip?"

"Well, it seems that Sulphur Springs has a little controversy going for it. One of the artists this year is going to exhibit a painting that is absolutely scandalous!"

"Don't tell me. A painting of Jesus waterskiing down at Lake Cherokee!"

That third martini had been stronger than the others!

"Clarence. You should be ashamed!"

"Well, what then?"

"Sarah Louise Upshaw is entering a painting called *A Room Full of Naked Men*."

Clarence thought for a moment. He was trying to picture just who Sarah Louise Upshaw was. "Is she the one who paints all those cross-eyed people?"

"Oh no, that's Lucy Pendergrass! Sarah Louise is the art teacher at the high school. She usually paints cats and flowers."

Clarence scowled. "It's probably a joke or something. You sure that Lucinda is not pulling your leg?"

"Oh no, it's true. Lucinda got it straight from the horse's mouth. A room full of n-a-k-e-d m-e-n!"

"And just who are these naked men?"

"I don't know. We didn't talk about that. Lucinda wants me to run a front-page story on it. Of course, she found out too late for this week's paper. It will have to wait till next week."

"Have you talked to this Sarah Louise Whatever-Her-Name-Is?"

"No, I haven't, but I will before the next issue."

Clarence thought. He tried to connect the name Sarah Louise with a face. It was no good, no face, but did that really matter? "I tell you what, Avis, I'll interview her myself. This might just be a great little story. A controversy right here in Sulphur Springs. Why, we might get this on the Associated Press wires!"

Avis looked at Clarence. He was actually interested in writing something for the paper. He hadn't shown so much interest since the roof blew off Billy Bob's 24 Hour Truck Stop and Foxy Ladies' Lounge in Hopkinsville during that tornado a year ago. He drove for an hour to cover that story. Now, Clarence had a smirk on his face. No, Avis thought, it was a smile on his lips. Pleased that something she had said had made him smile, Avis smiled too.

Clarence was smiling all right. He was thinking, *What kind of girl paints naked men?* That was the kind of girl he'd like to interview!

20

Every time a customer entered Dorphman's Hardware and Appliance, a little bell that hung above the door rang.

Michael Dorphman, waiting on a customer who needed the right size drill bit for a DIY project, looked up at the door and did a double take. A lady had just come in with a baseball cap pulled low down on her head, wearing sunglasses and with her hair pulled back in a ponytail. She had a determined look on her face that bordered on a frown.

Still talking to his customer, he watched as this stranger headed straight towards the back of the store, past the stoves and microwaves, to where all the art supplies were kept. She moved as if she knew exactly where she was going.

He turned his attention back to his customer.

"I'm sure that the quarter-inch bit, or the three-sixteenths, will do the job from what you've told me. If I were you, I'd buy them both, just to be on the safe side and avoid having to make another trip into town. Besides, sooner or later, you're going to need both these sizes for other projects."

"Well, that makes sense. I'll take them both."

Michael was a good salesman and personable, which was why Dorphman's Hardware and Appliance was still in business despite the proximity of two large building and home-supplies retailers in each of the neighboring counties.

Of all the Dorphman family enterprises, this was the one Michael felt most at home with. He had helped his father here as he grew up; and after his father's early death due to lung cancer, he had simply stayed on and posted a No Smoking sign by the front door. He could have had a job at the bank, the old hotel, the lumberyard, or the feed mill. After all, he had a college degree in business management. But he also felt he had a little grasp on what *happiness* was, and to his way of thinking, a certain amount of happiness lies in doing something you enjoy.

It was a concept lost on his wife. She didn't marry a "store clerk," she often said, implying that he was little more than just that. She had married a promising college graduate and president of Sigma Tau Omega, the most prestigious fraternity on campus. She no doubt felt that he was "going places."

Sulphur Springs wasn't what she had in mind when she thought of "going places." In fact, when they had married right after their college graduations, they had moved to Hopkinsville, and both gotten excellent jobs.

When, five years later, Michael's father had gotten sick and Michael was needed at the store, she thought it was only a temporary move. As it was, the next move was hers, and she took it—out of Sulphur Springs and out of Michael's life.

Michael often thought about the turn of events that led to his recent divorce, hypothesizing how things might have turned out differently *if*—but he always came to the same conclusion. He really didn't miss his wife, and in fact, he was actually a little relieved that she was gone.

After ringing up the purchase of the two drill bits, Michael looked around to see if there were any other customers needing help; and when he didn't see any, he headed back toward the art supplies to see what the stranger with the sunglasses might need.

There was something about her face, what little he could see, that had been vaguely familiar.

When he turned down the aisle with the painting supplies, the strange customer had pulled the sunglasses down to the end of her nose and was peering over them to get a better look at the tube of paint she held in her hand.

"Find what you're looking for, ma'am?" Michael asked as he stepped closer to the woman.

"Oh, hi, Michael. You startled me for a second," Sarah Louise spoke up.

Whoever the lady was, she knew who he was, yet he still couldn't tell who she was. He twisted his mouth in confusion and tried to peer closer at her face.

Sarah Louise caught his intent expression and realized there was a problem. "It's me, Sarah Louise Upshaw!"

"Oh, I'm sorry, Sarah Louise, I didn't recognize you...," he fumbled for words. "What with the hat and sunglasses and all! Trying to avoid the paparazzi?"

Feeling suddenly very silly, Sarah Louise pulled off the hat and stuffed it into her purse and pushed the sunglasses in after them. "There, recognize me now?"

"Yeah, although I don't think I've seen you with your hair pulled back in a ponytail since we were...on the swim team at the pool, back in—"

"Sixth grade! I'd almost forgotten!"

They both laughed.

Sarah had always had a soft spot for Michael. They had known each other all their lives and gone to school together. His family were Methodists, and hers were Baptists; but in a small town, they all mingled together in some form or another. Of course, the Dorphmans were in the country-club set, and the Upshaws weren't. But Michael had never shown any pretenses, and although they had never been close friends, they had been on the same swim team with the town's Summer Recreation League way back in the sixth grade.

"I told my grandmother about your painting."

Sarah Louise stared at Michael blankly at his sudden change of subject. She thought, *He knows...and now his sweet little old grandmother knows!* Then she said, "You told her about my painting?"

"Yes, I told her that you had bought a really large canvas and were going to paint a really large picture for the Spring Fling."

"Oh...you told her I was going to do a large picture. That's nice." Sarah Louise smiled an uneasy smile at Michael. "You didn't tell her what I was painting, did you? I mean, what I'm going to paint on the canvas, did you? I mean, the exact thing I'm going to put in the painting, did you?" Her voice was uneasy.

"No."

"You didn't?"

"How could I?"

"Yes, how could you?"

Something in her inflection when she made this last remark made Michael feel peculiar, as if he needed to explain further. "I don't know what you're going to paint, so how could I?"

Sarah Louise breathed a little sigh of relief. "Yes, I don't think I told you, did I?" She smiled and paused then added, "And you haven't heard anything about my painting, have you?"

"No, why? Should I have?"

"Oh, no, no...I just...I just thought that maybe you had heard something strange or something..."

Michael was going from confused to really confused. "Why? Is there something strange about your picture?"

Sarah Louise looked at Michael and smiled real big. "Let's just say it's not my typical painting...you know, cats and flowers, and more flowers, and more cats!"

The way she said this made Michael laugh. The bell on the door to the store rang, and he turned to see who had come in then turned back to face Sarah. "Another customer. Do you need any help? If not, I need to go check on them."

"Go right ahead, Michael. I need to browse a little more anyway."

He gave a very personable smile to her and turned and walked away. Sarah looked after him as he walked off. *So,* she thought, *that's one person in town who doesn't know. Not yet anyway!* She decided to only get one tube of flesh-colored paint for now, and she grabbed a purple and an orange to go with them to serve as a distraction.

When she got to the end of the aisle, she saw Michael was at the cash register with another customer, a middle-aged woman with a small child. Two teens had just walked in and were looking at the display of fishing lines.

Seeing them, Sarah Louise stopped. She thought for a moment and then reached inside her purse and pulled out the hat and sunglasses. Putting the hat on her head again and pulling it down as far as it would go, she then put the sunglasses back on and proceeded to the cash register. She wondered if this was how spies and undercover men operated.

21

The smell of garlic was heavy in the house when Claudette called Sarah Louise to supper. It was so strong that Sarah felt compelled to say something. "What are you cooking, Mother? It smells like a garlic factory in here!"

"Your mother is cooking garlic-roasted pork chops, with garlic-seasoned mashed potatoes, and garlic-and-cheese-flavored biscuits!"

This came from her father, Winslow, as he sat at the round kitchen table and pulled the tangerine-colored Fiesta ware salt-and-pepper shakers to his side of the table. He twisted in his chair, his back still bothering him.

"Don't tell me, Pop," said Sarah Louise as she sat down, "there was a two-for-one special on garlic down at Harry's Foodland."

"Good guess, Sarah Louise, but I don't let your father shop for groceries anymore…not since the time he came home with forty-eight cans of tiny Le Seur green peas."

"They were on special, Claudette, and a very good special at that! Besides, I like green peas!"

"Good, because when you get old and toothless, I'm going to puree those green peas and feed them to you three times a day!"

Winslow looked at his daughter. "They were at a really good price."

Sarah Louise looked back at him and made a sympathetic expression. "I know, Pop, and a penny saved is a penny earned. But you know, you're the only one in this house that eats green peas." She paused and then said, "So what's with the garlic if it wasn't a really good price at Harry's Foodland?"

Claudette set a small platter of pork chops on the table, with chopped garlic liberally sprinkled on top, and a bowl of garlic-seasoned mashed potatoes. She returned to the stove to check on the biscuits. Without looking back at the two sitting at the table, she tossed out, "And don't touch those potatoes till I sit down with the biscuits!"

Winslow put the serving spoon back into the potatoes with a slight frown.

Opening the door to the stove, in all its tangerine glow, Claudette peered inside. "Tell her, Winslow. Tell Sarah Louise why all the garlic!"

"This week is the Food Channel's Salute to Garlic!"

Then before he could say more, Claudette interrupted, "These are only three of the dozen recipes your father copied from the TV. Can you believe it? He gave me a recipe for garlic ice cream!"

"Garlic ice cream! Really, Pop!"

"Well, it sounded interesting."

Claudette pulled the pan of garlic-and-cheese biscuits from the oven.

"Need any help, Mother?"

"You can get the bowl of applesauce from the refrigerator."

By the time both women had returned to the table, one with a basket of hot biscuits and the other with a bowl of cinnamon-flavored applesauce, Winslow had two pork chops on his plate and was heaping the heavy-scented mashed potatoes beside them.

The meal then progressed nicely. The talk ran from recipes to the day's news, and they even discussed the weather. It wasn't until Winslow was loading his plate with seconds that the talk actually turned to the most pressing topic of the past few days—the painting.

"Oh, Sarah Louise…Hannah called me, right before I started supper, and told me that Herman will be here…around seven."

"Herman?"

"Her nephew…Herman."

"I know who Herman is, Mother, but why is he coming here?"

"He's Hannah's contribution to your painting. We drew lots, and Hannah drew first. Annie has Saturday, and Bonnie has Monday…I have Wednesday."

Winslow was buttering his third biscuit. "What are you talking about, Claudette? Hannah's nephew? Annie has Saturday?"

"You don't know, do you? Sarah Louise left them up to us…the men…the men in her painting…we have to supply her models…"

"So that's why Herman is coming over. But, Mother, Herman?"

"Let's don't go into it, Sarah Louise. Hannah almost died when I told her she would have to find me a man to pose for you. She never got past the word *naked*. She said she'd try to get Herman, and I said he would do. I mean, he is a man, a little geeky…but still, he's a young man. Well, anyway, he agreed, and she asked *when*, and you were at school, but I thought if he came at night—I don't want the neighbors to see a bunch of men coming and going from your studio. And with tomorrow off from school, you can sketch him tonight. And that gives you all day tomorrow to paint and then, Saturday…well, you get the idea."

Winslow still had the hot buttered biscuit in his hand. His mouth had dropped open wide enough to put two buttered biscuits in at the same time.

"You were going to let Hannah Bugleman's nephew Herman get naked in front of my daughter, and I knew nothing about it!"

"Oh, Pop, calm down! He's not going to get naked." Then, as suddenly as she said it, Sarah Louise started to snicker—then laugh right out loud. "Herman Bugleman…the thought of him without a shirt on is funny enough, but the thought of him…" She stopped there and put her hand to her mouth, trying to suppress her laughter.

"You mean you're going to paint real men? You're going to have real men in your studio, and you're going to draw and paint them...real, live, breathing men! If not naked—what?" Winslow said, raising his voice with each word till he was almost hollering by the time he finished.

"Oh, eat that biscuit, Winslow, before it gets cold. You heard Sarah Louise. She just needs to have a real model to look at to get her painting done. She's already told us that she's not going to really show them naked...just sorta naked...anyway, all they have to do is take off their shirts...right, Sarah Louise?"

"And their pants."

Winslow dropped the biscuit and stared at his daughter. Claudette stared too, and now it was her turn to drop her chin so that her mouth hung open—wide enough to hold three buttered biscuits all at the same time.

"Their pants?" Claudette muttered, her voice barely perceptible.

"Their pants!" Winslow shouted.

"Oh, Pop, I'll give them a pair of swim trunks or something to wear! I just need to see their body shape and their legs. I told you I'm not going to show anything...anything risqué, anything improper, anything—"

"You mean Herman Bugleman is going to stand in your studio with no shirt on and no pants! I don't think that's funny!"

"I guess it's a good thing you weren't at state when I had my live-figure drawing class." She looked at her father with a silly smirk on her face. It was a look she had perfected, and it always worked to dissolve whatever anger he had at whatever she had done or was contemplating doing.

It worked.

Sarah could tell because her father picked up his dropped biscuit and put it on his plate. He stared at his food for a second and then stuck a spoon into the potatoes and took a bite.

"If I put Herman looking out the window, I won't have to show his face...hmmm, yes, that would work. Although I might have to add a little muscle to his arms. He is a awfully thin, isn't he? I haven't seen him in a while. Is he still thin, Mother?"

Claudette had closed her mouth by now and was trying to take all this new information in. "Sarah Louise, I wish you'd told me...about the pants, I mean. I told the girls that all their models would have to do was take off their shirts. Maybe I should call them."

"Don't worry, Mother. Any man that will pose with his shirt off won't mind wearing a pair of shorts while I make my sketches. Do you have a pair of old Bermuda shorts I could borrow, Pop?"

Winslow swallowed another mouth full of potatoes then answered, "I'm not real happy about this, Lou. But I guess the sooner we get this painting and this Spring Fling thing over, the better. I'll look for a pair after supper." He paused then spoke again, "By the way, Claudette, what's for dessert?"

22

Herman Bugleman was thinking about dessert too. He was sitting at the small kitchen table in his aunt's house and finishing his meal. His Aunt Hannah liked to spoil him, and when she had invited him over for supper, he was only too glad to accept. She always fed him well.

Tonight it was fried chicken, scalloped potatoes, corn pudding, and homemade yeast rolls. His Aunt Hannah fed him better than his own mother. Even so, even with peach cobbler for dessert, Herman was as thin as the proverbial beanpole.

He couldn't help it. He was just naturally thin. His big ears, pale blue eyes, and heavy black horn-rimmed glasses didn't help any. They only exaggerated his thinness.

Herman looked around the small kitchen decorated with red checkered curtains, tablecloth, even matching pot holders. A white painted china cabinet was full of ancient china, stacks of cups and saucers, blue willow platters, and one shelf devoted to purple carnival glass—all antiques and all valuable. Herman knew what the carnival glass was worth because he had looked it up on the Internet. He looked it up because he knew that one day it would all be his. His Aunt Hannah had promised him her estate, had even shown him her will, naming him as the sole recipient, except for a few miscellaneous pieces to several of her friends.

Yes, one day, Herman would have the quaint little house full of antiques, family heirlooms, and years upon years of knitted, crocheted, cross-stitched, and embroidered pillows and armrest covers. His aunt had several lifetimes of memories in the tidy home. And Herman knew what every chair, plate, vase, and wardrobe was worth, thanks to the Internet.

He also knew what a new candy-apple-red Porsche cost, and he knew that one day he would be able to afford one.

The voice of his aunt brought him out of his deep thoughts, just as he was about to turn the key in the ignition of that candy-apple-red Porsche.

"Now, Herman, when you get there, I want you to take a good look at that painting Sarah Louise Upshaw is doing and you notice everything and you tell me what you saw when you get home. I want to know what kind of painting this is that she's doing. *A Room Full of Naked Men*—why, I can't believe it. You hear me, Herman?"

"Yes, ma'am. I'll look real good. But you said I'm the first feller to pose for her."

"That's *fellow*, Herman, not *feller*. Try not to sound like your mother's side of the family."

"Yes, ma'am. But I still don't get it. Why is she doing a painting of naked men anyway?"

"Because Claudette Upshaw has a big mouth! But never you mind why. You just take a good look around and ask questions, Herman. Lots of questions! I want to know what that painting's going to look like!"

"Yes, ma'am, lots of questions."

"You know how you are around girls, Herman. You either say the wrong thing, or you don't say anything at all!"

Herman knew. He wasn't comfortable around girls. Actually, he wasn't comfortable around people in general, mainly girls. He never knew what to say, and when he did say something, it always seemed to be the wrong thing to say. If only girls worked like computers. Press a button to turn them on and another to turn them off. You could turn the volume up or down on the computer, and you could delete!

"And another thing—here, let me get you another helping of cobbler. Don't let Sarah Louise make you do anything you don't feel right doing. You just take off your shirt. I don' t trust young women today. Why, a handsome, available young man like yourself—she just might try to get a hold of you and…"

Hannah didn't finish her sentence. *And just when it was starting to get interesting*, Herman thought. Besides, he rather liked the idea of Sarah Louise Upshaw getting her hands on him. He tried to get more information from his aunt. "And what would she do if she got her hands on me, Aunt Hannah?"

"What would she do? Why, she'd marry you! That's what! That's all any of those young women today want. They all want a man of their own. But she's not getting, my Herman! Now, finish your cobbler. It's almost time for you to be there!"

Herman sighed and took another bite of the hot peach cobbler. His mind drifted to a candy-apple-red car and Sarah Louise Upshaw getting her hands on him.

———✁———

As Herman was finishing the cobbler, across town, Clarence Lipowitz was climbing into his big black SUV. He turned the ignition on, and as he gunned the engine a few times, he adjusted the speakers to his surround-sound, high-fidelity in-car stereo system. It was the best money could buy. He turned the Italian-leather-covered steering wheel sharply and backed out of his driveway.

He had told his wife, Avis, that he had to attend a city council meeting, but he was going to pay a surprise visit to a certain Sarah Louise Upshaw. Avis knew he was going to interview her. It was just that she wouldn't approve of an interview after business hours, in the privacy of the attractive girl's home. Avis was more than aware of his weakness for other women, but she wouldn't argue about a city council meeting.

He pulled out of the subdivision, La Roma Hills. It adjoined the La Vista Country Club and 18 Hole Golf Course. It was the best address to have if you had to live in Sulphur Springs like he did. It took a lot of money to make Clarence tolerate living here. He didn't, he prided himself, come cheap!

<hr />

When Herman arrived at the Upshaw home, his predilection to do the wrong thing kicked in. He pulled into the driveway and parked. Then he worried if this was the right place to park. What if someone needed to leave and he was in the way? He backed out and pulled up in front of the house. He started to turn off the engine then decided that maybe he wasn't close enough to the curb. He spent the next five minutes trying to park the right distance from the curb before finally parking in front of the neighbor's house, where the lighting from the streetlight was better.

Another five minutes was wasted as he tried to decide whether it was better to go to the front door, the kitchen door, or the door to Sarah's studio at the back of the house. He had been here before, with his Aunt Hannah on several occasions, so he knew his way around. He finally decided to go straight to the studio door, where he ever so lightly knocked on the door; and when there was no answer, he just stood there, unable to decide what to do next.

It was the cat, Buford, who tipped Sarah Louise off to Herman's arrival. He had sat up from his place on the arm of the overstuffed sofa and looked in the direction of the door with his ears alert.

Sarah, busy at her canvas, noticed his change in position and looked toward the door. There, through the curtains, she could make out the shape of a person; and the ears—at a ninety-degree angle on each side of his head—were a dead giveaway that it was Herman. She reached over and turned her radio down and walked to the door.

When she opened it, Herman was relieved. He had decided to knock again but wasn't sure if he should knock louder or try knocking lightly once more. The world gave Herman too many choices.

"Come in, Herman. I've been expecting you."

"Hi, Sarah Louise. I guess my aunt told you why I'm here."

"Yes, Herman. I know why you're here. Won't you come in?"

As Herman stepped inside the door, Buford leaped to the floor, crossed the room, and scurried outside. Sarah looked at him as he ventured onto the patio and, when halfway across, decided that was as good a place as any to lie down. She hesitated before closing the door then decided to leave it open in case he wanted back in. It was a warm evening anyway and much too early in the year for mosquitoes.

As she turned to face Herman, in the glare of her overhead ceiling light, she realized how pale he was. Herman obviously didn't get out in the sun much. She wondered for a moment if she would be able to match his skin color. Then she noticed the nervous look on his face and realized that her next words shouldn't have anything to do with *get undressed*.

"Herman, thanks so much for coming. You don't know how much I appreciate this. Won't you sit down?"

"Aunt Hannah said you needed me to be a model for a painting. I didn't know you could paint well enough to paint people," he said, sitting down on one end of the sofa.

Sarah Louise, the slight derisive remark on her painting skills aside, continued to try to make him at ease. "Would you like something to drink…a Coke?"

While Sarah and Herman made polite conversation, Clarence Lipowitz pulled his SUV up to the curb two houses down from Sarah's address. It was a force of habit: never park too close to the lady's home. In a small town, you never knew who might notice.

He reached into his glove compartment and pulled out a small bottle of Eau Sauvage by Christian Dior and slapped a little on his face. After checking his smile in the rearview mirror to make sure he didn't have anything caught between his teeth, he stepped quietly from the car and started toward the house.

While Clarence was making his way down the street, Sarah Louise was peering into the refrigerator, trying to find a bottle of Miller Lite beer. She realized she had goofed when Herman agreed to having a cold drink. He had said yes and then specified what he wanted.

"Mother!" Sarah Louise yelled.

"Yes, dear, what is it?" Her mother's voice came from the den, where she and Winslow were watching TV.

"Do we have any beer?"

"Sarah Louise? Did I hear you right?"

"Yes, you heard me right!"

By this time, Claudette was in the kitchen. "I think your father has a few beers for when his fishing buddies come by. Look in the back."

"I did, and all I see are regular beers. I need a Lite beer." She faced her confused mother and, with one word, offered an explanation for her need, "Herman!"

"Oh…do you want me to have your father run to the store?"

"No. He'll just have to do with one of these." Sarah Louise grabbed the cold can and walked back down the long hall toward the studio.

Claudette followed her as far as the den and went back inside to join her husband. She wasn't sure he had noticed her absence. It was only when she sat down that she realized the decorating show she had been watching had been replaced by *Emeril Live.* "Winslow, turn back!"

"Okay, okay. Where did you go anyway? I thought I heard Lou's voice."

"You did. She needed a beer for Herman."

The next sound Claudette heard was the clickety-clack of the recliner mechanism as Winslow sat upright in his chair. "Herman?"

"Yes, Winslow. Herman wanted something to drink."

"You mean he's down in Lou's studio having a beer and parading around in his underwear?"

"Well…I don't know about the underwear, but he is down in the studio."

"Why didn't you tell me!"

"Why should I?"

"Because I want to be there to make sure nothing funny happens—and I don't mean funny as in ha-ha!"

"Oh, Winslow, Herman doesn't have an ounce of meanness in him. Then again, I wonder if Hannah knows he drinks beer. But I wouldn't be worried about him doing anything—what are you doing, Winslow?"

"I'm getting my service revolver out of my desk drawer."

"Winslow…you'll scare the poor boy to death!"

"I just want to scare him enough to keep his hands to himself!"

Claudette was up from her chair and standing in the doorway of the den, trying to run defense for the hapless Herman. "Now, Winslow…don't do anything rash…let's discuss this like adults!"

***

By this time, Clarence was making a slow circle of the house. He didn't know if this Sarah Louise lived alone or not, just that she was an unmarried schoolteacher who painted pictures of naked men, and he may or may not recognize her when he saw her. He did attend all the Spring Flings, and surely, he had run into her before. The name was vaguely familiar, but he couldn't put a face to it. Still, he wanted to reconnoiter the home to see where or if he needed to knock on a door.

As he neared the rear of the house, he saw the huge picture window of the studio, put there by Winslow to give Sarah Louise the natural light she needed to paint by. There, in the glow of the studio lights, he could see an easel and shelves of artists supplies. The room appeared empty of people. Herman was out of view, sitting on the sofa to the right of the huge window. As he took in the scene, Clarence saw Sarah Louise enter the room, a can of beer in her hand.

He studied her face for a moment. Yes, she would be an attractive person to get to know. He wondered if she had any more beer in her house, or maybe something a little stronger.

Outside Clarence's hearing range, Sarah Louise began talking to Herman. "This is the only beer I could find, Herman."

"That's fine, Sarah Louise. I didn't mean to put you to any trouble. Do you want me to take off my shirt now or after I drink my beer?"

"Well, I really do need to get started. Why don't you step behind this folding screen I've got set up here and let me explain just what I need you to do."

Herman stood up and stepped behind the large oriental screen, glad he didn't really have to drink the beer. He had never had a beer before anyway. It just seemed like a manly thing to do, and he so wanted to impress Sarah Louise.

"I really need you to take off your pants too, Herman. I know this may sound silly, but I need to see your legs. There's a pair of my father's old golf shorts there…put those on, if you don't mind. They may be a little big, so you may have to hold them up."

Clarence had made his way around to the door of the studio. Now, as he peered inside the open door, he saw Sarah Louise standing by the canvas, the beer still in one hand, her back to him.

Clarence cleared his voice to get her attention since there was no door to knock on. Then he said, "Sarah Louise?"

Sarah heard the voice, and even though it didn't sound exactly like Herman, she knew what he must be thinking. So without turning around, she spoke loudly over her shoulder, "Just take your clothes off and put them there on the chair. I'll tell you what to do next."

Clarence liked what he heard and with a sudden joie de vivre, he quickly obliged. In fact, he was undressed faster than Herman, who was just a few feet away on the other side of the oriental screen. Clarence hesitated when he got down to his boxer shorts. He was thinking perhaps he should stop there and inquire for further instructions when Sarah Louise turned around.

It is the law of statistics that things happen in threes. Plane crashes always seem to come in threes. Funeral homes will tell you that people die in threes. If you have one snow, you'll have two more before winter's over.

So it was that this night in Sarah Louise's studio, three things happened.

One, Sarah Louise turned around to find Clarence Lipowitz standing there in a pair of Ralph Lauren boxer shorts, red with a pattern of little white doggie bones, made of Thai silk.

Two, Herman stepped from behind the screen and, seeing Clarence, in surprise, let go of the belt loop of the oversized shorts he was wearing, letting them fall to his ankles and leaving him standing there in his briefs, only a shade whiter than his own skin.

Three, Winslow walked through the door of the studio, waving a service revolver.

23

Herman Bugleman had read, on the website Amazingfacts.com, that when a person is about to die, the last five seconds of their life will seem, to them, like five minutes. Everything will happen in slow motion, and the unfortunate victim will be able to take in every little detail of their demise. At the same time, they will, uncontrollably, reflect on their life and, in some manner, try to ascertain whether they are bound for heaven or the less desirable confinement of eternal fire and brimstone.

Thus it was that, as Herman's life flashed before his eyes, he also was able to observe every nuance of his predicament. Herman saw the surprised look on Sarah Louise Upshaw's face. He was also aware of the scream coming from her mouth, although the scream that came from his own mouth may have been louder.

He was aware that there was another man in the room, right next to him, who—it appeared—was also going to pose for the painting. Herman had no idea who this man was or why he was wearing such outlandish boxer shorts and not wearing a pair of old golf shorts like Herman was, although those shorts were now around Herman's ankles instead of his waist. Herman was pretty sure that this stranger was also emitting a kind of primal scream from his mouth.

Then there was Winslow. Herman saw Winslow, and the look in Winslow's eyes was not good. Winslow was waving a gun in the air, and the gun was alternately aimed at Herman then at the half-naked man next to him and then back at Herman and so forth. Winslow wasn't screaming like the others in the room, but there was another scream. It came from behind Winslow, where Claudette stood in the doorway with one hand placed beside her face and the other clutching her bosom as if she were having a heart attack—which was very close to the feeling Herman was experiencing.

Thus it was that Herman was sure of his imminent death but not sure whether the heart attack would get him before a bullet would, fired from the incredibly big gun Winslow was waving back and forth.

In slow motion, Herman saw Sarah drop the can of beer. He saw the man next to him grab a pair of pants from a pile of clothes on the stool beside him and turn toward the door. He saw Claudette make a grab toward the gun in Winslow's hand. He saw himself step out of the too-big golf shorts and start to turn to follow the half-naked stranger. But the last thing he saw was the puff of smoke that emanated from the muzzle of Winslow's gun, and then there was the awful boom of the gun as it went off.

That was the end of the slow motion for Herman.

When the gun went off, Herman went too—out the open door of Sarah Louise's studio, leapfrogging over the man in the red silk boxer shorts, across the brick patio, leaping over a fat furry creature that was also running for its life, and then running for his own life across the lawn in the general direction of town.

Mrs. Alma Peterman, the eighty-eight-year old neighbor of the Upshaws, also heard the gun go off. She was standing beside a flowerpot of geraniums that sat on the top step of her back porch. She was dumping a pail of lukewarm soapy water on them. It was the remains of her dirty dishwater, and she always used it to water her flowers for two simple reasons. One, she was convinced that the water department of Sulphur Springs regularly overcharged her for water that came out of her garden hose. She wasn't sure how they knew the difference, but she was sure they did. Secondly, when she was growing up on a farm in the Pleasant Grove community of the county, her mother had always used her dirty dishpan water to pour on her flowers, and her mother always had the prettiest flowers in the neighborhood.

So it was that as Alma was pouring the tepid water on her lovely red geraniums, she heard a gun go off next door.

Poor Alma dropped her pan in reaction to the sudden boom. She looked in the direction of the noise and saw not one, but two, half-naked men running across her backyard. One man, extremely thin and pale and wearing white briefs, was taking steps so big his knees were almost touching his nose. He dashed across the lawn and into the night. The other man was close behind, but he was wearing boxer shorts like Alma's late husband, Otis, once wore (but Otis only wore cotton boxers with a little printed design), and he was zigzagging across the lawn as if he wasn't sure what direction to take. He started to run one way then headed in another then turned and ran still another. He had what looked like a pair of pants clutched to his chest.

Neither man bothered to pass the time of day with Alma. They simply ran around her backyard and then disappeared into the darkness.

In the quiet that followed, Alma stood still for a moment then—yelling, "Perverts!"—she rushed back inside her house and locked the door behind her. The police, she decided, would need to hear about this.

Back in the house, Sarah Louise and Winslow were both standing over the prostate body of Claudette, who had fainted when the gun went off. Sarah Louise was fanning her mother with a magazine, and Winslow was holding one hand and patting Claudette's cheek with the other hand.

"Oh, Pop! You don't think she's dead, do you?"

"No, I don't think she's dead! She's just fainted is all. I know a faint when I see one. Why would she be dead?"

"Why? You just fired a gun. I don't know where the bullet went!"

"It didn't go anywhere!"

"It didn't go anywhere?"

"Yes, it didn't go anywhere. It was a blank! Do you think I'd keep live ammo in a gun I keep in a drawer in the den?"

Before Sarah Louise could respond, she noticed a slight movement by her mother. "Look, I think she's coming to!"

Indeed, Claudette was slowly coming back to the land of consciousness and gunshots and half-naked men.

"What happened?" was all she could muster as she looked up from her place on the floor into the faces of her husband and daughter.

"You grabbed at my hand, and the gun went off, that's what!"

"Don't fuss at her, Pop. What if she's hit her head on the floor and she's got amnesia?"

Claudette looked from husband to daughter and back then yelled, "I should be so lucky! Now help me up!"

They pulled Claudette to her feet and then walked her over to the sofa. Sarah Louise got her mother a glass of water from her bathroom faucet. After Claudette took a sip, she took a deep breath and then gave Winslow both an angry and worried look.

"Tell me, Winslow…please…be honest with me…did you just shoot one of those men? Is there a dead body around here somewhere?"

Winslow laughed. "If one of those fellows is dead, it's from fright. That gun only has blanks. It just makes a lot of noise and a little puff of smoke." He then turned to face his daughter. "And by the way, just who was that other man, and why did you have two men in their drawers in your studio?"

"One of them was Herman, right, Sarah Louise? I'm sure one of them was Herman," spoke up Claudette.

Sarah Louise gave her parents a perplexed look. "Yes, Herman was here. Poor Herman. He couldn't keep your old shorts up,

Pop, because he was so skinny, and…I don't know who the other man was. I turned around expecting to see Herman, and I saw a stranger in red silk boxer shorts standing there. I'm afraid I didn't get a good look at his face. I just screamed in shock, which is just when you came through the door, Pops."

"We were arguing all the way down the hall, Lou. Your mother was telling me you could take care of yourself when we heard you scream, opened the door, and saw two men…in their underwear…and I guess I thought the worse."

"You're sure there's no dead body outside your studio door, Sarah Louise?" Claudette asked again, concern still in her voice.

"Ohhhh, I guess I better go look for sure, but the way Herman Bugleman lit out of here, I'm sure he's in Timbuktu by now, and that other fellow, he grabbed his pants and was close behind him."

As Sarah Louise went to the door and reassured herself that there was no dead body lying around, Claudette was muttering over and over, "Poor Herman…poor Herman…what will Hannah say when she finds out that we almost killed the poor boy?"

Sarah stepped back into the studio. "No bodies, Mother, but there is something odd. A police car is over at Alma's house next door!"

24

When Alma Peterman called the sheriff's office, she wasn't hysterical or even scared, but she was mad, as mad as a wet hen, even madder! The thought that men would be running around her backyard in their underwear was more than she could bear. She didn't approve of the morals of today's generation by a long shot. The commercials on TV had gotten so bad that she only watched the game channel...As for movies, she hadn't been to a theater since Doris Day and Rock Hudson had stopped making films together.

Even so, she had picked up enough from the news, the radio, and the newspaper to know that the world was being run by people with loose morals. And now, those people were in her backyard!

When Judy Brown, the dispatcher, answered the phone down at the sheriff's office, Alma barked into the phone, "Let me speak to Ronnie Junior!"

Judy was used to that, of course. Many people, when they called, simply asked to speak to Ronnie Junior. That was the way people knew him. His father was Big Ronnie or just plain Ronnie. Both men had been in law enforcement all their lives, and both had served as sheriff—Big Ronnie for twenty years, and now Ronnie Junior for the last ten. People were so used to calling the men by their first names or nicknames that if you were to ask someone what their last name was, they would have to think about it.

When Alma said, "Let me speak to Ronnie Junior!" Judy simply turned her head to face the sheriff's desk and said, "Line one, Ronnie Junior."

Ronnie Junior laid his three cards facedown on the desk and pushed the button on the phone that sat next to him. He eyed the two deputies across from him with a serious look to let them know that they had better not look at his cards and spoke into the receiver, "Sheriff speaking…"

Alma was quick to respond, "Oh, Ronnie Junior, you need to come by here right now. You won't believe what I just saw in my backyard—two naked men! Well, they weren't completely naked, but they were pretty close to it. They were just wearing their underwear! And they were running around in circles in my backyard!"

"Is this Miss Alma?"

Ronnie Junior was pretty sure he recognized Alma's voice. Alma was a distant cousin on his daddy's side. Anyway, he knew the faces of most everyone in town, and he could recognize the voices of a good many.

Alma, again, was quick to respond, "Yes, this is Alma. You get over here right away. We can't have that sort of thing going on in Sulphur Springs!"

"Yes, Miss Alma, I'll be right there. You didn't recognize the men, did you?"

"Oh no. It was dark. I couldn't see well…just well enough to see that they were running around with no clothes on. What is the world coming to, Ronnie Junior?"

"I don't know, Miss Alma. You stay inside, and I'll be right there."

He rolled his eyes as his deputies' curious faces were trying to figure out what was going on from the one side of the conversation they were privy to. Ronnie Junior knew Alma was a responsible citizen, but he kind of doubted she had seen two men running around her yard in their underwear—maybe it was a couple of teenagers in shorts playing hide-and-seek in the dark.

Then Alma said something else. "And I don't know who fired the gun!"

Ronnie Junior sat up straight.

"Fired a gun! You mean someone was out there shooting a gun off?"

"Oh yes, didn't I mention that? A gun went off too. I don't know how many times. You don't think it's a drug war, do you?"

By now, Ronnie was standing up and motioning to his two deputies. "You just be sure you stay inside, Miss Alma, and don't you open your door to anyone till I get there, hear?"

<hr />

It was while Alma was on the phone that Winslow and Sarah Louise were busy reviving Claudette. At the same time, Clarence Lipowitz was diving into the passenger side of his big SUV. It was closer than the driver's side, and the sooner he got out of the gunsights of the madman in the studio, the better. Once in, he pulled the door shut and cowered on the floorboard. Only when he was sure there were no more guns being fired did he cautiously raise his head and peer out the window.

When he saw no one chasing him and no sign of the other fellow, the skinny kid in glasses and white underwear who had jumped over him in the studio doorway, he lowered his head and began fumbling with his pants—first, to find his keys and, secondly, to pull them on over his red silk boxer shorts with the little doggie-bone pattern.

<hr />

And Herman, he had run almost three blocks, through backyards, one alley, and one vacant lot before he realized he wasn't being chased by anything more dangerous than a stray wirehaired, flop-eared dog that had decided to join him on his evening jog. Gasping for breath, Herman stopped by a board fence and then sat down.

As the friendly stray mutt walked right up to him and began licking his face, Herman realized that he had absolutely no idea what to do next. So he continued to gasp for air, and the dog continued to lick his face.

When Ronnie Junior and his two deputies pulled up in front of Alma's house, they all three jumped out at once. They hadn't turned on their siren nor their flashing blue lights. If there were people out there with guns, Ronnie Junior didn't want them to run off, so he kept his presence quiet. He motioned to each deputy, one to head left and one to head right.

Speaking softly, Ronnie Junior directed them, "I'll go to the house. You both circle around, and I'll meet you in the backyard... keep quiet!"

Clarence was on his back, trying to pull his pants back on when he saw the lights of a car go by and heard the car stop, and it seemed very close. Then he heard the car doors shut. He very carefully raised his head again, just in time to see a deputy coming down the sidewalk, right straight toward his big black SUV.

Clarence Lipowitz curled up into a fetal position and made himself as small as possible. There, on the floor of the passenger side, he held his breath and tried to think of how he could explain to a deputy what he was doing there—on the floor of his SUV, at night, away from home—and why he was half dressed.

As he cowered, Alma let Ronnie Junior in her front door. She told him the whole story, beginning to end, as he walked through the house, making a quick survey of each room, just in case there were any intruders.

By the time he got to the back porch, Alma had repeated the story three times. Once there, his eyes scanned the backyard, and he stepped cautiously onto the back steps, motioning for her to stay inside the house.

When the two deputies appeared, Ronnie Junior joined them, and the three men talked among themselves. After a second, Ronnie Junior bounced back up the stairs and entered Alma's back door, where he asked her to turn on her back-porch light. With the added illumination, the three men gave the backyard the once-over.

Convinced there was nothing there, the sheriff spoke up, "Ryan, you check the Hardys' house next door. Scooter, you check the Upshaws' house. See if they heard anything or saw anything."

Ronnie Junior then rejoined Alma and gave the house another closer look.

It was while the men were in the backyard of Alma's house that Clarence, blue in the face from holding his breath, finally got the courage to again peer out his SUV window. Seeing that the deputy was gone from sight, Clarence pulled his pants up the last few inches needed to get them up on his waist where they belonged and then plunged his hands into his right back pocket.

He breathed a sigh of relief when his fingers made contact with his wallet and its precious contents, which would tell anyone who might find it just who he was. His identity safe, he flung himself into the driver's seat and started the car. He didn't gun the engine this time, and he turned the surround-sound, high-fidelity in-car stereo system off. Without turning his headlights on, he carefully put the vehicle into first gear and eased down the street in the direction of La Roma Hills.

Back at Sarah Louise's studio, the three Upshaws were standing nervously at the open door, looking in the direction of Alma's.

"What do you suppose the police are doing over at Alma's?" Claudette whispered.

"Do you think something's wrong?" Sarah Louise whispered back.

"Is something wrong? I guess hearing a gunshot and then seeing Herman Bugleman run across your backyard in his underwear would classify as wrong—or at least strange! And why are we whispering?" Winslow said, his voice as quiet as theirs.

"Oh no, Winslow. That deputy is coming our way...what should we do?" Claudette said, again in a whisper.

"We could all run inside and hide," Sarah Louise offered, also in a whisper.

"The first thing we'll do is quit whispering!" Winslow practically yelled. "Then we'll see what he wants. It may have nothing to do with us!"

"It looks like Scooter Davis...doesn't it look like Scooter to you, Sarah Louise?" Claudette offered, her voice still low.

"Yes, Mother, it looks like Scooter. That's good. He's not the kind to shoot first and ask questions later—like some people we know!" As she said this, she rolled her eyes at her father.

"Let's play it safe...confess to nothing!" Winslow said, his voice once again at a whisper.

By this time, Scooter was at the edge of their patio. He looked across the brickwork and saw the three of them by the door. "Evening, Mr. and Mrs. Upshaw. Hi, Sarah Louise. Sorry to bother you. Have you seen anything strange this evening?"

"Strange?" Claudette asked.

"Nothing's wrong with Alma, I hope," Sarah Louise said, hoping to change the subject.

"Oh, Miss Alma's fine. She called the sheriff's office and said she'd seen a couple of fellows in her backyard. Kinda spooked her,

I guess. She said they were running around in their…pardon me for saying…in their drawers."

"Drawers?" Claudette said, not sure what he meant.

"In their underwear, ma'am."

"Underwear?" she answered him, her hand to her chest.

"Oh, don't worry none, ma'am. We've looked around, and we can't find anyone. But you didn't see anything, did you?"

"Deputy, if there were men running around here in their BVDs, we'd have seen them. We were just standing here calling the cat when we saw you next door, and we were curious what was going on," Winslow explained.

"Well, she may have been seeing things, but she sounded pretty sure when Ronnie Junior spoke to her…could've been some kids playing games and just wearing their cutoffs."

"Kids?" Claudette said, her conversation seemingly stuck on one-word exclamations.

"Yes, ma'am. The first good, warm night of spring, and they stay out late, past suppertime, acting crazy. Well, if you folks haven't seen anything, I'll go."

Scooter turned to go and then spun back around.

"Oh, one more thing. You didn't hear a gun go off, did you?"

25

Herman Bugleman sat in the tall grass at the edge of the vacant lot and patted the stray dog on the head. The mongrel offered him a little companionship on what was possibly the worst night of his life. His aunt had forced him to go to the house of the one girl in Sulphur Springs he would most like to impress, and once there, he had somehow ended up standing in his underwear while being shot at by a crazy man. Now he was sitting in the dark in a bunch of weeds, afraid to go home, to his aunt's or back to his car.

He scratched at his bare leg and continued to pat the dog. Herman had never been in trouble in his life, and he still wasn't sure what he had done to get shot at. It was all very perplexing.

Herman took a deep breath. He scratched at his bare leg again.

The dog was sitting contentedly, wagging his tail, his tongue hanging out of his mouth and his fleas making the short hop from his furry hide to the nice white bare flesh of Herman.

Across town, Clarence Lipowitz pulled into his driveway and parked.

He was breathing easier now. In his mind, he went back over the events of the last thirty minutes. He had arrived at the address of Sarah Louise Upshaw just as it was listed in the phone book. When he got to her studio door, she had told him to undress, which he did. Then, in what was a blur of events, he had been screamed at, shot at, and had another man grab him by the shoulders and leap over him. The other fellow was confusing enough, but why the wild-eyed man with the gun had shot at him had Clarence really confused.

For now, he planned to sit quietly in his driveway until he could figure how to enter his house dressed as he was, unnoticed.

✦

In the doorway of the studio, the deputy was talking to the three members of the Upshaw family.

"Gunshots?" Claudette said.

"Yes, ma'am. Miss Alma said she heard gunshots right before the men in their, pardon me again for saying it, in their drawers ran around her yard. Did you folks hear any gunshots?"

"Did Alma say where the gunshots came from? I mean, did they sound like they came from far away…or…like they came… from close by?" Sarah Louise asked.

"Well, I didn't speak to her myself, but Ronnie Junior said to check all the houses nearby, so that's what I'm doing."

Winslow had been working his jaw back and forth with his hand, as if pondering the situation. "I tell you what, deputy, I'm willing to bet it was some of those wild teenagers you mentioned earlier, and I'm willing to bet they were shooting off some old firecrackers, probably left over from the Fourth of July."

"Firecrackers?" Claudette said in real surprise.

"Oh, that's good, Pops! Firecrackers! I bet that's what it was." Then realizing she may have said that too hastily, Sarah Louise added, "That's why the cat won't come when we call him. He's probably scared from the noise."

"Yes, deputy. I bet that's what it was," Winslow agreed.

"That makes sense now that you mention it. Well, I'll get back over to Miss Alma's and tell Ronnie Junior. If you like, I'll call for your cat while I'm looking around."

"Cat?" Claudette said, still stuck in monosyllables.

"Yes, ma'am, you said you were calling your cat."

Sarah Louise spoke up, "That's right, Scooter. The cat…our cat is out there somewhere. He's out there, and we were looking for him when you came by. The cat, I mean."

"If you tell me his name, I'll call for him."

Winslow took over the conversation since neither of the two women seemed to be holding up well under the pressure of the interrogation. "It's Buford, deputy—Buford! Yes, we'd appreciate it if you would look. That old cat means a lot to us. It's like a member of the family. Why, I wouldn't know what to do if something were to happen to old Buford!"

"I'll keep my eye out." And with that, Scooter turned and walked back to Alma's house.

With him gone, Sarah Louise and her father each gave a big sigh of relief. Claudette, however, stood there shaking her head.

"What's the matter, Mother? We got ourselves out of that okay."

"Yes, Claudette. We did pretty good. What's bothering you now?"

Claudette looked at her husband and daughter and once again muttered one word, "Herman!"

"Herman!" Sarah Louise echoed, shaking her head side to side like her mother.

"Herman!" Winslow agreed. "What are we going to do about Herman?"

When Scooter rejoined Ronnie Junior and the other deputy, Ryan, back at Alma's, he gave his report. Ryan had the same lack of success. Nobody had seen anything or heard anything. The couple that Ryan had questioned admitted that they had their

TV turned up loud, and he had had to knock three times before they came to the door.

Alma, however, was confident in what she had seen and heard, and she was convinced that there were perverts in her neighborhood involved in a drug war. "Ronnie Junior, they're fighting over their turf. It's just like on the evening news. What's our world coming to right here in Sulphur Springs?"

"Miss Alma, I don't think it's as bad as all that. Why, it could be some man came home early and found his wife with another man, and he started shooting."

"Two men, Ronnie Junior—two men."

"Well, maybe his wife was real accommodating, Miss Alma. But don't you worry. We'll take a walk around the neighborhood before we leave. You just get back inside and lock the door. And you call us if you hear or see anything else, hear now?"

"All right, Ronnie junior, if you say so. But I'm going to get a golf club out of Otis's golf bag and keep it beside the bed. If any pervert tries to get in the house, I'll club him good! It'll be self-defense—that's what it will be!"

Actually, as Alma locked the door and went to the closet to get one of her late husband's golf clubs, she wasn't sure what was more disturbing, the thought of a couple of drug-crazed perverts running around the neighborhood or that one of her neighbors was entertaining two men at the same time while her husband was out of the house.

When Clarence finally tiptoed into his garage, he sidestepped into the laundry room and grabbed a shirt and a pair of socks from the pile of dirty clothes and pulled them on. A pair of tennis shoes, stuck in the corner of the room, completed the outfit, and he quietly exited and went back outside.

Once there, he opened the SUV door and then slammed it shut and walked up to the front door, as if he had just arrived.

When he got inside, the children barely looked up from their spot in front of the big-screen TV to see who had entered the room. Avis was on the couch reading a magazine.

"How did your meeting go, honey?" she asked.

"Not quite as boring as they usually are." He plopped down beside her and offered nothing more.

Avis, always unsure what to say next, reached over and patted his hand. When he didn't immediately withdraw it, she spoke again. "My dear friend Lucinda Hardin-Powell called while you were gone. She wanted to know if we had interviewed Sarah Louise Upshaw yet. I told her you would probably call on her tomorrow. Lucinda said that she and BJ were planning a pool party when the weather gets good and warm and that we would be the first ones she planned to invite. Doesn't that sound nice?"

"Why? We have our own pool."

"I know, but it's a social thing."

"I don't want to socialize with Lucinda or her fat husband."

Avis got quiet. Clarence was in a sour mood again. She expected him to remain quiet for the rest of the evening, but then he spoke again.

"By the way, I think I'll let you interview that Sarah Louise person. You can leave me out of the Spring Fling Art Show and Antiques Auction to Benefit the Art Guild's Town-Beautification Project."

———※———

Across town, Herman was busy scratching at his legs and feet. Then he got up from his spot in the tall weeds and grass and scooted over several feet. Perhaps moving over would help. When he sat down again, he called to the dog, and it readily rejoined him, fleas and all.

For now, Herman's solution to his problem was to stay there until something happened. So he continued to pet the dog. The dog continued to wag its tail, and the fleas continued to bite.

As Herman sat there and waited, three blocks away, Ronnie Junior and his deputies, Ryan and Scooter, began walking up and down the street looking for drug-crazed perverts. And in the studio, the three Upshaws paced back and forth.

Claudette had finally broken free of her one-word conversations. "We have to do something about Herman. He could be out there getting in worse trouble. What if the sheriff finds him running around town dressed like he is?"

"Maybe you should go looking for him, Pops?" Sarah Louise said.

"Look? Where? He could be anywhere! And what about that other fellow? What happened to him? Where is he now...and who was he?" Winslow retorted. He looked down on the floor of the studio. "Whoever he was, he left his shirt, a pair of socks, and what looks like a pair of Italian-leather shoes!"

"That other man...I wonder...do you think that Bonnie or Annie got their days mixed up and sent their model over at the time we were having Herman?" Claudette suggested.

"Ohhhh, that makes sense, Mother. You'll have to call them and find out. Whoever it was, I doubt they will want to come back and pose." As she said this, Sarah Louise noticed the deputies had left Alma's yard and were walking up the street. "Pops, now, while the deputies are going toward White Oak Street, you go the other direction and look for Herman. We've got to find him before they do."

"She's right, Winslow...go!" Saying this, Claudette pushed her husband out the door of the studio.

Winslow stood on the brick patio for a moment, not sure he liked the idea of walking around his neighborhood, after dark, looking for a grown man in his underwear. He turned back toward the studio when Sarah Louise suddenly threw a pair of pants at him.

"You'll need these, Pops. They're Herman's!"

Winslow stood there for another moment or two then resigned to his mission, he started off into the dark calling in a restrained voice, "Herman! Oh, Herman…can you hear me, Herman?"

26

Hubcap Reynolds stuffed the last of his second chili dog into his mouth and wiped his greasy fingers on his blue striped coveralls. It was obvious that the coveralls doubled as a napkin, a towel, and a rag. It was splotched with grease, oil, ketchup, and a hundred other semi-identifiable stains. But then, the public doesn't expect a car mechanic to be prissy clean, and Hubcap wasn't.

He reached across the engine block of a '67 Chevy and grabbed a lukewarm half-full can of root beer. He polished it off in one prolonged gulp. Then he stood still for a moment, his cheeks filling up with air, and he let out a belch that approached four decibels.

Across the room, his companion, GW, spoke up, "Not bad, Hubcap. That's almost as good as that belch after the preacher's prayer last Sunday."

"Yeah. Boy, Rubie Lee like to a killed me for that one, and she woulda if it had been during services 'stead of during dinner on the ground."

Hubcap grinned from ear to ear at the memory of the Sunday belch.

After the church service, the congregation had gathered on the banks of the creek behind the plain whiteboard church for lunch, what people in Sulphur Springs called dinner on the ground. The preacher, trying to show his faith through his humility, had been the last one to go through the food line. By the time he got to the long white paper-covered tables, Hubcap was half through his meal and making plans for second helpings.

So when Brother Sowell bowed his head to lead the prayer, poor Hubcap had a stomach full of air. No sooner had Brother Sowell said amen that it just happened. The belch was, considering the surroundings, ungodly. Yes, if Rubie Lee had been close enough to reach out and hit her husband, she would have. As it was, Rubie Lee was still standing by the dessert table, slicing cakes and pies.

Hubcap laughed and shook his head. Of course, that wasn't the first time, nor would it be the last time that he would belch, break wind, or tell an off-color joke at the wrong place or the wrong time.

"Hand me that bolt cutter, GW," Hubcap said, his thoughts returning to his work.

GW crossed the cluttered floor of the garage and handed a pair of ancient bolt cutters to his brother-in-law. "Did you eat all the chips, Hubcap?" GW asked.

"Yep, I wuz hungry, GW. This is kinda late fer me to be a eating supper. If Rubie Lee hadn't bring them chili dogs and chips when she did, I mighta starved to death!"

"Hubcap, you got enough fat round your belly to keep you alive a week…maybe two!"

Hubcap laughed at GW's wisecrack. Hubcap loved a good wisecrack, even if he was the recipient. He and GW could exchange barbs all evening and never take them personally.

It was Hubcap's body shop, and he put in a full day, six days a week. Despite his demanding routine, on nice evenings, he would call his brother in-law, and the two of them would return to the shop to work on their own vehicles. The large double doors to the garage work bay were opened to let the warm night air in. They were working on Hubcap's Chevy, but last year, it was GW's '58 Ford truck. As long as it was old, had wheels and an engine, they were happy.

GW wasn't a mechanic by trade. He was what people in Sulphur Springs called a shade-tree mechanic. That is, he enjoyed working on automobiles in his spare time for the pleasure of it, like in the old days when a fellow would park his car under a big shade tree and tinker with the engine. You could do that in the old days. Today's cars were too complicated, with computerized components and parts that had to be factory authorized. Nowadays you just ordered a new part and plugged it in place. But the old cars had engines you could mess around with. Hit it with a hammer, clean it up and reuse it, or get a part from the junkyard and make it work. That was why, in their off time, Hubcap and GW restored old cars.

Just then, the faint strains of "Your Cheatin' Heart" came from GW's overall pocket. He reached into the deep pocket and pulled his cell phone out. "Yo!" he said as he hit the talk button.

The voice on the other end of the line talked a few minutes. "All right, see ya later, Sweet-ums," he replied, and closing the small device up, he put it back in his pocket.

"Sweet-ums! You musta been talking to Roberta!" Hubcap yelled across the garage. "Or have you taken to calling someone else Sweet-ums?"

"Yep, that was Roberta. She said to tell you that she and Rubie Lee were on their way to Walmart, and they might be late getting home."

"Lord, help us when those sisters go shopping." Hubcap laughed again. "They won't get outta there until they've done put us both in the poorhouse!"

As he and GW chuckled over the comment, Scooter stepped inside the open doors of the garage. "You boys workin' kinda late, aren't ya?"

The men both turned to face the deputy.

GW spoke first, "Hey, Scooter, what's up?"

"Oh, investigating some disturbance down the street. Miss Alma thought she heard some gunshots, and we're checking out the neighborhood."

"Gunshots?" Hubcap repeated in surprise.

"Yep, about a half hour ago. You fellows hear anything?"

GW looked Hubcap squarely in the face. "Hubcap...I told you to go easy on them chili dogs. That belch you gave out has done upset Miss Alma!"

The two men broke up in laughter.

"Was it that bad, GW? I wish I coulda been here to witness!" The deputy said; then he joined in the laughter, not so much from GW's comment as from seeing the two men laugh so hard.

"It was pretty strong, Scooter! If I do say so myself!" Hubcap said between gasps of laughter.

As the three men laughed, Herman moved one more time in the tall grass by the fence, not understanding why he kept itching. The stray dog kept by his side.

Finally, he turned to the dog and spoke to it, as if it would understand. "You know, pooch, there's something in this grass that's making me itch. I've gotta get out of here, and I don't know where to go!"

He stood up and looked around. Across the vacant field, in the backyard of a white clapboard house, he could see a clothesline in the faint moonlight.

"Pooch, I've just got me an idea. That clothesline has something on it. I might be able to find something to put on, something decent enough to let me at least walk down the street. What you say, pooch? Let's do a little investigating."

With that remark, the duo crept through the weeds toward the small house and its unsuspecting clothesline.

By the time Herman and the flea-bitten stray had reached the edge of the field, Hubcap, GW, and Scooter had stopped laughing long enough for Scooter to look under the hood of the Chevy and comment on the merits of Chevys over other makes. Then, remembering why he came, he told the men to keep their ears open for any more gunshots, and he headed out the open garage doors.

As he reached the doors, he turned and spoke up, "One more thing, fellows. If you see a stray cat, call the Upshaws. They're missing a cat, answers to the name Buford!"

With that, he headed out and crossed the street.

"Those guys sure have it tough. Loud noises in the night and lost cats! I wish my job was that easy," GW said.

"Go easy on 'em, GW. It just takes one looney with a gun to make up fer all the easy nights!"

"I reckon you're right, Hubcap."

The two men worked in silence for a while, each with their own part of the project to turn the car from a wreck to a showpiece. GW took the carburetor he was working on to the office to pull a catalogue from a shelf and try to match a part's number. As he did, he looked up when he saw something pass by the front window.

Five minutes later, when he went back to the work bay, he hollered to Hubcap, "Hubcap, you shoulda been in the office a minute ago."

"Why's that, GW?"

"I saw the strangest sight—"

Then before he could explain, another person stepped inside the open garage doors. The men both looked up to see Winslow standing there.

"Hello, Hubcap, GW. I saw your lights on and thought I'd stick my head in. What you two up to?"

"Just going broke trying to get this ole Chevy up and running again. I guess you're out looking for your cat. Scooter wuz just here. He said your cat was missing."

Winslow was, of course, looking for Herman. He had gone one direction and now was going in the other with no luck so far. He stuck his head in the garage in the faint hope that Herman had sought refuge here.

"My cat...oh yes, my cat!"

"GW wuz just about to tell me that he done seen something strange. What wuz it, GW, a cat?"

GW answered, "Not hardly. I saw something go by the front window of the office, and when I looked up, I saw the skinniest, ugliest woman I have ever seen. She had a towel wrapped around her head and the wildest combination of blouse and skirt I've ever seen, like she got her clothes at a secondhand-clothing store... and the dog that wuz with her wuz the sorriest-looking mutt I've seen in a month of Sundays!"

Winslow looked at GW with big eyes. "Was she wearing glasses...black-rimmed glasses?"

"Yep, I believe she wuz. Fellers, I wish you coulda seen her. Where is a camera when I need one?"

Winslow had a funny feeling in his stomach. "Which way did she go?"

"Oh, back toward town."

With that, Winslow turned and headed back out the garage doors. "See you guys later. I gotta look for that cat!"

Winslow took off down the street so quick that GW stepped to the open door and watched him for a minute as he disappeared into the night. When GW stepped back into the garage, he looked at Hubcap, who was back at work under the hood of the Chevy. "That's odd, Hubcap."

"What's odd, GW?"

"I thought Scooter said the Upshaws' cat wuz named Buford. But just now I saw Winslow running down the street and hollering, 'Herman, Herman!'"

27

There was a scowl on the face of the large gray cat. He was perched on the top of the barbeque grill that stood on the brick patio outside Sarah Louise's studio. Some cats have a natural scowl. Even when they're smiling, they appear to be in a bad mood. Then there are those like Buford. He had a complacent face, but when he felt put out about something, he could turn the corners of his mouth down, and the resulting scowl was definitely a sign of displeasure. He was displeased now because sleeping on the small welcome mat outside the door to the studio, there was a wirehaired mongrel dog. Buford was one mad kitty.

Things hadn't been going well for Buford lately. Last week, he had been chased about the house by a man with Kleenex up his nose. The last several days had been hectic with people in and out of the room he shared with his human companion. Then last night, while he sat comfortably on the warm brick of the patio, enjoying the night air, a loud noise had scared him so bad he was frozen in his place, not knowing where to run.

And just as he had decided to return to the safety of his home, two strange men had rushed out of the studio right at him. Buford had ended spending the night under the house. A gap between the foundation and the dryer vent was just the right size for Buford. Now, with the dawn, he had reemerged from the darkness of the crawl space to find a dog between him and home.

Home beckoned to Buford with its soft couch pillows and bowl of cat food. But home may as well have been a hundred miles away because Buford did not mess with dogs. In the relative serenity of his perch atop the barbeque grill, he sat there and scowled.

The dog, however, was reflecting on his relative good luck. A week ago, he had been dropped off on a lonely country dirt road. His owners, never the best of providers, had seen fit to get rid of him. He had tried to follow their car as it sped down the road, kicking up a cloud of dust, but he had lost sight of it. Every home he had stopped at, looking for a familiar face, people had only yelled at him or thrown rocks at him. Even other dogs he had encountered had barked and snapped at him. For days, he had lived as best he could. Then he had stumbled upon the big city of Sulphur Springs, where there were even more people to yell at you or throw rocks. But last night, he had been befriended by a skinny human who had patted him instead of hitting him.

It had been very exciting. The two of them had run together, sat in the tall grass together, and visited a clothesline together.

After that, the two had gone for a nice, long walk, the human talking to him the whole time. Another human had come running up to them, and after some yelling and a great deal of talking, the three of them had walked to this place, where he had been fed and given a place to sleep. The other humans, like the skinny one, had all been kind to him, particularly the young female one. With the warm sun starting to shine on the doorway, the dog pondered his fate and decided that he might just stay here.

There was a noise at the door to the studio, and both dog and cat looked to see what was up.

The door opened, and a woman stuck her head out. "He's still here, Sarah Louise. It's like your father said. You shouldn't have fed him last night!"

Another face appeared at the door.

"But he was hungry, Mother. You could look at him and tell that!"

"Well, he sure wolfed down everything you fed him. The refrigerator is empty of leftovers. I wish Herman had taken him home with him."

"Herman was having enough trouble last night, Mother. Pops had to practically drag him back here, and it took all three of us to convince him to go ahead and pose for me."

"Your father and I had to sit where he could see us the whole time. Oh, I hope he doesn't tell Hannah everything that happened!"

"He promised he wouldn't, Mother. He was just glad to get out of here alive."

"And…you got your sketches!"

"Yes, I got my sketches!"

Buford was observing all of this from his place on the grill. The strange dog was sitting up and looking at the humans, his tail wagging. That was a bad sign. Buford let out a cry of protest.

"Look, Sarah Louise. There's Buford, on top of the grill. Where has he been?"

Sarah Louise smiled at the sight of her spoiled cat and stepped across the doorway and onto the patio. She walked past the dog, which looked from her to Claudette, not sure whom to pay the most attention to. Picking her cat up, Sarah Louise talked soothingly to it and carried it inside. As she and Claudette closed the door to the studio, Buford looked over Sarah Louise's shoulder and gave the dog a smirk.

With the door shut, the dog sat down, not sure what to make of the cat and the now-closed door. He had seen cats before. They were of no interest, but the security of human companionship pulled at his vulnerable heart. He lay back down on the doormat, and a small plaintive whine came uncontrollably from his throat.

Inside the studio, Sarah Louise grilled Buford over his whereabouts during the night and why he hadn't come when she had called for him. Of course, he tried to tell her, but she couldn't understand cat talk, so he just purred and rubbed up against her, which seemed to satisfy her. A bowl of milk and some fresh-from-the-bag cat nibbles, and Buford was once again king of the studio. As he lapped the milk, the humans continued to talk.

"What are you going to do about the dog, Sarah Louise? We can't keep it. Dog hair and cat hair—it's all the same to your father. He woke up this morning with his eyes all red."

"I can't put him back on the street, Mother. Besides, he's a sweet little dog. Did you see how his eyes would light up every time I petted him last night?"

"Oh, I know he's a sweet little dog, but all animals are sweet to you. If we'd let you, you would have a zoo here—and your father said he has fleas!"

"I'm going to do something about that right now! Look under the bathroom sink, Mother. There should be some flea shampoo under there. I'll go to the shed and get a washtub. Pooch is about to get a good bath and combing!"

"And...after that?"

"After that, I think I'll take him to the vet's."

"The vet's?"

"I'm sure he needs shots, and the vet can look him over. He may need deworming."

"Why can't you just take him to the pound, Sarah Louise?"

"Because, after a week, the pound will...well, I don't like to think about it."

"They put them under, don't they?"

"Yes, Mother."

Claudette sat there and thought about the poor little dog on the doorstep. "I'll get the shampoo. And while you're giving him a bath, I'll look in the freezer."

"The freezer, Mother?"

"Yes, I have some stew meat in there. I bet he'd love it!"

So while his fate was being discussed, the stray mongrel lay on the doormat and whimpered, not knowing what his future may hold.

28

A parrot, a snake, and a Chihuahua greeted Sarah Louise and the pooch when they entered the All Creatures Great and Small Animal Clinic on East Main Street. Although his specialty was dogs and cats, Dr. Reuben Sneed was not too proud to doctor any animal. Like Sarah Louise, any creature suffering would pull at his heartstrings, and Doc Reuben would try to work his magic.

Sarah Louise checked in with the receptionist, and she and her new furry friend sat down in one of the hard plastic chairs that lined the walls of the waiting room. She looked at the others present. The kid with the snake was a high school student. She recognized him immediately. Sarah Louise had taught his older sister. The snake, some kind of a boa, was curled up into a ball in the boy's protective a rms. All Sarah Louise could wonder was, *How can you tell if a snake is sick?*

The parrot sat on an older man's shoulder. She didn't recognize the man. The bird was looking at the snake with a noticeable look of alarm. No matter how the old man turned or moved, the bird kept his eyes on the snake. For that matter, Sarah Louise also kept an eye on the snake. The dog, however, sat beside her, his tail wagging in various speeds from slow to ninety miles an hour.

"I didn't know you had a dog, Sarah Louise. I thought you were a cat person." The voice came from behind the receptionist's desk. "Does he have a name?"

Sarah Louise turned her face to the desk and spoke to the receptionist, although she couldn't see her from where she sat. "No name. He's a stray."

"Is he sick?"

"No, I just wanted Dr. Ruben to check him out. He probably needs shots. Don't all dogs need shots? I don't know much about dogs."

The woman with the Chihuahua put down the magazine she had been holding in front of her face and turned to face Sarah Louise. It was Ruby Stafford.

"I thought I recognized your voice. How are you, Sarah Louise?"

"Oh, hi, Miss Ruby. Is that your Chihuahua?"

"Yes, this is Miss Bitty. Say hi, Miss Bitty. She's not feeling well today. Miss Bitty is almost as old as I am—in dog years, I mean. We've been through a lot together, we have." Then, changing the subject, she added, "How are your folks, Sarah Louise? I haven't seen your father much since he retired."

"I'm afraid he spends all his time in front of the TV."

"My Harold used to do that. It would drive me crazy." She paused for a moment, and there was a touch of sadness in her voice as she continued, "It's been three years now. Three years in December." She paused again. "Now, it's just me and Miss Bitty."

Sarah Louise was at a loss for words.

Then the door opened, and the receptionist stuck her head into the room. "Jerry, bring Hercules in and let Dr. Ruben look at him...and keep him away from me!"

The small group in the waiting room laughed as the boy got up, holding his boa close to his chest, and followed the receptionist.

Ruby Stafford, concerned as she was about Miss Bitty, was anxious to bring up a different subject with Sarah Louise. Just two days ago, she had heard all about the now-famous painting at Pearl's Beauty Shoppe. With Sarah Louise right across from her, Ruby wanted to hear it straight from the horse's mouth. She was trying to work up just the right question when the door to the clinic opened, and another client walked in.

Naturally, everyone in the small waiting room turned to look at the intruder, who had stopped right inside the door. There, oblivious to the staring eyes of the others, he tried to pull a panicked cat from off his shoulders, where it had clambered up out of his arms. Cats, when they sense danger, head for the highest branch of the tree or, in this case, the person.

Sensing that his head was the next stop, Michael Dorphman pulled and pleaded to the panicky pussycat. "It's all right. Nobody's going to hurt you. It's all right!"

Miss Bitty stood up in Ruby Stafford's lap and began to hop around. The cat was just the right size for Miss Bitty to play with. The sick Chihuahua let out two high-pitched little barks.

"Now, now, Miss Bitty—be still!" Then, directing her attention to the newcomer whom she recognized, she said, "I'm sorry, Michael. Miss Bitty wants to play."

Michael, still tugging at the cat, whose claws were firmly caught in his shirt, replied to Ruby's comment, "I don't think she likes dogs, Miss Ruby." Then, as a claw managed to catch flesh, he exclaimed, "Ouch!"

Almost as quickly as he had said ouch, Sarah Louise was on her feet and at Michael's side. "Here, let me help you, Michael."

Michael cast his eyes from the tiny Chihuahua in Ruby's lap to the direction of the voice offering help. He immediately recognized Sarah Louise. "Oh, hi, Sarah Louise. This is the second time today that she's climbed up on my shoulder. I'm beginning to think she's the original scaredy-cat."

Sarah Louise stepped behind Michael and looked into the frightened cat's eyes, at the same time carefully pulling the offending claw out of Michael's shoulder and talking calming to the kitty. She patted the cat a few times on the head and talked some more. After a minute, the cat abandoned Michael for the security of her arms.

With the cat off his shoulders, Michael turned to face Sarah Louise. "Will you look at that! She took to you like a duck to water. I'm afraid I'm not very good with cats...I'm more of a dog person."

Sarah Louise laughed. "Is she sick?"

"I don't think so. She's a stray that wandered up to my grandmother's. They've been feeding her, and now she won't go away. I'm afraid Gramma will trip over her, so I took her off their hands!"

"Who is *they*, Michael? I thought your grandmother lived alone." Ruby, always attentive to other people's conversations, asked.

"Oh, Gramma and Ester Mae. Ester Mae comes by two days a week. I try to keep the two of them out of trouble!"

"So she's not sick?" Sarah Louise said.

By now, the mongrel dog had joined the two, afraid that its new owner wasn't going to return to his side.

"No, she's not sick. But I figured she would need shots, and I probably need to get her spayed."

As he said that, the pooch put his front paws on Michael's leg. "Whoa, what's this?"

Again, Sarah Louise laughed. "I'm afraid that's my story!"

With another dog now in the picture, the cat was starting to tense up again. Sarah could feel its muscles tighten beneath its hair. She began speaking soothingly to it.

"You have a way with cats," Michael said. He then bent down to pet the ever-friendly pooch, which quickly began to lick Michael in the face.

"It looks like you have a way with dogs," Sarah Louise said, returning the compliment.

Then the voice of Ruby Stafford again interrupted, "I think you two need to swap animals!"

They both laughed. Sarah Louise walked back to her seat and sat down, talking softly to the cat the whole way and holding it safely in her arms. She looked at Michael, who continued to pet the overly friendly pooch. Miss Bitty hopped about on Ruby's lap and emitted two more high-pitched barks.

"I think you're right, Miss Ruby, and it looks like your Chihuahua agrees with you. This pooch has already switched allegiances!" He turned his face to Sarah Louise. "What's his name?"

"Sarah Louise said he doesn't have one. He's a stray... right, Sarah Louise?" By now, Ruby was as much a part of the conversation as Michael.

"No name?" Michael said in exaggerated surprise.

"It just showed up at the house last night when...well, it just showed up and...I felt sorry for him, so I fed him. He was still there this morning, so I gave him a good flea bath and brought him here for a checkup." She paused a moment. "Does the cat have a name?"

Michael left his place by the pooch and came and sat beside Sarah Louise. "Sure, she does—Kitty."

The man with the parrot laughed.

"That's original!" Sarah Louise said, trying hard not to laugh as well.

"Let me see." She held the cat out at arm's length and stared at its face. "Mm, with that caramel color around her eyes and on her back, mm...how about Ginger? Short for gingerbread?"

"Sounds good to me!" Michael said.

"Your turn now, Michael. Give Sarah Louise's dog a name!" Ruby pleaded.

Michael put his hand to his chin. The dog was staring right at him, his tail in perpetual motion.

"Well, I do believe you look like....a Scamp! How's that?"

The dog could tell that Michael was talking to him although he had no idea of what he was saying. Even so, the inflection and the very tone in his voice were reassuring and the pooch joyfully let out a bark.

"See, he likes it!" Michael beamed triumphantly.

Miss Bitty agreed and let out a series of high-pitched barks only to be reprimanded by Ruby.

The door of the office opened and a smiling boy with the boa still clutched to his chest walked into the waiting room. The receptionist followed him into the room.

"Now, Jerry, don't be alarmed if he's not eating much. Doc Ruben says they take spells. I'll send a bill to your mom and dad!"

The boy nodded that he understood and as he left the clinic, the receptionist turned to face the man with the parrot.

"Mr. Lassiter, bring Gilligan back here to see Doc Ruben."

The older man got up and followed her into the inner office; the bird still on his shoulder.

The trio that remained returned to the subject of dogs and cats.

"Michael, the way that dog's taken to you and the way the cat's holding onto Sarah Louise, I think you two really should swap."

"I believe you're right, Miss Ruby. I've never had a cat before... always dogs." Michael looked at Sarah Louise, "What do you think, Sarah Louise?"

"Actually, it would be perfect for me. I can keep another cat in my studio...I have one already. And Pop wants me to get rid of the dog, I mean...Scamp!"

"Well, it's a done deal then!" Michael concluded. He turned his head to face Ruby. "Miss Ruby, you're a witness. It's an even swap!"

"Your grandmother won't mind?" Sarah Louise asked.

"Oh no, she was glad I was taking it off her hands. And, there's nobody at my house but me, so I don't need anyone's permission."

Sarah Louise gave the pooch a concerned look.

"He does look happy. Yes, a done deal!"

The two young people both smiled, the dog wagged his tail, and the cat began to ever so softly purr.

Ruby, with one hand trying to keep Miss Bitty still, was now free to return to her earlier concern. Michael's arrival had given her the inroad she needed to ask Sarah Louise about the painting.

Ruby tried to sound casual. "Michael, I guess your grandmother is busy getting ready for the Annual Spring Fling and Antique Auction to Benefit the Art Guild's Town Beautification Project."

"Yes, Ma'am, she's pretty busy. She's been looking forward to it since Easter."

Ruby paused a moment as if she were letting Michael's words sink in. Then she ever so casually turned her attention to Sarah Louise.

"Sarah Louise, I guess you're going to enter the art show. What are you going to enter this year?"

Sarah Louise looked at Ruby Stafford, then she looked at Michael, who had turned to face her in anticipation of her answer. She looked from Michael to the dog and then to the cat in her arms. Where, she thought to herself, *is a good earthquake when you need one?*

29

"Spinach is one pound for a dollar and ten cents; celery, eighty-nine cents; and seedless grapes are two twenty-five. These are just some of the items you'll find in the produce section of Harry's Foodland, locally owned, locally managed, and proud to serve the people of Sulphur Springs. Now we're back to *Ted and Sherry in the Morning* on station WQAK right here in Sulphur Springs. It's now time for our weekly agricultural report from Tom Abbott with the state agricultural extension service."

"Let's hear what Tom has to say, Ted. I know the local feeder pig market has gone up."

"Soooooweeee…let's do hear about those pigs…"

"We want to remind our listeners that the weekly agricultural report is brought to you by Harry's Foodland."

"The place to stop for all your food needs…"

Ted Bumquist switched a lever on the control panel, and the taped agricultural report took over the WQAK airways. He flipped two more switches and then turned to face his morning cohost, Sherry McGee. "Five minutes!"

Sherry pulled a set of earphones off her head and ran her one hand through her hair. She turned over a piece of paper that lay on the console in front of her, and after a quick glance, she looked up at the smiling face of Lucinda Hardin-Powell.

"Lucinda, it's so good of you to come down and be our guest this morning. Usually we don't report on the annual Spring Fling until a couple of days before the event."

"Oh, Sherry, we're just so excited about this year's show. We have more entries than ever!"

Smiling from ear to ear, Lucinda pulled a piece of paper from a huge purse that sat on the floor beside her. "I've got the full list right here!"

"Great," inserted Ted, "We can read that list of entries off. It's been a slow news day, and we're hunting for something to fill up our time."

"*Slow* isn't the word for it. Even Washington is quiet today—not a scandal in sight!" Sherry agreed.

"Give 'em a couple of days, Sherry. They never fail to disappoint us," Ted bounced back.

"That's why I was so glad when you called me this morning, Lucinda. We didn't have much on our agenda. The high school baseball coach cancelled yesterday's game…something about a band needing his ball field. There just wasn't much

"Well, I was sitting at home, going over my list, and the thought just hit me. Why not call the radio station and see if I can get on *Ted and Sherry in the Morning*. After all, half the people in the county will be listening."

This much was true. Half of the radios in the county, whether in cars or sitting on kitchen counters, were tuned to local AM 1129, WQAK. People were fiercely patriotic to their local station. It played a format that was heavily country music and gospel. That's why the other half of the residents of Sulphur Springs didn't listen—anyone under the age of eighteen. They preferred to listen to rap, pop, funk, hard rock, new age—anything but what the local station played. Does anyone ever wonder what the world will be like when that generation grows old and enters the nation's nursing homes? Wheelchairs and walkers will be moving up and down the hallways to the sound of "Pimp My Ride."

The station was truly the source of local news and a certain amount of gossip. Between Hank Williams Jr., Dolly Parton, and newcomers like Tim McGraw and Shania Twain, the station had its daily *The Living Word*, where local pastors had a chance to expound doctrine and remind listeners of upcoming revivals; the *Hospital Update*, where every new admission to the hospital was reported; *The Oglesby Funeral Home: Song of the Day*, where an old standard was played, like "Rock of Ages," and you could find out who was currently on display in their Rose Room. There was always the daily weather report, the fishing forecast, weekly news from each of the schools, the state agricultural report, local sports, and what was happening in the state legislature.

Yes, the little 400-watt radio station only broadcast to a small area, but it covered the local events and advertised all the local businesses. If you wanted to know what was happening around town, you just tuned in to *Ted and Sherry in the Morning*, from eight to noon, Monday through Friday.

Ted motioned to Sherry that the live feed was about to return, and he held out his hand, his five fingers extended.

"That's his cue to us, Lucinda. We have five seconds before we go back on the air.

Lucinda, oblivious to the fact that no one in the radio audience would be able to see her, sat up straight on the metal stool she was perched on and then used one hand to fluff up her hair and the other to pull her skirt over her exposed knees.

Ted lowered the five fingers, one at a time, till the last pinkie was down.

"Back to *Ted and Sherry in the Morning*. Thanks, Tom, for the agricultural report."

"Brought to us by the friendly local staff down at Harry's Foodland," chimed in his coanchor.

"Right now, the WQAK thermometer shows a balmy seventy-five degrees outside the studio with the sun shining."

"Sounds like a perfect day for fishing. Right, Ted?"

"Right, Sherry, and that's just where you might find me this afternoon! But right now, here in the studio, we have a guest. Tell us who we have here to grace our airwaves, Sherry."

"Ted, this morning, we have Lucinda Hardin-Powell with us. We all know Lucinda. She's a local girl."

"Born and raised right here in Sulphur Springs, right, Lucinda?"

Lucinda blushed. She hadn't expected to have to respond so soon. It caught her off guard, but she managed to clear her throat and blurt out, "Yes, Ted...I'm a local girl."

"Lucinda's husband, BJ, works down at the Merchants and Farmers Bank," Sherry said.

"And we want to wish all the folks down there a howdy from us and remind listeners that the Merchants and Farmers Bank is one of the sponsors for our daily *Hospital Update*!" Ted added.

"That's right, Ted, and Lucinda here is going to be talking about the Spring Fling Art Show. Right, Lucinda?"

Again, Lucinda was caught off guard. She leaned toward the huge microphone on the console in front of her as the realization hit her that she had to be alert. "Yes, Sherry." Feeling the need to say more, she added, "And Antique Auction."

"Let's not forget those antiques," Ted countered. "Tell me, Lucinda. What is the official title for the show, for our listeners."

There they went again, throwing something at her and expecting her to think on her feet. "It's the Annual Spring Fling Art Show and Antique Auction to Benefit the Art Guild's Town-Beautification Project!"

"So this is an annual event, Lucinda?" Ted asked this as if he didn't know.

Lucinda gave him a surprised look then realized he was playing dumb to get information out of her. "Yes, yes, it's an annual event.

This is the tenth year we have had it." Pleased with the sound of her voice and starting to get the hang of it, she decided to elaborate, "It just keeps getting bigger and better every year!"

"Where is this annual event held, Lucinda?"

This question came from Sherry, who, like Ted, knew the answer already, but Lucinda had become wise to what they were doing. There might be people out there who didn't know. So Lucinda began to take part in the interview with gusto.

"We hold the art show at the old Sulphur Springs High School, on Depot Street, at the corner of Dorphman Avenue, right here in the center of Sulphur Springs. We use the old school year round. It's the headquarters of the Art Guild. We have all of our offices there. And we offer lessons during summer months and one-day classes during the rest of the year. You know, painting or ceramics—the ceramics class meets every Thursday morning."

She rather enjoyed this, the sound of her voice—hundreds, if not thousands, of people listening to her every word. Lucinda opened her mouth to say more, but Ted cut her off.

"Let's stop there, Lucinda, for a station break and a word from the good folks down at the co-op who help sponsor our show."

He flipped a switch, and both he and Sherry took off their headphones. "Five," Ted said, and he turned in his seat to sort through a pile of tapes on the table behind him.

Sherry looked at Lucinda, who sat there with her mouth open. "We're off again, Lucinda. Five minutes."

Lucinda politely closed her mouth.

"You aren't nervous, are you?"

"Oh no...I'm fine," Lucinda answered. It was a white lie at best.

Lucinda was nervous. Her efforts to get the public upset over Sarah Louise's painting were not going as fast as she had hoped. The paper wouldn't run anything until next week. Yes, the gossip mills were going strong, but no one was demanding that the Art Guild do anything. Her calls to the school board members' wives evidently had no effect, and that was puzzling. Maybe, Lucinda reasoned, maybe not enough people were aware yet. Here, now, however, with the airwaves at her disposal, she was prepared to remedy that. Yes, she was a little nervous but also a little hyper with the power that lay before her in that little microphone just inches from her mouth.

Sherry began to make small talk with Lucinda to while away the break. They discussed the difficulty of getting their children to Little League practice, and Lucinda spoke of her efforts to get BJ to lose weight.

In no time, Ted turned back around and held up the five fingers again.

"We're back with our guest, Lucinda Hardin-Powell, with the Sulphur Springs Art Guild. Lucinda, tell us, just when is the art show?" It was Sherry doing the questioning now.

Lucinda was ready. "The Tenth Annual Spring Fling Art Show and Antique Auction to Benefit the Art Guild's Town-Beautification Project is next weekend, April 2 and 3. That's Saturday from ten till five and Sunday from one to five at the old Sulphur Springs High School, on Depot Street at the corner of Dorphman Avenue."

"Tell us about the antique auction, Lucinda. Where is it held? Is it at the school also?"

"No, the auction is Saturday evening at the VFW Hall, downtown, next to the post office. The auction is from six till… who knows. We just go till we run out."

"Who does the antiques, Lucinda? Does the Art Guild do that, or do you have someone come in and do that, like an antiques dealer?"

Ted suddenly reentered the conversation. "This is the part of this annual event that my wife and mother-in-law look forward to. Every year, my wife comes back with at least one piece of Depression glass, and she never tells me how much she spent!"

The two women laughed.

"We have Mavis and Earl from Granny's attic in Bowling Green do the antiques every year. They bring in a truckload of stuff. We never know what they'll have exactly, but they always have a variety of stuff—something for everyone! You can spend a little, or you can spend a lot. The Art Guild gets a percentage of the evening's sales…"

Lucinda was on a roll. She had the mic and was enjoying every minute of it. For the next thirty minutes, the three discussed the art show and the antiques and the beautification project, along with the occasional word from the sponsors.

As the time drew to a close, Lucinda pulled her little piece of paper closer to her and prepared to read the list of entries. Lucinda had arranged the entries in such a way that paintings were last, and the last name she intended to read was, "Sarah Louise Upshaw, acrylic painting." She was pleased with herself.

As Ted once again held up his five fingers, Lucinda let her eyes skim the paper in front of her till they rested on Sarah's name. There, the last words Lucinda expected to say were—right there, underlined and in big letters—"a painting titled *A Room Full of Naked Men.*"

Lucinda clutched the paper close to her ample chest and smiled. She smiled a smile no less ample than her bosom.

30

"The nice thing about living in a small town, Malvenna, is that when I don't know what I'm doing, someone else surely does!"

"Why, Huey? What makes you say that?"

"Malvenna, honey, I've had three people ask me what I was going to do with Sarah Louise's painting! I just don't know how so many people have found out about it. Why, when I stopped at Danny's Donut Den on the way here—you know I can't drive by there without stopping—"

Malvenna interrupted him, "Oh, me too! Booger would eat three meals a day there if I let him. He could live on their fried pies!"

Not minding the diversion, Huey had to ask, "The chocolate?"

"Oh no, the apricot!"

"Well, sweetie, you tell him to try the chocolate and to be sure to ask Wong Fu to sprinkle extra sugar on top."

"Oh, Huey, it's not Wong Fu. It's Cam Tang. *Cam*, like short for *camouflage*, and *Tang*, like in the drink. That's how I remember!"

"Wong Fu, Cam Fu! I know why he calls it Danny's Donut Den. Can you imagine driving up to a place called Wong Fu's Donuts and Chop Suey? What are they anyway?"

"Vietnamese, Huey. We fought a war with them, remember?"

"If America had known how good the Vietcong could cook American pastries, there wouldn't have been a war! Now, where was I—and hand me another doughnut, that one with the sprinkles on top."

It was true. Cam Tang and his wife, Mai, had the monopoly on doughnuts in Sulphur Springs. Not only did they open the popular Danny's Donut Den, but they supplied doughnuts to three area restaurants. And their oldest son, Tu, ran the doughnut and pie counter at the new super-Walmart on the bypass.

People stopped by the shop on their way to work. It was only open mornings because the Tang family got there by 4:00 a.m. every day, making for a full day by noon. People like Huey had to buy enough when they stopped to get them through the day—or night, if you had a heavy sweet tooth like Huey.

What most people didn't know was that Cam, a boat-people refugee from the war, had gotten his training in a traveling carnival and could deep-fry anything. But his secret to success was to keep the back door of the small kitchen open so that the odor of fried dough bounced around the intersection of West Main and Dorphman Avenue, the town's busiest intersection. It was a trick he had learned in the carnival: throw a handful of onions, on the grill, and the odor pulls people in like flies to a watermelon at a July picnic. If Cam ever got tired of fried dough, he could make a living cooking burgers and hot dogs. The man was a wiz at American food. It had been years since his tongue had tasted rice.

"You were saying something about people knowing what you're doing. You know, in a small town like ours," Malvenna finally answered Huey, all the while licking the powdered sugar off her fingers so she could pop a piece of gum in her mouth.

"That's right. I was getting my dozen doughnuts when Charlene Gooch put her peroxide pompadour in my face and asked me where I was going to put *A Room Full of Naked Men*.

She was getting her sugar fix and getting an éclair to take to Pearl at the beauty shop and said that the girls down at Pearl's all thought I should hang it behind a curtain and charge people extra if they wanted to see an X-rated painting!"

"That's not peroxide, Huey. She's a natural blonde!"

"My left foot, Malvenna. Hair doesn't come that blonde. Marilyn Monroe would look like a brunette next to Charlene Gooch!"

Malvenna shifted in her chair and unconsciously fluffed up the back of her blonde hair. She knew all about peroxide. "She may touch it up with peroxide, Huey, but I know a peroxide blonde when I see one! So what did you tell her?"

"I told her I hadn't seen the painting yet, only heard about it like she and Pearl had. So I'd have to wait. But I told her that if we could charge extra to see it, the money would be going to a good cause, the Annual Spring Fling and Antique Auction to Benefit the Art Guild's Town-Beautification Project."

"I guess that explains how so many people know about it. Say something in the morning at Pearl's Beauty Shoppe, and by noon it's halfway 'cross town."

"Oh, that reminds me. Lucinda told me to be sure to listen to *Ted and Sherry* this morning. Turn that radio on, Malvenna, while I get me another cup of coffee."

As Huey made his way across the tiny office to the coffeemaker, Malvenna turned to the radio and moved it to the edge of her desk. She then stooped in her chair to unplug the electric pencil sharpener. The old school had not been wired for the electronic age, and now that the computer got first dibs on the plugs, everything else had to take turns.

"Did she say why, Huey?"

"No, she didn't, but I somehow have a feeling it has to do with the Spring Fling and a room full of naked men!" As he walked back to his desk, he added a terse, "Wanna bet?"

"What would she be doing at the radio station? And if she was, it's not her job to go to the station and talk about the show. She's just the membership secretary!"

Huey knew he had stepped on a nerve and couldn't resist the opportunity to say more. "Five will get you ten!"

"Now, Huey, I like Lucinda as well as anybody can…why, I was the first person she told about that painting. But she doesn't run the Art Guild!"

"No, she doesn't. Not now anyway."

"What do you mean by that?"

"I mean, just look at her eyes, honey. Look at her face when we have a meeting. You may know peroxide when you see it, but I know ambition when I see it. Lucinda won't be happy till she has—"

"Louise's job!" Malvenna exploded. "Oh no! I'm next in line for project chairman. I've been here longer than any Lucinda Hardin-Powell!"

"Don't get your panties in a wad, Malvenna! She doesn't want to be any old project chairman. She won't be happy till she's got Biederman's job—VP!"

"VP?" Malvenna echoed.

"Bet your sweet bippy!

We can't let Lucinda get that. It's the Biedermans' and Dorphmans' money, and well…it's who they are that keeps the Art Guild going. Lucinda's nothing. Why, her husband just works at the bank!"

Huey felt the responsibility to remind Malvenna that her husband was no higher up the social ladder. "Booger drives a backhoe, Malvenna."

"My Booger may drive a backhoe, but he owns his own business! That Lucinda better not try to be a social climber around me!"

"Oh, sweetie, I agree. But I'm just telling you the truth. You can have your project chairman when Louise gives it up, but

Lucinda wants the VP spot—just you wait and see. Now, turn that radio on!"

Malvenna wasn't sure if she should be mad or glad, glad that Lucinda wasn't after the very position she lusted for or mad that Lucinda had higher aims that she had not even considered. She clicked the switch, and the radio hummed on.

A voice they both recognized as that of Ted Bumquist was speaking. "Tell me, Lucinda, what is the official title for the show, for our listeners."

Huey sat there. He was wearing his favorite Hawaiian shirt, the one with the bare-chested surfers on the front. He brushed a pink sprinkle off the leg of his white slacks, and he watched Malvenna's face closely as she listened to the voice of Lucinda Hardin-Powell answer Ted, "It's the Annual Spring Fling…"

31

"And our last entry in the acrylic-painting category is by Sarah Louise Upshaw."

There was a calculated pause. "I believe she's the art teacher at Sulphur Springs High School. Her entry is a painting, quite large, I'm told, called"—there was another pause—"it's called *A Room Full of Naked Men*."

Before Ted or Sherry could say anything, Lucinda was quick to add, "And that's the full list of entries so far. Of course, we accept entries up to the morning of the show. Sounds like an exciting display to me."

If Lucinda expected to climb down off her stool and make a quick exit, she was wrong.

Ted seized on the announcement. "What was that last thing you said, Lucinda? I'm not sure I heard it."

Lucinda fumbled with the piece of paper. She had made her point; now she just wanted to leave and let things take their course. She didn't want to have to discuss a painting about naked men, especially since Mrs. Dorphman hadn't been impressed with the subject matter and, even more so, since she hadn't consulted Louise or Mrs. Biederman about appearing on the radio show.

Lucinda wanted to appear naive about the whole thing, if that was possible.

Radio announcers, however, don't like a pause in their programming. It makes the listener feel like they are lost in space. You fill up every second with entertainment or advertising. One minute of nothing is a minute wasted.

While Lucinda played with her piece of paper, trying to think of something to say, Sherry came to the rescue. "I believe, Ted, the last thing Lucinda told us was that the Art Guild will accept entries up to the morning of the show. Is that right, Lucinda?"

Lucinda looked up from the crumpled paper to face Sherry. Her mind was blank. Is that what she had said? She was so nervous that she wasn't really sure what she had said.

It was Ted who came to the rescue this time. Any pause longer than one second put his mouth into gear. "So if I wanted to go down to Dorphman's Hardware and Appliance—who, by the way, sponsors our daily *High School Coaches' Minute*—and purchased some canvas and some kind of paint, I could do a painting and have it ready by the morning of the Spring Fling?"

Lucinda blurted, "Yes, that's right, Ted. You could…I guess. You'd have to work fast…but yes…you could."

"So, Ted, just what kind of painting masterpiece do you have in mind?" Sherry queried him.

"Well, Sherry, I'm not a great painter like I'm sure most of the artists in the Spring Fling will be, but my mama has a flower bed in the backyard, and every summer, she has a bunch of *surprise lilies* come up. Are you familiar with surprise lilies, Sherry?"

"Yes, I am, Ted. One day the ground is bare, and the next day there is a huge ole lily there, like a big surprise."

"Then I guess you know what else they call surprise lilies, Sherry. If not, maybe you do, Lucinda?"

Lucinda wasn't sure where this conversation was going. She wanted to be going somewhere herself, out of the radio station. Her mind went blank again—surprise lilies, another name?

"I sure do, Ted. They call 'em *naked ladies!*" Sherry replied.

"That's right, Sherry. So maybe I can do me a big old painting of surprise lilies and call it *A Room Full of Naked Ladies!*"

Sherry laughed, and Ted guffawed at his wit. Lucinda, a tattered piece of paper in her hand, sat there with her mouth open.

"But right now, let's have a station break and update of today's weather before we finish today's show." And Ted hit the switch on his control panel.

Sherry was still laughing when she turned to face Lucinda.

Lucinda was easing off the stool and trying to make a quiet getaway. She had accomplished her goal, and she wasn't sure of what to think of Ted's humorous remark. Did it call the right amount of attention to the controversial canvas by Sarah Louise, or did it make the whole thing sound like a joke?

"Don't go yet, Lucinda. Ted and I will want you to give us the days and hours of the Spring Fling one more time."

Caught, Lucinda eased back up onto the cold metal stool.

"And, Lucinda, what gives with that last painting? Is the Art Guild going to display a nude painting?"

"Not *nude*, Sherry."

Ted joined the conversation, having pressed the buttons that automatically played a blue grass version of the station's call letters and a station promotional tape.

"Nudes! Didn't you hear what Lucinda said? It was a *room full* of naked men, not one!"

Sherry looked to Lucinda again. "Is that right, Lucinda? Is the Art Guild going to bare a little flesh for the matrons of Sulphur Springs?"

"Uh, I haven't actually seen the painting myself, so I don't know exactly what that woman is painting…but I think the title gives us a good idea."

Lucinda suddenly found herself almost being defensive, but she needn't worry. Ted and Sherry found the whole thing amusing.

"I definitely am going to see this, Ted. Maybe we can do a live show that morning and question people before and after they see the show."

"Mmm, we might be able to do that. The station is doing a live show this Saturday for the opening of the Little League season down at the park. Live shows two weekends in a row. I'll check with Casey."

Casey was the station owner and sole announcer every afternoon and the DJ. He kept his payroll small.

<hr />

As Ted and Sherry tossed about the idea of a live radio show the day of the Spring Fling and Lucinda placed a shredded piece of paper in her purse and took a few deep breaths before she was back on the air, and while Huey and Malvenna tried to decide how to deal with Lucinda's sudden sense of self-importance, and while Sarah Louise sat in the vet's waiting room and tried to change the topic of conversation with Ruby Stafford, other people were reacting to the disclosure that the normally benign, even boring, Spring Fling Art Show was going to feature a painting of naked men.

One of them was Lucy Pendergrass.

To be sure, some people merely chuckled at the news of the racy painting. Then there were those people who immediately put their tongues to wagging, not to mention what it was doing to their imaginations, which were in overdrive.

But to Lucy Pendergrass, the news was liberating.

Lucy clicked off the flashy neon-pink radio above her kitchen sink, and a smile crossed her face, making its way into her double chin.

Why was she smiling so big?

Lucy, it seems, had always wanted to do a nude, but convention had always held her back. She had tempted fate with her Venus de Milo with arms, but she hadn't gone the full monty.

She turned from the sink to gaze at the kitchen she shared with her sister, Calpurnia. The kitchen was huge, with white cabinets that covered every wall and counters on all four sides. The house had once been a hotel for drummers and traveling salesmen, and the kitchen and adjoining dinning room once served meals to the salesmen. It had ten bedrooms. The sisters had, since inheriting the old home from an ancient uncle, turned the former bedrooms into other things. Three rooms were working studios for Lucy: one for oils, one for acrylics, one for everything else. Calpurnia used one room for an office. And the other rooms served to display knickknacks from travels abroad.

Lucy had spent her adult life living in New York City, where she worked for a big travel agency. She had been everywhere not once but twice.

And, of course, there were her paintings. She had started painting because the walls needed something, something big. She had never touched a paintbrush in her life, she liked to tell people, till she had retired and moved back to little Sulphur Springs. Most people didn't find that hard to believe.

Picasso had his Blue Period and his Pink Period and so forth. Lucy had her "really bad" period, her "just plain bad" period, and was now in her "bad" period. It was the serious hope of everyone who knew her that she would one day work herself into her "not so bad" period.

There was a good reason that Lucy Pendergrass never sold her paintings. That didn't mean that her artwork didn't grace the walls of many homes in Sulphur Springs. They did. Every relation to Lucy and Calpurnia suffered with a Lucy Pendergrass original over their living-room couch—or worse, over their bed. Lucy told people where to hang her gifts, and she fully expected them to be there the next time she visited.

Some people dread a visit to the dentist, but the people of Sulphur Springs knew real dread: the sight of Lucy Pendergrass walking up their front steps with a large canvas under one arm.

As Lucy stood at the sink and the wheels in her head turned, the gleam from almost one hundred cookie jars shone in the pupils of her eyes. Lucy had collected cookie jars on her travels; and now, thanks to eBay, she had an enviable collection. They were her children—good substitutions for the real, flesh-and-blood kind. Lucy had never been married.

If Lucy had her way, when she died, the rambling old former hotel would become a museum dedicated to her cookie jars and paintings. The cookie jars covered every spare inch of the countertops and peered through the hundred-year-old glass cabinet fronts. And the paintings, they hung everywhere—hallways, bathrooms, even the back porch had *A View of the Matterhorn*.

The gears in Lucy's head continued to turn. If Sarah Louise Upshaw could paint a naked man, Lucy Pendergrass could paint—a naked woman. Yes, a naked woman, and not just any woman. She wouldn't paint the Venus de Milo again. Nothing Greek or Roman this time around. No, she would have to be something special.

As she thought, her eyes flitted around the room. Cookie jars in every possible incarnation glared back at her. Dutch flower girls, Howdy Doody, Shakespeare's Globe Theatre, the Eiffel Tower, a motorcycle, a totem pole, the Pillsbury Doughboy—then her eyes caught a rare piece. It was a Little Black Sambo. His white eyes flashing against his glazed ebony skin, with his bright-red shirt and blue pants, he was a charmer.

Then it hit her. With a president in the White House with a black heritage—that was it. She would do an African queen, a temptress in black with a skimpy leopard skin skirt, and Lucy could picture it now. There would be bangles and beads. The queen leaped off the canvas and danced in Lucy's imagination.

If Sarah Louise Upshaw thought she was going to win any ribbons with her naked men, she would have to arm wrestle with Lucy's jungle woman first, and Lucy would make sure her ebony queen won!

32

Sara Louise pulled her car into the family driveway. Her mood was mixed. She had solved her problem with the dog by giving—no, swapping—it with that nice Michael Dorphman. That was good.

She had been held captive by Ruby Stafford's leading questions about the art show. True, she had managed to avoid any specifics till Ruby and Miss Bitty were called into the vet's office. Ruby, the old bag, Sarah Louise thought, knew about the painting already. She wasn't asking innocent questions. She was digging for dirt, the kind of dirt you collect and then run to the phone to share with the other gossips in town. That was bad.

She had a new cat. The cat was under the car seat just now, scared of the car's noise and motion. But it had taken to Sarah Louise, and Sarah Louise had taken to it. She had scheduled another trip to the vet to get it spayed; but for now, her cat, Buford, would have a companion to replace her last cat that had passed away of old age. That was good.

She had gotten behind a car on Dorphman Avenue, whose driver had a cell phone in one hand and the steering wheel, occasionally, in the other. She, the teenage driver, appeared to be texting someone. As a result, the car veered from one side of the lane to the other, as if it was toying with the idea of changing lanes and plowing headfirst into oncoming traffic. Sarah Louise was as agitated as the cat under her seat, and even though she had been able to turn off on New Providence Road to her street, Sarah Louise was still agitated from the experience. That was bad.

Then there was the whole situation caused by her mother, the painting, the art show, the near shooting of two innocent men by her father, and a half-finished painting with the torso of Herman Bugleman sketched out. She did, however, have the weekend and the whole week after it off from school, which should—thanks to spring break—give her enough time to finish her painting. That was good.

Now, she had to pull a frightened cat out from under her car seat, get into the house before her father saw her new companion, get back to work on her canvas, and be ready for another model when Claudette made the arrangements.

Yes, her mood was mixed.

As she turned off the ignition to her car, she gave a furtive look toward the kitchen door to make sure her father wasn't standing there watching. With a little luck, he was having a tête-à-tête with Rachel Ray or Anthony Bourdain, compliments of the Food Network.

Inside the house, her Pop was indeed in front of the television, but it didn't matter who or what was on because Winslow was oblivious to anything. He was soundly sleeping. If you walked into the room and woke him up, he would try to tell you that he was only "resting his eyes," but he was asleep. The snoring was a dead giveaway.

Claudette was on the phone. She had seen Sarah Louise drive up, but her attention was so caught up with her conversation that Sarah Louise could have pulled an elephant out from under the car seat and Claudette wouldn't have noticed. "Can't be too sure about that, Bonnie, but I think in the morning would be best…

that is, if you are sure the young man can make it. I don't want to make things any more difficult for you."

Claudette listened to Bonnie's response for several minutes before she said anything again. "If he has a bathing suit, that would help. Herman didn't bring one, and when he put on a pair of Winslow's old shorts, the ones he used to wear on the riding mower—well, they were just too big and kept falling off. The poor dear. I didn't know a boy could be that scrawny. I only had girls, you know, and Winslow was never that scrawny…leastways not when we married. He's always been a tad overweight…yes, don't all men after they reach forty?"

Bonnie took the conversation over for a while, and then it was Claudette's turn. "She's home now. I saw her drive in a few minutes ago…I guess around eight or nine…Yes, she's always up and around by then. If she tells me otherwise, I'll call you…You'll be at home…Oh, is that tonight? I can call after that, but that will be late, and you'd still have to call that boy and get a hold of him…I'll go ask her right now, and if you don't hear from me in the next fifteen minutes, you tell him between eight and nine tomorrow morning. And, Bonnie, I do appreciate this…I do. A friend in need is a friend indeed!"

Claudette hung up the phone and walked over to her tangerine-toned stove and checked the pot of boiling water. She turned the burner to low and put a wooden spoon in. A pot with a wooden spoon won't boil over, and she headed down the long hallway to Sarah Louise's studio apartment.

Sarah Louise looked up from the bowl of cat food she was pouring and turned to face the door when she heard the tapping there. That was her mother's tapping. She knew the soft sound by heart. Her father had a staccato knock, like a machine gun. So her mother was on the other side of the door—but was she alone, or was her father with her? To be safe, Sarah Louise stepped in front of the chair where the new cat was sitting next to Buford, the two still making introductions to each other.

"You can come in, Mother."

The door opened, and Claudette walked in and carefully shut the door behind her. She knew the consequences of a door left ajar.

Sarah looked past her mother, and sure she was alone, she stepped back to her small kitchen counter and finished pouring cat food.

As she did, her mother noticed the new cat. "Where did that come from, Sarah Louise?"

"The cat, Mother?"

"Yes, the cat, Sarah Louise! What do you think I'm talking about? Oh, if your father finds out...a cat and a dog...all in the same day!"

"Her name is *Ginger*, short for *Gingerbread*. See the lovely color on her back? Reminds me of the color of gingerbread. You agree?"

"I only agree that your father will have a conniption fit—where's the dog? You left here with a dog and you come back with a cat. I don't like the looks of this."

"Relax, Mother. I swapped the dog for the cat. Let me explain..."

While she told the story, Sarah Louise put the cat food on the floor in front of the chair, and both cats jumped down to investigate. Buford pushed the new cat away and tried to hog the bowl for himself till Sarah Louise picked him up so the new cat could eat.

By the time Sarah Louise had given all the details of her afternoon adventures, the new cat had eaten and then made its way around the perimeters of the studio apartment and was now investigating a pile of clothes by the door.

Sarah Louise and Claudette both watched as Ginger made herself a depression in the stacked garments and lay down.

"Whose clothes are those? I don't recognize those."

"Yes, you do, Mother. Those are the clothes Herman was wearing last night when Pop found him. I don't know what to do with them. I can't go looking for clotheslines in the neighborhood to see if they are missing a flowered blouse and a plaid skirt and purple towel. What taste in clothing! I might be doing the social scene a favor by taking those out of circulation."

Claudette nodded.

"I haven't seen a flowered blouse like that since the '70s. And that purple towel…I hate to think it might match someone's bath."

"Careful, Mother. Your kitchen is lost in the '70s itself. Does the color tangerine inspire anyone today?"

"I guess you're right."

"And I don't know what to do with the shirt, socks, and shoes left by the stranger who was standing there in his boxer shorts last night. I guess if he wants them bad enough, he knows where he left them."

"Still no clue to who he was, I guess—oh, that reminds me why I came in. Bonnie…yes, I just got off the phone with Bonnie. Oh, it's been longer than fifteen minutes now! And the eggs! Well, I guess they're hard-boiled by now anyway."

Sarah Louise looked at her mother, trying to follow her train of thought. "I guess you called Bonnie to see if the mysterious stranger was a model she sent last night."

"Yes…and no…I called…and she didn't…but she is sending someone over in the morning, between eight and nine, a young man who works part-time for Dewey down at the tire store… says he's a nice, clean-cut young man, needs a little extra cash… so she's paying him to come here. I told her not to tell Hannah because no one offered Herman any money last night. I didn't, did you? No, I'm sure you didn't, and I know Winslow didn't…I didn't expect anyone to have to pay out any money…"

There she went again, hopping from one thought to another. It was so like Claudette. She never finished one sentence before she started another. But that didn't matter. Sarah Louise wasn't listening. She was realizing she had to get to work finishing her painting of Herman if she was going to be ready in the morning for another model—a room full of naked men one at a time.

33

The first sense Michael Dorphman experienced Saturday morning was a warm, wet touch on his nose, followed by an unmistakable smell of dog fur. When he opened his eyes, somewhat startled by the previous two sensations, his visual sense confirmed what his brain was piecing together from the clues his body was sending.

There, in front of him, nose to nose, was the furry face of a dog. It was the orphan dog he had gotten through his swap at the vet's the day before.

As soon as he opened his eyes, the dog, which did answer to the name *Scamp* (the name Michael had given him)—but which would have answered just as well to *Ignatz* or *Beauregard*—took that as a sign of approval and responded by licking Michael's face.

Maybe it hadn't been such a good idea to let the dog sleep on the bed with him. "Whoa, boy…," Michael sputtered, pushing the mongrel off him. "That's not my idea of a morning bath!"

The fact that Michael was speaking to him made the dog all the more responsive, and he bounced from one side of the large bed to the other. Having gone from being an abandoned hound to having a place of his own in only twenty-four hours was almost more than the dog could bear, and he barked loudly.

The bark said nothing special other than, *Here I am!*

But Michael, not a professor of dog behavior or dog communication and relying on the experience of owning dogs in the past, deduced something else. "Wanna go out, don't ya, fella?" He bounced out of his century-old cast-iron bed and stepped quickly to the door. The dog, of course, followed.

Michael opened the door and stepped out into the morning sunshine, and the dog bounded after him and then ran off ahead of him off the porch and into the dew-covered grass.

This is living, the dog thought. He sniffed the air so full of scents: grass, trees, hay, cows, horses, animals from the forest. The dog turned to see if Michael was sucking in the lovely odors with him, but Michael was gone, the door to the rustic cabin closed.

Disappointed, the dog looked about him. Should he return to the cabin porch and look for his new companion or investigate the world around him? He had already run around the yard yesterday when he had first arrived and, with Michael, had visited the nearby barn and its horse smells. But right now, the odor of rabbit was tempting him. It was just past the fence there, only a few feet away; and he really did need to empty his bladder, not to mention leave his own scent on every tree between there and the house.

So the hunt for Michael lost out to the hunt for rabbit, and Scamp dove headlong into the tall grass of the pasture that surrounded the cabin on three sides.

Michael, meanwhile, had turned on his TV to catch the news and put the coffeemaker to work. Then he walked into the bathroom and clicked on the wall heater. He closed the door as he exited so that the room would warm up. He did so like to step out of the shower into a warm bathroom.

He poured a cup of coffee and stepped back outside. He looked for the dog and finally spotted the tip of his tail in the tall pasture grass.

Content that the dog was happy and hadn't decided to run off, Michael sat down on a wooden chair on the old porch. He was still in his pajama bottoms and T-shirt, his routine sleeping attire, but he didn't worry about neighbors seeing him. For that matter, he could have been wearing less. He often walked out on the porch with just his large bath towel around his waist, taking in the clean country air. He had no neighbors!

While he sat there keeping an eye on the dog, other people were waking up in Sulphur Springs.

Lucinda Hardin-Powell had poured two bowls of sugarcoated Fruity Pebbles and stationed her kids, BJ Jr. and Princess, in front of the TV. She had then gone back to bed, where her husband, BJ, lay oblivious to the noise of the TV, the opening and closing of doors, or even the commotion around town his wife was causing. For her part, Lucinda planned to stay in bed as long as possible. She had done enough in the last three days. Maybe she should lie low for a while.

Huey Pugh was cooking an omelet for his breakfast. He poured just a dash of sherry into the egg mixture. Huey had taken every class in French cooking offered within a one-hundred-mile radius of Sulphur Springs. As the eye on his stove warmed up, he pulled a plate from the armoire that he had converted into a dish cabinet. Should he go with the white plate with the lovely scrolled border or go with the faience plate that looked like a cabbage leaf? Decisions, decisions. He went with the cabbage leaf. Later in the day, he would return to the old school building and begin setting up tables. His would be a busy day.

Pearl was already at her beauty shoppe, spelled with two *p*'s. Fridays and Saturdays were her busiest days. All the little old ladies of Sulphur Springs were entrenched in the belief that one should look their best on Sunday for church, so they all had standing appointments to have their hair done as close to Sunday services as you could get. The younger generation wasn't so motivated. They came to the shop when they felt like it.

One reason, of course, was that the younger generation didn't go to church on Sundays. They went to the lake. The other reason was that, as Pearl had long observed, girls today didn't go to any beauty shop. They just let their hair hang any which way or shoved it up under a baseball cap turned backward. But Pearl didn't worry. She figured her old ladies would all die off about the same time she did, so what the younger generation did was not her problem. Besides, today was Saturday, and it would be full of good gossip, not the least of which was all the talk about the painting of naked men at the Spring Fling next weekend.

<hr />

Lucy Pendergrass was already at work in her studio. She was putting the background on a large canvas, the largest she had in her studio. Oranges and yellows were streaking the top of the canvas—an African dawn as Lucy visualized it.

Lucy had told her sister, Calpurnia, about her revelation, only to find out that Calpurnia already knew about Sara Louise's painting but had neglected to mention it. For sisters, they were almost polar opposites. Lucy was large and a commanding presence in any crowd. Calpurnia was petite and thin; but with her fifties fashions and thick horn-rimmed glasses, she was no less a presence. Lucy had never married while Calpurnia was twice married and twice divorced, taking back her maiden name each time and with one child from each marriage. She had grandchildren scattered from Kentucky to Georgia. Lucy would spend her day painting; Calpurnia would spend her day preparing news releases about the upcoming Spring Fling for the papers in the surrounding towns. And yes, she would mention that there would be some interesting artwork.

———— ∞ ————

Clarence Lipowitz was a late sleeper. He would stay in bed till the boredom of lying there overpowered the boredom of his life. If Clarence had his way, he would—but what was the use of thinking otherwise? He knew where he was. He was in a hick town, in a hick state, and married to a woman whose only redeeming quality was that she was rich and Clarence needed her to sign the checks. His life was one of toleration. He tolerated his kids, his job, his wife, his neighbors, his—well, everything. Maybe he should get up and go by that attractive teacher's house again. He had left an expensive pair of shoes there. But on second thought, there was that guy with the gun. No, Clarence would lie there as long as he could.

———— ∞ ————

In the old Dorphman home—just short of being called a mansion because it wasn't fancy, just big—Clara Dorphman put her silver butter knife into the stick of real butter on her kitchen table and spread the golden glob across her piece of whole-wheat toast.

Michael insisted she eat whole wheat instead of white for her health. It did taste good. This was her second slice, or was it her third? She couldn't remember. Not that it mattered. She would spend all morning reading the paper from Bowling Green. Sulphur Springs had a weekly, not a daily, so she subscribed to the Bowling Green daily paper.

She so enjoyed reading the obituaries. This was the second time she had read them this morning—or was it the third?

Her beloved Michael had taken his shower and got dressed. Scamp was back inside and wolfing down his dog food. He had learned early in life to eat whatever was given to him and to eat it all. You never knew when you might be fed again, and if you left anything, it wouldn't be there when you came back. It would be a hard lesson to unlearn. Poor Scamp, he didn't realize that his days of hunger and loneliness were over.

"Scamp, you do realize that you are the first dog I've had since I was in high school? Couldn't have a pet in college, and when I got married, my wife's first purchase as Mrs. Michael Dorphman was a white couch. And when it was delivered, she told me, in no uncertain terms, 'Dog or cat hair will never touch this couch!' She was a woman of her word because when we divorced, she took that couch with her."

He sat down on the worn leather sofa beside the fieldstone fireplace and reached down to put on his shoes. The dog finished his meal and came bounding over to Michael, where he again licked his face, it being so handy because Michael was still bent over and now tying his shoelaces.

"Whoa, boy!"

Michael sat up and glanced at the clock as he used the back of his hand to wipe dog drool off his cheek. He still had a little time left before he rushed by his grandmother's for a bite of breakfast and then to work. He patted the seat of the sofa beside him, but the dog only wagged his tail. It took a few more pats on the sofa before Scamp got the idea and jumped up there. It was the first sofa he had ever sat upon. In a few seconds, he had rested his head on Michael's lap and was having his ears scratched.

"Just you 'n' me, Scamp. But that's all right. For now anyway," Michael mused out loud.

In the last two years, Michael had left a good job in a big city, returned to Sulphur Springs to help his ailing father, buried his father beside the mother he had lost to cancer as a teenager, and then seen his wife of five years leave him.

Yet he wasn't miserable.

He was back home.

He had never realized how much he had missed his childhood home till he got back. Even the slow pace of the hardware and appliance store was good. He had good employees, and he personally knew just about everyone who came in the store.

Of all the cousins, he was the closest to his grandmother. After his mother's death, he and his father had moved in with Clara. One day, he would probably live there again. But for now, he was happy in his grandfather's old hunting cabin. His grandfather had never hunted anything larger than rabbits, but the old board and batten cabin had been there for Michael when he left the apartment he and his wife had shared.

The cabin had once been a simple tenant's house and was over a hundred years old. His grandfather had taken it over and added indoor plumbing, electricity, and the large front porch. Michael was doing some updating. He had added insulation, put in new wiring, and central heat and air-conditioning. His next project would be to upgrade the bathroom and its antique shower.

He looked around the room as he continued to scratch behind the dog's ears. The walls were pine boards with a beveled edge. They were kind of plain, and there above the sideboard, where many a country breakfast had been served to a crowd of hungry rabbit hunters, was a bare space.

"You know what, Scamp?" Michael asked the dog, which wagged his tail faster at anything Michael said. "I think we need some artwork to go there. The next time I see Sarah Louise Upshaw, I'll ask her to paint me a barn picture to go there. Whatcha think, Scamp?"

The dog only wagged his tail faster.

34

The large canvas in Sarah Louise's studio had seen some dramatic changes in the last three days. What had started out as *A Room Full of Cats* had been reconfigured as *A Room Full of Naked Men*.

The original painting, as she had sketched it out and begun painting, had a couch in the center. A window was visible on the wall behind the couch. A coffee table was in the foreground, in front of the couch. To the viewer's far left was a plant stand with a beautiful pot of fuchsia flowers.

Fuchsia flowers! Isn't that where this all started?

The original concept was for Sarah Louise to be sitting on the couch surrounded by cats—hence, the title *A Room Full of Cats*. It was to be a self-portrait. Yet it was to be more than that. It was to be a reflection of her life.

In all great art, as any art critic worth their salt would tell you, a great painting is more than a reproduction of what the artist sees outside his window. The painting has to reflect something of the artist's psyche.

Yes, there were artists who prided themselves on their ability to depict an apple, a sailing vessel, a ballerina, or an elephant so lifelike that it seemed to breathe. But if there was no emotion there, you may as well have used a camera to capture the same image. On the other extreme, there were artists who used pure emotion to attack the canvas with colors, lines, swirls, or bursts of paint. They could be appreciated on a different set of values.

Artists can become famous for being different, even so much so that being different is all that some artists are. But truly great art happened when the artist revealed a part of his soul on the canvas.

In the middle, between those artists trying to be different and those obsessed with capturing reality on their canvas, were artists like Sarah Louise. They painted what they wanted to paint. They weren't commercial in that they didn't paint to make money. They painted because it pleased them. They may be realistic or abstract, but they put their heart into what they did. Their paintings were like their children, and once complete, they had trouble letting them out of their sight.

Sarah Louise was a good artist. She knew she would never be great. For one thing, her emotions were too common. She was a happy person. She couldn't paint an emotionally draining painting. Her emotions didn't drain. Although right now she was in a dither, it wasn't enough to inspire anything controversial.

Wasn't it odd, then, that someone so average and innocent should be setting half the tongues in Sulphur Springs to wagging! In her original concept, Sarah had done that little bit of self-revelation that a good painting needs. She had placed herself on the couch. In her hands, she had a book. It was open, and she was holding it up so that it obscured most of her face. She was reading it. The title of the book was to be *Welcome to My World*.

The viewer would have had to tilt their head to read the title because it was to be painted on the book's spine. Few people, Sarah Louise reasoned, would have gone to the trouble. But if they had, they would have grasped what the painting was saying.

The painting was a reflection of her. The canvas was to be full of clues to who Sarah Louise Upshaw was.

First, there were the cats, lots of them. She had no one significant in her life, not counting her immediate family, of course, so her cats were her companions. On the coffee table was to be a stack of books. Each book's title would be a clue to Sarah Louise. There would be books on her favorite artists: Salvador Dali, Norman Rockwell, Andrew Wyeth, and Vincent Van Gogh. It was a mixed bag of artists. One book was to be *Man's Search for Meaning*, the famous book of philosophy, and another was to be the recent tome *The Purpose Driven Life*—both of which she liked.

If there was room, she would add other titles that meant something to her.

On the other end of the coffee table was to be a teapot and a cup of tea and an atlas. One represented her idea of a nice day—a cup of tea slowly sipped as you watch your life go by. The atlas was a hint of a desire to travel, a desire that she had heretofore neglected.

The open window was to represent the world that was out there. It beckoned to her. The flowers were her love of color, nature, and beauty. Somewhere, she intended to place an artist's palette, a tube of paint, and a paintbrush.

To her, it all made sense.

The average viewer would look at it for a few seconds and either like it or not and move on down to the next painting on display. Maybe that was best. Do we ever really want people to stop and examine our lives, our inner selves, our hopes and dreams, our—

Now, Sarah Louise had to drop the cats and add naked men. Five of them!

Odd numbers work better than even numbers, as all artists know. And less than five wouldn't have really been a "roomful," so five it was.

She stared at the canvas, reconfigured as it was.

She had stretched the couch so that she now sat in the middle. That would give her room to place a man to each side of her. Herman was already looking out the window behind the couch.

Poor Herman. With his homely face, she couldn't have him face the viewers, so she put him looking out the window. Still, his rather big ears and skinny body were a bit silly. Maybe she could flesh him out a bit.

She would put one man behind the pot of fuchsia flowers. They were already there on a plant stand. The fifth man would be on the viewer's right, entering the room. But what would she have these men doing? Just sitting or just standing there?

Sarah Louise put her pencil down. She walked over to an overstuffed club chair and sat down, laying her head back so it rested on the back of the chair. She closed her eyes. Maybe, if she closed her eyes tight enough, it would all go away…

Then there was a loud knock on the outside door. Sarah Louise jumped at the sudden intrusion. For a moment, she thought, *Who can that be?* Then a quick glance at the clock, and she realized it was ten minutes after eight. Where had the morning gone? It must be the young man that Bonnie was sending over.

She hurried to the door.

The boy who stood there looked a little sheepish, despite the fact that parked behind him in the driveway was a large wrecker with "Bobby Ray's Towing" painted in garish colors on the side. He cleared his throat and said, "Miss Bonnie give me this here address. She said you was a painter and that you needed some help."

From the way he said it, Sarah Louise thought, *Surely, he doesn't think he has come here to help me paint my house. What will he do when I ask him to start taking off his clothes?* She smiled and took a deep breath. "Yes, I need some help. Did Bonnie tell you what I needed you to do?"

A silly grin came across his face, and he blushed a deep pink. "Yes, ma'am. She said you needed me to stand still and let you paint me half naked."

Well, Sarah Louise thought, *he does have the right idea.*

In a few minutes, he stood in the center of the studio wearing the most outlandish bathing suit she had ever seen. It was a bright yellow with colorful clown fish strewn about it. The bright yellow made the boy's pink skin look all the more pink. He had a suntan on his face and forearms, but otherwise, he was as pink as a newborn baby.

She worked through a few quick sketches, having him face her, turn sideways, and even sit while she sketched.

Winslow had been instructed to put his gun up and stay away, but Claudette had come in with cookies and Kool-Aid to make sure nothing was out of the ordinary.

The boy seemed harmless enough, so she left and told her anxious husband to relax.

The boy's name was Carney Teague. Sarah Louise recognized the last name. She had taught several Teagues, but this boy was from up the road. He had moved here after high school. He was getting married in a few months, so he was working as many jobs as he could. He filled in at Dewey's tire recapping but worked full-time at Bobby Ray's Body Shop. That was why he was driving the tow truck. He was on call today. If a wreck happened, he would have to leave, so he kept his cell phone next to him.

He had a pleasant face. There was still a bit of a childish look about him, but he was showing signs of maturity. He would, Sarah Louise figured, make a handsome man someday. There was a wisp of a mustache across his upper lip. It was black, as was his hair, and it almost gave him an exotic look.

Exotic?

Yes, Sarah Louise thought, *he has a bit of the exotic to him.*

He talked the whole time, a sure sign of nervousness. He spoke of his family, his girl, her family, their plans for the wedding. He talked about towing cars and some of the bloody wrecks he had seen.

Sarah Louise only half listened, just enough to make occasional comments back. But she was thinking. She might be able to salvage this painting yet. If she sat Carney Teague to her right on the couch and, instead of an atlas on the coffee table, had him holding a globe—that would still represent her wanderlust.

Yes, she might be able to put herself in this painting yet.

35

"Ub hr 2 nite?"

"may-b," she texted back.

"Time?" was his reply.

But before Casey Taylor could text her boyfriend again, she heard the familiar rapid footsteps of Professor Ifama approaching.

"Gotta go," she quickly texted, tossing her cell phone into her open purse and just as quickly grabbing a stack of papers on the crowded desk in front of her.

And just in time. The professor hit the door of her office at the same fast clip that she did everything in life, as if she was already late for her next appointment and what she was doing now had to be gotten out of the way so she could make it to that next appointment.

"Mail, Taylor?"

"On your desk, Professor Ifama."

Professor Ifama, dressed in a dashiki covered with big yellow flowers, sat her large woven fiber purse on her desk chair. The professor had stage presence. If you saw her, in a crowd or by herself on a campus sidewalk, she stood out. From her large size—not large as in *fat* but large as in *build*—to her striking African garments, the woman had a way of grabbing your attention.

The professor picked up a stack of mail and began to go through it.

As she did, the student assistant took advantage of the professor's distraction to look down at her purse to see if her boyfriend was still texting. She had to be careful. Professor Montricia Ifama kept a tight schedule, and she expected her student assistants to do the same. Once they walked in her office door till the time they left, they had better be busy.

Just as her eyes were about to focus on the tiny screen of her cell phone, an envelope was thrust in her hands.

"Taylor, this is the schedule for graduation next month. Put it on my calendar."

"Yes, Professor Ifama."

And lest Casey Taylor had any thoughts of dillydallying, the professor added, "Now, Taylor!"

"Yes, ma'am!"

Casey Taylor jumped up from the desk she and the other student assistants shared and rushed over to the door of the office. She pushed it close so that the back of the door was now clearly visible. On the back of the door was a very large calendar, each day of the month given at least three square inches.

Professor Ifama lived by her calendar.

Three months—March, April, and May—were thumbtacked to the back of the door so that, at a glance, the professor could see what lay ahead. There was always something written in the weeks ahead because the popular African studies professor kept a very busy schedule.

Casey Taylor reached into a plastic cup, also tacked to the back of the door, and retrieved a bright-orange marker.

She had a choice of colors because the plastic cup held every color in the rainbow, but all school functions were in orange. Yellow was used for her class schedule, blue for speaking engagements, purple for her exercise class, and so on.

The professor led a very hectic but very organized life.

A little agitated, the professor spoke again, "Why do I keep getting mail addressed to the Social Studies Department chair? Taylor, take these two down the hall to Stauber's office!"

Casey grabbed the two letters before Professor Ifama had the chance to add, "Now!" The professor sat down in her chair, not removing the large purse but merely pushing it to the side with her rear end so that she and the purse shared the space. She wouldn't be here long, the professor reasoned, so why move it and then have to hunt for it?

There was just so much time in a day, so the professor made short work of the mail, tossing almost half into the trash can. The rest of the mail she sorted into three large color-coded bins on her desk. That taken care of, she pulled her tortoiseshell glasses off her face and set them down carefully on her desk so she could rub her eyes. Having done that, she closed her eyes tightly and took ten—she counted them slowly—deep breaths. With that done, she pulled her right desk drawer open and pulled out a jar of African shea-butter hand lotion and was soon spreading the magic ointment over her hands.

Professor Montricia Ifama was a busy woman but allowed herself the occasional moment to pamper herself (the expensive lotion) and to relieve stress (the ten deep breaths). She was a complex woman, driven yet devoted to taking time for herself— if for no other reason than to stay healthy so she could do that much more with her life.

Her busy schedule was the result of several things. She had a full teaching load because she was one of the most popular professors on campus. Her African studies classes were a must-have for the university's black students and, as a social studies elective, popular with students whose skin was anything but black.

And she took her job seriously.

She didn't know about Africa from reading books. She had embraced the land of her ancestors. She had traveled there. She had led student trips there. She dressed African. She cooked African. She decorated African.

Her office, besides the two desks piled high with papers and books and the large calendar on the back of the door, was festooned with African tribal masks, pieces of bright African fabrics, carved granary doors, decorated calabashes, and African clay jars used functionally to hold pens, pencils, umbrellas, etc.

Even her name was African. But it hadn't always been. She was born Montricia Jones in Washington, DC. From a poor family, she had early seen the rewards of hard work and not being shy about speaking your mind or taking the lead while the others in the classroom timidly sat there.

She had gone from the crowded stoops of Anacostia to the halls of academia and shed her name in the process. *Jones* didn't fit her African persona. So she had dropped it in favor of *Ifama*. It meant "everything is all right" in one of the dark continent's many tribal dialects.

The choice had a double significance for her. Besides the actual meaning, it was also the name of a strikingly good-looking doctor she had met in Ghana on her first trip to Africa. He was everything she had wanted in a man—self-confident, dedicated, handsome, witty—and the one thing she didn't want: he was already married with four children.

While he probably wouldn't remember the bright-eyed summer volunteer who was always underfoot, she had never forgotten him. When she had returned to the United States, she informed the eighty-year-old grandmother who had raised her that she was no longer a Jones but an Ifama.

She was content not to have a love life anyway. She didn't have the time. There were students to educate and inspire. The world needed to be a better place. She could make a difference. Even now, at the age of forty-five, she was still the little girl in the dingy classroom in Washington, DC, raising her hand for attention.

Confident that she had rested enough, Professor Montricia Ifama got up and went over to the door. She mentally crossed off the day's events so far: the morning lecture at the museum, two hours to be spent in her office. At noon, there would be a lunch meeting with two other professors. She then glanced at what the week ahead had to offer: church on Sunday (tomorrow), classes all week. Then, next Saturday, there was something written in the square, but it had been printed so small she couldn't see it without her glasses.

She walked over to her desk, picked up her glasses, and returned to the door.

There she saw in bright green—green for volunteer work—letters: "Judge, the Tenth Annual Spring Fling Art Show and Antique Auction to Benefit the Art Guild's Town-Beautification Project, Sulphur Springs."

36

Claudette put the half-full Tupperware pitcher of Kool-Aid back in the refrigerator and set the empty plate in the sink. Between Carney Teague and Winslow Upshaw, the stack of raisin oatmeal cookies had disappeared.

She sat down at the kitchen table trying to decide what to do next. If she went back to Sarah Louise's studio, she might appear to be prying. After meeting the young man with the thin black mustache, she felt confident that he presented no threat. He was politely sitting in a chair eating cookies when she had left them, Sarah Louise sketching away.

If she went and sat with Winslow, she would have to watch *ESPN Highlights* till her husband was sure he had caught up with what was happening in the world of sports. Then he would turn to the Food Network. Neither sounded interesting to Claudette.

The house was clean.

The laundry was done.

She got up and returned to the fridge. She pulled out a large tangerine-glazed mixing bowl topped with wax paper: the rest of the cookie dough. Perhaps baking all morning would keep her busy, busy and calm.

Calm—she longed for a week of calm.

There was so much going on now. It really would have been simpler if Winslow had shot her as she had asked him to. The situation wouldn't be resolved, but at least she wouldn't be around to have to witness it. It reminded her of the country-music song "If I Had Gone Ahead and Shot Her When I First Met Her, I'd Be Outta Jail By Now."

But she was here, alive and breathing. She had to live every minute of every twenty-four-hour day till next Saturday, when hopefully everything would be over.

Since that Lucinda Hardin-Powell had blurted out *A Room Full of Naked Men* on *Ted and Sherry in the Morning*, there had been no less than ten phone calls from neighbors, family, friends, and busybodies—wanting to know "if the rumors I've heard about Sarah Louise are true."

There was no denying it.

Claudette told everyone who called, "Sarah Louise is painting a harmless little picture for the Spring Fling, nothing to get alarmed about. Just wait till Saturday next, and you will be able to see for yourself. Don't let the title of the painting confuse you..."

Finally, after spending thirty minutes with her own Great-aunt Gertrude, on her father's side, she had disconnected the phone.

She rolled out the dough and used an inverted jelly glass to cut out her cookies. Just the right size, that jelly glass. She had been using it since she and Winslow first married. Once the oven was at the right temperature, she slid the cookie sheet in.

She sat once again in the kitchen chair. *Now what?* she thought. Read the morning Bowling Green paper again? Did she really care what was happening in Bowling Green? Claudette was toying with the idea of defrosting her tangerine freezer when the doorbell rang.

"That's odd," she mumbled to herself. Anyone who knew them came around to the kitchen door. Only strangers came to the front door.

She stepped to the window above the kitchen sink and leaned over so as to get a view of who or what was at the front door. "Oh no"—she audibly gasped—"Brother Armstrong!"

If Claudette was nervous about the preacher coming to visit, the preacher was no less nervous about being there. Brother Armstrong was the minister at the "Sulphur Springs First Baptist Church, Founded in 1822," as the sign out in front of the church said in large Old English letters.

Brother Armstrong had been there since the previous minister had run off with the wife of the Methodist Church's choir director. That was almost seven years ago.

That minister had been young and full of personality. The church had been proud of his dynamic sermons, his chiseled good looks, and his superb tenor singing voice. When the Methodist Church's annual Easter cantata needed a tenor to fill in for their tenor, a victim of strep throat, the Baptists had volunteered their minister. It was to be a source of pride to the Baptists that the star of the Methodists' annual cantata was their own minister.

And he had sung spectacularly.

As they found out two weeks later, it was because he had something to sing about. They had never lived it down.

When they immediately began looking for another preacher, they took the polar-opposite route. Brother Armstrong was short, fat, and sang like a frog. His looks, if they were chiseled, were chiseled by a nearsighted sculptor. Then there was his hair. He hadn't any.

Yes, he was the exact opposite of their beloved Brother Donnie, who had insisted they call him by his first name. No one would ever choose Brother Armstrong to have an affair with. They could only assume, since he was married with three grown children, that he had once been, possibly, good-looking. Mind you, that was only an assumption.

Then there were the sermons. Brother Donnie had the congregation in the palm of his hands. They took in his every word. He was dynamic behind the pulpit! We can only assume that he was dynamic away from the pulpit as well. Mind you, that was only an assumption.

Dear old Brother Armstrong was not dynamic. He put people to sleep. But he had managed to stay at First Baptist and even work his way into his parishioners' hearts. He hadn't done it through skillful speaking but through subterfuge.

His technique was to start off every sermon with a joke. They looked forward to his latest joke. Nowadays he got them off the Internet, but he had "*Reader's Digest* Collection of Fun and Laughter'" to fall back on.

The next trick up his sleeve was the sermon itself. While the actual sermon wandered from here to there with the occasional route of scripture, he always ended the sermon with a pithy statement. He would tell them, "So I leave you with this parting thought, the very soul of what I have been speaking on..."

It worked like a charm.

Everyone sat up and paid attention to the last words. They might have been dreaming during the sermon, but they were wide awake for his parting thought. And they remembered it. They left confident that they had understood the sermon. He had put all fifteen rambling minutes into a short memorable quip.

Oh, if only all preachers would do that.

Other churches might depart their sanctuary thinking to themselves, "Now, what was that sermon about?" But the attendees of the Sulphur Springs First Baptist Church knew exactly what their preacher's sermon was about because he told them. And consequently, because they could, they were convinced that he was a great preacher.

While that might seem like a stroke of genius, the sermon was not the real strength of Brother Armstrong.

In any church, it isn't the depth, breath, soul, or clarity of the sermon. The true success of any preacher in any denomination is who you did or did not make mad!

The best of preachers, if they make their church's biggest benefactor irate, was out of there in a skinny minute. It is the bookkeeper who runs the church. When the bookkeeper clues the trustees or elders or board of disciples, on to the fact that Mr. and Mrs. So and So have stopped putting their big checks into the collection, heads start to roll.

Brother Armstrong knew that. Not handsome, not dynamic, he was smart. "You don't bite the hand that feeds you"—it had been one of his pithy statements.

The congregation had liked it. "It was true" they had all agreed, and Brother Armstrong knew just how true.

"Never make anyone mad." That was his guiding mantra.

Now, here he was at the door of three of his most faithful. And they were good "givers" too. He had called the church book-keeper at home to find out just how "good" they were. Not only were they good givers, but Claudette baked scrumptious lemon pound cakes that always showed up at the monthly pot-lucks and wrapped up on his doorstep every Christmas.

No, it wasn't Claudette who was nervous. Brother Armstrong was even more nervous.

Still, he had to confront the family because of all the rumors and all the stories going around and the radio show and all the phone calls he too had received.

Short of preaching a sermon on public nudity, the only solution was to visit the Upshaw home.

He rang the doorbell again.

Claudette answered it.

They smiled nervously at each other, and she invited him in.

An hour later, Brother Armstrong absent mindedly licked his forefinger tip to make it wet, then pressed the wet finger onto the small plate in front of him to get the last crumbs from the wonderful raisin-oatmeal cookies Claudette had plied him with.

All in all, he reflected to himself. It had gone well.

There had been no need to involve Winslow or Sarah Louise herself. He and Claudette had gone over everything, the sequence of events, the silliness of it all.

He was satisfied that the morals of Sulphur Springs were not to be corrupted.

Yet, there was a sermon to preach.

Should he mention the painting in the sermon?

To repeat the story as Claudette had told him would be an embarrassment to her and the family. Keep everyone happy. He couldn't tell how Claudette had simply opened her big mouth. Keep Claudette happy. He couldn't tell about Winslow and the gun now could he. Keep Winslow happy. Nor should he mention that Sarah Louise was having men come to her studio and pose half clothed. Keep Sarah Louise happy.

Maybe he should just avoid the topic all together. He did already have a sermon written and a pithy statement all lined up. But, people were expecting him to do something to save the morals of Sulphur Springs.

A bead of sweat began to appear on Brother Armstrong's forehead.

He was getting nervous again.

37

After Carney Teague left, Sarah Louise took her sketches and walked over to the canvas. She had covered the canvas with an old sheet, one she used as a drop cloth when she painted. The sheet had so many paint drops and paint spills that it was starting to resemble a painting by Jackson Pollock, the famous Expressionist.

When she painted, except for perhaps her own parents, Sarah Louise liked to keep her projects to herself. Of all the paintings she had ever done, this one especially needed to be kept out of sight.

Carney Teague didn't know enough about art to ask to see "how the painting is coming." He probably wasn't even aware that there was an art show only a week away. He had simply shown up as a favor to a friend and for a little cash.

It is amazing what people will do for money.

Taking your clothes off for money was probably one of the least things people did. To watch television, you would think that nothing was sacred anymore. People bared their personal life to twenty million viewers every night between seven and ten. Their marriage spats, sibling rivalry, drug addition, corporate greed, their weight problems, ruthless ambition, talent or lack of talent—it was all there for the public to see.

If you fell flat on your face walking across the stage at your college graduation and your family was nice enough to catch it on film, it would likely show up on *America's Funniest Home Videos*. Not only was it embarrassing enough to have it happen to you in the first place, but you now had the added joy of knowing that most of America would witness it and they would be laughing at you. As if that wasn't bad enough, thanks to reruns, they would be laughing at you again and again and...

But it would be "okay" because you could win $10,000.

So Americans everywhere were doing things, the kind of things you once kept private, and were doing them in front of camera crews. And if you went on the Internet, there was little or nothing that people wouldn't do for a little recognition, a little fame, a little money.

Wasn't that a sermon that Brother Armstrong had preached? Sarah Louise thought. Yes, she remembered it now. She couldn't recall anything between the opening joke and the end, but she remembered his closing remarks: "The love of money is the root of all evil."

Maybe, she thought, *he should have added, "The love of fame is pretty evil too!"* It wasn't fame that Sarah Louise was pursuing. If anything, she would have, at this moment, been pursuing anonymity.

Sarah Louise had no idea that her pastor had spent the morning with her mother. If she had known, she would have panicked. Claudette had a way of speaking first and thinking second. As it was, Claudette had no intention of telling either Sarah Louise or her father of the preacher's visit.

With the drop cloth now on a heap on the floor, Sarah Louise was trying to mentally picture how Carney Teague would look sitting next to her on the sofa. She tried to picture a globe, big enough to obscure most of Carney Teague but not so big as to hide him or so big as to make the painting off-balance. Aesthetically, even if the subject matter didn't please her, the painting must have balance, proportion, depth, etc. It must still be a work of art.

Satisfied, she spent the next hour drawing her young model onto the canvas. She started by sketching lightly with her pencil till she was sure she had her scale right. This meant stepping back from the canvas every few minutes to see if things looked right.

Once she was confident things were to scale, she used her sketches of Carney to actually draw him into the picture. With that done, she had begun painting.

She worked fast because her choice of mediums, acrylic paints, dried fast. If she had painted in oils, she could take her time blending and shading, but the painting wouldn't have been dry in time for the art show on Saturday. Acrylics, because they have a plastic base as opposed to an oil base, dried fast—almost too fast—so she had to hurry as she painted.

She squeezed the last of the flesh-toned paint from the tube and onto her palette. She looked about for another tube. That was when it hit her. She didn't have any more flesh-colored paint.

She had been cautious when she bought the tube down at Dorphman's Hardware and Appliance because she was afraid of what someone would say if she had bought five tubes of skin-hued paint.

The clerk, as Sarah Louise had visualized it in her head, would say. "My, that's a lot of flesh-colored paint! Whatcha painting? A room full of naked people?"

Of course, she would have to correct the clerk by saying, "No, I'm not painting a room full of naked people. I'm painting a room full of naked *men!*"

As it had turned out, it was Michael Dorphman who had waited on her. He probably wouldn't have been so brazen as her imaginary clerk, but he would have been smart enough to notice—and then what would he have thought?

Not that it mattered anymore. The whole town surely knew by now.

She glanced at the clock; it was 11:45 a.m.

"Oh no." She gasped to herself. "Dorphman's closes at noon on Saturdays!"

She flung her brush into a glass of water and grabbed her palette with its last bit of flesh-colored paint. She used her other hand to grab her purse and car keys and raced to her studio door, clumsily pulled it open, and ran down the hallway to her parents' kitchen.

Claudette was mixing egg salad for lunch when her daughter burst in.

"Take this, Mother," Sarah Louise hollered as she pushed the wet palette into her startled mother's hands. "Put that in the refrigerator! I'll be right back! I've got to get to Dorphman's for more paint before they close!"

With that, she was out of the kitchen door.

Claudette looked at the palette of paint in her hands. She had absolutely no idea why it should go into her tangerine refrigerator, but she would do as her daughter said. As Claudette placed the paint palette into the aged refrigerator, and as Sarah Louise pressed her gas pedal and sped out of the driveway—two cats, Buford and Ginger, tread softly through the door of the studio and into the off-limits part of the house. Sarah Louise, in her haste, had left the door open.

As she raced across town, Sarah Louise didn't have to worry about getting a speeding ticket. One reason was that, even though she did go over the speed limit on the straight stretch between the BP station and the bypass, she wasn't "reckless."

In town, the local police force was more concerned with dangerous behavior than they were with speed—unless, of course, you had an out-of-town license plate.

The other reason, was that all the local police were down at the ballpark. Today was Rally Day for the T-Ball, Little League, and Babe Ruth League ball teams. The park was bumper-to-bumper traffic as every child in the program showed up for the first official games of the season and for their team pictures. The photos had to be made today and made before those first games so the uniforms would be crisp, clean, and white. What policemen who weren't there with their children were there to direct traffic.

Sarah Louise pulled into the parking lot of Dorphman's Appliance and Hardware just as her car showed 12:00 noon. The parking lot was, except for her car, empty.

Hardly waiting for the car to stop, she threw the gear into park and pulled her keys from the ignition. She leaped out of her vehicle and rushed to the entrance of the business and gave the doorknob a twist—it turned!

Sarah Louise breathed a sigh of relief and bolted inside. She looked around the store. There was no one in sight. Then she heard a click sound, and the lights in the back of the store went out. Another click, and the lights in the middle of the store went dark. A third click, and the lights at the front, where she was standing, went out.

"Wait," she hollered, hoping that whoever was flipping the light switches would hear her. "I just need a tube of paint," she added, with her voice lost among the vastness of the huge hardware store.

There was a sudden movement to her left, and she turned in that direction. Out of the darkness came a rush of movement, straight at her. She stepped back toward the door only to have the paws and face of an excited dog in her face.

It was Scamp, the dog she had rescued only two days earlier.

38

"What do you want, Annie?"

"Hannah, how did you know it was me?"

"Oh, Annie, let me tell you! I've got caller ID. I can look at the phone, and it will tell me who's calling before I even answer it!"

"It talks to you?"

Annie Whittier was terribly behind the times. She had no idea what caller ID was, what computers did, and would have argued that *tweeting* was something birds did.

"Oh no, you ninny!" Hannah Bugleman was blunt with everyone, and Annie, although one of Hannah's best friends, was no exception. "The phone doesn't talk to me. It has a little screen-like place, and that screen shows who's calling!"

As Annie absorbed this new bit of technology, Hannah continued, "My brother, Alvin, insisted I get one because I was always complaining about people calling me, trying to sell me stuff. Lord, Annie! They were calling me every night. So Alvin and Herman came by last week, and they had this box with them, and I said, 'What have you got there?' and Alvin said, 'Sister'— 'cause he calls me *sister*, you know—he says, 'Sister, I am making you a part of the technology revolution.'

"Well, I was just floored when he got this here new phone out. It doesn't look anything like my old phone. Let me tell you, it came with a book of instructions, like I don't know how to use a phone. And guess what! It has so many extra features that I feel like I'm one of those spies in one of those spy movies. Why, it has something called *callback* that I haven't figured out yet, but Alvin says I will like it once I get used to it."

Hannah could have, and would have, talked an hour or more about her new phone, but Annie finally spoke up. She had called for a reason. "Hannah, that's all very nice, but I need to talk to you about something else."

"Spit it out, Annie. What's bothering you?"

"Oh, Hannah. I don't know what to do about my naked man…I mean, the naked man I'm supposed to find for that painting by Sarah Louise."

"Now, Annie, I told you, and Claudette told you. You just don't listen. You aren't supposed to find a naked man. You only have to find a man who will take his shirt off. Understand, Annie? Or do I have to repeat myself?"

"Yes, yes, I know. But I can't go around asking men if they will take their shirts off. What if they think I'm a pervert?"

"You don't look like a pervert, Annie!"

"How do you know what a pervert looks like, Hannah!"

"I just know. They bleach their hair, wear too much makeup, wear clothes two sizes too small—and they all have had breast augmentation! Breast augmentation, Annie!"

"Breast augmentation?"

Annie didn't do well on words over three syllables, and the subject matter was one she certainly was not familiar with.

After explaining, in plainer words, what she meant, Hannah returned to the reason Annie had called. "You haven't found someone to pose for Sarah Louise?"

"Oh no, Hannah. I haven't even started. I don't know where to start."

"You've got a son and a grandson, don't you?"

"I thought of them, but Robert Jr.'s wife is the jealous type. I don't dare ask him, and my grandson is only twelve. I don't think he is what she had in mind."

Hannah, despite her brash manner, did feel a little compassion for Annie. After all, she herself had fainted when Claudette first told them to go out and each find a naked man. But Hannah had simply used her nephew, so she was spared a real search.

"If it's any consolation to you, my nephew, Herman, said it was an easy thing to do. He just stood there while Sarah Louise made some lines with a pencil on a big pad of paper."

"What else did he say?"

"Herman doesn't say much. You know, it's a sign of genius. I read that myself in the *National Geographic*."

"The *National Geographic*?"

"Yes, it said that people who were quiet were really just sitting there thinking. Quiet people are probably geniuses…like Einstein. Herman is quiet just like Einstein."

"Didn't he say anything else?"

"I don't think he wanted to talk about it. I had to bribe him with an apple pie."

"What did he say after the pie?"

"He said he took off his shirt and that she handed him a pair of Winslow's old Bermuda shorts to put on."

"Did he change right there in front of Sarah Louise?"

"Oh no, Annie. He changed behind some kind of screen. All artists have screens, you know. Don't you ever watch the movies? Models always get dressed behind a screen!"

"That's a relief, I guess."

"What are you going to do, Annie?"

"I don't know. I'm supposed to have someone by Monday. I'm supposed to call Claudette by Sunday night and let her know."

Hannah was quiet for a moment. But not for long. "I tell you what, Annie! I don't know why you didn't think of it yourself.

Doesn't your sister, Florence, have a grandson in college? He's the one that got a football scholarship. You told us all about it! Remember?"

"Oh, I don't know why I didn't think of him myself! Luther! Of course! He's in school in Hopkinsville. I'd have to get his number from Flo. And Hopkinsville, that's not too far for him to drive...if he doesn't have classes on Monday, that is. Oh, Hannah, you're so clever!"

"Yep, it's a good thing you called me. I better hang up now so you can call Florence."

"Oh, wait, Hannah! One more thing! Did Herman say how the painting looked? I mean, how much of Herman is she showing? I don't want Sarah Louise to show too much of Luther!"

"No, Herman didn't say. I told you, he's a genius, and they don't say much. But you and I will find out for ourselves on Wednesday!"

"We will!"

"Are you on another planet, Annie? Wednesday is our weekly card game. We'll all be there, and we can go down to Sarah Louise's studio and see for ourselves!"

"Oh, Hannah. Do you think she will let us? I mean, aren't artists supposed to be temperamental?"

Temperamental—that was a big word for Annie.

"I'd like to see her try and keep us from seeing that painting. After all we're doing to help out in this crazy situation! I'm going to see how my nephew, Herman, looks on that canvas or else!"

Or else indeed!

39

A dog may be man's best friend, but mankind is certainly one of dog's best friends. Scamp, the abandoned mongrel, had at least two friends in this world; and in true dog fashion, he would never forget either one.

No doubt, when Sarah Louise entered Dorphman's Appliance and Hardware, the dog's ears and nose went on alert. Whether it was the smell of her perfume or whether he recognized her voice when she hollered out, "Wait—I just need a tube of paint," the fact remained that a friend from his past had returned.

He had bounded in her direction with the wild abandon that only a half-grown dog has and stopped only when he was practically wrapped around her feet.

The intruder to the hardware store crouched down and, on the personal level of dog to face, began to pet, scratch, and pat the joyful pooch. "Why, it's Scamp! Now, what are you doing here?"

She said this as if the dog would understand a single word she said and would actually answer her question.

But he didn't have to. As Sarah Louise continued to pet the friendly hound and the dog licked her hands, Michael Dorphman appeared from around the corner. "I thought I heard a voice!"

"Oh, hi, Michael. It's you. I'm sorry to get here right as you're closing. I just need to run back to the art section and get a tube of paint. It will just take a second."

"No problem. Let me flick the lights back on. It's dark back there!"

"Oh, I hate to make you go to a lot of trouble. I was painting, and I realized I was out of..." She hesitated for a moment, trying to decide if she should say *flesh* or not. "A certain color. I would have come earlier if I had been paying attention to what I was doing."

"Like I said, no problem." Then, changing the subject, he added, "I see Scamp recognized you."

"I'll say. I wasn't expecting to see him here, and when he came rushing at me just now, he almost frightened me."

"I was afraid to leave him at the cabin all morning by himself, and I hate to tie a dog up...maybe later after he feels more at home there. So I brought him to work with me."

"How did he do?"

"Well, you're the only customer he has tried to lick to death! I would say he makes a great hardware-store dog. I just may bring him back."

They both stood there alternately looking at the dog and then each other, never sure how long to stare at each other but not wanting to be rude and ignore each other. Much like a couple of teenagers at their first dance.

Michael felt the awkwardness first. "If you head on back to the art corner, I'll get the lights." He turned and headed toward the back of the store.

As he did, and as she turned to go in the other direction, she hollered back at him, "You don't know how much I appreciate this."

Scamp, meanwhile, stood there. He wasn't sure which of his two new friends to follow. Decisions, decisions! The friend who had shared a bed with him or the friend who had fed him on the dark lonely night when he had first arrived in town?

He looked in the direction of Michael and then in the direction of Sarah Louise. Deciding that beauty beat brawn, he loped off in the direction of the lovely female.

By the time that Michael got to the art corner, having flipped the light switch on, he saw that Sarah Louise was alternately petting a frisky dog and looking through the tubes of acrylic paint.

"Here, boy! Come here and let Sarah Louise alone for a minute!" He slapped the side of his leg with his hand, and Scamp excitedly rushed over to him.

"Thank you, Michael. First the lights, now the dog. I hope you don't think I'm making a major purchase here...I'm just getting a tube of paint."

Michael sat down on a large wooden case that held an assortment of pastels but kept the dog's collar in one hand. "Whatcha painting?"

Sarah Louise turned to face him. "You don't know?"

Embarrassed at his ignorance, Michael tried to think, but he really didn't know. "Uh...if I remember right, you got a large canvas about a week ago...but I don't think you told me. Maybe you were going to enter something in the Spring Fling? Yep, I remember now. You said you were going to enter something in the Spring Fling."

"So you don't listen to *Ted and Sherry in the Morning?*"

Confused but game to know more, he said, "I keep the radio behind the counter on WQAK, but if I'm busy, I don't know what they're saying...the usual stuff, I guess. Why?"

"Then you didn't hear what Lucinda Hardin-Powell had to say on Friday's show?"

"Lucinda? The same Lucinda that graduated with us, married to BJ down at the bank?"

"Yes, her!"

"I guess not...why? What did she say?"

Michael was smiling, like he expected Sarah Louise to say something amusing. If only he realized how serious this was, she thought. Yet it came as no surprise. Her recollection of Michael from growing up to the present was that he was a happy person. In fact, he was a nice guy. He wouldn't think of something bad coming out of the local radio station.

"Oh, I could tell you, but you probably have to be someplace. I'm probably keeping you from something."

"No, Scamp and I have no further plans for the day except to go back in the cabin and share a ham sandwich. So what did she say?"

I may as well tell him, she thought. *He'll find out sooner or later. Besides, it would be nice if someone besides my parents and Dotie knew my side of the story.*

While she was deciding where to start, Michael spoke up, "Oh, before you tell me, I need to ask you a favor."

"A favor?"

"Yes, and if you can't do it, or don't have the time to fool with it, just say so. But I need a painting to go on one wall of my cabin."

"Your cabin!"

"Yeah, since my ex-wife and I parted company, I've been living at my grandfather's old hunting cabin. It's off Honeysuckle Lane, on the back of Gramma's farm."

"I've been out Honeysuckle Lane before. The Durhams live out that way."

"Yeah…the Durhams. They're my closest neighbors. Anyway, I need a painting…" He paused to extend his hands in front of him to try to show how large a painting he needed.

"Yea big!"

Then he continued, "I'd really like an old barn."

"Old barn?" Sarah Louise echoed.

"Yeah! You do old barns?"

Old barn. That's a relief, she thought. *With my reputation right now, he might have asked for the Dallas cheerleaders au natural!* She laughed to herself at the prospect.

Seeing her smile, both Michael and the dog reacted. The dog wagged his tail; Michael grinned.

Sarah Louise stared at Michael. He had a cute grin—almost boy-like but a hint of the man there. Then, realizing she was being silent, she said, "Old barn…yes. I've never done one before…but I can…that is, if I see one…I mean…"

She was starting to sound like her mother. She regained herself. "Michael, I can only paint something I've seen in person. I don't make up things very good…do you have a barn in mind?"

"Actually, I do. There is a barn next to the cabin. My cousins and I used to play in the hayloft when we were kids. When my mom gave me a pony one Christmas, I kept it there." He paused at the recollection. "Well, anyway. It has a lot of good memories."

Sarah hated barns as much as she hated lighthouses, but somehow this request didn't seem so bad. But there was the problem of seeing what she painted. "If you don't mind me coming over some time and doing some sketches…"

"No, not at all. It looks like you're gonna be busy today, but I'll be home all day tomorrow. After church, of course."

"Tomorrow?" There she was again, simply repeating what he had said.

"Sure. And you can see my cabin. Maybe you can give me some decorating ideas. I'm not helpless when it comes to that. My ex was convinced I was hopeless, but I can do a little of that. Decorate, you know."

"Decorate?" She wasn't very original in this conversation.

"Yes, decorate."

She had never been asked to help a man decorate his home, or paint his barn for that matter. She felt a need to say something. She needed to explain things, but was this really the time? Then she threw caution to the wind. "Tomorrow…that's good for me. Say one o'clock? And if you can wait till then, I'll tell you what Lucinda said. I could tell you now, but it's a long story…a very long story. But I do need to get back home. I left my mother with egg salad in one hand and my paint palette in the other."

Michael laughed. "Deal," he said.

"Deal." She laughed back.

40

After the choir led the congregation in singing "How Great Thou Art," Brother Armstrong walked over to the pulpit of the Sulphur Springs First Baptist Church, founded in 1822. The building wasn't nearly as old, dating to 1970—before people began to appreciate old architecture and everyone was in a rush to "modernize." Besides, the Methodists had just built a new church house, making the Baptists look cheap.

Great song, Brother Armstrong thought. *Everyone likes that one. Off to a good start. Keep everyone happy.*

He looked out over the sanctuary. Not quite full. A few heads lost to golf or fishing. It had been a nice sunny morning, so that was to be expected. All eyes and ears were directed at him. He knew why. It wasn't the sermon they were looking forward to; it was his opening joke. Late night talk show hosts have their monologues; the preacher had his bit of humor.

No warm-up, he started right in. "A Sunday school teacher looked at the circle of bright-eyed children in front of her. She had just finished her lesson and was about to let her young charges loose on the world. *Have they learned anything today?* she thought. After all, it had been a difficult lesson on sin and forgiveness. Dare she ask the children what they had learned?"

There was a subtle laughter in the sanctuary as the parishioners realized where the joke was going. It was to be one of those out-of-the-mouth-of-babes stories. They loved those.

"She took a deep breath and, throwing caution to the wind, asked, 'Now, children, who can tell me what we all must do before we can expect forgiveness of sin?' The little classroom was quiet. The children appeared to be giving it great thought. Then Little Bobby spoke up."

There was another wave of stilled laughter. They were familiar with Little Bobby. He was a recurring character in the preacher's sermons. If Little Bobby was in the story, it was Little Bobby who would cause mischief. Little Bobby never failed to disappoint them.

The preacher continued with his story. "Little Bobby looked his teacher in the eye. She had asked the class, 'What must we do before we can expect forgiveness of sin?' 'Teacher,' Little Bobby said, 'first we've got to sin!'"

It worked.

The faithful flock of churchgoers gave a hearty laugh. Even the little ones caught on. It was a mixed group of the faithful. Middle-class Sulphur Springs mingled in with a few successful businesspeople and a few old money—a blend of young and old, mostly old because young people today were too busy to go to church. The farmers and ranchers went to the small churches out in the country.

Good so far, Brother Armstrong thought. *Keep them happy.* Careful to let them get most of their guffaws out first, he plunged right into his sermon.

An elderly woman on the front row, now that the joke was over, opened her Bible and laid it across her lap. It was Miss Amelia Caplinger. If there was a thorn in Brother Armstrong's side, it was her.

When he quoted scripture, she turned to the chapter and verse—not to read it to herself to reinforce the lesson. No. She looked it up to make sure the preacher had quoted it correctly. If he had, she nodded her head succinctly.

Woe to Brother Armstrong if he left out a word or added one. She would pull a bookmark out of her purse, with great ceremony, and mark the spot. That meant that, on her way out, she would open her Bible and point out his error.

Miss Amelia favored the King James Version. There was no other as far as she was concerned. It didn't matter that the Baptist Sunday School Board had approved more recent versions. If Brother Armstrong didn't quote from the King James, she would pin his ears back, so to say.

Brother Armstrong had learned in the first month he was there to only use the King James. Not that it mattered to him. Keep them happy.

His scripture bounced about anyway. He made sure to always quote from both the Old Testament and the New. *Don't leave anyone out.* They liked Matthew, so he quoted Matthew regularly. They also liked First Corinthians. But if he wanted to wake them up or make them uneasy in their seats, all he had to say was, "In the book of Revelation..."

Yes, the book of Revelation was like a rocking chair in a room full of cats. It made them all nervous.

He rarely quoted Revelation. Keep them happy.

Today he wound his sermon this way and that way. When he had quoted his scripture, Miss Amelia seemed content. Good sign. Keep them happy.

Then he began his wind up.

There was usually a subtle change in voice, tempo, or perhaps the way he stood—whatever. People seemed to know when he was about to finish. Maybe they knew that he timed his sermons to be exactly fifteen minutes, and their internal clocks were at work.

"In our bit of humor at the start of this week's sermon, Little Bobby made the observation that to receive forgiveness, we had to sin first. I think that was very observant of him. Our problem in the world today, even here in Sulphur Springs, is that sometimes we are convinced that someone has sinned and we are ready to make judgment…be it forgiveness or to pick up stones and prepare to throw them.

"'We must sin first,' Little Bobby said. But I ask you, What if a person has not sinned? What if we only think they have sinned? What if we have only been told they have sinned? What if we haven't witnessed the sin ourselves?"

He paused.

They knew his pithy statement was coming. They didn't know that today he had a double whammy. Today he was about to give them two pithy statements.

"So I leave you with these two thoughts, the lessons that I have been preaching today. I tell you that when it comes to sin, appearances can be deceiving!"

Pause.

"Therefore, we should not be hasty to throw our stones— because 'Judge not that ye be not judged'!"

As the choir director stood and announced the closing hymn, Claudette breathed a sigh of relief. She had worried all morning about what the preacher might say. She had asked him not to say anything specific, and he hadn't.

Winslow, beside her, was unaware of the preacher's visit. To him, it had been just another boring sermon. He had spent most of the sermon with his eyes on Miss Amelia to see if she pulled out any bookmarks.

On the other side, Sarah Louise seemed content.

She had, that morning at breakfast, suggested they not go to church. After all, Winslow's eyes were still a little puffy from his latest exposure to cat dander—two cats this time. Then there would be the stares.

Claudette had insisted, but it ended up a draw. They skipped Sunday school and just went to the service. That way, they avoided the intimacy of the Sunday school rooms, where someone might pointedly ask questions.

Now, Claudette thought, *as soon as this song is over—we're out of here.*

———∞———

Across town, Lucinda Hardin-Powell, at the Pentecostal Church of the True Believer, was quick to answer any and all questions people might have. And if they didn't ask, she would bring the subject up.

The sermon at the Pentecostal service was the same as it had been the week before and was the same as it would be the next week, the unerring word of the Bible.

———∞———

Michael had sat next to his grandmother at their pew in the Methodist Church. His uncles and their families sat both in front and behind. It was the Dorphman section of the church. They could be counted on to sit in the same spot every Sunday.

The Methodist preacher hadn't mentioned anything about the Spring Fling. Like the Baptist preacher, his job depended on keeping away from controversy and keeping his congregation happy. Besides, Methodists got upset about so little. They accepted most things with a shrug—unless it had to do with the church budget!

———∞———

Sunday in Sulphur Springs had been fairly uneventful. The Pentecostal Church was small, so Lucinda hadn't swayed a lot of opinions. The three largest congregations—the First Baptists, the First United Methodists, and the Church of Christ—hadn't stirred anything up.

The Baptist service had been vague enough to not make anyone mad but had enough depth to make some people think. The Methodists had avoided it altogether, and the Church of Christ sermon had been spent condemning the Baptists and Methodists for not being Church of Christ.

41

"I have to hurry, Mother, if I am to get to Michael Dorphman's by one o'clock. I told him one o'clock, and I don't want to be late."

"I understand, Sarah Louise. You've told me three times already—slow down, Winslow—but I told you I have lunch made…well, pretty much made. All I have to do is bake the rolls. Everything else, except the apples, of course, is in the Crock-Pot. I said slow down, Winslow."

"How can I slow down with you two hollering at me?"

"I wasn't hollering, Pop. I just said, 'Why don't you pull into Randy's Pit Stop and let me get a barbecue sandwich at the drive-through? It'll save some time.'"

"I don't call a barbecue sandwich from Randy's a good lunch… not when I have a pot roast at home."

"Turn here, Winslow, if you're going by Randy's."

"Yes, ladies!"

As they sat in the drive-through line at Randy's Pit Stop, Sarah Louise had time to think about what she should wear. Change out of her Sunday clothes, for sure. But what if he was still dressed nice, a shirt and tie? No, the Dorphmans would all wear suits to church; after all, they were the Dorphmans. Yet

Michael was different. A little more laid-back, perhaps. Still, she should definitely change from skirt and heels. Jeans—but which ones? She had a pair in her closet, washed and ironed.

Then again, maybe that would look too…too something. Jeans aren't supposed to be ironed, are they? Shorts—it was warm. No, she might have to hike out into a field, and she didn't want to get her legs scratched by weeds. Besides, they were pale from being out of the sun all winter. No to the shorts. A pair of jeans, yes, but not her best ones. Besides, the best ones, the ironed ones, were tight. Not too tight, mind you, but sexy tight. Not that there was anything wrong with being sexy, but did she want to give Michael the wrong idea?

She wasn't looking for a relationship, and this certainly wasn't a date. Still, he was an attractive man, her age in fact. For all she knew, he might already have a girlfriend. He had been divorced long enough to respectfully be dating again. What if she got there and he had a woman with him? She would certainly feel funny if that happened and she was wearing her sexy jeans.

"Two Randy's special pork barbecue sandwiches, one fries. One medium sweet tea," Winslow ordered.

"Seven dollars and fifty-six cents," the boy at the window said.

Winslow reached into his back pocket for his wallet.

"Did you order two sandwiches, Pop? I can't eat two!"

"Where were you when I ordered, Lou? Asleep?"

"No, Pop. I was just thinking."

"Don't bother her, Winslow. She has a lot on her mind. Besides, Sarah Louise, I know who the second sandwich is for—your father!"

After the exchange of dollar bills and loose change, Winslow handed the sack of food over to the backseat where his daughter sat. "Remember, Lou, one of those sandwiches is mine!"

"Yes, Pop. Now get me home. I need to change clothes."

Pulling a sandwich out of the paper sack and grabbing a loose fry, Sarah Louise returned to her thoughts. *Blouse! I have a nice yellow one...no, too bright. Maybe white. No, I don't want to look squeaky-clean. This is a farm I'm going to. Scratch the white. What about a T-shirt?*

Later, as she drove down the road toward Michael Dorphman's cabin, she reaccessed her wardrobe. Jeans, but not her best ones. A T-shirt with an unbuttoned long sleeve on top. Tennis shoes. Casual, but not too casual. Why was it people had to work at it to look casual? Didn't that defeat the purpose?

The road would end at his driveway, he had told her. A big mailbox on an old tree stump for a post. Yes, there it was.

He hadn't told her about the cattle gaps or how rough the driveway was. It was gravel and seemed to wind and twist forever. Then she saw a cabin ahead with a big old barn to the side.

She pulled up beside an old pickup truck and stopped. The hood of the truck had a sport coat and tie lying on it. There was no parking spot as such, just a flat place in the grass where the gravel drive sort of disappeared as if the grass was slowly devouring it.

As she got out, she reached into her backseat for her sketchpad. She decided to leave her purse in the car.

"Hey!"

She heard a voice and tried to figure where it had come from.

"Here!"

She looked to her left and saw Michael standing at the huge open doors of the rumbling old barn. She waved.

He waved back, just as the tip of a dog's tail began making its way through the tall grass of the pasture between her and the barn. It had to be Scamp. Sure enough, the dog was soon at her feet, begging to be petted.

Then Michael appeared. "I just beat you."

"Beat me?"

"Yeah, I just drove up myself. I had the dog in the barn while I was at church. Didn't want him to try to follow me or to run off. Had lunch yet?"

"Yes, I grabbed a bite at Randy's. I'm not keeping you from lunch, am I?"

"No, I got me a burger at the Sonic. Usually I eat a big Sunday lunch at Gramma's or with one of my uncles. The family always gets together somewhere, but today I didn't want to stay that long—we eat and visit for hours!"

"You didn't have to change your schedule for me. I could have come later!"

"Oh no...I wanted to be here. It's too nice a day to sit inside. One of the first really nice weekends this spring. 'Sides, I was a little worried about leaving the dog alone too long."

Sarah Louise looked around. "You have a nice place... quiet, for sure. I don't guess you have any trouble with door-to-door salesmen?"

"No. If you show up at my front door, you're either coming to see me or lost!"

"I like it. Peaceful. Just the type of place an artist would live." Then, casting her eye at the cabin, she added, "So this is the cabin you're fixing up? The one with the wall that needs a painting?"

"Yeah, let me show you!"

During the tour of the old cabin, Michael had enthusiastically shown her every detail from the old cast-iron bed that sat to one side of the room to the kitchen table made from wood cut off the farm.

The cabin was really just one big room. When his grandfather had converted it from a tenant house to a hunting cabin, he had taken out all the inside partitions so that it was now one big multipurpose room—kitchen, dining room, living room, bedroom. The back porch of the cabin had been enclosed to make the bathroom and pantry. It was furnished with farm machinery made into functional items like lamps, some real antiques, and a few nice pieces left over from Michael's divorce.

"My ex-wife would call this style of decorating eclectic. I call it *me*!"

They both laughed.

Sarah Louise wasn't sure if he was being so hospitable because he had very few visitors or because he really enjoyed talking to her. She was flattered by his attention, especially when he asked her what she thought of this or that piece of furniture or where he had placed something.

No, she said to herself, *he just hasn't had anyone to talk to for a while. He's lonely for conversation, and I just happen to be here.* Still, she felt comfortable with him.

He produced a folding lawn chair and carried it outside to a small rise overlooking the barn.

"I'm sorry you have to tramp through this hay. It's almost high enough to cut. Then it won't look so bad. After we cut it, we'll let the cows and horses back in," Michael said.

"That's all right. I have cousins who live on a farm. I've hiked through a lot of hayfields."

"How's this? I don't know what an artist looks for when they are picking a spot."

"This is fine." She looked in the direction of the barn.

"Well, maybe a few feet to your left. I like the way the trees behind the barn line up."

As she took her spot and sat down, pulling a pencil from a pocket, Michael looked back at the cabin and spoke again. "If you don't mind me leaving you here alone, I'll run back to my cabin and change. I'm still in my Sunday slacks and shirt. But I'll be right back...or do you want quiet while you draw? It just dawned on me that I might be in your way."

When he said that last line, he seemed a bit disappointed, as if he really wanted to watch her draw. Sarah Louise really didn't like for people to look over her shoulder while she sketched, but she had picked up on the disappointment in his voice. "Oh, I don't mind."

"Good! I'll make us a pitcher of lemonade while I'm down there. How's that sound?"

"Great!"

She watched as he hurried down to the cabin. She didn't know why he was in such a hurry. *Is he anxious to get back to her?* she wondered. No, he was probably just anxious to get out of his Sunday clothes. *Yes, that's it*, she reasoned.

By the time he returned, the dog having followed him to the cabin and back, Sarah Louise had already done a quick sketch.

"Wow, I'm impressed. It would take me a week to draw that!"

"It would take me a century to do what you've done to that cabin!"

They both laughed again.

"So you like this view?" Sarah asked.

"Yes, that's exactly what I had in mind!"

They made small talk while he poured her a glass of lemonade, and she sketched away. The dog was hyper, so he left her to run around the field, playing fetch with an old stick. Finally the dog tired and lay down to rest.

Michael returned to the rise and sat on the ground beside the folding chair. He took a minute to catch his breath.

"Oh, I almost forgot, Sarah Louise…you were going to tell me what Lucinda said on the radio?"

42

Annie Whittier had hardly got off the phone with her great-nephew when she dialed up Sarah Louise. When her great-nephew had agreed to pose for the painting, it had taken a load off Annie's shoulders. Now she was anxious to call Sarah Louise and get her contribution to this controversial painting over with.

"Hello?"

"Sarah Louise, this is Annie. Your mother told me to call and let her or you know who I've got to pose for you tomorrow."

"Did you find someone, Miss Annie? I hope it wasn't too much trouble."

"I'll be honest with you, Sarah Louise. I fretted over it for two days. Then I was talking to Hannah, and she suggested my sister's grandson. He is going to college in Hopskinville on a football scholarship, you know. I don't know why I didn't think of him myself. So I called him. I was afraid he might have classes he had to go to, but he said he was through with classes by two o'clock. You didn't say when I had to have someone there, so I told him to come after that. Will that be too late for you, Sarah Louise?"

Just lucky to have someone, Sarah Louise was hardly in a position to be picky. "Miss Annie, that will be fine. Does he know how to get here?"

"I gave him your address, and he said he could use his computer to find his way. I don't see how his computer can do that, but there's a lot I don't understand about computers!"

"What's your nephew's name?"

"Luther...Luther Evans. His grandmother is my sister, Florence. Now, he won't get there till around four, and I told him I'd have supper ready for him when he gets done. I wanted to give him a little something for his trouble, but he said he wouldn't take anything. But he did say that his fraternity is selling chances on a keg of beer, and if I would buy some from him, that would do. He's going by his grandmother's before he leaves and sell her some chances too. What will I do with a keg of beer if I win one, Sarah Louise?"

After she finished telling Annie she could donate the beer keg to the next Lion's Club rook tournament, Sarah Louise thanked her and hung up. She didn't set the phone down, however. She immediately dialed up her friend Dotie.

"Hello?"

"Dotie, this is Sarah Louise—"

Then before she could say anything else, Dotie took possession of the conversation and hardly let go.

"Oh, Sarah Louise, I'm so glad you called. I've been worried about you. I told Moose all about your mother and the painting. I thought I was going to have to call the doctor. He laughed so hard. Now, Sarah Louise, you have to admit it is funny. Moose even told me to call you and tell you he would pose for you. I told him, 'Honey, she doesn't want to put two hundred and fifty pounds of flesh on that canvas!' I think I went and hurt his feelings, but not for long. As soon as I pulled a tray of butterscotch clusters out of the oven, he was all hugs and kisses again. But seriously, Sarah Louise, what is going on? I heard that it was on the radio. I missed it because I had to take the kids to the dentist to have their teeth cleaned. It's so much easier to do them both at the same time..."

It took a while, but Sarah Louise was finally able to get a word in edgewise. She updated Dotie on what had happened since they had last seen each other. Dotie listened some and talked some and then talked some more.

"Right now I'm finishing up my second man, the young man who posed for me on Saturday morning. I have someone else on Monday."

"That makes three, Sarah Louise. You just told me you will have five naked men in that painting."

"Don't call them naked, Dotie. But you're right. Five! Claudette is supposed to have someone here on Wednesday, and I have no idea where she is getting someone. She just tells me not to worry. I guess I'll have to trust her, and it looks like I'll have to find the fifth man myself...and I have no idea where I'll find someone."

"I can send Moose over, but you'll have to close your eyes when he takes his shirt off. It's not a pretty sight."

"I'll figure something out. To change the subject, though, Dotie, do you remember Michael Dorphman?"

"Michael...of course, I do. We had a bunch of classes together in high school. He and Moose roomed together on the senior trip. Why?"

Sarah Louise wanted to know what Dotie might have heard through the grapevine about Michael's marriage and divorce. She was, she told Dotie, "just curious"; but since he was the first man Sarah Louise had mentioned since that dreadful investment banker from Atlanta, Dotie got excited. And when she was excited, she talked even more!

When Dotie finally got off the phone with Sarah Louise, she picked up the cookbook she had been looking at before Sarah Louise had called. Putting her forefinger down on a recipe for pecan minibites, she dialed up Malvenna Botts.

"Hello?"

"Malvenna, this is Dotie Fisher. I finally found that recipe. Sorry it took so long."

"Oh, thank you, Dotie. I have to take something to the Art Guild's kickoff party on Wednesday, and I remembered how good those were when you served them at Homer Goolsby's retirement party."

"And, Malvenna, they are so easy to make, and you can make 'em and freeze 'em, and no one will ever know!"

"My kind of recipe!"

"What is the Art Guild doing with a kickoff party? Sounds like a football game!"

"Right before the Spring Fling, we always get together, all of us that are in the guild, and have finger foods. It's kind of the last chance we'll have to socialize before the real work begins. From Thursday till Sunday, we'll be so busy it will make our heads spin. Every year, I say I'm not gonna do it again, but then by the time it rolls around again, I guess I've forgotten how much work it takes!"

She was right. It took a lot of work and a lot of time and a lot of planning and a fair amount of intrigue, which is why, as soon as Dotie hung up, Malvenna dialed up Baby Huey.

"Hello?"

"Huey? It's me, Malvenna."

"Oh, hi, sweet thang!"

Huey called her and all other women a variety of pet names.

"Two things, Huey." She paused to put a fresh piece of bubblegum into her mouth. "One, you don't need to look for a pecan-tart recipe. The high school home-ec teacher, Dotie Fisher, had one. I just got off the phone with her."

"Don't tell me that, Malvenna, honey. I have spent the last two hours looking for that recipe!"

"Don't lie to me, Huey!"

"Thirty minutes, I swear!"

"Enough about that. Here's the other reason I called. What did Mrs. Biederman say about Lucinda? You said you were going to ask her if she had heard Lucinda on the radio when you and her went over Saturday's schedule."

"Oh, Lady M, let me tell you. She was fit to be tied, just like you and I were. Now, don't you go and tell anyone I told you this because she swore me to secrecy. But she said she had the radio on down at the store, and she thought she recognized Lucinda's voice, and she said to herself, 'What's she doing on the radio?' And when she turned up the volume and heard Lucinda carrying on about the Spring Fling, she said she almost hit the roof."

"I would love to have seen that!"

"Me too! Well, she didn't get a chance to talk to Lucinda till Saturday, around noon, just before she met me down at the gym. But she said she told that girl in no uncertain terms that it was her job, not Lucinda's, to go on the radio."

"What did Lucinda say? I mean, what was her excuse?" Malvenna was chewing her gum at a frightening pace.

"Mrs. Biederman said the girl claimed the radio station had called her and that she didn't think anyone would mind!"

"I'll believe that when I see pigs fly!"

"Let's not get personal now, Malvenna!"

"Oh, Huey...but what is she going to do about it?"

"She's already done it!"

"What'd she do?"

"Biederman was going to have the kickoff party at her house, there on the ninth hole at the La Vista Country Club and 18 Hole Golf Course. So she told Ms. Prissy Pants that since she felt so special, then she could just have the kickoff party at her own house! Now Lucinda will have to clean up her house and decorate and set up tables—serves her right! That's a hoot! I bet she has some of her old tole painted knickknacks in every room of her house. I bet it's tacky, tacky, tacky!"

"I've never been in her house."

"Me either. That address is too uptown for little ole me!"

"You know, they can't afford that house on his salary down at the bank. I've been told that her parents made their down payment for them."

"I wondered how they could afford to live at La Vista."

They continued to diss Lucinda for a little while, and when Malvenna hung up, Huey only paused long enough to pour himself a little more white wine before he was dialing up Lucinda Hardin-Powell.

"Hello?"

"Lucinda Sweets, this is Huey!"

"Oh, hi, Huey. What do you want? I was just getting ready to put the kids to bed."

"I'll just be a minute, dear. I was talking to Mrs. Biederman yesterday afternoon"—he paused for dramatic effect—"and she said that you had volunteered to have the kickoff party at your house. That's so sweet of you, girl."

He paused again. Of course, that was a lie. Huey wondered if she would correct him or let it stand.

"I...uh...I thought it might take some pressure off her...I mean...she has so much to do to get ready for the Spring Fling."

"That's why I called. I wanted to volunteer to help you with the party. I can do a flower arrangement for you, or a table decoration..."

They discussed the party, and admittedly, Lucinda was glad for the offer of help. Huey didn't care if he helped or not, but he did welcome the chance to show off his decorating skills. His tastes went from extravagant to over-the-top in everything he did—flowers, table arrangements, decorating—much like Huey himself.

As soon as Huey hung up, his offer to help accepted, Lucinda began to worry. The radio station wasn't the only place she had stepped over the line. There was her visit to the *Sulphur Springs Sentinel*, the local paper. She quickly picked her phone back up and dialed Avis Lipowitz.

"Hello?"

"Oh, Avis, this is Lucinda Hardin-Powell."

"Oh, Lucinda, it's so good of you to call. But I shouldn't be surprised now that you and I are such good friends!"

Oh, darn, Lucinda thought. She had told Avis she wanted to be friends, and the attention-starved Avis had believed her—and worse, she had remembered.

Before she could say why she had called, Avis continued, "I bet I know why you're calling!"

"You do?"

"Yes, you said that as soon as warm weather gets here, you and BJ would have Clarence and me over for a cookout!"

Double darn, Lucinda thought. Yes, she had said that. She, of course, was just saying that the same way you say, "We must do this again sometime," but don't really mean it. Avis had absolutely no social skills. Nuance in conversation was something she had never heard of.

"Oh, I do...yes, I do...I do want to have you both over, but—"

Before she could say more, Avis was at it again, "You know, we usually work till late at the paper on Tuesdays and Wednesdays. Tuesdays we set all the ads up, and on Wednesdays, we put the paper to bed. That's newspaper talk for...for...well, it means...we put the paper to bed..."

"Finish it."

"Yes, that's it. Tuesdays wouldn't work because we stay till we get done. But Wednesdays, we leave at five and let the staff finish up—so I guess this Wednesday would be great because we could leave the paper and come right to your house."

What Lucinda really wanted was to make sure that Avis didn't tell Mrs. Biederman about their little visit and the editorial that Avis had promised to write. Lucinda was in enough trouble with Biederman as it was.

"Actually, Avis...I'm having the Art Guild over this Wednesday, and—"

Before she get another word out of her mouth, Avis jumped in, "Oh, that would be great! Why, we'd love to come. I do so want Clarence to get out more and meet people. He spends all his time at work or at the golf course or in front of the TV. You do know that I am a bit of an artist myself. I got a 4-H ribbon one year for my popsicle-stick Christmas star. I think I might just join your Art Guild!"

Avis had done it. She got herself and Clarence invited to the Art Guild kickoff party. Lucinda ended up asking her and Clarence to come early at 5:00 p.m., as soon as they left the office. That way, she could clue Avis in on keeping quiet about the upcoming editorial; and that way, BJ, who hated these affairs, would have another man to commiserate with.

By the time Lucinda hung up, Avis Lipowitz was the happiest she had been all week, even in a month of weeks. She didn't have anyone to socialize with, and now she did. Lucinda's efforts to merely use her had gone over her head. She smiled as she picked up the phone. She dialed Clara Dorphman. Her conversation with Lucinda had reminded her that she needed to ask Clara, the official head of the Art Guild, a few things about the Spring Fling.

"Hello?"

"Miss Clara, this is Avis Lipowitz, with the *Sulphur Springs Sentinel.*"

"Oh yes, I know you, Avis. I knew you before you were a Lipowitz, when you were a...a..."

Clara's memory failed her.

"I was a Stump. George and Elizabeth Stump were my parents."

"Oh yes, I remember now. What can I do for you?"

"I was talking with Lucinda Hardin-Powell this evening about the annual Spring Fling, and since I am writing an article about the art show and all, I thought I would ask you a few questions."

"Yes, Avis. And let me tell you, dear, we need that to go on the front page. We always go on the front page."

"Oh, certainly. I think that Lucinda said that Mrs. Biederman would bring by a press release on Monday, but since you are the official head of the Art Guild, I thought I might get a few quotes from you." That was correct. Avis wrote most of the paper herself.

She asked Clara Dorphman whose idea it was to have a Spring Fling when it initially started.

Unfortunately, Clara couldn't remember whose idea it was, so the conversation turned to the kickoff party. Avis was quick to tell Clara that she and Clarence would be there. Clara then had Avis hold on while she went to her purse to retrieve her appointment calendar. She wanted to check to make sure she had jotted down the kickoff party for Wednesday. She had. So, relieved, she returned to the phone. If she put things down in her appointment calendar it—well, it helped. The truth was she often forgot to consult it.

After the two hung up, Avis sat by her phone smiling. She was excited by the party. When was the last time they had been invited to a party? She couldn't wait to tell Clarence. Then, on second thought, maybe she should wait and tell him at the last minute—yes, that seemed like a better idea.

As soon as Avis Lipowitz hung up, Clara Dorphman took the phone and dialed her grandson Michael. In looking at the appointment book, she had noticed that beside "Kickoff Party," she had written, "Call Michael." Now, for the life of her, she couldn't remember why.

"Hello? Michael?"

"Gramma? Is something wrong?"

"I don't think so. Why do you ask?"

"It's kind of late to be making a social call. Do you need something?"

"I'm not sure..." She then explained the notation in the little, purse-sized appointment book. "Why," she asked him, "am I supposed to call you?"

"Because I am supposed to take you to the party. Uncle Jeff couldn't make it, so I told you I would since you don't drive at night, but you were going to call me and let me know when to pick you up."

"Oh yes, I remember now." She kind of did. Then she turned to another subject. "Why weren't you here for lunch today? I know I saw you at church."

"I guess I forgot to tell you, Gramma," But he hadn't. "I had to get back to the cabin because I had someone coming to see me about a painting."

"A painting?"

"Yes. I asked Sarah Louise Upshaw to do me a painting for the wall of the cabin, there above the sideboard. You remember Sarah Louise Upshaw, don't you? She enters the Spring Fling every year."

Clara tried to put faces and names and bits of information together. "Isn't she the art teacher at the high school?"

"That's right, Gramma." He was surprised she remembered.

She thought some more. "She's the one who always paints cats...cats and flowers!"

"Yes, Gramma. And you know what else? She's really nice." He laughed.

"Why are you laughing, Michael Dorphman?"

"At something Sarah Louise told me. She had this really funny story about her painting this year, but I'll have to tell you some other time...it's a long story."

He thought his grandmother didn't need to hear of any possible controversy concerning the Tenth Annual Spring Fling Art Show and Antique Auction to Benefit the Art Guild's Town-Beautification Project.

But of course, he could have told his gramlmother because she would have forgotten by morning. If only everyone else could.

43

"Sorry I'm late for breakfast, Mother."

"I figured with no school today, you would sleep late. It's there, in the oven."

Sarah Louise was in a pair of cotton pajamas covered with a pattern of little cats and little cat paw prints. Her hair was pulled back into a loose bun held in place by a pencil. She looked half awake.

Claudette saw how tired she looked. "Why don't you sit down? I'll get it."

"Would you? Thanks, Mother."

As she set the plate down in front of her daughter, she cautioned, "Plate's hot!"

The plate had three biscuits, two sausage patties, and a good-sized helping of scrambled eggs.

"This is too much, Mother. I'm not a horse!"

"Just eat what you can. What you don't eat, your father will. He'll be in here for another cup of coffee, any minute now. Milk or juice?"

"Milk."

As Claudette poured her daughter the glass of milk, she commented, "Those pajamas are getting pretty worn-out. Didn't I get you some new ones, this last Christmas?"

"Yes, but these are so soft. The new ones are nice, but they're still a little stiff. Anyway, I needed something comfy last night."

"Trouble getting to sleep?"

"Not getting to sleep, staying asleep! I went right to sleep, but I woke up about two this morning, and when I did, I made the mistake of thinking about all the things I have going on right now. I don't know when I got back to sleep."

"I didn't hear from Annie yesterday. Should I call her now that you're up?"

"No need to, Mother. She called me last night. Her great-nephew is going to be here around four this afternoon."

"Florence's grandson, I bet."

"Yes, name's Luther Something-or-Other."

Sarah Louise took a biscuit and pulled it apart then buttered one half. "By the way, Mother, have you got someone to pose yet? I need him on Wednesday, in the morning."

Claudette flustered. "I'm working on it…don't worry…don't you need jelly for that biscuit?"

"Don't change the subject, Mother."

She knew her mother too well. It was obvious Claudette didn't have anyone lined up yet, just one more thing for her to have to worry about.

"I'm not trying to change the subject, Sarah Louise…but since we have, now tell me more about Michael Dorphman's cabin and your visit."

So as Sarah Louise ate—and she did end up eating everything on the plate—she told her mother again how quaint the cabin was, about the dog, the barn, and she kept commenting on how nice Michael had been.

"You know, Dotie said his ex-wife was a real snob. I never met her, not that I recall. You'd think in a town as small as Sulphur

Springs you would run into everyone sooner or later. Anyway, he didn't have her picture anywhere in the cabin—and I wasn't about to ask for one—so I could see what she looked like. But according to Dotie, his ex thought Sulphur Springs was beneath her dignity."

"When did you speak to Dotie about Michael?"

"I called her last night...I...uh...I had something about school...something I had to ask her...anyway, she knew all the dirt."

As Sarah Louise said that, she realized she really was starting to talk like her mother. *Make complete sentences!* she chastised herself.

"Dirt? What is the dirt on, Michael or his ex-wife?"

"Oh, not on Michael. He's just like I remember him from high school. He's just a nice guy. But according to Dotie, his ex was a social climber, and Sulphur Springs society was at the bottom of her ladder. Dotie says that when he came back here to help his father at the store—when his father was so sick—that Michael's ex thought it was going to be temporary—but then his father got worse, and when Michael decided to stay and run the store, they parted company."

"How does Dotie know all that? She doesn't mix in the Dorphman social scene."

"Moose's brother lived beneath them at Robin Hood Manor, those apartments on Maple Street. Evidently, he and his wife heard a lot. To make a long story short, Michael's ex treated him terrible. And there he was—with no mother, his father dying, his grandmother going fruit loopy—and trying to keep the family business going. And evidently, she yelled at him for everything."

"Sounds like she was a joy to come home to."

"He certainly didn't act like he missed her, so I guess you're right. Moose's sister-in-law says she left him for another man."

"The poor boy...guess I should say *poor man*. I still picture him in a bathing suit that comes down to his knees. I haven't seen him in ages...maybe I saw him at his father's funeral. Has he changed?"

"Well, he doesn't still go around in a bathing suit that comes to his knees, if that's what you mean. He looks pretty much the same as he did in high school. Taller, of course. He's filled out some. I guess his hairline is receding a bit, kind of makes him look more mature…but still cute."

"Did you say *cute*?"

"I don't like your tone of voice, Mother. I am not interested in Michael Dorphman. Yes, he has a cute face, but our relationship is strictly business. He's hired me to do a painting, and that's as far as it goes."

"How much are you going to charge him, for this painting you're doing?"

"Oh, I can't charge him, Mother—not after all he's been through!"

"Strictly business…I see!"

Before Sarah Louise could refute her mother again, Winslow walked in. "There you are, Lou. Did you leave me anything?"

"Oops, Pops. I guess I was pretty hungry."

Winslow looked at the empty plate in front of his daughter. He scowled. He turned to face the refrigerator, its tangerine color glowing in the morning light from the kitchen window.

"No, you don't, Winslow. Nothing there, not for you anyway. Sit down, and I'll get you some fresh coffee."

"Not even a paint palette?"

They all laughed.

"Oh, Pop. I had to keep the paint from drying out while I ran to the hardware store."

"I thought it was frosting for a cake. I came this close"—he held his fingers slightly apart—"to eating it!"

He sat down, and Claudette poured him a cup of coffee. "Sarah Louise?"

"No thanks, Mother."

Claudette sat down, and the three sat quietly for a while. Claudette was moved by the tranquility, especially in light of the last few days. "To see us sitting here, you would think we were living the normal American life."

"Normal?" Winslow repeated. "Normal?"

"I'd say," Sarah Louise added, "*normal* around here is just a setting on the washing machine!"

44

By the time Luther Evans arrived, Sarah Louise had been painting all day, and she had accomplished a lot. She had finished with Herman. He stood serenely looking out the window. His bare shoulders were about all you could see of him because, standing where he was, the man who would be sitting on the couch would hide most of Herman's skinny physique.

"For all anyone could tell, Herman, you could be wearing a hula skirt."

Sarah Louise had said this out loud, with only Buford and Ginger to hear. The two cats were curled together in a large woven basket that doubled as a cat bed. It was the right size for just one cat, but the small stray Ginger seemed to think it was made to be shared, and Buford didn't seem to mind.

Without realizing it, having said *hula skirt*, she absentmindedly began humming "Tahitian Love Song" from an old Don Ho album that her mother used to play. Claudette had played it so much that Sarah Louise knew the lyrics of every song on the old vinyl disk. She could probably sing "Tiny Bubbles" backward.

She then cast her eye over to the image of Carney Teague. His slightly exotic looks made him stand out nicely, sitting on the right side of the couch. The globe had turned out well. The globe, combined with the coffee table, had Carney prudently covered up. Where Herman had sloping shoulders, Carney had strong shoulders. They looked good, she thought.

The globe had been tricky, simply because of the detail required. Carney was holding the globe so that France faced directly outward. That was her intention since she had always wanted to see Paris and all its wonderful art museums.

Staring at France, in its subtle shade of pink, she began to sing, half out loud, "I love Paris in the springtime…"

Sarah Louise had finished her own figure and the book she was holding in her hands. The book had no title yet because she wasn't sure she wanted to go with her original choice, *Welcome to My World*. With a room full of cats, books, flowers, and a globe, that had seemed appropriate. Now that the painting was full of naked men, she was pretty sure she would have to ditch that title.

The flowers on the plant stand had been the first thing she had painted. Nice fuchsia flowers. Sarah toyed with the idea of putting more flowers on the canvas to fill in any bare spots. The good news was that she had painted flowers so often that she could do a vaseful in record time. If, at the last moment, she needed flowers, that wouldn't be a problem.

She planned on putting her fourth model behind the fuchsia flowers—although, if her fourth model showed up and he had red hair, that wouldn't work.

"I need a good profile," she said again half out loud. This put a stop to her rendition of "I Love Paris."

Glaring at the spot behind Carney Teague, Sarah Louise decided that if Luther Evans had a good profile, she would put him entering the canvas from the right. He would have a tray in his hands with a teapot and a cup and saucer.

Without thinking, "Tea for Two" popped into her head, and she hummed the first stanza over and over to herself.

The pile of books on the coffee table was half done, which led her eyes to the missing figure that was to sit on the left side of the canvas. She twisted her mouth, trying to decide if she should go ahead and work on this figure, even though she had no model, or paint more on the books.

Bored with books, she picked up a pencil and began to rough out the outline of another man. Of course, she didn't have one to look at, so she just used her imagination to do a basic head shape, shoulders, etc. She sketched lightly with the pencil because the actual outline would have to wait for the anticipated fifth model.

From out of the thin air, she found herself half humming, half singing "Love is Blue." Then it dawned on her that the sofa was blue. *Of course*, she thought, *blue is on my mind...how silly of me. Or maybe I should be singing "Blue Moon." I could follow that with "Blue Eyes Crying in the Rain."*

She looked at the clock to check the time. It was almost four. Annie's great-nephew should be arriving soon.

Sarah Louise stepped back from the canvas to look at what she had accomplished. The outline of the man, the one she had just drawn from her imagination, looked almost familiar, as if it was the outline of someone she knew.

"That's impossible," she said, once more out loud.

But before she could give it more thought, she heard footsteps coming down the hallway to her studio. Without a knock, the door opened, and her mother stood there with a pleasant-looking young man beside her.

"Sarah Louise, this is Annie's great-nephew, Luther!"

A baby-faced tall, thin young man stood beside her mother. His blond hair went well with the few freckles on his face, and his smile was shy, yet genuine.

Fifteen minutes later, Luther was changed from a pair of fashionably faded blue jeans and a long-sleeve plaid shirt to the pair of cutoffs he had brought with him. He emerged from behind the screen to stand, a little embarrassed, in the center of the studio. He looked down at his feet. "Do I need to take my sandals off?"

"No, your feet are fine. Just stand over here and face the window. I'll probably have you stand in several different poses."

He faced the window.

Great profile, Sarah Louise mused. Then, to help him relax, she engaged him in a little conversation. As she spoke, she picked up her sketchpad and sat down in the big overstuffed chair in the middle of the room. "What's your major, Luther?"

"I have a double major!"

"Really? I'm impressed."

"Music and business."

"And what do you intend to do with those?"

"I want to be a country-music star. I know how hard it is to do that, so with those two majors, I can at least get a job in the music business. Maybe one will lead to the other."

Sarah Louise was very impressed. Evidently this side of Annie's family wasn't as clueless as Annie usually was. "Do you play any instruments?"

"My music emphasis is voice, but I've been playing guitar since I was twelve. I can play a little piano too."

The aroma of cookies baking in the oven slowly entered the room by way of the air vents Sarah Louise shared with the rest of the house. "I think my mother is baking us some cookies, Luther. Is that okay with you?"

"I wouldn't turn 'em down if they were offered!"

Luther seemed like a good kid. Sarah Louise wondered what kind of songs a young boy like himself would write since so much of country music seemed to be about the turmoil of love. Was he old enough to know about love—its frustrations, its joys, its heartbreaks?

She had him face left. "Have you done any writing yet?"

"Gosh, yes. I've been writing songs since forever!"

"Let me hear something you've written. Luther!"

"Sure, but it would sound better if I had my guitar with me."

He cocked his head at an angle, as if he could hear music being played somewhere in the distance. Then, closing his eyes—in a pleasant, tight voice—he began, "Babe, you've gone and done me wrong. / That's my heart you're standing on, / I hate to hafta sing you this song, / But that's my heart you're standing on."

He stopped, opened his eyes, and looked to Sarah Louise for her reaction. She was laughing.

"That's country, all right. I liked the melody—catchy!"

He laughed at her words.

"Don't you have something a little more romantic?"

"I can do romantic."

"Let's hear something romantic then."

Luther pursed his lips together as if trying to recall something. "I'm not sure I can remember all of it, but this is one I wrote when I was in the eighth grade."

He turned his head slightly again and shut his eyes. His voice, when he began, was a little softer and a little more wistful. "If I could wish, / Upon a falling star, / And know my wish, / Would come true, / Then I would wish, / To make you mine, / And I'd spend, / Eternity with you."

Sarah Louise stopped sketching. "That's lovely, Luther. You wrote that in the eighth grade?"

"Yep! I didn't write the melody till the ninth grade, but I liked the two together so much I've used it on every girlfriend I've had since then!"

"And these ladies from your past, have they all liked it?"

He blushed.

Sarah Louise decided that maybe, despite his young age, he did know a lot about love.

Later, after he had gone, with a sackful of Claudette's cookies to take back to his dorm, Sarah Louise worked some more on the canvas.

As she did, she hummed to herself the little melody Luther had written, the romantic one. She repeated the few lines he had spoken till she began to tire of them, yet—she paused to think for a moment—"If I could wish upon a star and know my wish would come true…"

"What would I wish?" she said out loud.

45

The smell of gasoline, old oil cans, and rusty car parts have a strange effect on men. Just as a woman can swoon over a vanilla-scented candle or a bowl of harvest apple-and-pumpkin potpourri, a man is drawn to the odor of a garage like a moth to a flame.

So it was at Hubcap's garage.

Every day, Hubcap Reynolds could expect a varied assortment of Sulphur Spring's male population to just drop in. There were the "onetimers." They only came by because they needed Hubcap's expertise. They had their regular mechanics but had been told, "I've done all I can, buddy. You might try Hubcap!" And they were often right because if it was an old vehicle, Hubcap could at least tell them what was wrong.

There were his usual customers. They always brought their cars to Hubcap: little old ladies who had driven the same car for the last thirty years; kids who had been given the old family car or who could only afford to buy the castoffs of their parents' generation; little men who—for lack of a better word—were too "cheap" to ever buy a new car or truck, so they drove till one hundred or two hundred thousand miles showed on their odometers; and the old-car enthusiasts who loved old models, old hood ornaments, old bumpers, old leather seats, old anything associated with an old set of wheels.

And then there were his *regulars*.

They didn't need anything; they just stopped in to "jaw" some—talk, that is. They might stop by every day or just when they were in the neighborhood, but they stopped by and sat in his combination office/waiting room and were as much of a fixture as the tattered Naugahyde couch and folding metal chairs.

Today there was Ernie. His real name was Ernest. He was retired and in his wife's way. The garage was his retreat.

Hardtimes was another. He couldn't work because of something or other in his back. He signed his checks "Jesse Pike," but at the garage, he was Hardtimes. To listen to Jesse talk, he had never had a good day in his life. Something was always going wrong for Jesse.

Duffy was there. He was the gossip, the joker, and the most talkative of the regulars. He always knew a good joke, the latest gossip, and could tell you who was going to win Friday night's game—pick your sport! Duffy had a job nights, so he spent at least part of every day checking in with Hubcap and whoever else was around.

Today these three were talking politics. They were taking sides on the upcoming election of the town mayor and the town commissioners. It was months away, but the candidates were already declared and campaigning.

As they argued who would lower taxes and who would raise them, they paid little attention to Herman Bugleman.

Herman was there with his aunt's car.

Hannah Bugleman had sent her favorite nephew to Hubcap's to have him give her '85 Pontiac Grand Prix its annual spring tune-up. Hannah was a fanatic about tune-ups and oil changes. It had paid off because she was still driving it. Another reason was that she hardly drove any distance. The car had never gone much beyond the city limits in its lifetime. The odometer hadn't hit seventy-five thousand miles yet.

Herman's job with computers gave him some flexibility with his work hours, so he was able to take the car in. This was just one of many chores she expected him to do for her. After all, she regularly reminded Herman that the Grand Prix, the house, her antiques would one day be his. She pushed Herman here and there with a combination of bribery and guilt trip.

As Hubcap changed the oil, Herman stood in the bay of the garage watching. He didn't wait in the small office of the garage because Duffy, Hardtimes, and Ernie were there. Other men intimidated Herman.

In the other bay of the garage sat the '67 Chevy that Hubcap and his brother-inlaw, GW, worked on at least one night a week.

So Herman stood quietly out of Hubcap's way, hoping the mechanic wouldn't make any small talk with him about cars or car motors or knives or guns or hunting or football or women or any of the things other men talked about.

Hubcap, however, had to have some kind of noise going on. Since he was too far away from the regulars to take part in their conversation, he had the radio on the "oldies" station in Bowling Green. Right now, Tommy James and the Shondells were doing the "Hanky Panky," and Hubcap's body was gyrating to the beat. Between twisting his torso and draining the car's old oil, he found time to pull a doughnut from a white paper bag labeled "Danny's Donut Den."

It was at this time that a big black SUV drove up with its sound system turned so high that you heard it vibrate with a *thumpa, thumpa, thumpa* before you actually saw where the sound came from. It pulled right up to the garage, stopping sideways so that it blocked both bays of the old cinder-block building.

A tall dark-haired man stepped out. He left the motor running, the air-conditioner on high, and the sound system going, *thumpa, thumpa, thumpa.*

He was wearing sunglasses that wrapped themselves halfway around his head. He glanced toward the open bay door where Hubcap was suspended half in and half out of Hannah's engine. The dark glasses kept him from seeing anything there, so he stepped instead to the adjoining office.

Duffy, Hardtimes, and Ernie had stopped their discussion when the expensive SUV drove up, part curiosity and part a lull in the arguing.

The man realized he would have to take off his sunglasses if he wanted to see, and he fashionably placed them on the back of his head, as if he had eyes there. It was the way all the Hollywood stars did.

He stood, looking at the three quiet regulars. Not saying a word but seeing that Hubcap wasn't there, he walked across the office through the open door to the inside of the garage.

"Sociable type, wasn't he?" Ernie mumbled.

Seeing the chance to get a good laugh, Duffy spoke up, "He looked at you like you wasn't even there, Hardtimes!" And after seeing the frown that put on Hardtimes's face, he added, "And he must not have been too impressed with you or me either, Ernie!"

Ernie laughed as Duffy grinned. Hardtimes continued to scowl.

Once inside the garage, the newcomer saw Hubcap and walked the three or four steps to the front of the old Grand Prix.

"Here's the number you needed, Reynolds!"

Hubcap looked up. He had been so engrossed in what he was doing that he hadn't seen the man drive up or walk in. Hubcap did, however, recognize the tall dark intruder. He reached across the motor of Hannah's car and took a piece of paper from him, not bothering to wipe the oil or powdered sugar off his fingers.

"That looks like the number I need. If I can find the part in Hopkinsville, I'll order it this afternoon. I may have to call Bowling Green or Nashville, but I'll let you know when it gets here."

As the silent man stood there listening to Hubcap, he noticed that only a few feet away, a gangly, scrawny young man with glasses was staring at him, staring at him almost as if in a trance. It made the man nervous, and he looked back at Hubcap.

"Call the office when it comes in, and I'll bring the Corvette by," the man said.

He turned to go, having—he felt—said enough. As he did, he saw that the bespectacled young man was still staring at him; but now he had turned his head slightly, as if to get a better view. His stare was a little unnerving.

The man walked briskly to his SUV, not bothering to go back through the office area. In a minute, he was gunning his engine and heading down the road.

Hubcap put the scrap of paper into one of his overall pockets and plunged back into the Grand Prix's engine.

"Mr. Hubcap?"

"Yeah, Herman?"

"Who was that man, that man that was just here?"

"That's Clarence Lipowitz, from down at the paper. Why?"

Herman answered, "I think I've seen him somewhere before..."

Clarence Lipowitz was thinking the same thing about Herman as he drove to the *Sulphur Springs Sentinel* office. *I think I've seen him somewhere before...*

46

She pressed the remote control in her hand, and the large screen lit up with the elongated figure and face of a woman.

"This is by Amedeo Modigliani, from the early twentieth century. Notice the exaggerated nose line and flat plane of her face. Her eyes are just slits in the face—no emotion there."

The students were quiet, absorbing everything Professor Ifama said, if not out of respect, out of fear. You did not talk or whisper while Montricia Ifama had the floor.

There was another press of the remote. An African tribal mask appeared on the screen.

"This mask is from Zaire, one of the places I've been blessed to visit." She paused. "And if you are ever there, in Brazzaville, there is a grass shack with a tin roof on the beach that has the best roast pork and fried bananas you will ever have the glory of putting in your mouth! It's called Little Boo's Pig Meat Palace!"

The class laughed.

"But if you go, don't drink the water!"

They laughed again.

She was firm, but she could toss such tidbits into her lectures so that the students never failed to enjoy her class. Her asides about bathrooms in the Congo had them rolling in the aisles.

"See how similar the face of this mask by the Itumba tribe is to the face by Modigliani? The flat face, the slits for eyes, the pronounced line of the nose?"

The two faces were almost identical.

"Now, class, I see it's about time for the bell. I want you to read the next chapter in your text and be able to tell me, when we meet again, what other European artists were inspired by the African art that was making its way into the museums of Paris. Be prepared!"

"Be prepared"—that meant only one thing: a pop quiz when the class met again! When the bell rang and the class emptied the room, Professor Ifama handed the remote to the student assistant who was in charge of the PowerPoint screen and projector for the Art Department.

The assistant, a medium-height young man with a ponytail, reached to take it from the professor. As he did, his sleeve pulled taut, revealing a tattooed forearm.

"Is that a new tattoo, Jeremy?"

The student had a bit of bravado about him. Rather than answer outright, he immediately pulled the sleeve up to show his entire arm. "Do you recognize the symbol, professor?"

"Celtic, early eighth century. Druid funeral ceremony."

She didn't like being quizzed by a student. Of course, she recognized the design. If he thought her world started and ended with only Africa, he was mistaken. She could lecture him on Celtic interweaving designs or Andean pottery or Sanskrit swastikas—not to mention a lecture on respect.

Jeremy was taken back but tried hard not to show it, instead giving a smug nod of approval.

She didn't stop there. "I wear a Celtic cross around my neck." As she spoke, she intently watched his eyes and deliberately paused to give him time to absorb what she was saying. "And an Egyptian Eye of Horus, and a Swahili sun symbol."

It was a sly smile Jeremy now offered in response.

He was a rare student who could bring up a topic Professor Ifama knew nothing about, but Jeremy wasn't above trying. And he didn't try just Professor Ifama. Jeremy was a student who was convinced he was smarter than any of the old geezers who taught at the state university, and he was equally suspect of them all.

Certified genius by an IQ test in the second grade, Jeremy had been the darling of his elementary school. His mother had insisted that he "be challenged"; and so he had received individualized instruction, hours to himself in the library so he could "explore his interests," and use of the office computer.

He was the ideal student. Then he became a teenager.

The staff of his high school handed him his diploma, with glee, when he was only sixteen. They were thrilled with his academic success but more thrilled to see him leave. No one likes a student who catches every spelling mistake on the board, every equation error on a worksheet, every mispronounced name in a history lecture.

Now in college and a sophomore at only eighteen, he was no less precocious. He questioned every philosophy of education laid before him, and he did it to his professors' faces—no after-class teacher-to-student discussions but a Spanish Inquisition while the rest of the class watched. When he raised his hand in class, his professors called on him with a mixture of dread and homicidal thoughts.

The solution was to give him a lot of "independent study."

Since he was on a scholarship tied to the school's work-study program, he also did small jobs in the Art Department. He had brains, but he didn't have money.

The tattoo was a luxury he had saved a semester to afford.

After Professor Ifama left the lecture hall, Jeremy locked up the equipment and took the keys back to the office of Professor Reingold, the head of the Art Department. Reingold was on the phone when Jeremy walked in.

"Yes, we do have a class like that. We call it Life Studies, not 'nude people drawing.'" It's a part of our studio series for first-year students. Why, may I ask, do you want to know?"

Jeremy couldn't hear the other side of the conversation, but he didn't mind eavesdropping on what he could hear. He sat, with a slouch, on a chair opposite the professor's desk and twirled the key ring around his finger.

"We have several people who model, but if you want to apply to be a model, you have to come by my office and fill out an employment application." The professor was quiet for a moment, listening to his caller again.

"Oh, I see…you need a model. Well, we don't make it a habit to send our models to people's homes! An emergency? I don't see how needing a model to pose nude is an emergency that…Oh, just take off their shirt…But still, I'm sorry, ma'am, I can't…I'm sure you will pay them, but…"

It was obvious the person on the other end of the line was not giving up easy. They needed a model, and they were willing to pay.

Jeremy sat up straight and began to wave his arms, trying to get Reingold's attention.

"Just a moment, Mrs.—? Upshaw!…Yes, I'm sure you are a good Christian woman…Oh, your daughter went to school here?…Oh yes, Sarah Louise. Yes, I recall her…but—just a second, Mrs. Upshaw, I have a student that needs me…No, I won't hang up, just hold on for a second…" He placed his hand over the phone. "What do you want, Jeremy? Can't you see I'm on the phone with a crazy woman!"

"Me, professor!"

"What do you mean *me*?"

"The lady on the phone. She needs a model. I model for the Life Studies class. I do it all the time! If she's paying, I can use the job!"

Professor Reingold thought hard for a moment. Yes, he recalled, the ponytailed young man had worked as a model—not as a part of his work-study, of course, but as extra-employment to earn money.

The professor wavered for a moment. A strange person was on the phone, for sure—was it wise to send a student to their home? Then he remembered how obnoxious Jeremy was. If he told the young man no, he would just argue till—"Madame, I may have a student who will pose for you...Oh, it's for your daughter... uh...I'm sorry, but I think I have to go to a class right now...I'll just hand the phone over to this student and let you two make all the arrangements..."

47

Tuesday had dawned on Sulphur Springs with a warm breeze and the sweet scent of blooming lilacs. It would be another nice spring day. Birds were singing. It seemed like just another day in the neighborhood, but of course, for some of the residents of Sulphur Springs, it was anything but just another day.

Herman had spent the morning at Hubcap's garage getting a tune-up for his aunt's car. He was glad when he was able to leave the intimidating world of cars and motors. As he drove the '85 Grand Prix down White Oak Street, he continued to wonder why Clarence Lipowitz looked so familiar.

Sarah Louise had spent all morning painting a half-naked man onto the large canvas in her studio. He was her third model, and she was almost finished with him. The prospect of who might be her fourth and fifth models loomed over her.

Lucinda Hardin-Powell was vacuuming rugs, dusting shelves, scrubbing toilet bowls, polishing furniture, and alternately yelling at and chasing her children from one room to the next to keep them out of her way. With this being spring break, they were out of school and underfoot, just as she had to prepare her home for fifty guests on Wednesday night—make that fifty-two guests!

Huey Pugh was pushing tables around the gym of the old Sulphur Springs High School, trying to get an arrangement that would let a crowd of people flow—and he was anticipating a crowd!

Avis Lipowitz was at her desk at the *Sulphur Springs Sentinel*, going over a list of things to get written up by the paper's Wednesday deadline. As she looked over the different pages, she checked off the articles: the sports page and the fishing forecast, the main page and the break-in at the pool hall, the editorial page and her editorial about the painting by Sarah Louise Upshaw. Avis remembered that she hadn't interviewed Sarah Louise yet. She stopped what she was doing and reached for the phone book.

Calpurnia Pendergrass was also at the old Sulphur Springs High School in her Chamber of Commerce office. She was faxing news releases to all the neighboring towns with an update on the Tenth Annual Spring Fling Art Show and Antique Auction to Benefit the Art Guild's Town-Beautification Project. She had already sent all the necessary information about the annual event a month earlier. Weekly updates kept people from forgetting. But this update was a little spicier than previous ones. There was one line in the fax that began, "A controversy has gripped this usually staid event as local artist and high school art teacher, Sarah Louise Upshaw, has decided to enter a large acrylic painting called…"

Ester Mae Washington was cleaning another closet at Clara Dorphman's home. This time, it was an upstairs bedroom closet. Every box that Ester Mae pulled out Clara opened and went through piece by piece: photos, newspaper clippings, sweaters, socks with no match, quilt pieces waiting to be sewn into a quilt top—a lifetime of memories.

Clara would get excited by each box, bringing back years of recollections with their appropriate laughter or tears. Since Ester Mae had witnessed most of those recollections in their origin, she laughed and cried right along with Clara.

They never found what they were looking for because Clara had never been sure what it was she was looking for in the first place. But the day went along that way, the two women bound not by blood but by shared experience.

Claudette had spent all morning on the phone trying to find a model for Wednesday, her day to have a man to pose for Sarah Louise. There were no modeling agencies in Bowling Green, Louisville, or Nashville that had men in their employ. She had even tried Cincinnati. She called state university as a last straw, but it had worked. A nice-sounding young man had agreed to "take off his shirt" for her daughter. He would be there Wednesday afternoon.

"Wednesday afternoon," Claudette said to herself. Then she said it again, only much louder, "Wednesday afternoon! The girls will be here for cards...oh no...oh yes...maybe that's okay...or maybe it's not..." Claudette sat there pondering it all.

Michael Dorphman was behind the counter at Dorphman's Appliance and Hardware. Behind him, against the wall and out of the way, was a large striped canvas dog pillow with a very contented dog plopped in its center.

Scamp had taken to his job at the hardware store very well—store mascot and greeter. He stayed behind the counter, but there, he was able to see every customer come and go. It was like a live TV broadcast just for him.

When Lucy Pendergrass walked in the front door, Michael turned to his employee behind the cash register and said, "John, I'll take care of her, if you'll take Scamp out back for a little walk."

"Sure thing, Michael." Then, turning to face the mongrel, John said, "Hey, Scamp, let's go outside!" And the two of them left by a back door so Scamp could tend to business of his own.

"Howdy, Miss Lucy! Can I sell you a toaster oven or a pound of nails?"

"Don't be silly, Michael Dorphman, or I'll turn you over my knee! You know why I'm here."

"If you didn't come in here once a week and buy paint, I'd go out of business, Miss Lucy!"

She chuckled as she made her way back to the art section of the store.

Michael followed. "I guess you have something to enter in the Spring Fling?"

Lucy stopped and turned to face Michael. With a dramatic thrust of her hand into the air—which caused the huge orange-and-green muumuu she was wearing to look like an empty parachute in mid-descent—she looked him straight in the eye and declared, "Michael, I am creating a masterpiece! This is the painting that will make people remember Lucy Pendergrass!"

His eyes grew wide in response to her declaration, but before he could comment, she had spun around and continued in the direction of the art supplies.

"Feathers, Michael! I need feathers!" she hollered at him.

For the next thirty minutes, Michael searched boxes and shelves for the odd assortment of objects Lucy demanded. First she had to have feathers. There were feathers in a box left over from the macramé craze, and while they were going through the macramé supplies, Lucy had suddenly been inspired to get beads for her painting.

Michael showed her every box of beads in the store till she found a double handful that pleased her. Then she wanted bits of rope and scraps of leather and finally ended up adding two tubes of black paint to her purchases and making her way back to the front of the store and the cash register.

After she left, John, who had returned from walking the dog a long time ago, turned to his boss. "I was starting to get worried about you. You back there with Lucy Pendergrass! People might start talking!"

"The next time someone wants art supplies, they're yours! I must have dug through every box of beads in the store!"

"Is she into macramé now?"

"No, she said she needed them for her painting for the art show this weekend. I can't, for the life of me, imagine what she is painting!"

As they were talking, Louise, the bookkeeper, walked up to Michael from the office around the corner from the front counter. "Michael, I need to ask you about this invoice for two freezers on back order."

As Michael turned to face Louise, the bell on the door rang again, and John looked up to see Sarah Louise Upshaw walk in.

"Can I help you?"

"I just need some art supplies. I know where they are."

"No problem, I'll be glad to help."

John started from behind the counter to follow this pretty customer back to the art section and be of assistance. But before he could get two steps, he felt his boss's hand on his shoulder. "I'll take care of Ms. Upshaw, John. Louise needs you to look over some invoices."

Sarah Louise shifted her gaze from John to Michael. "I can get what I need. You really don't need to bother."

"Oh, it's no bother!" Michael said.

As if on cue, the dog recognized Sarah Louise's voice and bounded up from the pillow and over to her, causing her and Michael both to laugh. Then the three of them made their way off to the rear of the store.

John turned to face Louise. "He just got through telling me that he didn't want to wait on anybody else that needed art supplies. I don't get it!"

Louise laughed. She got it. She handed the invoice to John. "You can look at this all you want, but when Michael returns, give it to him to look over—if he returns!"

48

"You're going to buy all the flesh-colored paint I have, Sarah Louise Upshaw!"

She took the last two tubes of the paint from their place on the shelf. As she did, she pursed her lips, as if doing so could help her concentrate. "This may be enough. Of course, I can always mix the color…it's so much easier to buy…the premixed that is. I'm boring you with this, aren't I?"

"Oh no. I need a break from selling nuts and bolts." He paused a moment, suppressing a laugh as Sarah Louise twisted her mouth again. "So how do you mix flesh-colored paint?"

"It's not that difficult, just a matter of proportions. Start with white, add just a hint of red to make a very light pink. Then you mix in a dab of yellow—and voila!"

"Just how much is a 'hint' and how much is a 'dab'?"

"Why? Are you planning on painting a roomful of naked people too?"

He laughed. "So how is the infamous painting coming?"

"Three down…two to go!"

"Still nervous about the big unveiling on Saturday?"

"No, but only because I have enough other things going on to keep my nerves on edge!"

"Like what?"

"For one, I have an interview with Avis Lipowitz, this afternoon. And she's coming by the studio!"

"Are you going to make the front page?"

"I hope not!"

"There's more?"

"Mother won't tell me who my next model is and—"

Just then, John walked up. "I hate to interrupt, Michael, but Mrs. Newsom is here to pick up her washing machine, and I'm not sure which one is hers...there are four on display."

"Tell her I'll be right there, John."

John returned to the front of the store.

Michael turned to face Sarah Louise. "Sorry, gotta go...I'd like to hear the rest..."

"Oh, I've bored you enough, Michael, but it is nice to just be able to talk to someone who sees the humor in it all...well, back to the scene of the crime!"

Since she had what she had come for, she headed to the front of the store alongside Michael, the pooch between them. No one said anything.

Right before they turned the corner at the sinks and commodes, Michael stopped. "Hey, I've got an idea! Let me take you out for supper tonight. You can finish telling me your problems, and I'll tell you how much fun it is to load and deliver washing machines!"

She was speechless. Her first inclination was to say, *Oh, I'm really too busy right now* or *You don't want to hear my problems*, but then, the thought of a nice dinner out—when had she last eaten out with someone besides family?

"I guess I can...of course, I can. I told Avis four o'clock. I should be through by—"

"How does six o'clock sound?"

"That should do."

"Your address?"

"It's 175 Tulip...just off New Providence Road."

He repeated the address, "Okay, 175 Tulip, just off New Providence Road."

"Oh, Michael…nothing fancy…please…just to get out of the house…Randy's Pit Stop will do, really!"

He laughed and walked toward the washing machines, calling the dog as he went, "Here, Scamp! Come with me!"

Once back at the studio, Sarah Louise tried to tidy up her work space. It wasn't dirty, just cluttered. She never seemed to have enough time to put books back on the right shelf or to put her brushes up. They just lay about here and there.

She walked around picking up cat toys and pushing furniture an inch or so to the left or right till it suited her.

There, by the door, was that pair of expensive Italian leather shoes, a pair of socks, and a silk shirt. She picked them up, not sure what to do with them, which was why they were just sitting by the door in the first place. If only she had a box marked, "Deal-with-Later Stuff." But as she mused over the clothes, she heard a noise and saw Avis pull into the family's driveway in her green Corvette.

Sarah Louise quickly laid the shoes and shirt on the first clean spot she saw, the table beside the couch, and rushed to the door. "Avis, won't you come in?"

"Thank you, Sarah Louise. I've never been on this street before. It's a charming little neighborhood."

Poor Avis, in trying to be nice, she was only condescending.

"Sit right here, on the couch, and I'll get you a Coke or something?"

"No, that's all right. We'll just do a few questions. I need to get back to the paper. Tuesdays we lay out all of our advertising."

Avis sat down, placing her purse on the table beside the couch. "So, Sarah Louise, I hear you've stirred up a little controversy right here in Sulphur Springs."

"I guess I have…but I can assure you…I didn't mean to!"

There she was, sounding like her mother again. That made twice today. First at Dorphman's Appliance and Hardware with Michael, and now with Avis Lipowitz. *Don't be so nervous,* Sarah Louise told herself. *Use complete sentences!*

"Why paint a room full of naked men, Sarah Louise?"

For a half hour, Sarah Louise spun out the story from beginning to end, explaining—mostly in complete sentences—how Claudette had created the problem and how she had decided to go ahead and paint but do so in a way that would prove harmless. There were things she left out, like the visit to Coach Hatton's office and the events of the night Winslow fired his service revolver.

Avis appeared to understand as she took notes on a little steno pad, although she seemed to be a little disappointed, to quote the song, "Is that all there is my friend?"

"May I see the painting?"

"Of course, Avis." Sarah Louise got up and walked over to the canvas, draped with the paint-splattered sheet.

Avis stood up to follow Sarah Louise to the other side of the room where the canvas and easel stood. She reached over for her purse since she was going to leave as soon as she finished looking at the controversial work of art. As she did, her eyes came to rest on the silk shirt—the silk shirt of Clarence Lipowitz.

She recognized it immediately. She had bought it for him in Miami last summer. *No,* Avis thought, *just a coincidence.* Yet she picked up her purse and ever so slightly pushed the silk shirt back an inch to see what lay beneath it.

Sarah was tugging at the sheet, which had snagged on the corner of the canvas, when she heard Avis say sharply, "I don't need to see it, Sarah Louise. I've seen enough for one day!"

A second later, she was gone.

49

Dino's Little Italy was the nicest restaurant in Sulphur Springs. Its tablecloths were real cloth, not oilskin or plastic. Mama Dino insisted on a touch of class. It was called *Dino's* because, at one time, the restaurant's owner and chef had looked a little like the Italian singer and celebrity Dean Martin, who was called Dino by the press. That was some thirty years and one hundred pounds ago.

Angelo Capelli, his real name, had served in Vietnam with local boy Steven Freedle, who now ran the co-op. Steven had invited Angelo to visit him one day. Angelo had and, since every street corner in his New Jersey neighborhood already had an Italian restaurant, decided to make Sulphur Springs his home and open up his own eatery. It was slow at first since the only Italian food Sulphur Springs had ever heard of in 1980 was spaghetti.

One summer weekend, Angelo, now called Dino by everyone here, returned to Jersey for a family reunion and came back with Mama Dino. Mama Dino, real name Simona, was as svelte as Angelo back then. But thirty years of pasta, garlic bread, and Alfredo sauce can do a number on a person's waistline. Yet it was Mama Dino who put the little restaurant on the map. She had style. With her arrival came the red-and-white checkered tablecloths, the wine bottles used as candlesticks, the real wicker bread baskets, and the cannolis and the cheesecakes on the dessert menu.

The people of Sulphur Springs had adopted the Capelli family and made them their own. Food has a way of breaking down doors that might not have been opened otherwise. After all, Angelo and Simona didn't sound very Southern when they spoke. The next generation of Capellis had been conceived, birthed, and raised here. The three Capelli offspring, aside from their olive complexions and coal-black hair, looked and dressed and sounded like any other Sulphur Springs child. Tony, the oldest, had played quarterback his senior year at Sulphur Springs High School. Gina and Maria had both been cheerleaders. Now, it would be their children who would be washing dishes in the back and clearing tables.

Mama knew everyone in Sulphur Springs because, at one time or another, everyone in Sulphur Springs had eaten there—and Mama remembered. She smiled big when she spoke your name, unless you had once stiffed her on the tip.

As Michael and Sarah Louise sat down, Mama Dino handed each one a menu. "And how are we tonight, Sarah Louise?"

"Fine, Mama Dino. It smells so good in here. What are you cooking?"

"Dino's been playing with his calzone recipe all day! And how are you tonight, Michael? I see you brought someone here besides your gramma…that's good maybe, I think?"

Michael blushed. "Yes, that's good…uh, I hope Dino has some of his experimental calzone on the menu tonight!"

While Mama Dino and Michael and Sarah Louise made small talk at the restaurant, Avis Lipowitz was sitting at her desk at the *Sulphur Springs Sentinel*.

She had closed the door between her office and where employees Edward, Julie, and Rebecca were working on ad layouts. Clarence had taken their kids to McDonalds and was going to take them home after that. They were old enough to stay by themselves for a little while, so he would return to the paper to help wrap things up.

Avis wanted to pick up something and throw it against the wall. She would have if she had been there alone, but she couldn't with her employees in the next room. She tried so hard to keep the problems with her marriage hidden. So instead of throwing things, she put her head in her hands and tried to hold back the tears.

Every time she thought Clarence had stopped seeing other women, something like this happened. The shirt was his, and the shoes, the expensive Italian-leather shoes—no wonder he had been wearing his Adidas the last few days.

Avis tried to put two plus two together. Clarence had offered to interview Sarah Louise, and he had then changed his mind. Why? Then there was that night meeting he had attended. Why did she let him go to night meetings? She knew better! And why did he leave his shirt and shoes there—was he planning on going back?

This time, she wasn't going to pretend she didn't know what was going on. She would tell the three employees they could go home, and when Clarence returned, she would demand answers!

——◦◦◦——

Back at the restaurant, the supper date was going well. Because neither of them was actively looking for a significant other, they were relaxed and talkative. No attempts to impress each other as people do on the first few dates before they start to let their guards down. Michael and Sarah Louise had let their guards down a long time ago.

"I don't want to sound sappy, but I don't know when I've had such a good time…you know, just talking and having a good time."

"Me too, Sarah Louise. I haven't been out with a member of the opposite sex other than my grandmother since Sophie left. Oops…I promised myself I wouldn't bring her name up. Dates don't like to hear about the ex!"

Date—the word bounced around in Sarah Louise's head. Was this actually a date? Maybe it was, but still it didn't really seem like it. Then again, she had spent an hour getting dressed, most of that time spent sitting in her bathrobe staring at her open closet and mentally trying on every outfit in there. Yes, maybe it was a date—or maybe it wasn't.

***

When Clarence walked back into the office of the *Sulphur Springs Sentinel*, he noticed that the three employees were gone. That was good. It meant that the ads were all done. Why hadn't Avis called him on his cell phone and told him? It would have saved him a trip back down there.

He walked into Avis's and his private office. His wife was standing, staring out the window. She turned around to face him, and he didn't like what he saw. She was mad—she didn't get mad often. In her hand, she clutched a nice silk sport shirt.

"Do you know where I found this, Clarence?"

Clarence looked from the shirt to his wife's face and did what he did best—he lied! "You've been over to that art teacher's! I hope she told you how she tried to get me to undress for her and how I had to leave to keep my virtue intact!"

Virtue—did anyone in Sulphur Springs really think that Clarence Lipowitz's virtue was intact?

"What are you trying to say, Clarence?"

"What I am trying to say is, I went to interview the tramp, and she asked me to take my shirt off so she could draw me…

for that crazy painting of hers...the one that everyone is talking about. I agreed just to be nice!"

A line in Avis's forehead softened. Clarence noticed it. He could read his wife like a book, a first-grade primer at that. And he kept talking. It was all downhill from here.

"I got suspicious when she asked me to take off my shoes, something about not getting footprints on a rug she wanted me to stand on. So I did...but then she insisted I sit down on the couch while she poured me a glass of wine. I almost fell for it... but when she practically sat on my lap, I realized what she was up to!"

"She tried to sit on your lap!"

"That little schoolteacher is a slut. I hope the school board knows that...but I guess it's best to keep things like that, quiet... which is why I didn't mention it to you, Avis..."

"You should have told me, Clarence."

"I pushed her away from me and started to leave, and the brazen hussy grabbed my shirt. I was afraid of what she might do next...you know people like her."

"People like her?"

"Yeah, people like her try to get people like us in a situation where they can try to blackmail us."

"Blackmail?" Avis was aghast at the word.

"Yeah, blackmail...I left as fast as I could. I didn't realize I had left my shoes behind till I got back to my car, but I wasn't going back into that woman's den of inequity!"

Poor Avis, she looked somber. Now came the icing on the cake. Clarence stepped over to his desk, sat down in his chair, and put his head in his hands. His voice got quiet and heavy with emotion. "And to think you didn't trust me."

Avis rushed over to his desk and threw her arms around him and, through her tears, pleaded, "Forgive me, Clarence, please forgive me!"

50

When the old pickup truck had pulled into the Upshaw driveway at 6:00 p.m. sharp, Winslow and Claudette took note and returned to their supper. They had already been clued in by their daughter that she could answer the door by herself, which was a more polite thing to say to one's parents than, "Mind your own business."

There were, however, other eyes in the neighborhood watching Michael's arrival. Alma Peterman was using her late husband's binoculars to see the license plate numbers on the back of Michael's truck. She then jotted them down on a pad of Big Chief notebook paper. She also wrote down the minute, hour, day, month, and year of his appearance at the Upshaws.

There was a one-woman neighborhood watch program for Tulip Avenue, and Alma was it. Since the night she had heard a gunshot and then seen two half-naked men run through her backyard, Alma had been convinced her neighborhood was about to be taken over by Communists. Then a series of conversations with a cousin, who watched Fox New religiously, convinced her that Communists were no longer a threat. They were probably members of the Mexican drug cartel or, worse, crazed Arab terrorists!

Ronnie Junior, the sheriff, didn't seem to be properly upset about the situation even after three phone calls, but he had suggested she watch her neighbors closely and take down the license numbers of any suspicious vehicles.

To Alma, they were all suspicious.

Every UPS or FedEx delivery to every neighbor in sight was written down. The mailman had better be on schedule, or it went down on Miss Alma's pad of paper. She had never realized how many people drove up and down her street till she started taking notes. The daily traffic kept her going from one window in the house to another. But after dark, she was even more apprehensive.

This wasn't the first strange vehicle to show up at the Upshaw house. Alma had always kept up with who visited her neighbors on either side of her simple 1930s white clapboard home because she was...well, she was nosy. But now she was twice as nosy and had a pencil and a pad of paper to boot.

Later that evening, at 8:25 p.m., as Alma wrote it down, a dark-red pickup truck, license plate number 615-75BH had pulled into the Upshaw driveway. It was the second time the truck had been there that night.

<hr />

When Michael pulled back into the Upshaw driveway, he had gotten out to politely escort Sarah Louise to her studio door. There, she thanked him again for the nice night out. It was probably the tenth time she had thanked him, but at least she had done it in complete sentences!

Since they had, among a slew of other things, discussed over supper the lurid artwork she was creating, Sarah Louise had nervously asked Michael if he wanted to see it. "Of course," he had replied. So as he walked her to the door, she asked him again, "You still want to see my scandalous painting?"

"If you don't mind me seeing it. Aren't artists moody about people seeing a work in progress? I don't want to make you moody!"

He was right. Most artists prefer to keep their work under wraps. When people see a half-done canvas, they ask such silly questions: "You're not leaving this blank, are you?" or "I hope you aren't going to put another tree right here?" or "You know what I think would look cute right here?" No artist wants to hear the word *cute*. Sarah Louise was the same. No one ever got to watch her paint, unless she was doing a demonstration for her students; and no one ever got to see her half-finished canvases, except for her family. But for Michael, she was willing to make an exception.

"You won't make me moody, I promise!"

Once inside, Sarah Louise pulled the sheet from the canvas and revealed her painting.

Michael didn't say anything. He put his hand to his chin, as if in deep thought; and rubbing his chin a few times, he gave out a *mmm* sound, then another *mmmmm*, more drawn out and louder, and then another *mmmmmmm*.

"Oh, stop that, Michael!"

He laughed.

"Tell me what you are thinking!"

"Really?"

"Yes!"

"It looks tame enough to me. I don't think the PTA could get up any charges of 'immoral' or 'improper' behavior based on what you've got here!"

"That's a relief!"

"I think everyone will get a good laugh out of this. I would pay more attention to those fuchsia flowers than I would—is that Herman Bugleman looking out the window?"

"You recognize him?"

"With those ears, who wouldn't?"

They both broke up with laughter, and at that exact moment, the door to her parents' hallway opened, and Claudette burst in. She didn't realize that Michael was still there, and because she was so anxious to know about Sarah Louise's night out, she spoke right out loud, "Tell me, Sarah Louise...how was your date with Michael? Bet your—ooops!"

The couple immediately broke into giggles again.

"Oh, I'm sorry...I thought you were gone, Michael...it's me, Sarah Louise's mother...I haven't seen you in ages...but Sarah Louise told me you were still cute—oh, I shouldn't have said that...I think I'll come back later..."

"That's all right, Mrs. Upshaw. I was about to leave anyway... and it's nice to see you again. It has been a long time! But it's even nicer to know"—his eyes darted in the direction of Sarah Louise, just long enough for her to take notice—"that I am still *cute!*"

Claudette's face flushed, and that caused Michael and Sarah Louise to laugh again.

Claudette looked from Michael to Sarah Louise, and despite her embarrassed feeling, it was plain to see that Sarah Louise was happy. It was the first time she had seen her laugh in a while, but there was something else. Sarah Louise kept exchanging glances with Michael as they laughed. There was a certain familiarity there. It was a look a person has when they have been around someone long enough to say or do what they want without worrying what the other person will say because they know the other person will accept them for who they are. Claudette and Winslow showed that look once upon a time...before they had both grown old and cranky.

"I told you, Michael...my mother is liable to say anything... that's how I got in this fix in the first place!"

Claudette didn't speak up in her own defense. She was enjoying this interplay between the two young people.

"Sorry if I embarrassed you, Mrs. Upshaw! I'll make it up to you. What do you say, after all this is over, on Saturday, you and Mr. Upshaw and Sarah Louise come to my place for supper?"

Sarah Louise turned to Michael. She placed her hand on his forearm. "You don't need to—"

"I insist! I cook a mean burger on the grill, and I'll pick up a quart of slaw from Randy's Pit Stop." He turned from Sarah Louise to Claudette. "What do you say, Mrs. Upshaw?"

Claudette was speechless, not about the invitation but because Michael had unconsciously placed his hand on top of Sarah Louise's.

"Well, I accept, Michael...and I'll bring Claudette and Pop with me. Maybe I can get my mother to make some of her fudge brownies for dessert."

It was right after Michael closed the door and started toward his truck that Claudette's tongue returned. "You like him...don't you, Sarah Louise?"

"Of course, I do, Mother. Gosh, we've been friends since junior high."

"No...I mean...you really like him!"

"Mother, there you go again! I don't like that tone of voice of yours. We're just...good friends...that's what we are."

Claudette walked over to the painting. She hadn't seen it for several days. "Sarah Louise, this sketch you've started...the man who is going to sit beside you on the couch...behind the stack of books...who is it?"

"What do you mean, who is it? I haven't got a model yet. That's just a rough sketch I made up!"

Claudette looked out the studio window as Michael Dorphman opened the door to his truck and got in. His silhouette, against the glow of Alma Peterman's back porch light, was identical to the silhouette Sarah Louise had sketched on the canvas.

"Sarah Louise...I think your subconscious is at work..."

———— ❧ ————

And as Claudette studied the half-finished painting, Alma Peterman jotted down the time of Michael's departure.

Later, content that her neighborhood was quiet for the night, Alma prepared to go to bed. She double-checked all her doors to make sure they were locked and pushed one of her kitchen chairs up against the door from there to the back porch as an extra precaution. After changing into her gown and putting her false teeth into a glass of water beside her bed, the last thing she did—before turning off the Gone with the Wind lamp on her bedside table—was to place her late husband's number seven golf club beside the bed. She would be prepared the next time anyone ran across her backyard!

51

The speed limit on State Route 51E varied between twenty-five and forty-five. It seemed to change every half mile. To the driver of a car or truck, this was frustrating, particularly if you had a clutch and manual transmission.

As Jeremy Finch took the curves and straight stretches astride his beat-up motorcycle, he was glad he wasn't driving a car to Sulphur Springs. It was pretty obvious that this road had been laid out in the days of horse and buggies. The road followed the contours of the land. It skirted every large hill and went up and over all the small hills.

The warm spring weather was another reason he was glad he couldn't afford a car and was on his motorcycle. He got a natural high from the rushing air as it hit his face. He had undone his ponytail so his hair flew out behind him; he looked a little like a banshee in flight.

Jeremy wasn't using his helmet on this old road. Laws, like the one requiring motorcycle riders to use helmets, cut away at Jeremy's sense of "I know what's good for me and what isn't." Besides, he liked to push the limits on authority of any kind. The helmet was strapped behind him on his seat. If he came to a town, he would put it on then remove it again when he got to the town limits.

If he was stopped, he would plead that the chin strap on his helmet was broken, and it was. He had taken care of that. We told you he was certifiably a genius. He loved it when he could put one over on the police, or any other person or agency or authority figure that tried to control his free spirit.

Posing for the life studies class was just one example of how he flaunted life's conventions. The black leather jacket he was wearing with the hand-painted skull and the two joints of marijuana in his hip pocket were another.

When Jeremy got to the city limits of Darlington, the town closest to Sulphur Springs, he had dutifully put his helmet on. As he had ridden through the small town, he had stopped at the only traffic light in town. Waiting for the light to change, he looked to his right and admired his reflection on the window of Gump's Flower Emporium and Gifts.

Inside the shop, a slightly plump middle-aged woman was looking in his direction. She let out a heavy breath of air then turned to the woman beside her, "That reminds me."

"What reminds you?" the other woman said.

"I need to order another teddy bear in a black leather jacket. I used the last one on Joe Bobby Smith's funeral two weeks ago, and you never know when one of those motorcycle people are going to get themselves killed."

"I thought he got shot in a barroom brawl over in Covington."

"He did, but his motorcycle buddies all chipped in to get him a wreath with 'May you ride the big Harley in the sky' on it. I talked 'em into putting the little bear on it. And his mama took that bear home with her after the funeral, and I've been told she keeps it on top of her TV, where she can see it and be reminded of Joe Bobby."

From what I know of Joe Bobby, I don't think I'd want to be reminded!"

Ronnie Jean Gump looked back out the window in time to see Jeremy ride off down the street. As the owner of Gump's Flower Emporium and Gifts, she had a window literally on everything that happened in Darlington. She made flower arrangements for its birthdays, graduations, weddings, operations, and funerals.

Despite the ordinary sound of her last name—she had been a Townsend but married a Gump—her flower shop was considered one of the best in the three or four towns around. Folks even came to her from Sulphur Springs, fifteen miles down State Route 51E and with two flower shops of its own. A flower arrangement with the name Gump on it was considered a touch of class.

It didn't take much to bring a touch of class to the rural landscape of towns like Sulphur Springs and Darlington. But that didn't stop Ronnie Jean from going over the top. Her floral arrangements went from humongous to outrageous. No single rose in a bud vase for her. If someone was to be so cheap or naive as to order a solitary flower in a simple bud vase, Ronnie Jean added enough baby's breath, colored tissue paper, and curled ribbons to make it a showpiece. Maybe it was that something extra that Ronnie Jean did that made people want her to put flowers into their lives from birth to death.

"Tootie, call down to the funeral home and make sure they're not getting ready to lay someone out."

"Why, Ronnie Jean, what a question to ask!"

"Oh, silly, I've got to judge that Spring Fling Art Something-or-Other in Sulphur Springs Saturday morning. If they have somebody dead down at the funeral home, I need to know. I don't want to leave you here alone with a big funeral to get ready for!"

"Amen to that!"

"I have to be there early. The judges go in before it opens to the public, and we pick the winners. This is my first year as a judge, but how hard can it be to pick a pretty picture and put a ribbon on it?"

"And you've got such good taste, Ronnie Jean. It won't be no trouble for you at all!"

Ronnie Jean stopped curling ribbon long enough to look around her shop at her assortment of balloons, stuffed animals, dried flowers, silk flowers, live flowers, plants, candlesticks, scented soap, silver baby spoons, ceramic churches, and resin angels. She had eight different resin angels to choose from, all of them designed so they could be placed on the edge of a tombstone so that they looked like they were sitting there, for eternity, watching over the dear departed. Even Joe Bobby's grave had one.

"Who else is going to judge 'sides you?"

"Mrs. Biederman told me, and I wrote it down somewhere. Let me see if I can remember. There's me, some professor from the state university, and Hamilton Goodpasture from over in Greenbrier. You know him. We did his house for that Christmas open house two years ago!"

"Don't he run a bank?"

"That's him."

"What's he know about judging art shows?"

"Probably nothing, but you gotta have at least one judge with money...you know, them big bucks. People think if you've got money, you've got good taste!"

"Ain't that a hoot!"

"If people only knew how tacky some rich folks are...but that's where I come in. If they could put flowers in a vase themselves, I wouldn't have a job."

Tootie put the last dried flower in the arrangement she was working on. "Whatcha think, Ronnie Jean?"

Ronnie Jean gave the vase a critical eye. "You didn't put any feathers in it, Tootie! What have I told you? Dried flowers need something to give them a little pop! Hand me that box of peacock feathers!"

In a few minutes, the simple dried-flower arrangement had gone from boring to bang—just leave it to Ronnie Jean!

"I do love feathers! Now, don't that look better, Tootie?"

Tootie had to agree, it did, and as the two women admired their handiwork, Jeremy Allen Finch was fifteen miles clown State Route 15E, pulled over to the side of the road. He reached behind him and begrudgingly grabbed his helmet.

52

Winslow Upshaw stuck his forefinger in the icing on the two-layer German chocolate cake then, pleased with the taste, looked around the kitchen to see if the icing's mixing bowl was sitting out.

He spied it by the sink, with the spatula lying beside it. In a split second, he had the spatula in his hands and was scraping leftover icing out of the bowl. As he was getting the last out, he heard his wife and daughter coming down the hallway.

"That young man said he would be here around two...that's all I can tell you...he didn't tell me anything else...except his name...I've already told you that! I told him to come around back...everything will go smoothly...I promise."

"I just wish you had told him to come in the morning, Mother."

"Why?"

"Because that means he'll be here the same time your card-playing cronies are here, and I don't want them to interfere."

"Now...how would they interfere? We'll be playing cards...here in the dining room...you'll be in the studio. I don't see a problem."

"I see a problem—Hannah Bugleman!"

By this time, they were in the kitchen, where Winslow, now seated at the kitchen table, was privy to their conversation.

"Don't worry, Lou. I can take care of Hannah Bugleman. What do you want me to do with her? Tie her up and throw her off the river bridge? I've been wanting to do that for years!"

"Hush, Winslow...she just doesn't want the girls to come down there and bother her...like we would...well, maybe Hannah would..."

"That's it Pop. I can just see Hannah making it her business to come into the studio and critique the painting, my model, and probably my life!"

"Lou, she critiques everyone's life! But if you don't want her there, it's as good as done. I'll park a chair right in the hallway. She won't be able to get by me."

"Promise, Pop?"

"Promise!"

"Now that that's settled, I'm going back to the studio. Remember, I don't want anyone barging in while I'm working—and, Pops, no guns!"

As Sarah Louise left to return to her studio, Claudette was giving Winslow a hard stare. "Your sugar, Winslow!"

"What about my sugar?"

"I thought you were going to go easy on sweets!"

"I am!"

"Oh yeah... what's that smudge of icing I see on your cheek, huh, Winslow?"

Winslow's tongue darted out, and in no time, the evidence was gone. "Case closed!"

"Oh no, it isn't, Winslow...and you're not getting any of this cake either...it's for the girls...and the leftovers go home with them...there won't be any left sitting around to tempt you... besides, I made you some sugar-free dessert...Jell-O!"

"Oh boy!"

"Don't be sarcastic with me, Winslow…now get out of here…I see Bonnie driving up now…Hannah and Annie will be right behind her…"

Claudette had been right, and by the time the clock struck one, the four ladies were all there and making their way to the dining room to play their weekly game.

Everything seemed to be going smoothly.

It was a minute till two when Jeremy rolled his motorcycle into the driveway on Tulip Avenue. Actually, his disdain for rules included a disdain for time schedules—unless money was involved. He didn't wear a watch, lest anyone accuse him of being a slave to the timepiece, but he did use the blinking time screen on his cell phone to keep on schedule, if it suited him.

Today, because he was getting paid handsomely, it suited him to be on time. Besides, he was looking forward to this job—the chance to pose for an older woman, in her home, just the two of them.

Sarah Louise opened the door to her studio and stood where Jeremy could see her.

Before he turned off the ignition on his motorcycle, he gunned the engine a few times. This was strictly for show. Like the caveman who beat his chest to impress his cave ladies, Jeremy was saying, *Look at me, I'm bad!*

And Alma Mae Peterman did look at him.

She had seen him ride up and pull into the Upshaw driveway, and she ran through her house from the living room to the dining room to the kitchen to keep up with him. She lay her binoculars down and grabbed her pad of paper.

"So," she grumbled to herself, "is this what it's come to? First, that Sarah Louise Upshaw has men in pickup trucks coming and going all hours of the night…now she is seeing motorcycle hoodlums!" He had to be a hoodlum, she reasoned. He was wearing a black leather jacket with a large grinning white skull on the back!

Alma laid the pad and pencil down long enough to go to her bedroom. There, she grabbed Otis's number seven golf club and, in only a minute, was back at the window. There, with the pad of paper, the binoculars, the club, and with a pot of coffee on the stove, she sat. *If only*, she thought, *Otis were here.*

Jeremy hopped off the motorcycle and pulled the helmet off his head. He shook his head so that his long hair hung in all its glory then turned to face Sarah Louise.

What have we here? Sarah Louise thought. *Is this the model Claudette got? Why, he's just a kid—and a cocky little kid at that!*

"I'm Jeremy!" he hollered across the driveway.

Sarah Louise swallowed hard. "Come in right here, Jeremy. I'm Sarah Louise Upshaw. I've been expecting you."

Once inside, Jeremy pulled off the leather jacket and laid it across the arm of the chair, careful to arrange it so that the gleaming skull was fully visible.

Sarah Louise, meanwhile, was trying to size this kid up, and he was indeed just a kid. She wasn't sure he was old enough to shave. His face looked awful smooth. And that long hair! Then there was his motorcycle and the way he walked—with a slight swagger. Yes, she knew his kind. She had students like him before. She had never let them intimidate her, and she wouldn't let this Jeremy character either!

"Like the skull? I did it myself."

"That's cool, Jeremy. Did you use fabric paint or acrylics?"

"Acrylics...why?"

"I've found that fabric paints hold up better on leather, especially when exposed to weather. If it starts to peel, get some Prang brand fabric paint to touch it up."

Jeremy chaffed. He had goofed by using the wrong paint. She was right because it was already starting to peel in places. He didn't like it when an adult knew more than he did. Sarah Louise, on the other hand, knew she had shown her authority. She went on to the next step—be firmly in charge!

"If you'll step over here…this is where I'll need you to stand. Did you bring a pair of shorts to change into?"

"I usually pose nude, so I didn't bother. I'm not ashamed by my body… we're all naked under our clothes, aren't we?"

Sarah Louise wasn't prepared for this, but she rallied back. "Aren't we! The other models I've used were more comfortable changing into shorts or a bathing suit, but I've certainly sketched nudes before!"

Then before he could do or say more, she added, "In your case, I think I'm only going to need you to take off your shirt. Actually, I was hoping for an older model, more muscular perhaps, but you'll do."

That took some of the wind out of his sails!

"How old are you, Jeremy?"

He paused for a moment, seriously considering lying. Would twenty-one make a difference?

"Eighteen… but I'll be nineteen in August. I'm already a sophomore!"

"That's an accomplishment! What are you studying?"

He pulled off his shirt and tossed it on top of the jacket. Then he pulled a rubber band from a pocket and pulled his hair back into a ponytail before answering, "Calculus and philosophy—a double major!"

Oh boy, Sarah Louise thought, *I hope he doesn't want to discuss Nietzsche.* She decided not to comment on philosophy or on his now-exposed tattoos. If that was how he wanted to invest in art, that was his business.

"Stand facing this way, please, Jeremy, and I'll get my sketchpad."

Yet things were still going smoothly, just as Claudette had promised.

53

"Oh, hi, Malvenna…I wasn't expecting you!"

"I wanted to get these pecan minibites to you. I know Mrs. Biederman said we were to deliver our food between three and four, but I was having my hair done then, so I just brought them now…I knew you wouldn't mind."

Malvenna popped her gum a really big pop. Lucinda smiled graciously. What else could she do? She knew Malvenna was probably still miffed at her for her being on the radio station. She couldn't be rude to her now and risk alienating her entirely.

"I'll take them!"

"Oh, no trouble! I'll bring them in and set 'em down for you… where's your dining room?" Malvenna barged right in. "Down this way?"

She stopped halfway down the hall at the living room. "Is this your living room? It's so big! I bet you love that fireplace, don't you? Ohh…" She stepped inside the room and walked over to the couch.

"Where did you get those throw pillows? I saw them in *Town & Country*, and I have looked all over for them!"

Lucinda followed her into the room. She smiled graciously again. Before she could answer Malvenna, her intruder started over to the window. "Are these silk? They sure look it! I found some fabric at Biederman's that looks like silk but costs half as much...you could have saved a bundle. Did you do 'em yourself, or are they ready-mades?"

Malvenna loved going in other people's homes. She never missed a home show, and she stopped at every Open House sign in town on Sunday afternoons, not because she wanted to buy a home but just to see how other people lived.

She popped her gum again.

"Is that you, Malvenna Honey? I thought I heard your voice!"

Both women turned to see Baby Huey standing in the doorway. He was wearing a bright-red-and-green Hawaiian shirt with a pair of very large white shorts, which revealed his stubby and almost-as-white legs.

"Oh, Huey! You here?"

"I've been here for an hour, Malvenna. I've been helping Lucinda decorate the serving table!"

"Oh, let me see!"

Huey escorted Malvenna farther down the hall, both talking a mile a minute. Lucinda smiled graciously, although there was no one in the room with her to appreciate it. By the time Lucinda joined them in the dining room, the two had settled down in chairs and were talking about the large buttercups in Huey's arrangement.

"You know, Huey. When I saw those big buttercups and sprigs of peach blossoms, I said to myself, 'That looks just like something you would have gotten from Gump's!'"

"Really?"

"Sure enough! Wanna know what else I think, Huey?"

"Malvenna, sweetie, if I want your opinion, I'll ask you to fill out all the necessary papers!"

"Oh, hush, Huey...you need one of those artificial birds stuck in there. You know, the kind made with real feathers. Wouldn't that be cute?"

"I don't do *cute*, Malvenna."

"Well, I think one would be just perfect there. What do you think, Lucinda?"

Lucinda smiled graciously and opened her mouth to say something, but—

"This is just my first arrangement. I made a smaller one to go by the pool, where the drinks will be served."

"The pool? I didn't know you had a pool, Lucinda. Where is it?"

"Right this way—but first, let me show you Lucinda and BJ's master bedroom. The bed is a king size, and if it has one French lace pillow, honey child, it has fifty!"

"Oh, I just love French lace. Lead me, Huey!"

As the two of them left on their tour of her house, Lucinda sat down and stopped smiling graciously.

———✦———

Across town, Avis Lipowitz was sitting at the keyboard of her computer.

> A moral outrage that could seriously damage our town's image and place us with the great sin cities of the past, Sodom and Gomorra…

Maybe that was a little strong. She hit the Delete button.

> an affront to the sensibilities of our fair town and an insult to the reputation of our esteemed annual art show…

Yes, that was better.

Libel laws prevented Avis from expressing a strong opinion on the front page of the *Sulphur Springs Sentinel*, but the editorial page was different. An opinion was an opinion, and Avis certainly had an opinion. Still, she had to be careful about naming names in an editorial.

She hit the letters on her keyboard with a determination she rarely had. Not only had that brazen hussy tried to ensnare her husband, but the attempt at blackmail was reprehensible.

She stopped and reread what she had just written. It met her approval, and she attacked the keys again.

> Such brazen attempts to sully our community's noble and virtuous name call for unprecedented action! People such as this should be ostracized or at least denied a job on the public's payroll! A teacher needs to be fired, and we all know who she is!

Pleased with the next two paragraphs as she continued to write, she double-clicked on the Print button, and the scathing editorial emerged from the printer.

Avis took a yellow Post-it note and neatly printed, "Clarence, look at this and make any changes, then give to Julie or Rebecca to paste on to the layout. I'm going to take the kids by the babysitters and then go ahead and change clothes for tonight. Remember the party I told you about this morning."

She placed the editorial and its little note on the desk opposite hers and left. Clarence, she noticed, had been gone over an hour getting an update from the sheriff's office on a wreck that happened last night. She couldn't complain. It was a good sign that Clarence took his time when investigating a story—the paper had to get all the facts and get them right. Still, she didn't know why he couldn't have just called the sheriff's office.

As Avis pulled out of her reserved parking space beside the paper's office, Malvenna was back in Lucinda's dining room.

To Huey's credit, he had shown her not only the master bedroom but every room in the house. The two of them, when they were sure they were out of Lucinda's earshot, had dissected the decorating scheme of every room they came into. Since Huey and Malvenna didn't share the same design aesthetic, they ended up arguing over every wall color, artificial plant, and tole painting in the house.

While they had been gone, Lucinda had placed silver trays and cut glass bowls around the table. On each empty serving dish, she had a folded index card with a person's name and the food item they were supposed to bring.

Malvenna walked around the table until she found the one with her name. Lucinda was busy in the kitchen. Malvenna looked at the silver tray set aside for her pecan minibites and frowned.

"Oh, Lucinda dear...I can't have my pecan minibites right here. You have Georgia Robinson's bourbon bonbons next to me! I'm just gonna move my minibites over to the other side of the table...right here next to Clara Dorphman's chess pie...won't that be nice...if she remembers to bring it."

Lucinda stepped to the doorway between her kitchen and the dining room.

"Well, I gotta go! See you, Huey! You think about what I said. An artificial bird would look really cute in that arrangement. Bye, Lucinda! I just love your house!"

Lucinda bit her tongue to keep from saying anything. She did, however, smile graciously one more time.

When Clarence did return to the paper, his breath smelling slightly of olives and martinis, he read the note Avis had written. He sat down and looked over her editorial.

Picking up the page from his desk, he walked to the door of his office and stepped into the work area of the paper.

"Rebecca!"

"Yes, Clarence?"

"We won't be having an editorial this week. Put in one of those cartoons we get from the wire service. If Avis asks, tell her I took care of things."

"Yes, sir."

He stepped back to his desk and wadded Avis's editorial up and tossed it into the trash can beside his desk. In a tight voice that only he could hear, he spit out, "I'm supposed to be excited about a party where I can mingle with the leading rednecks of Sulphur Springs and an editorial that would get us both sued for libel—I should have stayed at the 19th Hole Lounge."

54

"I can't wait to sample that German chocolate cake, Claudette. It looked delicious!"

"Don't worry about that cake, Bonnie, play a card. It's your turn!" Hannah answered instead.

"Oh, relax, Hannah. I know it's my turn."

Bonnie studied the three cards left in her hand. Finally, but only after she heard steam coming from Hanna's ears, she laid down a five of hearts.

"Your turn, Annie!" Hannah barked.

"Okay, but..."

"But what?"

"I don't think you're gonna like it." Annie laid down a ten of hearts and smiled big. "I've kept up with the cards. You don't have a heart higher than a ten, Hannah."

Hannah gleamed real big at Annie. "You're right, Annie, but I do have a trump card! In fact, that's all I have are trumps!" She laid down her remaining cards.

Claudette surveyed the damage. "Annie...looks like we got skunked...again!" She threw in her hand, as did the other two girls.

Annie conceded, "I'll say!"

As Hannah picked up the cards and began to shuffle, Bonnie looked to Claudette. "How about that cake, Claudette?"

"I can do that...this is a recipe that my mother got from the back of a box of Duncan Hines cake mix...I don't know how long ago that must have been...I found it the other day looking for a recipe for cream-cheese pound cake...I had forgotten I had it."

"I'll help you!" Bonnie offered as she got up from her chair and followed Claudette into the kitchen.

Annie turned to Hannah. "Are you still gonna go see the painting...you know, the one Sarah Louise is doing?"

"What other painting would you be talking about, Annie? Of course, I am. I told you I was."

"Yes, but didn't you hear what Claudette said when we got here? She said Sarah Louise is busy, and we shouldn't disturb her."

"So what?"

"I mean, you don't want to make anyone mad, do you?"

"Why not? It won't be the first time I've made someone mad. If somebody doesn't like the way I do things, that's their problem!"

"Oh, Hannah...Claudette's your best friend. You can't make her or her daughter mad!"

"They'll get over it. I'm going to see that painting and see what she's done to my precious Herman. If she has painted him totally...well, if I see...I mean...she better not have done anything to embarrass the Bugleman family!"

While Hannah and Annie discussed the wisdom of dropping in uninvited on Sarah Louise, and while Claudette and Bonnie were cutting the German chocolate cake, Winslow was sitting comfortably in the doorway of the den, his chair halfway in and halfway out of the hallway. No one could get by him unnoticed. He was watching *Throwdown with Bobby Flay*.

"Let me add a little vinegar to this. You wouldn't think that a little vinegar would add to the flavor of this pork barbecue, but it does!" Bobby gushed.

Winslow's mouth watered. He leaned forward to get a better view, but he was too far away from the screen to see how much vinegar Bobby was adding. Without thinking of the consequences, he got up and walked into the den to get a better look.

In the studio, Sarah Louise was almost finished with Jeremy.

While she sketched, she had solved her problem with his flippant attitude by asking about his philosophy professors. All college students like to talk about their professors. If they like them, they will tell you why; and if they don't like them, they will tell you why in great detail.

Since Jeremy didn't really like any of his professors, he had talked nonstop for an hour. All she had to do was make the occasional comment like, "Really?" or "You're kidding!" She had decided not to worry about his legs since the only way he would show them was to strip completely. She would have to use her sketches of Herman's legs. She was almost finished with the young show-off.

Things had gone smoothly.

But Jeremy wasn't finished with her! "You haven't said anything about my tattoo!"

"What would you like me to say, Jeremy? That the number one plastic surgery procedure in America today is tattoo removal?"

He had to smile at her quick comeback. She was clever, he had to admit. Yet Jeremy had another trick up his sleeve. "The design at the top of my arm is yin and yang. I'm sure you know that one. The one on my forearm—it's my newest one—it's a nice Celtic design."

"I like Celtic designs, Jeremy. I love the way they intertwine… but the problem with being an art teacher is there are so many designs that I like. I could never settle on just one or two. If I were to actually waste my money on a tattoo, I'd have to have them all…I'm afraid I would be the tattooed lady of the circus!"

Jeremy laughed, and Sarah Louise laughed at his response.

"I have one more. It's the first tattoo I got. I got it a long time ago, before I turned eighteen, the legal age!"

Sarah Louise pretended to be interested. "What is it? Don't tell me it's a heart with an ex-girlfriend's name!"

"No." He laughed again. "I'll show you."

Sarah Louise had the sketchpad in her lap, and she turned it up to face her and hold it at arm's length so she could get a better look at her last sketch of Jeremy from the back. When she did, she temporarily blocked him from her view.

Sarah Louise was vaguely aware of what Jeremy had just said, "I'll show you." She imagined he would lift his pants' leg to show her a small tattoo on his ankle, maybe a Tweety Bird or a Tasmanian Devil! Teenagers!

What she didn't realize was that the hidden tattoo was on his left cheek—that's *cheek* as in posterior, not facial. On his left buttock was a nice Alfred E. Neuman, the mascot of *Mad* magazine. The tattoo made Jeremy laugh every time he got out of the shower and stood in front of a mirror. He sincerely hoped that, one day, someone of the opposite sex would find it equally amusing. Now was a good time to find out!

Jeremy stepped out of his jeans and boxers and stood, his backside to Sarah Louise, as naked as the day he was born—to paraphrase, Sarah Louise was about to see what the stork saw!

She wasn't the only one!

Walking down the hall toward the studio was Hannah Bugleman followed by a nervous Annie. "Hannah...I don't know...," she said.

Claudette and Bonnie had just walked back into the dining room. "Where's everyone?" Bonnie asked.

Claudette set down the two plates of dessert she was carrying. "Oh, I suppose they are in the den talking to Winslow...peek through the doorway there and call them."

Bonnie peeked. "They're not there!"

Claudette walked across the hall to the den to see for herself. "Winslow!"

"Yes?" He turned from the TV to face her.

"Are Hannah and Annie here?"

"No."

"Winslow…I thought you were guarding the hallway!"

"I was…why?"

"Oh no…," Claudette stammered. She ran to the door and looked down the hallway. She could only see to the turn that led to the studio, but she could hear Annie talking, and it was coming from that direction, "I don't think this is a good idea, Hannah!"

Claudette took off down the hallway. Winslow ran to the doorway, looked at his wife as she made the corner, and started off after her.

Bonnie stood there for a moment, not sure what to do, then decided she would follow the troops and headed down the hallway. She was still holding two dessert plates, each with a slice of German chocolate cake.

Sarah Louise was about to set the sketchpad back down and take a look at Jeremy's tattoo when she heard the door behind her open. She twisted in her seat to face that way and see who was about to enter.

And things had been going so smoothly.

55

It was all very confusing to Alma Peterman. To read the headlines of the paper each morning was to be convinced that our nation—no, our world—was going down the tubes.

If only her Otis were still alive. He could explain everything to her. When she saw men and women marching on TV with signs saying "Gay Pride," she didn't see why being happy was something to protest. Otis had to explain it to her. When men started wearing gold chains around their necks and earrings, it was Otis who made her understand the changing times. Otis explained why there were popular movies about wizards and witches and why skirts kept getting shorter and tighter.

Even when people destroyed buildings in New York City, buildings full of innocent citizens, Otis explained what the culprits meant when they said it was done in the name of religion. Religion, Alma thought, sure wasn't what it used to be.

She was sure that Otis would know what was going on next door. The Upshaws had always been such good neighbors. It was hard to believe that sweet little Sarah Louise was now dealing in drugs. But the proof was right there on her pad of paper. The cars of the Wednesday card players she had recognized, but it was those others—a wrecker, an old pickup truck, and now a motorcycle! She had it documented, all those strange men, at odd hours, coming and going from the back of the Upshaw home.

Maybe it was one of those meth labs she had heard about on the six-o'clock news. Alma decided that people in America needed to take back their streets and make them safe for—she wasn't sure just what—but drug dealers and perverts and terrorists were about to meet their Armageddon because Alma was armed and dangerous.

Grabbing the number seven golf club, Alma Mae Peterman left the security of her kitchen and opened the door to her back porch. She was one her way to the OK Corral!

It was precisely at this moment that Hannah, with her hand on the doorknob to Sarah Louise's studio, heard Claudette yell.

"Oh, Hannah…don't go in there…please…I promised Sarah Louise!"

"I'm going to see that painting, Claudette! Try and stop me!"

Hannah jerked the door open.

Sarah Louise was already looking to the door. Now, hearing someone hollering, she suddenly had a sense of impending disaster.

The door swung open, and Hannah Bugleman looked at Sarah Louise and then let her eyes go past Sarah Louise's shoulder and rest firmly on a portrait of Alfred E. Neuman—on a man's bare rear end!

She screamed.

When she did, Annie, easily frightened anyway, screamed because of the suddenness of Hannah's scream. Claudette arrived at the door just then. She looked in the direction of Hannah's stare, and seeing Jeremy's bare tush, she screamed.

Winslow—running as fast as he did when he played right tackle over forty years ago on the football team of Sulphur Springs High School—ran right into the roadblock caused by the three women, pushing them all three into the studio, kind of like a chain-reaction car accident on icy roads.

Hannah, pushed into the room a couple of feet, panicked at the thought of being so close to a naked man and threw both arms into the air and fainted.

Annie reached for Hannah to catch her, but being smaller, she couldn't hold the now-limp form of the overbearing Hannah. Annie fell back—right into Claudette, who grabbed the falling Annie and, overwhelmed, fell back into the arms of her husband, Winslow, who fell backward, unable to hold up three women at one time.

There was, however, no one to catch him.

Bonnie, the last to arrive, had wisely not tried to catch anyone. She stood back and let the four others collapse in a heap in the doorway. She had her hands full anyway, with the two plates of cake. She looked in the studio, where Jeremy's bottom was still the center of attention.

Now, Bonnie screamed, dropped both plates of cake, and put one hand to her chest and the other one to the wall to steady herself.

Sarah Louise had seen the whole affair in a kind of slow motion. She had been transfixed by the screams and collapse of, first, Hannah, then Annie, then her mother, and then her father, and now the reaction of Bonnie as two plates of German chocolate cake went flying into the air.

Everyone was staring at her—no, they were looking just past her. What were they looking at that had caused such panic and hysteria?

Sarah Louise turned around.

Jeremy, too, had beard the noise and commotion. He turned his head to look behind him, where the noise was coming from, twisting his upper torso to get a better look. It was then that he heard another scream.

It was from Sarah Louise as she realized he was standing butt naked in front of her.

This wasn't quite the reaction he had intended!

He turned to face the others, not to further expose himself but to reach for his jeans, the ones be had just stepped out of. He picked them up and held them modestly in front of him, with his exposed rear now facing the studio door to the outside.

And there was another scream—more anger than fright or surprise yet very intense. This scream came from the door of the studio. Jeremy spun around.

Alma Mae Peterman stood there, with a raised number seven golf club in one hand and a pair of binoculars in the other. She was approaching him with killer instinct.

Jeremy screamed. He stood paralyzed, his only thought, *What nuthouse have all these people escaped from?*

And to think it had all been going so smoothly, just like Claudette said it would.

56

"Yoohoo, Lucinda! It's me!"

In the kitchen, Lucinda cringed, much the way a person does when someone scrapes their fingernails across a chalkboard. Then she heard the patter of footsteps down her hallway.

"Oh, there you are! I didn't knock because I knew you were expecting us!" Avis beamed.

Lucinda gave that smile she had perfected earlier in the day. "Certainly, Avis! What is a doorbell for between friends?"

"Can I be of any help? It looks like you've got your hands full."

A look around the kitchen revealed Saran-wrapped plates of assorted finger foods and sweets. Lucinda was having to deal with which ones to keep refrigerated, which ones to put in the oven to warm up, and which ones could go out on the table in the dining room now.

"Yes, you can, Avis. You can start by rinsing off these grapes in the sink here…" Lucinda stopped because she was suddenly aware of Clarence standing there with a look on his face that said anything but, *Howdy, I'm so glad to be here!* "Clarence, B J is out on the patio by the pool. I bet he could use some help…he's getting the drinks ready."

Drinks? That was all the motivation Clarence needed. He didn't ask what direction to go; he simply trusted his instincts to get him there, and he left the two women alone.

Lucinda turned back to Avis. "The grapes go on that fruit tray on the counter, and then we have to cut up the apples…"

And somewhere in the next few minutes, she would have to work it into their conversation that Avis was not to mention to anyone at the party their tête-à têtes over the last few days or the explosive editorial Avis had promised. It would take a little cunning and subterfuge—but Lucinda was getting good at that.

Out by the pool, BJ was pouring another bag of ice from the Quick Mart into an oversized ice bucket made from the bottom third of a Jack Daniels whiskey barrel. He looked up when Clarence walked through the double French doors from the den.

"Hey, Clarence! Good to see another man here."

Clarence didn't waste any time with small talk. He cut to the chase. "What you got to drink?"

BJ, whose taste ran from Bud regular to Bud Light, turned and pointed to an assortment of beverages he had arranged on the bar behind him. The bar was, appropriately, made from barnwood, supported by two more old whiskey barrels.

"I have your basic brews here: Bud, Coors, Sam Adams, Michelob, Miller—name your poison!"

"That all you have?"

BJ was a little taken back. What else could you possibly want? But he did have more, for Lucinda had coached him on the tastes of the Art Guild women. He pointed to a cloth-covered card table. There—beside the obligatory Coke, Pepsi, and Sprite—was an array of bottles with cute labels.

"I have wine in brown bottles, wine in green bottles, wine in yellow bottles, and wine in clear bottles."

To BJ, there was a difference in wines based on the color of the bottles. He didn't touch the stuff. Men—real men, that is—drink beer, and that was as far as his liquor education had ever gotten.

"You don't have anything stronger?"

BJ thought for a moment. "I think I have a little tequila in the pantry, left over from the Super Bowl."

Clarence smiled. "Now you're talking!"

In the kitchen, Avis had proven to be a big help. Not that she was particularly gifted in kitchen skills but because she took directions so well. If asked to slice, dice, mash, or blend, she did as asked. It was how Avis had learned to operate over the years: do as you are told, and there are fewer arguments, fewer frustrations.

She and Lucinda worked well together for the half hour they had alone till a few more members of the guild arrived to help. Then there were the people who always arrived early at any gathering, and they too poured into the kitchen and dining room.

Most members of the Art Guild were women, Huey being the most obvious exception. Artists are not limited to the female gender, but joining art guilds seemed to be. Yet the women had husbands, and as the men arrived, they were directed to the patio by the pool.

Clarence hadn't offered any help to BJ other than to help him empty the bottle of tequila. That didn't bother BJ any. A man is always more comfortable with another man around, even if he just watches him work.

By the time the party officially began at 6:00 p.m.—not that a trumpet blew or a bell rang—people were scattered across Lucinda and BJ's home.

Lucinda had abandoned the kitchen to mingle, and people were snacking and talking. Even in small towns, people will turn to one another and say, "What have you been up to? I haven't seen you in ages!" There was talk of recent operations, trips to Florida over the winter, new cars, new grandchildren, "How much did you pay for that dress?" and, "You must try the pigs-in-a-blanket I brought tonight."

At least, that was the talk of the women.

Out on the patio, by the pool, the men carried on entirely different conversations. To them, it ran to, "How about those Braves?" "Been fishing yet?" "Who you gonna vote for in the mayor's race, the councilmen's races, the tax assessors' race, the sheriffs' race?" "Have you had any luck with Rogain?" "Did you hear the one about the traveling salesman and the..."

Both groups had their small talk. Both groups had their social circles.

Mrs. Biederman was sitting on the couch in the living room, talking to Mrs. Moore, the doctor's wife. Mrs. Newman, wife of the circuit court judge, had—upon entering the room—gone straight to the two women to visit.

Huey and Malvenna were huddled by the fireplace in the den. It was a two-fireplace home because they also had one in the master bedroom. They had grabbed Lois Womack and Jessica Sims and were talking about Lucinda's choice of paint color for the den walls.

Several older women were standing by the dining-room table with Clara Dorphman, admiring the cut glass bowls and silver trays.

And so on. Everyone had a little group of people they were comfortable with. Except Avis, who went from group to group, testing the waters.

The men were no different.

The judge and the lawyer and the doctor somehow managed to find one other. Businessmen like Michael Dorphman were talking to other businessmen. Malvenna's husband, Booger, the backhoe driver, was talking shop to two men in the construction business.

By the pool, BJ manned the bar.

Clarence stood close by, if only because BJ had command of the bottle of tequila. But the two men carried on a little conversation, even if Clarence's end of the conversation ran from snide remarks to outright character assassination. As they talked and Clarence's speech got a little slurred, Travis Morgan walked up.

Travis was new to town. He had made a substantial investment in the chicken business, raising chicks into "fryers." He had purchased a large farm east of town and had built rows and rows of chicken houses.

Anxious to "belong," Travis and his wife, Stacey, had joined every organization that fell their way: Rotary, the Baptist Church, the Chamber of Commerce, the PTA. Stacy did a little watercolor, so it was she who had joined the Art Guild.

BJ knew Travis well because everything Travis had done, business-wise, had been financed through the bank where he was a loan officer. "Hey, Travis!"

"BJ! I see your wife has put you to work."

"I'd rather be in front of the TV...the Braves are playing the Cubs."

"Yeah, I hated to miss that game too, but I'll catch it later on TiVo." Travis noticed the glum-looking man standing beside BJ. Anxious to know everyone—it was good for business—he extended his right hand. "I don't believe we've met. I'm Travis Morgan. I own the River Bend Poultry Ranch, east of here."

BJ realized his lack of etiquette and jumped in, "Excuse me, Travis. I should have introduced you. This is Clarence Lipowitz. He and his wife, Avis, have our local newspaper, the *Sulphur Springs Sentinel*."

Clarence didn't show a lot of enthusiasm, but he did extend his hand, and the two men shook.

"So how's business, Travis?" BJ was quick to ask.

"I'm sending five hundred fryers a week to a processing plant near Paducah."

"Wow," said BJ, trying to make up for Clarence's lack of interest, "that's a lot of hot wings!"

"Yeah, I'd like to have someone build a processing plant closer. I drive the truck myself, every Saturday. But it's a bigger investment, and no matter where you put one, the neighbors complain. They all want their fried chicken, but no one wants a chicken chop shop in their backyard!"

Clarence, for some reason, found that funny and laughed. BJ, glad to see Clarence do something besides smirk at everyone and everything, laughed too. And Travis, wanting to be a part of his new home, took it as a sign that he was being accepted in this tight little community, and he laughed.

If Clarence and Travis only knew what strange ways their lives would intertwine before the week was over, they would neither one be laughing.

57

Alma took the last bite of German chocolate cake from her plate and swallowed it. She laid her fork down and smiled nervously. "You're sure that young man is going to be all right?"

Claudette reached over and patted the older woman on the shoulder. "Yes, Miss Alma...I'm sure...the bump on his head went right down with the ice pack...Winslow offered to drive him back to school...but he said he was okay...he's gone now anyway." Claudette took her glasses off and used the edge of her tablecloth to clean them.

"Besides, Miss Alma," Sarah Louise interjected, "he was laughing... afterward, I mean...when we got Hannah revived and—"

"When he was sure you no longer had that number seven golf club in your hand! Where did you get that club, Alma?" Winslow said, trying to change the conversation.

"Otis played golf for a few years...after the war...World War II. My son-inlaw says those clubs are antiques and worth something. Said I should take them to the *Antiques Roadshow* the next time they come to Nashville or Louisville."

Winslow was impressed by the age of the old number seven club, not as impressed as he was by the way Alma had swung the club herself, but he decided not to comment on that.

"And he wasn't too upset? I mean, he understands why I called him a pervert just before I...I conked him good?"

"Yes, he understood. He just didn't think little old ladies could pack such a wallop, but we explained it all...when he came to."

"And Hannah's going to be all right?"

"Oh, Hannah...that's not the first time I've seen her faint... but she fainted before you even entered the studio...I guess the sight of that young man's...," Claudette hesitated, not sure whether to say *butt, posterior, rear end, buttock, tush, hienie...*

"Now, who did you say that man was again? The man on that poor boy's butt?" Alma had no trouble saying it.

"Alfred E. Neuman...he's from a magazine."

"There was an Alfred somebody that ran for president once, but this wasn't him?"

"No, Alma...it was just a silly cartoon face...young men today...tattoos...it's a fad, I guess."

"I thought Hula-Hoops were a fad, Claudette...but tattoos of faces on a person's butt? I guess I'm glad my Otis is not around to see this..." Then, as if the thought had just occurred to her, said, "You don't have a tattoo of someone's face on your butt, do you, Winslow?"

Winslow had to laugh, and soon all four of them were laughing.

"Now that you've finished your cake, what you say, Alma, that I walk you back over to your house?"

"Oh, Winslow, you don't have to do that. I've caused enough trouble for you all."

"I insist, Alma!"

"Please, Miss Alma...we should have called and let you know about Sarah Louise's painting...and all her models...and, well... anyway...we'll do better next time...you go home and get a good night's sleep!"

"Yes, Claudette, a good night's sleep. And, Winslow, I need my golf club back. I do sleep better if I know it's beside the bed."

"I'll go get it, Pop...it's still down in my studio... I put it in the closet."

In a few minutes, Alma Mae Peterman had her golf club and was safely back home; and Winslow was back in the family's kitchen, where his wife and daughter were washing dessert dishes. Winslow plopped himself down in one of the chairs at the kitchen table.

"I think making her sit here with us and finishing that piece of cake was a capital idea, Claudette!"

"Yes, Mother, one of your better ideas."

Claudette received their compliments and responded, "I sent a big piece home with Hannah."

"That crazy Hannah! If she had just left well enough alone! And if I hadn't left my place in the hallway!"

Sarah Louise sat down heavily on the chair beside her father.

"Let's face it, folks...If I hadn't decided to go ahead and do a crazy painting called *A Room Full of Naked Men*, if I had just swallowed my pride and called that Lucinda Hardin-Powell and explained—"

Claudette interrupted, "Don't blame yourself, Sarah Louise... we all know whose fault it is...mine...me and my big mouth..."

Winslow spoke up before Claudette and Sarah Louise beat each other and themselves up trying to place blame. "Hey, you two! It is funny! At least, it will be a week from now. My mom used to always say to me, when I was a kid and I was worried about something, she'd say, 'A week from now, you'll have forgotten all about it!'"

"If only, Winslow!"

"No, I mean it. One day...all right, maybe not next week...but one day, we'll look back at this and laugh! And it could have been worse! Alma only knocked Jeremy out. She could have cracked his skull, and we'd have a murder on our hands!"

"Murder! Oh, Pop…don't say that!"

"Yes, a murder! And Hannah could have hit her head when she fell. It could have been a double murder!"

"Winslow…if you think that is making us feel any better…"

"Look, all we've lost is two broken cake plates. Everyone went home happy…well, mostly happy."

"You're right, Pop…it could have been worse. Jeremy was laughing when he left."

Claudette added, "I hope he was happy…I doubled what I was going to pay him…and I made him promise that he wasn't going to sue anyone!"

"Just how much did you pay him, Claudette?"

"Don't worry, Winslow…I used my butter and egg money… it's all said and done!"

Sarah Louise picked up where she had left off. "So that's Jeremy! And Hannah was happy enough with the painting. She thought Herman looked very masculine standing there looking out the window. Bonnie was the only one who left here sad."

"I told her I have plenty of those dessert plates…not to worry… but that's Bonnie…let me fix everyone an egg-salad sandwich… we haven't had supper yet…and I don't feel like cooking!"

"That's fine with me, Mother. I'm not real hungry after that cake, and then I'll go back to my studio. I've got to start painting Jeremy into the canvas. Maybe nothing else exciting will happen in Sulphur Springs tonight!"

And then again, maybe not.

58

"Look at that Lucinda over there, showing off her tole tray to crazy old Clara Dorphman! The only reason she decorates her home is so people will think she has an interesting life!"

"What do you mean, Huey?"

"Well, Malvenna Sweetie, look over there by that piano, which I bet no one in this home can play. She has that shelf with a metal reproduction of the Eiffel Tower and a framed menu from a French restaurant and a pair of cheap wineglasses."

"So?"

"So, toots, she ain't been to Paris! She just wants people to think so!"

"You sure, Huey?"

"I know for a fact she's never been past Scottsboro!"

"Oh, Huey…you must make this stuff uplft."

While Huey and Malvenna discussed the hostess for the evening, the host was still busy on the patio dispensing drinks.

Clarence continued to stand by him, although the contents of the bottle of tequila were long gone, and he only clutched a glass of faintly tequila-flavored ice. Clarence was enjoying his perspective—standing where he was, just a few feet from the deep end of the pool and out of the glare of the backyard security light, from there he could see everyone on the patio, even if most of them couldn't see him.

There is an old saying that if you can't say something nice, you should at least have the decency to be vague. Clarence had no such decency. With his lips well greased by liquid libation, he nimbly skewed first one person and then another. Fortunately, only BJ got to hear the tart tongue.

After Joseph McGill, a local attorney, left the bar, Clarence leaned over to BJ's ear. "BJ, you know the difference between a lawyer and a catfish?"

"No, Clarence, I don't."

"One's a bottom-feeding, scum-sucking, slimy creature—the other is a fish."

BJ didn't laugh immediately because it took him a while to get it, but that didn't stop Clarence, who enjoyed laughing at his own wit. That was no worse than what Clarence said of the town mayor: "If he were any more stupid, he would have to be watered twice a day."

BJ had gotten that one and had laughed appropriately.

Like a shark drawn to the smell of blood, anytime BJ laughed at what Clarence said, the wit got nastier and more frequent. Clarence, his inhibitions loosened by the tequila, was on a roll.

"Is that Harper Bailey over there, BJ? The president of Heritage Savings and Loan?"

"The heavyset man talking to Travis?"

"Yeah, the fat guy! I've played a few rounds of golf with him. You know what, BJ, if you stand real close to him, you can hear the ocean!"

That was a zinger, although it took BJ half a minute to get it. Since Harper Bailey was a competitor in the banking and loan business, BJ laughed so hard he had to take another drink from his third beer, or was it his fourth?

About this time, Lucinda walked up with a plate of bite-size foods from the dining room. "BJ, honey, I brought you a little something."

Still laughing, he replied, "Thanks, Cindy-poo, but I'm not hungry!"

Cindy-poo, that was the name BJ used for his wife when he wanted to be cute or perhaps romantic. He never used that name in public—unless he had had too much to drink.

Lucinda eyed him funny. "Eat, BJ." She shoved the plate of tuna in a tart shell, pecan minibites, sausage cheese balls, and stuffed mushrooms in his face. "Eat, BJ—now!"

Her tone of voice sobered him as much as the food would. BJ knew better than to drink on an empty stomach. He also knew, from the look in Lucinda's eyes, that he was going to regret his indiscretion.

As BJ munched frantically, Clarence wisely stepped from behind the bar and sidestepped in the direction of the pool. If it had been Avis, he would have acted differently; but the wrath of other men's wives, he avoided.

He stopped a few feet away from BJ and Lucinda and turned to look around. Maybe someone else would appreciate his cutting insight. Two feet to his left, three businessmen were talking. Clarence recognized them, or at least thought he did. His eyes were getting a little blurry. He ambled over to them.

The closest of the three was Charlie Simpson, the manager of the new super-Walmart. He knew Clarence because the paper did their advertizing. "Hey, Clarence, how's it going?"

Clarence shrugged his shoulders.

"Clarence, I guess you know Richie Vance here, from the Ford dealership, and Michael Dorphman, from Dorphman's Appliance and Hardware?"

Clarence looked at both men and nodded slightly to each as a way of acknowledging their presence. He could have extended his right hand and shaken theirs, but he was still clutching his glass of ice, which now only remotely tasted of watered-down tequila.

"Richie was just telling us that he heard someone wanted to put a pizza place where the old Shell station is."

Clarence wasn't impressed with this bit of news. "So?"

"That's good news, Clarence. That's the old gas station next to City Park. It's the place the Art Guild wants to tear down as their beautification project this year!"

Clarence responded, "We must make Sulphur Springs presentable in case anyone with taste should happen to visit!"

The three men looked at Clarence, not sure if they should laugh or be offended.

"Actually, it is a good thing, Clarence. The old gas station is an eyesore. The city took it over for back taxes, and it has just set there. If the Art Guild will clear the property, and if a pizza place wants to build there…for one thing, it would"—Charlie paused to choose his words carefully—"make our town a little more presentable."

Charlie had chosen his words carefully because he was aware that Clarence, by virtue of his position with the paper, was someone to keep on your good side. But he was also aware, from Clarence's glassy stare, that the latter had been drinking too much.

So it was the age old question: do you humor an old drunk or walk off and leave them to their own company? Charlie was being gracious.

Clarence mumbled in response, "Oh yes, the Art Guild beautification project…the Art Guild…that's why we're all here tonight! Look around you, guys. This is Sulphur Springs's high society, and we are honored just to be here!"

There was something snide in his tone of voice that got under Michael Dorphman's skin. He didn't have a particular opinion of Clarence Lipowitz, one way or the other. His business dealings with him had been that, strictly business. But to hear him put down his hometown, even if it was the booze talking, irritated Michael.

Richie spoke up, trying to put a more pleasant spin on things. "My wife, Kristie, has three photographs to enter in the art show Saturday."

Michael turned his attention from Clarence to Richie. "What's she got pictures of, Richie?"

"One of that last snowfall we had and two close-ups of flowers from our garden last summer."

"My wife has a cross-stitch and a patchwork quilt," Charlie responded.

Clarence didn't like that the conversation was going without him. "What? Nothing controversial?"

Charlie looked at him, "Controversial?"

"Don't you keep up with the local gossip mill, Charles? Little ole Sulphur Springs has a real controversy abrewing. In our little town where people are so narrow they can look through a keyhole with both eyes, we have a controversy!"

Michael stiffened. No one, since he had arrived at the kickoff party, had mentioned Sarah Louise's painting. He felt strangely defensive.

"I haven't heard of any controversy." It was Richie, who was equally ignorant.

"Then you don't know about the art teacher at the high school and her X-rated painting? I believe it's called *A Room Full of Naked Men!*"

Charlie and Richie looked at each other in surprise.

Yet Clarence wasn't through. "But what can you expect, gentlemen, from"—he leaned forward, and his voice got a little lower, as if he were about to impart a secret—"from the local slut."

It wasn't that he really thought Sarah Louise was a slut, or a tramp, or a woman of loose virtue; it was simply that he felt the need to trash anyone and everyone. Not that it mattered why he said it—only that he had said it—because before he straightened back up, he felt the hard fist of Michael Dorphman hit his large New Jersey nose; and the force of the blow made him reel backwards.

Inside, by the double French doors that led outside, Huey just happened to glance out to the patio. He squealed in delight, "Oh, Malvenna, baby, this party is finally going somewhere. People are jumping into the pool!"

59

Lucy Pendergrass was on a creative roll. In her attempt to paint the winning entry in the Art Guild's Spring Fling, she was tossing convention to the side. The first rule of general propriety to go had been the decision to paint a nude woman. Having heard that Sarah Louise Upshaw was doing a painting called *A Room Full of Naked Men*, she had decided that she was just as capable as the high school art teacher, and she too would paint someone naked.

She had always leaned toward the Greek ideal—hence, her previous painting of the Venus de Milo with arms, arms that were discretely folded in front of her so that her modesty was preserved. But to make an impression on the judges in this year's art show, she had decided to go in an entirely different direction.

So it was that the large painting in front of her now was an African Zulu queen. In one hand, the Amazon-like woman held a spear, and the other hand rested upon the head of a slightly cross-eyed spotted leopard.

The woman stood tall and proud, except for the fact that she, like the leopard, was a little cross-eyed.

There was no garment about the Zulu woman's chest. She was as topless as a *Playboy* magazine centerfold. If Lucy Pendergrass wanted the judges' attention—she had them with the ample bosom on display.

Farther down, Lucy had painted the briefest of skirts about her waist. It was the short skirt that now took Lucy's attention and her creativity to task.

Cutting up bits of the leather she had gotten from Michael Dorphman, she layered paint and leather until the two were one. The viewer couldn't tell where the leather left off and the painted leather began. It is a technique called *collage*. The effect was three-dimensional.

But Lucy wasn't through. She now added strings of leather, beads, and feathers.

She stood back and admired her handiwork. "Genius!" she said out loud, obviously pleased with the effect.

Then, as she was prone to do in every aspect of her life, she went overboard. She grabbed the paintbrush and—taking more leather strips, more beads, and more feathers—she put a three-dimensional necklace around the black maiden's neck. Next, she attached a similar piece to the end of the spear and finally a collar around the spotted leopard's neck.

Once again, she stood back and admired her work; and once again, she mouthed, "Genius!"

Not content to take in the masterpiece alone, she stepped to the door of the studio and hollered out to her sister, "Calpurnia, get up here this minute! You must see this!"

While Lucy Pendergrass awaited her sister, Sarah Louise was also in a painting frenzy.

This was Thursday, and tomorrow afternoon, she had to deliver her finished painting. Her schedule was tight Now she was painting the face of her tattooed exhibitionist, Jeremy, onto the canvas. Oddly enough, the model who had revealed the most was the most covered up on the canvas. By placing him behind the vase of fuchsia flowers, only his head and shoulders were visible. Another pot of flowers at his feet covered up his legs, which were really Herman's legs anyway.

Sarah Louise had left off Jeremy's tattoos and ponytail. She had also added a few lines to his face so that he didn't look quite so young. It was bad enough she was painting herself in a room full of naked men. She didn't want to appear to be robbing the cradle on top of that!

She painted fast yet accurately; and now, still early in the day, she was almost finished with this, her fourth model. Taking a break, she sat down on her overstuffed chair and tried to breathe slowly and deeply. She had seen on one of those TV self-help features where breathing like that would lake away stress. *Ha!* she thought. *It's not working!*

Stress!

There are all kinds of stress in a person's life. The stress from the struggle for survival is, for most people, mitigated by the comforts and security of modern living. That is, we don't have to worry about a saber-toothed tiger attacking us on our way to the mailbox.

Then there is the stress that comes from family and friends. Dysfunctional families are textbook examples of this kind of stress. It is what makes people run away from home or at least move three states away the first chance they get.

There is financial stress. Everyone worries about money to some extent. Even rich people worry, perhaps not to the same degree as the working poor, but they worry nevertheless. Just knowing that at the end of each month we still have a dollar or two in our checking account keeps that stress in control for most of us.

Sarah Louise wasn't suffering from any of those types of stress. Her stress would be classified as the "train-schedule" stress. The train leaves at 6:00 p.m., and you're afraid you will miss the departure. It's the kind of stress that makes you wake up in the middle of the night from a dreadful dream, a dream where you find yourself in a hurry and in a giant parking lot, but you can't find your car—or even your car keys!

Sarah Louise's train was leaving at 5:00 p.m. on Friday. That was when she had to have a completed painting done and handed over to Baby Huey, who would be standing in the gym of the old Sulphur Springs High School underneath a huge sign with big letters spelling out, "Tenth Annual Spring Fling Art Show and Antique Auction to Benefit the Art Guild's Town-Beautification Project."

It would be nice to miss that train, she thought; but after having gone through so much, after involving so many people, after gunshots, stray dogs, crazy neighbors, people fainting, cracked skulls, and broken dessert plates—she had to go through with it.

The problem wasn't that Sarah Louise couldn't paint. It was that her canvas was missing the fifth man. The vacant spot on the couch was to be Sarah Louise's model. She had told her mother that she would get the fifth model, if Claudette would get the other four.

Sarah Louise had fully intended to ask someone to pose, but everything was happening at such a frantic pace, she hadn't had time to go look for someone. And now, here she sat, and the only person she could think of was Baby Huey!

Laying her brush down, she closed her eyes and tried to breathe deep and slowly. But it wasn't working. Her mind kept darting from one thought to another and, in between, kept picturing Huey standing bare-chested in her studio.

There is power in prayer, or at least every church in America operates on that principle. Sarah Louise guiltily felt the need to pray for a solution to her problem. Then again, should a person pray to the Lord for a man to pose half naked when people were starving in some third-world country and really needed prayers?

So not able to cross the threshold of faith for something so trivial, she sat there and breathed deeply.

It was when she had counted to seventy-five—breaths, that is—that one of the cats jumped onto her lap. Opening her eyes, she reached to pet it when she noticed that it was staring toward the window. There was someone standing at the door of her studio, about to knock.

It was Michael Dorphman, and his first words to her, after she answered the door, were, "I hope I'm not bothering you, Sarah Louise, but may I come in for just a moment? I have something I need to tell you...before you hear it from someone else!"

She politely invited him in and asked him to sit down on the couch, but in her head, she was trying to imagine what he might possibly have to tell her...before someone else did? As she sat down beside him, she could feel stress from her toes to the top of her head. *Breathe, slow and deep*, she told herself; and she braced herself for what had to be, she reasoned, really bad news.

Michael didn't exchange pleasantries or comment on the weather. He went straight to the matter at hand. "Sarah Louise, last night at the kickoff party for the Art Guild, I punched a man in the nose because of a crude comment he made...he made it about you and your painting...I don't think I helped the situation any...except that the man I punched was too drunk to remember what he had said to get his nose busted, and maybe that will help...but I shouldn't have lost my temper like that. Oh, I'm not sorry I punched him, but I don't want you to think I'm a violent person.

"I guess I was afraid you would hear that a drunken brawl had taken place and that I was in the middle of it...and...well, I don't want you to think bad of me... I don't want you to think I am a drunk and a ...a brawler..."

Sarah Louise's eyes were as wide as saucers. She was... speechless. But then the strangest thing happened—she began to laugh. Michael's eyes now grew wide. He was taken off guard by her reaction. Then, strangely, he began to laugh too. Soon they were both clutching their sides, unable to speak and breathless.

Finally, Sarah Louise took a deep breath and held it long enough to stop giggling. "Oh, Michael…I would never think you were a drunk and a…a brawler…I remember you from high school…from the swim team. I've seen how nice you treat your grandmother…you're the last person I could think bad of."

"Really?"

"Really. But tell me, why and who did you punch? And it was all because of me?"

60

M ichael Dorphman had been right when he told Sarah
Louise he was afraid she would hear about the punch in
the nose from someone else. To be honest, the news had been
circulating around Sulphur Springs all morning.

It went something like this:

"Good morning to all of our listeners out there in Sulphur
Springs. It's eight o'clock, Thursday, the thirty-first day of March.
Tomorrow is April 1—April Fool's Day."

"That's right, Ted. So if you haven't made plans to fool someone
tomorrow, this is a reminder! On tomorrow's *Ted and Sherry in
the Morning*, we'll have a list of the ten best all-time April Fool's
Day stunts."

"Sherry, that sounds interesting. We have lots of local and
national news, and it looks like a big weekend ahead!"

"You're so right, Ted. This weekend, we have the Tenth Annual
Spring Fling Art Show and Antique Auction to Benefit the Art
Guild's Town-Beautification Project. And we'll be doing a live
broadcast from the show, which I hear is expecting a large crowd."

"Sherry, as I recall from our interview with Lucinda Hardin-
Powell on last Friday's show, the Art Guild was going to have

their kickoff party last night, so I guess all the members of the guild are now in combat gear for this weekend."

"I bet they are! After their kickoff party comes the hard work of getting the gym ready and setting their displays up! And, Ted, I've heard from Calpurnia Pendergrass at the Chamber office that a TV crew will be here from Hopkinsville to cover the event. But right now, we will switch to our CBS News Radio headquarters in New York for this morning's world and national news…"

That word sparked conversation downtown at Pearl's Beauty Shoppe.

"News—I have some news, Pearl!"

Pearl looked up from the sink, where she was washing out several combs and brushes. She turned the radio down a notch. "Kinda early for news, isn't it, Charlene? We haven't had any customers yet."

"I got this off the phone from Miss Ruby. She called me at seven this morning. She knows I'm up by then, and she couldn't wait to tell me."

"Ruby Stafford?"

"Yep, Ruby Stafford!"

"Well, tell me, Charlene. Don't hold it in—it's not good for your digestion!"

"It's about that kickoff party they was just a talking about on the radio…that there Art Guild party."

"What about it?"

"Ruby says her niece belongs to the Art Guild, and she went to that there party, and she told Miss Ruby it wasn't nothing but a bunch of drunks pushing each other in a *swimming pool!*"

It was those exact two words that were being spoken at that same moment at the old Dorphman home across town.

"Swimming pool," Clara Dorphman said it half out loud.

"What's that, Miss Clara?"

But Clara was a bit fuzzy on why the image of a swimming pool kept entering her head. "Oh, nothing, Ester Mae, I was just thinking to myself...did you already put the butter up?"

"Yes, ma'am. Michael done told you that you had enough butter on yore toast."

"Did he? I guess he did. He came and left in such a hurry. He told you how nice our party was last night...the kickoff party?"

"He did, Miss Clara. He said you both left a little early...he didn't say why."

Suddenly it clicked for Clara. "The swimming pool!"

"There you go, talking to yoreself again, Miss Clara!"

"I remember now, Ester Mae. Michael said someone fell in the swimming pool at Lucinda's last night. I was in the living room, and there was some kind of commotion. Then Michael walked in and told me we needed to go. And I asked him why because the party wasn't over yet, and he said someone had fallen in the pool—how silly. But he wouldn't let me go look. I think that's what the commotion was...it was everyone else wanting to look."

"Sounds like you folks done had a wild party. That's what them Hollywood folks do. They have parties, and they start pushing each other in the pool. Good thing Michael done got you outta there, Miss Clara...I think you'uns had you a wild party!"

A half mile away, that sentiment was being repeated. "A wild party! That's what I heard!"

"That so?"

"Yep, Hubcap. I heard it was a drunken brawl, and you know what else I heard?"

"No, I don't, Duffy, but I reckon you're gonna tell me!"

"Sure am. I heard that everyone there ended up in the pool... clothes and all."

"I didn't know that BJ and Lucinda had a pool big enough for all the Art Guild. I've seen some of those Art Guild people—they're big! Musta been packed in there like sardines, Duffy."

"I guess since they was all drunk, it didn't matter how close they were!"

It was difficult for Hubcap to keep up his end of the conversation because he was on his back under the rear end of a '62 Cadillac. ""Duffy, 'stead of running your mouth, do something useful, like hand me that one-half-inch hex wrench—there, by your foot!"

"Sure thing, Hubcap...but the only thing about it, I don't know why I never get invited to any parties like that!"

"You 'n' me, we don't belong to that country-club set. Them folks want me to fix their car, and you to make parts for their air-conditioner, but they don't want us to sit on their sofa in their living room—or even jump into their swimming pool, Duffy!"

"All the same. I wish I coulda been there..."

<hr />

Elsewhere in Sulphur Springs, that same phrase was being spoken.

"I wish I coulda been there...they say that two people almost drown, that they had to pull BJ's wife, Lucinda, outta the pool and do CPR on her!"

"Lucinda? Why, that would have been a sight to see. Where did you hear all this, Cam Tang? Did you go to the party?"

"No, Preacher Armstrong...but I hear it exactly from the horse's mouth...that right?"

"That's right, Cam, except that we usually say *straight* from the horse's mouth."

"Crazy language, English!"

"So who was the horse's—I mean, who did you hear tell about it, the party and the pool and all?"

"Mr. Biederman. He always get a dozen glazed to go every morning to take to work with him. Him good customer at

Danny's Donut Den. He tell Coach Hatton all 'bout it. Coach on way to golf course. Coach Hatton laugh a lot. I think maybe he laugh to think BJ's wife, Lucinda, need CPR."

<hr />

Lucinda's fate was being discussed by others this morning. "Lucinda need CPR?"

Huey laughed.

"Was she hurt, Huey Eugene? I heard she almost drowned!"

It was Alma Peterman doing the asking. She had already been called twice by people and decided to call someone who would know the whole story.

"She didn't almost drown…let me tell you how it happened, sweetheart. Someone pushed Clarence Lipowitz in the pool. When I saw that, I said out loud so everybody could hear, I said, 'This party is finally going somewhere. People are jumping into the pool!' I didn't know who it was at first, just that somebody was in the pool. So everyone rushed outside to see, and there was Lucinda standing at the edge of the pool, yelling at BJ to get Clarence out before he drowned!"

"Why was Clarence in the pool, Huey? I heard he was drunk!"

"Hon, he and BJ had done polished off a bottle of tequila all by their lonesomes! Two people saw them passing the bottle back and forth. Well, Clarence was standing with Michael Dorphman and Charlie Simpson and somebody else, and they say Clarence said something smart about Clara Dorphman or about the Art Guild. And Michael—he's Clara's grandson, you know—well, he just punched Clarence in the nose, and Clarence fell back into the pool. That's when Lucinda ran over to the edge of the pool and started hollering for BJ to jump in and save Clarence."

"What did BJ do?"

"He jumped in, Miss Alma—he jumps when Lucinda tells him to jump!"

"How did Lucinda end up in the pool?"

"Let me get to that. I was right behind her, and she was leaning over, trying to grab Clarence and help pull him out... and...well"—Huey paused as if not sure what to say next—"I guess she just lost her balance!"

"But, Huey Eugene, I heard you were in the pool too!"

"Just let me finish, poopsie. BJ let go of Clarence and went after Lucinda, and they were all three just splashing around. It looked like so much fun that I couldn't help myself. I yelled, 'Cannonball!' and jumped right in!"

"You didn't!"

"Yes, toots, I sure did. It was the best cannonball dive I ever did, splashed half the water outta that pool—that's why everyone at the party was soaking wet!"

That subject too was being discussed in town and, in this case, at the scene of the previous evening's fiasco.

"Soaking wet—this carpet is still soaking wet!"

"You want me to go by the hardware store, Lucinda, and rent one of those rug cleaners? You know, the ones that suck up water... they have them at Dorphman's Hardware and Appliance."

"Dorphman—don't mention that name in my house, BJ! If Michael Dorphman hadn't clobbered Clarence in the first place, none of this would have happened."

"Tell me what to do, Lucinda. I'm late for work already, and I've got a splitting headache to boot!" BJ's voice sounded recalcitrant.

Lucinda looked at the wet carpet. "I'll put some more towels on it and leave the patio doors open...and I'll get BJ Jr. to look in the garage for a window fan."

"That sounds like a good idea...a fan will help it to dry faster." BJ looked dejected, and it was plain to see that he felt somehow responsible for the evening's dramatic end. "Want me to take your dress to the dry cleaners?"

"The dry cleaners won't do any good—my dress is ruined! It was getting a little tight anyway...but I oughta make Huey buy me another one!"

"Huey?"

"Yes, Huey Eugene Pugh!"

"But, Lucinda, you were already soaking wet and in the pool when he jumped in and splashed everyone!"

"BJ...you didn't see what happened. I was leaning over the edge of the pool, reaching for Clarence, and Huey came up behind me, laughing and carrying on. And then everyone else was standing there, and just as I got a hold of Clarence's hand, somebody pushed me in—and, BJ, I am sure as I am standing here that it was that Huey Eugene Pugh!"

Lucinda wasn't the only person in town thinking about Huey.

"Huey Eugene Pugh. He was the one that got everyone wet—when he did a big ole cannonball dive."

Julie began to laugh at the memory of it.

Edward and Jennifer both laughed at the thought of three hundred pounds of Huey doing a cannonball dive into Lucinda and BJ's pool.

"But you don't belong to the Art Guild, Julie!"

"No, my mom does. She couldn't get my dad to go with her, so I went. I told her that if all their parties were this much fun, I wanted to go to the next one. She didn't think that was funny."

The three staffers of the *Sulphur Springs Sentinel* were goofing off because Avis hadn't come to work yet. This week's issue of the paper had been delivered from the printer an hour earlier and was stacked in several piles by the front door. Edward would have to start deliveries to all the stores in town soon, and the girls would have to address the local subscriptions and get them to the post office by noon. But since their boss wasn't there to crack the whip, they were taking their time.

"I bet Clarence doesn't show up for work today!"

"He doesn't show up most Thursdays anyway, not if the weather's nice and he can go to the golf course...I wish he would show up, though."

"Why's that, Jennifer?"

"Avis wrote an editorial about the Spring Fling, and he cut it. I have a feeling she won't be happy about that, and I don't want to take the blame!"

Edward looked down at the paper in front of him. The headline was impressive: "Controversy Surrounds the Tenth Annual Spring Fling Art Show and Antique Auction to Benefit the Art Guild's Town-Beautification Project."

Julie looked over his shoulder. "This is one art show that will go down in history."

———

Julie's opinion was echoed three blocks away.

"This is one art show that will go down in history, Lucy. This is one that will put Sulphur Springs on the map, on the map, on the map!" Calpurnia, having said that, adjusted her horn-rimmed glasses.

"Do you think you should call the TV station in Nashville again? They don't know about the free-for-all at the kickoff party last night."

"I'll fax them an update, but I don't need to say anything about the drunken swim party. They have already said they would send up a TV crew if things were slow down there. I know for sure that Hopkinsville is sending a live film crew, and I may still get coverage in Bowling Green."

"I want lots of people there when my Zulu maiden wins the ribbon for first prize at the art show, maybe even Best of Show. This is my magnum opus. I just feel it, Calpurnia—and I want media coverage!"

"Don't worry, little sister, I'm getting as many news people here as I can. Just remember, you don't know what this painting by Sarah Louise looks like, and you may have some real competition, competition, competition!"

Lucy frowned for a moment. "I need to see that painting *A Room Full of Naked Men*."

But Lucy wasn't the only person curious about the painting.

"*A Room Full of Naked Men*—that's the name of Sarah Louise's painting, the one that started all this hullabaloo. And it's her painting that caused the big fistfight and all those people being thrown into the pool last night!"

Hannah Bugleman spoke with the air of great authority.

"I had heard about the painting on the radio, but I didn't know about the brawl at Lucinda's till I stopped for gas at the Quick Mart. They were talking about it inside when I went in to pay."

Hannah pushed her grocery cart closer to Florence Barton's cart. "I know all about it! I know all about it because I've had four people call me this morning already!"

Florence pushed her cart a little closer to Hannah's. "Do tell!"

"I heard they had to call the police to break up the fight and that two people almost drowned and had to be taken to the emergency room, and…"

Yes, the news was making its way around Sulphur Springs, and accuracy was of little importance.

61

The knock on the door was almost imperceptible. It was only after the third time that Sarah Louise looked in the door's direction and saw a short person wave at her through the window.

It was Dotie!

Sarah Louise rushed right to the door and opened it. "Dotie, it's so good to see you. Come in!"

"Oh, Sarah Louise, I hope I'm not interrupting you, but I've been so worried about you…I just had to come see you in person to make sure you were all right!"

Sarah Louise was moved by Dotie's confession, and she threw both arms around her best friend. "That means so much to me, Dotie. I swear this has been the longest spring break ever. I can't wait for this weekend to be over and to get back to my routine!"

After the two sat down on the studio sofa, Dotie began the conversation. "Are you okay, Sarah Louise? Tell me the truth! I wanna know!" Then, before Sarah Louise could respond, Dotie kept talking. "There have been so many stories flying around. Not that I believe half of what I've heard, but there was Lucinda on the radio, and she told the whole world the title of your painting, and then I heard that the Art Guild members had a fight at their kickoff party last night and that Michael Dorphman pulled the first punch, and I knew that you were asking me all about him the other day, and I stopped at city hall to pay my water bill, and in the newspaper rack was this week's *Sentinel,* and the headlines said "controversy," and I was worried how you were taking all this, and…"

Sara Louise took advantage of Dotie's brief stop to take a breath. "Pop went out and got a paper at lunch, Dotie, so I've read the article. It doesn't say much…and Michael came by and told me about the party. It really was funny the way he told it…"

"Funny? I don't think fights and rumors are funny, but Moose did laugh when he told me about Huey jumping in the pool at Lucinda's—yes, that part would have been funny. What did Michael say?"

For the next thirty minutes, Sarah Louise caught Dotie up on all that had taken place since they last spoke to each other, including Michael's explanation of the fist in Clarence's face. After all that, the two walked over to the painting.

"I'm about to start painting my last model. If I work on him tonight, I should be able to finish in the morning and have it to the gym by five o'clock. That's the deadline for getting artwork there."

Dotie stood in front of the canvas. "So that one on the left, behind the flowers, is the notorious Jeremy, and I recognize Herman. That's him looking out the window. These two men I don't know, and I see you've started drawing your last model. When did Michael pose?"

"How did you know Michael posed for me? I haven't told you yet."

"Look, Sarah Louise, you've got his outline started right there. I know Michael Dorphman when I see him."

"Mother said the same thing when she looked at my sketch, but I just made that man up—it's no one in particular!"

"Sure looks like Michael to me! So he posed for you?"

"Yes, I've got my sketches of him right here. After he told me all about the party and we got through laughing, he asked who I had for my fifth model, and I told him I didn't have anyone yet, and he volunteered! I don't know what I would have done if he hadn't offered. He's a real..."

She wasn't sure what word would fit best to complete her sentence. *Friend* seemed too impersonal. While she labored to find the right word, Dotie looked at Sarah Louise's face and tried to read what she wasn't saying. And after a few seconds, she knew what was there.

"You love him, don't you?"

"Love who?"

"Michael!"

"Michael?"

"Yes, Michael Dorphman, and don't you deny it because I can see it written across your face! I heard it in your voice when you talked about him, and I knew something was up when you asked me over the phone what I knew about him—can't fool me!"

But evidently, Sarah Louise had fooled herself.

After Dotie left, she sat perplexed on the couch. Was she in love with him? More importantly, was he in love with her?

"No," she said out loud to herself, "no...it's all going too fast...a week ago, he was just a former classmate...a friend... from friend to lover in a week...no...that happens in movies... movies and fairy tales...and...no...and here I am sounding just like my mother again!"

After supper, Sarah Louise painted like a madman, or madwoman if you prefer. She was anxious to get Michael down right, to do his face justice. He wasn't terribly handsome, but he had good features and a kindness about him that made him attractive. Blond hair and blue eyes. She had always wanted to fall in love with a man who was tall, dark, and handsome, and maybe a little "mysterious."

If she was falling in love with Michael, her dream man had evaporated because Michael was average height, not dark, nice-looking—well, maybe handsome—but not mysterious. He was, she hated to say, as comfortable as an old shoe. Maybe that was it. Maybe Jane Austen and all the romance novels were wrong. Maybe a man of mystery was not it. She stopped painting for a moment to gather her thoughts. Maybe she didn't see Michael as a love interest because she was so relaxed around him—like an old pair of canvas Nikes.

When her mother walked in a short while later, Sarah Louise had a question posed for her. So after showing her mother the progress she had made, she asked Claudette to sit down.

"Mother, I don't think I've ever asked you this—maybe it's too personal—but what made you fall in love with Pop?"

Claudette didn't hesitate to answer. It was as if she had crammed for a marriage exam and was ready for whatever the professor threw at her. "Because I was happy when I was around him…I don't mean silly happy like a starry-eyed teenager…just comfortable…no pretense around him…I didn't feel like I had to be in my best dress or have my hair just right…he would come by the house and sit on the porch with my father and visit…and I got kinda used to him being around…like a piece of furniture. One afternoon, I walked out on to the porch, and he wasn't there, and I realized I wanted him to be there…that I missed him when he wasn't around…you know, I could have married Ralph Tinsley…his father and grandfather owned the funeral home in Greenbriar; he still does today…Ralph always wore a tie and drove his father's Lincoln Continental…but Ralph was the kind to buy a girl flowers, and your father was the kind to dig a hole in the yard and plant you flowers."

It was the longest discourse she had ever heard her mother give. "Why do you ask?"

Sarah Louise was trying to put it all together, what her mother had said, what Dotie had said, what Michael had said.

"Sarah Louise…did you hear me? I said, 'Why do you ask?'"

"Sorry, Mom…I guess I was thinking…why did I ask? Oh, no particular reason. I guess I can finish this in the morning. Do we have any cake left over? A piece of cake and a glass of milk would taste good right now."

"I have some pound cake in the freezer…it will take just a second to thaw it out in the microwave…you wash up your brushes and come to the kitchen….it will be ready when you get there."

As Claudette walked down the hall, past the den where Winslow had fallen asleep in his recliner, and into the kitchen, she reviewed the conversation she had just had with her daughter. Sarah Louise was talking about *love* again, something she hadn't done since the investment banker from Atlanta. That was significant.

But another thing stood out—it was the first time Sarah Louise had called her *mom* since she became a teenager and had decided *mother* was more age appropriate.

"Mom, yes, it was nice to be called *mom* again!"

62

Cecil Womack brushed the crumb of his blueberry muffin from his crisp white shirt. He prided himself on his neat professional appearance: white shirt, black tie, shiny badge. The badge was brass, and he had polished it to the luster of gold. It read, "Sulphur Springs Rescue Squad and Emergency Response." Above it was another brass badge. This one had "Captain" emblazoned upon it. The crisp white shirt with its shiny adornment was stretched to accommodate Cecil's expansive girth.

"That muffin as good as it looks, Captain?"

"Sure 'nuff is, Stubby—gotta watch those crumbs, though!"

"Been wantin' to try one of his muffins since he started making 'em, but I can't seem to get my eyes past the honey buns!"

"Oughta try 'em…better for you than that sugarcoated honey bun you're chompin' on. How many times you reckon Mr. Tang dips that thing in sugar? Two? Three?"

Embarrassed, Stubby wiped sugar from his lips and took a sip of his heavily sweetened coffee.

If Cecil Womack was eating the blueberry muffin because he thought it was healthier than the honey bun Stubby was eating, he was operating under a delusion. The honey bun was coated in sugar, but the muffin was loaded with fat grams.

There was no sign on any wall of Danny's Donut Den that read "Warning: Arteries may be clogged by some items on our menu." There were no calorie or fat-gram disclosures. The muffins only looked healthy. It gave people an excuse to eat two of them instead of one of the sugarcoated delights that were the staple of Cam Tang's business.

"Mr. Cecil, you need more coffee?"

"No thanks, Mr. Tang. I'm good to go!"

A few minutes later Cecil and Stubby were in the Sulphur Springs Rescue Squad and Emergency Response vehicle, number one.

"Hand me the clipboard, Stubby."

"Sure thing, Captain."

Cecil Womack ran a tight ship. Even though he used George Browning's nickname, Stubby, when he spoke to him, he expected George and all the other members of the squad to address him as *Captain*. Everything Cecil did, he did in a very professional way. Whether it was a cat stuck in a tree or using the Jaws of Life to pull a teenager from a car crash, Cecil took his job very seriously. He had gone from being a skinny high school volunteer fireman to the head position and one of the only two paid positions of the Emergency Response Department of Sulphur Springs.

Cecil was proud of his rise through the ranks of the mostly volunteer squad that not only saved lives but also directed traffic and parked cars at the Sulphur Springs High School football games. Even though be had started out as a fireman, he had been lured to the EMT by the adrenaline of seeing blood and hearing screams of pain at an accident; and although he had never intended to pursue higher education after high school, he took the rigorous training needed to be an emergency medical technician. From the ambulance crew to being the director, or "captain," of all the city's emergency operations, his position had been hard-earned, and he wore his badge with a little swagger, if not a slight waddle due to his expanding waist.

"What's on the agenda for today?" he said half out loud, not expecting an answer from Stubby but from himself.

"Meet with the mayor at ten o'clock to go over request for a new fire engine for the fire department. Pick up the ambulance service's budget proposals and deliver them to the bookkeeper down at city hall…"

He then turned to face Stubby, who was popping a piece of sugary bubblegum into his mouth. "It ain't on here, Stubb, but we need to call Larry and make sure he has his people lined up to park cars at that there Spring Fling on Saturday. From all the talk that's going around, I reckon we are gonna have a big turnout!"

Fifteen miles down the road, in the neighboring town of Greenbrier, Hamilton Goodpasture was also concerned with his appearance. He held an expensive imported silk tie up to his neck and looked at it in the mirror. He could never remember if you wore stripes with stripes or stripes with solids.

"Trisha! Trisha!"

His wife stepped from the bathroom to see what her husband wanted, but as soon as she saw the tie in his hand and the helpless look on his face, she knew. "No, no, Hamilton, you can't wear a striped tie with a striped shirt!" Then crossing the room to the expansive walk-in closet, she looked till she found a nice solid-colored tie and placed it in his hand.

She didn't bother to tell him that she had told him how to pick his ties a thousand times because—well, she had told him a thousand times before, and it hadn't sunk in yet. She waited till he had it tied in a half-Windsor before she spoke again, "Pull your pants' legs up!"

He obliged. "Don't trust me?"

"No."

She didn't. He had absolutely no fashion sense. She thought she had solved the sock problem by only buying one color—black.

But Father's Day gifts and Christmas gifts from the employees down at the bank had left him with pairs of patterned and bizarre-colored socks; and true to fashion, if she didn't check, he put on whatever his hands grabbed first in his sock drawer.

"Okay...this time, Hamilton...gray...gray will work."

She started making the bed but suddenly stopped and turned to her husband, right as he was preparing to leave the room. "What time do you have to be there tomorrow?"

"Where?"

"That art show you're supposed to judge in Sulphur Springs. You told me about it a month ago. It's on the calendar in the kitchen."

"Oh, that...I think early. Why?"

"I need to make sure your new khakis are pressed, and maybe your denim shirt..."

She had to dress him everywhere he went. From underwear to hat and gloves, she bought all his clothes and then told him when to wear them. Fortunately, he was better at banking than he was in matching ties to shirts.

Hamilton walked over to the bed and gave his wife a peck on the cheek. "Thanks, honey!" Then he looked kind of serious for a moment. "How am I supposed to judge an art show...I don't know anything about art!"

She pressed her tongue against the inside of her cheek as she tried to think of what to tell him, short of offering to go with him and hold his hand. Then it came to her. "Hamilton, just let the other two judges do all the picking and all the tallying. You just agree and nod your head. If I've heard right, from my cousin in Sulphur Springs, they had a little controversy brewing with some kind of painting of naked people. You just play it safe. Let the other two judges do all the work!"

Hamilton liked that suggestion.

In Nashville, south of Sulphur Springs but easily the largest town within driving distance, the director of programming of the city's largest TV station, WKAZ, sat with her own clipboard, except hers was on her Blackberry.

"Controversial painting in Sulphur Springs..."

She was scanning the e-mails from Calpurnia Pendergrass: "high school teacher...normally staid exhibition...*A Room Full of Naked Men*...local residents upset ..."

The program director pushed a few buttons. There was a ringing and then a pickup.

"Lassiter?"

"Yes!"

"Lassiter, I want you to take a film crew and the mobile unit to Sulphur Springs tomorrow—since you have the weekend shift. I want you to cover the town's annual art show."

Sissy Lassiter was understandably surprised. "Art show? Is nothing happening in Nashville this weekend?"

"Not just any art show, Lassiter. Barring any terrorist attacks on Music Row, I want you there. Seems we have a little controversy concerning a painting, and controversy gets viewers! We like controversy!"

"Yes, we do!"

"I'll send you the details."

As Sissy Lassiter hung up, she twisted her lips and considered the assignment in light of her career goals. The attractive blonde newscaster took a deep breath, difficult to do in the tight skirt and revealing blouse she was wearing, and wondered if this change in her weekend schedule would be good for her or keep her in the background. Sissy did not want to be in the background. Sissy wanted to be in front of the camera and on prime time. She was trying to get a spot on the local nightly news at six o'clock, but after a year at the station, she was still stuck with the ten-o'clock news and weekend reports.

She needed something besides Girl Scout cookie sales and crowded conditions at dog pounds. At last, a little controversy. She would do the best she could with this. What was it again—an art show? There was a gleam in her eyes.

63

Buford took a swat at Ginger, and Ginger reciprocated with a wallop, which made Buford lean back so far he fell out of the wicker basket the two had been sharing.

Distracted by the commotion, Sarah Louise looked around the edge of her painting. "Play nice you, two!"

The two cats looked in her direction. Their expressions gave no clue to the motives behind their brief boxing match. Now, they were distracted by the voice of their owner, master, caretaker, and—if the truth be told—servant.

Seeing the look of innocence they both displayed, Sarah Louise put down her brush and walked across the studio to the outside door and opened it. "Why don't you two go outside for a while?"

The two cats rushed to the open door but stopped right at the threshold. There, each one gave the patio and backyard a good look—we can guess—to make sure there were no large birds of prey or ferocious dogs around. Once sure it was safe, first Buford and then Ginger stepped outside into the warm sunshine.

With her concentration now broken by the cats' interruption, Sarah Louise didn't go straight back to her painting. She put the wet paintbrush into a glass of water and took off her robe. She was still in her pajamas, having risen early and begun painting. Now she was comfortably far enough on the canvas to stop and get cleaned up and dressed.

Before she stepped into the small bathroom that adjoined the studio to turn on the shower, she took another look at the canvas. *Yes,* she thought, *I made it work!* And for all practical purposes, she had.

She had accomplished what she had set out to do. She had, thanks to Claudette, created a little buzz about her painting. The buzz had turned into more of a roar, but she had managed to shift the subject of the painting from cats to naked men and do so in a manner that shouldn't cause a riot. Notice we said *shouldn't.*

With the help of her mother and her card circle, she had gotten her first four models with little fanfare, the incident with Winslow and the gun being one exception and the head-cracking Alma being the other. She had gotten a new cat and met back up with an old friend and possibly begun a relationship that held potential. That friend, Michael, had come to her rescue by being her last model—he had also come to the rescue of her reputation by punching someone in the nose at the Art Guild party.

Yes, she had accomplished what she had set out to do, and now the painting was almost done.

Oh yes, there was one more thing. She had forged a new relationship with her mother. The two had become closer. Even though she had felt like strangling Claudette only a week ago, now the two were more like the friends that they had been since she was a child and believed her mother could do no wrong. As a teenager, Sarah Louise had flipped to her father as her confidant and advisor—but now, she and her mother had reacquainted, so to say. Sarah Louise even found herself sounding like her mother.

Sounding like her mother? She looked in the mirror. If she gained forty pounds, pull on a pair of glasses, put her hair up, and wore double knit—she would be her mother!

Sarah Louise blinked her eyes to get the mental image out of her mind and hurried to the bathroom to take her shower.

⌁

At the gym of the old Sulphur Springs High School, Huey, Malvenna, Lucinda, Mrs. Biederman, Louise Smith, and a handful of others were busy.

While most of the Art Guild members were receiving artwork and sorting them by category, Huey was still arranging tables and folding panels. Malvenna stood close by, popping her chewing gum and giving such comments as, "More to the left, Huey" or "Looks a little crooked to me." She was, despite such observations, a big help.

"Is this the last one, Huey?"

"Yes, Malvenna, baby, and it's about time."

"Sorry I couldn't help you yesterday. I had to go to Bowling Green to get a part for Booger's backhoe. Took all day!"

"That's all right, sweetie. I like working by myself anyway. I worked late yesterday, after the others were gone. You wanna know why...promise not to tell?"

Malvenna, not able to resist a secret, walked over to Huey's side and leaned her ear close to his mouth. "Why, Huey?"

"So I can sing opera, baby!"

She straightened up. "Opera?"

"Not so loud, Malvenna!"

"Opera, Huey?"

"The echo in this old gym is wonderful...it's like singing in the shower, only better!"

Malvenna looked around the gym and tried to visualize Huey prancing from one end to the other singing, "La Pagliacci!"

"Oh, take that look off your face, Malvenna! I have a good voice, in case you didn't know, and I just sing at the top of my voice, and nobody can hear me...'cept me...which is good, 'cause I don't always remember the words."

Mrs. Biederman walked up just then and put an end to the revelation. "Can we start hanging things now, Huey?"

"Yes, Mrs. Biederman. This was the last panel."

Mrs. Biederman looked around as if to give a final approval. "This is where the paintings go? Like we did last year?"

"Yes."

She twisted her mouth, and it was evident she was considering something. "Where do you intend to hang it?"

When she said *it,* Huey knew what she was talking about. Malvenna, standing there, also knew.

"Well, let me tell you what I've done, Mrs. Biederman. I have three spots where it can go. When Sarah Louise shows up—and I guess she is still going to show up?"

"As far as I know, Huey. I haven't heard otherwise."

"If it's tame—that is, if it's not too…too…"

"Naked!" Malvenna supplied the missing word.

"Yes, if somehow it's not too 'naked,' it will hang right here, in the middle of the gym. Because I know that everyone who comes to the art show will want to see it for themselves…I didn't want to make it difficult to find. But if it's a little more…more…"

"Naked!" Malvenna again offered up the word.

"Yes, that's it. If it's a little more 'naked,' I will hang it over there. He pointed to the far corner. "It won't be so obvious, kinda hidden, but not…so people will have to make an effort to see it. They won't accidently walk up to it with their granny or little kids in tow and be embarrassed."

Mrs. Biederman nodded in approval. "You mentioned a third place, Huey."

"Yes, Mrs. Biederman. If it's just too…too…"

"Naked!" Malvenna almost beamed as she once again found the right word.

"Yes, if it's just really naked, I'm gonna hang it in the old girls' locker room and charge people a dollar extra to see it!"

"Huey!"

"Just kidding, Mrs. Biederman—about the dollar, that is. If it's too bad, we'll have to do something…"

"If it's too bad, Huey, I don't know what we're going to do!"

The three of them stood there considering all their options, agonizing over what *A Room Full of Naked Men* might look like, which is why they were totally unprepared when Louise walked up to them.

"Isadora, sorry to interrupt you and Huey and Malvenna, but we have a problem."

"Sarah Louise?" Mrs. Biederman asked nervously.

"Oh no…Lucy Pendergrass just got here, and…"

64

Clarence Lipowitz leaned over the sink to get a closer view as he shaved. Pulling the razor from his ear to his chin, he jutted his jaw out slightly to make the side of his face smoother. In so doing, the muscles around his nose were stretched, and Clarence let out an expletive.

"Did you say something, Clarence?"

Clarence fought the urge to say something smart back to his wife. "Nothing, Avis."

Avis stuck her head in the door of his bathroom. Their master bath was actually two baths. They—rather, Clarence—had designed it that way. This way, either one of them could bathe and get dressed without bothering the other one. No double sinks here like middle-class America. It was, in truth, very practical; but its real purpose was to give Clarence that much less time around Avis, a fact that never dawned on her.

"Do you need anything from Walmart? I'm taking the kids to shop for a birthday present, then to Randy's Pit Stop for lunch. We may go to a movie. This is the last day of their spring break, and I thought we'd make a day of it. Tomorrow, I expect to be busy. I have to take Sophia and Arnold to that birthday party, and you need to cover the Spring Fling."

"Me?"

"Yes, you."

Saying that, she left the room.

Clarence didn't like being told what to do, but he bit his tongue again. Since the scene he had made at the kickoff party, Avis had been on his case. He was walking a tightrope, and he knew he had to keep his balance—even if it meant letting Avis have her way.

"Two weeks," he mumbled to himself. Two weeks of playing the obedient husband, and he should be able to step back into his old routine, although he had made a mental note to himself to be more careful about combining liquor and snide remarks, especially when Michael Dorphman was around.

He stretched his jaw again, a little more carefully this time, and pulled the razor across his cheek and the nose, much less puffy than it had been the day before only slightly pained him.

"Two weeks," he mumbled again.

<hr />

While Clarence shaved and Avis shopped and Sarah Louise got back to her painting, Lucy Pendergrass was the center of attention at the gym of the old Sulphur Springs High School. She had dutifully entered her painting, *Shakila, the Zulu Queen*, but rather than hand the canvas over to the Art Guild ladies at the sign-in table, she had taken it and headed straight toward Isadora Biederman, Louise Smith, Huey Pugh, and Malvenna Botts.

There was no stopping her, not that anyone in the Art Guild would have been foolish enough to try.

"Isadora!" Lucy hollered across the gym, and what eyes weren't already on her now were.

Louise turned to Mrs. Biederman. "I tried to warn you!"

"Isadora! I'm so glad you're here. You have got to see this. It's this year's winner of the Spring Fling!" She turned the large canvas so that it faced the four of them: Isadora, Louise, Huey, and Malvenna.

Their jaws dropped.

Lucy's painting literally jumped out at them. There was no way to adequately describe it. Was it a work of art, a trashy work of art, or just trashy? Perhaps *tacky* would better apply, and then again, the word *centerfold* came to mind.

The Zulu queen's bare chest seemed to take up most of the upper half of the painting. The exposed bosom walked the line between *nude* and *naked*. There was a difference, and the African woman's chest stood precariously on the line.

To make matters worse, in her typical style, Lucy had painted her cross-eyed. But Shakila—a name she had found by looking at rap music CDs at Walmart—wasn't just cross-eyed. She was cross-eyed and looking at her own chest. It was as if she too was dismayed by their size.

Huey shot a glance over to Malvenna, whose face was a bright red. Isadora Biederman had shut her eyes for the moment, but when she reopened them, the naked woman was still there. Louise meekly left the group and walked back to the sign-in table. Lucy didn't notice any of this. She wasn't looking to them for approval anyway. She was staring at the large panel behind Huey. "Take this, Huey!" she barked.

Huey, although he matched her pound for pound, obeyed.

Lucy placed a hand on each hip and stared at the panels in front of her. She was mentally trying to find just the right spot for her masterpiece. "Malvenna, grab one of those hangers!"

Malvenna, her face still flushed, picked up a little hook from a box on the edge of the closest table.

"Huey, bring Shakila here!"

Huey looked over at Isadora Biederman as if to seek rescue, but Mrs. Biederman had stepped back and was holding on to a chair for support. She looked about to faint.

In a few short moments, Lucy maneuvered Huey and Malvenna until the three of them had her painting hung in the very center of the wall of folding panels—the very spot Huey had reserved for Sarah Louise's *A Room Full of Naked Men*. Isadora had, by this time, sat down.

Lucy clasped her hands together in front of her. She was beaming from ear to ear. Her ebony queen stood triumphant. There was a bright orange-and-yellow African sunset behind her, those colors standing in stark contrast to the rich chocolate tones of her skin. Her hair was a combination of Afro and braids copied from hair-product ads in an issue of *Ebony* magazine. The three-dimensional effect of her necklace and skirt, with their beads and feathers, made her presence all the more real.

Then there was the spotted leopard. The animal's fur was so smooth it looked like a carved sculpture rather than a living, breathing furry animal; but few people would notice because they would be staring at the feline's eyes, which, like its companion, were slightly crossed.

It was lost on Lucy, who swooned at the effect her painting had. She turned to face the others. "Isadora, this is the spot! She's perfect here! Calpurnia says she had two, maybe three, film crews here tomorrow. I want them to see this when they walk in!"

She turned to Huey. "Huey, don't move her! This is where she's going to hang!"

No one had ever told Huey where they wanted their artwork to hang or sit or anything. That was Huey's job, and really, no one cared. But now, Lucy was demanding top billing. What could he do? Malvenna shot him a quick look.

Huey looked at Mrs. Biederman for help. Her eyes were open, but they had a glazed-over look to them, and she had one hand to her forehead as if she had a migraine beginning. So with no moral support, Huey crumbled. "Yes, Lucy, honey!"

Lucy turned to go then, just as quickly, turned back around. "Is Sarah Louise Upshaw's painting here yet?"

Malvenna spoke up, "No, Lucy. We were just discussing where it should go when you arrived…"

Lucy set her eyes on Huey again. "Don't move my painting, Huey!" Then she turned and left.

Huey looked over to Malvenna, and then the two of them looked over at Mrs. Biederman, who now had both hands to her temples and was looking a little cross-eyed herself.

65

Claudette, Winslow, and Sarah Louise sat beside one another on the sofa in the studio. They were scrunched together because it was a small sofa, but that was of little concern to them. A large easel, with Sarah Louise's painting, was directly in front of them, and that was where their attention was focused. Winslow also had his attention on two wads of tissue up his nostrils because he was in cat territory.

They sat there quietly for several minutes.

"Lou, I don't see anything in that painting that should get you or anyone else in trouble. It looks like *A Room Full of Men without Their Shirts* instead of *A Room Full of Naked Men*. His voice was slightly muffled due to the tissue.

"I agree, Winslow…of course, if you wanted to believe they were naked, you could…not that you would want to…believe they were naked, that is…but you could."

"I know what you're saying, Mother. The title works for the painting, but I could just have easily called it *Me on a Sofa*."

"You did a really good likeness of Jeremy, Lou. It looks just like him."

"Sarah Louise, you should paint people more often…you're very good at it…maybe this is the start of a new style for you!"

"Oh no...it's back to cats and flowers for me! The only exception is the barn I promised Michael."

"Speaking of Michael," Claudette spoke up, "he called right after lunch...not long after you left the kitchen, Sarah Louise... you really need to give him your cell phone number...he wanted to know how you were doing and if you needed any help taking the painting to the gym..."

Sarah Louise turned to her mother. "What did you tell him, Mother?"

"I told him you were almost through...and like you told your father and me at lunch, that you weren't going to take your canvas to the school until right before five o'clock...you wanted as few people as possible to see it before tomorrow...but I told him I was sure it was okay for him to see it and that we just might need some help...so he said he would meet us at the gym at a quarter to five."

"You should have called me to the phone, Mother. Anyway, I—"

"You don't want his help?"

"It's not that...I just hate to bother him..."

Claudette smiled in a peculiar manner. "I don't think it's any bother to him at all!"

Winslow thought about what Claudette had just said and leaned forward a bit and turned his head to get a better look at his daughter. "Have I missed something?"

"What do you mean, Pop?"

"He means, Sarah Louise, that he is the next to the last one here to realize that Michael Dorphman likes you...a lot...and the last one to know that is you."

"Oh, Mother!"

Then Claudette skillfully changed the subject, letting what she had said sink in. "Show your father what you put on the book... the last thing you painted...what you showed me earlier..."

Still aggravated by what her mother had just said, Sarah Louise pointed to the painting. "See the spine on the book, Pop? The book I'm holding in my hand? See what it says?"

Winslow pushed his glasses farther down on his nose to focus on the words in the painting. Then he read them out loud, "*Much Ado About Nothing* by William Shakespeare." He thought about it for a moment then laughed a big laugh. "That's good, Lou! Much ado about nothing—good choice! I hope the judges see it. I hope Lucinda What's-Her-Name sees it. I hope Coach Hatton sees it. I hope the people at the *Sentinel* see it. I hope every busybody in Sulphur Springs sees it!"

Sarah Louise and Claudette chuckled at his tirade.

"I don't care who sees it, Pop. I don't care if nobody sees it… it's how I feel, and I'll be glad when it's all over!"

Claudette spoke up, "We need to get a move on it…it's four-thirty now…I'll get my purse…Winslow, you load the painting into the car."

"Let me wrap a sheet over it first, Pops—and take the Kleenex out of your nose!"

When they arrived at the school, Claudette leaned over and whispered to her husband, "Let Michael carry it in…pretend you have a bad back or something…"

There were few cars there. Most of the volunteers had gone home already. Even Lucinda Hardin-Powell had left, reluctantly, because she was anxious to see if Sarah Louise would show up, but she had to pick her kids up at her mother's and start supper. Huey's car was there, and Malvenna's, and Isadora Biederman's, and—Michael's.

Winslow faked a backache well, and Michael carried the canvas into the building. When they walked in, only Malvenna was sitting at the sign-in table. Huey and Mrs. Biederman were hanging up a couple of watercolors that had also been late in coming.

Upon hearing the gym doors open and close, Isadora and Huey turned to face the Upshaws and Michael.

"Darn," Isadora said in a hushed tone that only Huey could hear. "I was about to believe that she wasn't going to show!"

Huey tried to cheer her up. "Now, Mrs. Biederman...Sarah Louise's painting can't be any worse than Lucy Pendergrass's... can it?"

"Let's hope not," she answered, and then taking a deep breath, she summoned up the courage to go meet the arrivals.

When Huey and Mrs. Biederman got to the sign-in table, Malvenna was finishing writing up this last entry. "Sarah Louise Upshaw...acrylic painting...and title?"

"*A Room Full of Naked Men*," Sarah Louise replied.

The room was ghostly quiet as Malvenna wrote the title down. It was Huey who decided to break the silence. "Sarah Louise, sweetie, take that bed sheet off that painting and let me see what all this uproar is about...I've been waiting all day to see this, so show it to us before I pee in my pants!"

That more than cut the serious tone of the last few minutes, and they all laughed, even Sarah Louise. She pulled the sheet away and stepped back a few feet so everyone could get a good look.

Isadora was the first to say anything, before Huey could toss out any more of his witty repartee. "Oh, Sarah Louise...it's just fine. I was, I have to admit, a little worried...but I should have known...it's just fine!"

For the next ten minutes, the small group laughed and visited. Michael stood by his "portrait," and they all commented on the likeness. Huey asked him to take off his shirt, but he declined. Then Isadora told them about Lucy's Zulu queen, and they all tramped to the center of the old gym to see it and where they all had an opinion to express.

Finally Malvenna said she had to leave and Isadora too. They left it up to Huey to finish and close up.

Sarah Louise was a little curious to see who else had their work on display, if any of her former students had entered the Spring Fling, and Michael accompanied her down the first row of exhibits.

Winslow had started to follow them, but Claudette made a little kick at his shin to get his attention and whispered, "Leave them alone, Winslow." She pointed him toward the door, saying, "Wait for me out in the car."

Once he was safely out the door, she stepped over to Huey, who was rehanging a few pastels to make room for Sarah Louise's entry. Claudette talked to him in hushed tones for a minute, pointing to Sarah Louise's painting, and then she stepped around the corner so that Sarah Louise and Michael, at the other end of the row, were able to see her.

"Hey, you two…Winslow has an upset stomach, and we have to rush back to the house…you two stay as long as you want…Huey says he's going to be here awhile…you don't mind bringing Sarah Louise home, do you, Michael? And Sarah, you'll have to grab yourself a bite somewhere. I haven't done a thing about supper!"

Before either of them could say anything, Claudette was gone, leaving the couple to look at each other in surprise and then to laugh at her sudden departure.

"Ms. Upshaw?" Michael spoke up. "Since you haven't had supper yet, would you be my guest…say, Ronnie's Steak House in Greenbrier? It's just fifteen minutes down the road."

"That's awful nice of you…I can't believe my mother ran off like that… but…"

"But nothing! I insist on taking you out to supper, a kind of thank-you for not painting me too fat or making my nose too big or"—he thought of Lucy Pendergrass's painting—"making me cross-eyed!"

Al that, Sarah Louise broke out laughing; and the two of them laughed the rest of the way down the row of needlepoint and cross-stitch, and all the way over to the patchwork quilts and appliqué!

66

After Sarah Louise and Michael left, Huey locked the old double doors to the gym behind them. He, however, remained inside. There were still things to be done. He walked up and down each row of tables and folding panels, moving and rearranging artwork as it suited him.

The last row he visited was the one where *A Room Full of Naked Men* hung, next to the pastels and at the beginning of the acrylic paintings. He stopped in front of Sarah Louise's painting and appeared to be giving it deep thought. He then disappeared across the gym and into the old classroom wing where the summer art classes were taught. When he came back, he had a paintbrush in one hand and an artist's palette in the other—and one more thing, he was singing opera to himself.

Huey is not the only one we are interested in.

Across town, in the La Vista Country Club and 18 Hole Golf Course subdivision, Lucinda Hardin-Powell was sitting down to supper. The chicken was baked, not fried. The rolls were whole wheat. The vegetables were steamed. As the children ate, BJ, her husband, tried to smile as he took his first bite of broccoli—but it wasn't easy. If only his cholesterol had been lower, he could be eating fried chicken and mashed potatoes, and his mind created a repast of forbidden foods.

At the opposite end of the table, his wife was no less preoccupied. She wanted to call someone to see if Sarah Louise Upshaw had delivered her painting, but the only people she might call—Huey, Malvenna, or Mrs. Biederman—were the very ones she had already made mad. Best to leave them alone. What if Sarah Louise had decided not to enter her painting? That would be the worst-case scenario. It would be as if she, Lucinda, had made much ado over nothing! No, Lucinda secretly hoped Sarah Louise had brought her shockingly risqué canvas and that tomorrow Lucinda would be vindicated for all her hysterics.

In La Roma Hills, Isadora Biederman sipped a double martini as her husband massaged her feet, and she told him everything that had happened that afternoon. The martini helped her see the humor of it all, and her description of Lucy Pendergrass's painting made her husband anxious to see it for himself.

Down the street, Avis and Clarence and their children, Sophia and Arnold, were eating delivery pizza and watching reruns of *America's Funniest Home Videos* on their big-screen plasma TV. It did Clarence good to see other people fall flat on their faces, get hit in the groin, or stumble into swimming pools.

Winslow and Claudette were also eating. Contrary to what Claudette had told Michael, she and Winslow were having pot roast. Banana pudding, made with Splenda, was waiting in the tangerine refrigerator.

Their neighbor Alma Peterman sat in front of her TV eating a TV dinner. The microwave was one of the few modern conveniences she tolerated. Beside her, she had her phone, her binoculars—and her trusty number seven golf club.

At Dotie Fisher's home, dessert was already on the table, the family having made short work of her sloppy joes and oven fries. Dotie was serving up the last of her peaches from the freezer, baked into a deep-crust cobbler. As she dished out a big scoop of vanilla ice cream onto each plate, she wondered if she should call Sarah Louise and check on her again.

Sarah Louise was also on the mind of Coach Hatton. Tomorrow morning, he intended to be one of the first people in line to see the Spring Fling Art Show. He had instructions from the school board to see the painting for himself and decide if charges of indecency should be brought up. At times like this, he wished he was back coaching football.

Pearl was working late at her beauty shop. Fridays and Saturdays always ran late. The gossip for the day had centered on the tenth annual art show. There was a lot there to talk about: a painting of naked men, a brawl at the kickoff party, and then the rumors about another scandalous painting—this one by Lucy Pendergrass. My, how news travels! Pearl got it from Charlene. Charlene got it from Ruby. Ruby got it from her niece…

At the radio station, Ted Bumquist packed the last of the equipment he would need for Saturday's live radio broadcast. Sherry would meet him there. He stepped into the sound booth long enough to tell Terry, the night disk jockey, that he had started a fresh pot of coffee. And then he was out the door and headed home. *Tomorrow,* Ted mused, *should be interesting!*

Two blocks from the radio station, Hubcap was working on a Ford Pinto. His brother-in-law, GW, sat in the driver's seat, turning the ignition key off and on in response to Hubcap's request.

"You 'bout ready for supper, Hub?"

Hubcap rubbed his chin and considered the proposition. He reached into his overall's pocket and pulled out a twenty. "Take this and run down to Randy's and get me a number two special—and ask for extra hot sauce. You get yourself something outta that!"

While GW hopped into his truck and headed to Randy's Pit Stop, Herman Bugleman was sitting in front of his computer. He was on his Facebook page. Herman wanted all his Facebook friends, small in number as they were, to know that he would be in a painting at the Sulphur Springs Art Show on Saturday. Since most of his Facebook friends were other computer geeks in other cities, it was doubtful they would come; but if Herman wanted to feel like a celebrity, that was fine. He knew for sure that his Aunt Hannah would be there.

Farther down the road, Clara Dorphman was sitting on her recliner by the TV. She was watching the Weather Channel. She had been watching it all day because she had punched the wrong button on her remote and couldn't get it to change channels. Michael had shown her how to fix that, but she had forgotten how. She hadn't forgotten about the big art show tomorrow. She would be there…now what time did they tell her to be there?

Lucy Pendergrass and her sister, Calpurnia, were baking cookies and placing them in a cookie jar in the shape of Elvis Presley. The ladies of the Art Guild might not see fit to provide refreshments tomorrow, but Lucy was going to stand by her painting and hand out cookies!

There were people in other towns looking forward to Saturday's big event.

An hour's drive away, at the state university, Professor Montricia Ifama was chewing a candy bar and walking on her treadmill. She was watching *Nova* on the public television station. Unaware of any controversy, Montricia was mesmerized by the TV as it explained, in layman's terms, the big bang theory.

Likewise for Ronnie Jean Gump. She too was not aware of the two attention-getting canvases. She sat in her flower shop and put another handful of funeral ferns into a large pot while reaching for a ribbon with "In God's Hands" in gold glitter. Ronnie would have to hurry back to the flower shop after judging the art show because one of Darlington's finest citizens had choked on a chimichanga at the Mexican restaurant and gone into cardiac arrest. The orders for funeral sprays were piling up.

The third judge, Hamilton Goodpasture, was aware of some type of problem at the art show, but he had the instructions of his wife on what to do; and as a banker, he knew prudent advice when he heard it—let someone else take the blame.

In Nashville, at TV station WKAZ, Sissie Lassiter was laying out her outfit for Saturday. She wanted to look her best and since she always looked good in red, red it was. She picked up her bottle of peroxide. Sissie didn't care what any painting would look like tomorrow, only that she looked good.

In Greenbrier, Sarah Louise and Michael were enjoying their time together. The talk was of this and that, no mention of the art show. Sarah Louise hadn't realized how comfortable it was to just have idle talk. Maybe it was like her mother said—someone you were comfortable with.

While all of this was going on, Huey was singing the "Anvil Chorus" from *Carmen*. He sang at the top of his voice, not caring if he hit a few flat notes or substituted a few la-la-las for forgotten lyrics.

Huey passed by his own entry in the art show, a nice still life. On the canvas were a pair of red and black pumps, from Huey's collection, the ones he kept in his locked closet. The shoes had a high luster to them, which made them pop off the canvas. Huey wanted to touch them every time he walked past.

He stepped back from the painting by Sarah Louise where he had been busy. Huey wasn't sure why Claudette had him make two changes in her daughter's painting, but he had complied— as a favor to Claudette and because she had promised him fifty dollars for a job well done.

Picking up the brush from the palette, he stepped over to the painting again and added just a speck of white to each of Michael Dorphman's eyes. Content that he had done his job well, he started back to the old classroom to return the supplies he had borrowed.

Getting to the center of the gym, Huey couldn't resist the urge to stop and do a few lines from "La Bohème." So he stood there in his white slacks and gaudy Hawaiian shirt and poured out his soul. It went perfect, if he did say so himself. The acoustics, enhanced by the folding panels, were excellent. Huey took a bow to the imaginary audience and then another. A glass of sherry at the moment would have been perfect.

He turned to continue his journey, and there she was—right in front of him—*Shakila, the Zulu Queen*! He couldn't take his eyes off the statuesque woman in ebony hues. He was transfixed by her cross-eyed expression. Huey hated to see a painting, even a mediocre one, ruined by incompetence.

"Shakila, sweet thang, I wish could help, but…" Huey pondered for a moment. "But…maybe…"

67

"Hand me a pin, Huey."

"Yes, Mrs. Biederman...will one do?"

"Maybe you better give me two, and hurry...I expect the judges to be here any moment. Are the doors locked?"

"Yes, Mrs. Biederman."

"I don't want anyone in here, Huey, except you and me, Louise, and the judges—understand?" Then before Huey could respond, she added, "That especially means Lucinda Hardin-Powell!" Isadora Biederman was emphatic.

Huey helped her down from the small stepladder, and the two Art Guild members stood back to better examine their handiwork.

"I'll be with the judges while they're walking through...but if I get called off by something, you know what to tell the judges!"

"Yes, Mrs. Biederman. The two paintings with the drapes over them, they are to be viewed last."

"That's right. I don't want any rumors or preconceived notions to affect the judging. On their initial walk-through, Sarah Louise's and Lucy's paintings are out of view. After they have had a chance to see everything and after I explain things, then we can take down the drapes and let them start judging."

"Yes, Mrs. Biederman."

Huey didn't use any of his pet names with Isadora Biederman.

"You watch the doors and keep people out. If Calpurnia shows up—she has her own key—you keep her up front, away from the judges! If she has Lucy with her, call me!"

Huey put the stepladder to the side and walked to the doors of the old gym. He had on his best pair of white linen slacks and his newest Hawaiian shirt, straight from the Nieman Marcus online catalog. It had every color of the rainbow and then some. Huey looked like a walking fruit salad on a shiny white platter.

At the door, Huey could see the parking lot was clear, except for his car and the cars of Mrs. Biederman and Louise Smith. Louise was outside, waiting for the judges to appear. At the far corner of the parking lot, Larry and two civil defense volunteers were setting out orange cones to direct traffic.

It was all Huey could do to keep from breaking out in an aria from *The Barber of Seville*. This was going to be an exciting day, no way around it. There would be crowds of people, Ted and Sherry would be doing a live broadcast, and Malvenna had already called him this morning to say that TV station WKAZ in Nashville was sending a reporter. Finally, the sleepy town of Sulphur Springs was getting a little media attention!

It was eight o'clock sharp when all three judges appeared, right on schedule. The three judges were people whose careers involved timetables and deadlines—punctuality was in their blood.

The Tenth Annual Spring Fling Art Show and Antique Auction to Benefit the Art Guild's Town-Beautification Project would be open to the public at ten o'clock. That gave the judges plenty of time to see every category and display and choose a first-, second-, and third-place ribbon. There would be one additional ribbon—the coveted Best of Show. Last year, the Best of Show went to a papier-mâché Statue of Liberty, entered by Miss Beva's third-grade class from Sycamore Elementary. Its artistic merits were debatable, but it won the judges over with its decidedly unprofessional approach—it was made entirely of recycled materials and got an A for effort, so to say.

Upon their entering the doors, Isadora introduced herself and then let the judges make their acquaintances. Louise got together a handful of ribbons, and Huey locked the doors back.

"I don't know if you have heard anything about this year's art show or not…"

Isadora scanned the faces of the judges to see if there was any response. Hamilton Goodpasture had on his banker's face, the smile he used when he was about to repossess a car—totally unfeeling. Ronnie Jean Gump's face gave no indication that she had heard of a scandalous pointing by a local high school teacher. The face and eyes of Montricia Ifama were harder to gauge, like she was anxious to start more than anything else

"But we've bad a little controversy!" Isadora continued. Then she turned. "If you will come this way, I'll explain…"

As Isadora Biederman "explained," the sleepy town of Sulphur Springs was anything but. People all across town were up and moving.

Clarence Lipowitz was getting dressed. He had to cover the show. He was a little nervous, not because he had never covered a local event but because there were people he wished to avoid.

Herman Bugleman was having breakfast with his Aunt Hannah. He would be driving her and Annie to the show.

Cecil Womack and Stubby were at Danny's Donut Den and preparing to check on Larry and his crew at the parking lot.

Michael Dorphman had eaten breakfast with his grandmother and reminded her that she was to be at the art show at nine-thirty for pictures. He was at work now. Saturday mornings were always busy with do-it-yourselfers. Even so, he had arranged to meet Sarah Louise at ten o'clock at the old gym for moral support. His employees would cover for him.

Hubcap was at his gas-station-turned-into-repair-shop. Duffy was there and a couple of the other regulars. Their talk was still about the art show.

Pearl was busy at her beauty shop. She and Charlene were using enough hair spray to add another degree to global warming.

Ted Bumquist was getting in his car and heading out to the gym to set up the radio station's live hook up.

Coach Hatton was also at Danny's Donut Den, trying to control his nervous attack with a jelly-filled doughnut—raspberry—his third one.

Lucinda Hardin-Powell was washing dishes at her home in La Vista and anxiously watching the clock. She had been told by Mrs. Biederman to be there at ten o'clock and not a minute sooner. *The old biddy,* she thought.

Malvenna was doing her nails before she had to show up to work the art show. She was watching *Design on a Budget* on HGTV. "That green is all wrong," she tried to tell the TV host.

Ronnie Junior, the sheriff, was releasing two teenagers from the jail, where they had spent the night after getting caught rolling a classmate's lawn with toilet paper. The classmate's parents didn't think it was funny.

Travis Morgan, down at his chicken farm, was getting the last of five hundred chicken coops loaded on his large flatbed truck. The clucks and peeps from five hundred leghorns filled the air.

Calpurnia and Lucy Pendergrass were taking the last cookie sheet from the oven. They had baked enough to fill three more cookie jars. Calpurnia was in a hurry. She had made arrangements to meet the news crews from Nashville, Hopkinsville, and Bowling Green at nine-thirty at the gym.

Claudette and Winslow and Sarah Louise were trying to keep busy around the house, halfway pretending this was just a routine Saturday.

Back at the gym, having finished a quick walk-through, Mrs. Biederman led the group to the draped painting by Sarah Louise.

"This is the first painting...the one that people in town have been concerned about...Huey, remove the drape. I'll let you decide for yourselves."

The three judges stood politely silent as Huey grabbed the stepladder and moved it to Sarah Louise's canvas. His three hundred pounds weren't safe very far up the stepladder, so he only made it to the second step and stretched to undo the pins holding the drape.

As he pulled the cloth away, Isadora spoke up, "The title of this painting, as I mentioned earlier, is *A Room Full of Naked Men*." She paused to let them take it in.

Montricia, the most vocal of the three, spoke up first, "I'm a little let down, Mrs. Biederman. From the way you were talking, I thought I was going to see a little more flesh...I've seen more skin on the 'green' on our campus when the students lay out to work on their suntans!"

Ronnie Jean had to agree. "I didn't notice the bare chests. I was admiring those fuchsia flowers. They look so real—some kind of daisy?"

The three women discussed flowers for a few moments while Huey got down from the stepladder, and Hamilton remained quiet.

Finally, Montricia summed up her feelings. "It's a nice composition: excellent flowers, good color balance...but if your public is coming here expecting controversy from that painting, they're going to be disappointed!"

"You're right, Professor Ifama—may I call you Montricia? It seems so formal to call you professor!"

"Go right ahead, and I'll call you Ronnie Jean...if that's okay?"

"Yes, Montricia, it is. That's all I've ever gone by. But I think you're right. It is a nice painting, but I don't think the morals of Sulphur Springs are in any danger. Mr. Goodpasture, what do you think?"

"I agree, ladies...you're absolutely right!" Hamilton was following his wife's instructions to a T.

Isadora was pleased with their response. She turned to take them to the center of the gym, where Shakila *Zulu Queen* awaited them. "Huey, bring the stepladder!"

As Isadora, Hamilton Goodpasture, the professor, and Ronnie Jean stepped away, Huey looked again at Sarah Louise's painting. Because it was the judges' first look at the painting, they had not noticed the two slight changes Huey had made per Claudette's request. Even Isadora hadn't noticed. But Huey knew there would be two people who would notice—immediately.

"I don't know how to prepare you for this painting. We weren't expecting this canvas…it caught us by surprise. All I want to say at this point is that it shows a little more flesh than the painting we've just seen…Huey!"

Huey got back upon the stepladder. He stretched again and pulled the pins out, letting the drape fall to the floor.

Hamilton Goodpasture had somehow ended up closest to the painting, and as the drape fell, he found himself face-to-face with the oversized bosom of the Zulu queen. He stepped back in surprise, almost tripping over Mrs. Biederman. Again, he was speechless, but this time, from shock.

Then Ronnie Jean and Montricia stepped back also—and Isadora and Huey joined them. The five of them stood quietly and stared.

Hamilton Goodpasture didn't know if it was polite to stare at the half-naked woman so long and turned his eyes toward the gym ceiling.

Ronnie Jean, still quiet, stepped up to the canvas to examine it. She touched the leather skirt as if to make sure her eyes were not fooling her. It wasn't an optical illusion. The skirt was actually sticking out from the canvas. The effect was spooky.

She then reached to touch the necklace but realized it might look like she was about to fondle Shakila's breasts and stopped, stepping back to the others. "I've never seen anyone paint like that…I mean, putting real stuff on the canvas…can you do that?"

Isadora assured Ronnie Jean that you could. "Yes, it's called *collage*, and it's technically a type of painting. I agree the effect is dramatic."

Then the professor spoke up. Her voice was full of emotion. "I am overwhelmed! This is the most beautiful painting I have ever seen…it captures the soul of my Africa! Don't you see it! This woman represents the tragic, tortured past of my people as she steps from history to face the world, brave and resolute—look at her eyes!"

It was then that Isadora noticed that something about the life-size painting had changed. Maybe it was because she was too close, but now she stepped farther back and studied it. The eyes! They were no longer cross-eyed! All of a sudden, the painting had gone from a naked African woman looking at her own very large chest to a noble queen looking out over the African savanna, her face confident and proud. What had happened?

The professor continued, "Yes, her eyes…see how she looks forward, unafraid of what lies ahead, ready to lead her people, the oppressed women of Africa—no, the oppressed women of the world—to freedom!"

Ronnie Jean clasped her hands together. "Oh, Montricia…I see it…I do! You're so right! And I must say, I love the way she used those real beads and feathers!"

It was over-the-top, to be sure—right up Ronnie Jean Gump's alley.

Isadora cast a suspicious eye toward Huey.

Hamilton Goodpasture didn't know what to do. He didn't care what the others said. All he saw was a naked woman, a naked woman that had one of the largest bosoms he had ever seen! Yet he remembered what his wife had said. "Ladies, I agree 100 percent, absolutely and emphatically—do I sense Best of Show?"

And it was agreed upon, right there.

Huey's trick with his paintbrush had changed the picture from an embarrassment to a masterpiece. Even the spotted leopard was no longer cross-eyed. It looked confidently across the African landscape. Of course, she was still brazenly naked. From the waist down, it was a very skimpy skirt; and from the waist up, she was really out of proportion—was it humanly possible to be that large and not lose your balance?

It didn't matter. The judges' decision had been made.

68

Outside the gym, over two hundred people had gathered. Huey had been correct in assuming that notoriety guaranteed a good crowd. Not that anyone said right out loud, "I've come to see that painting of naked people!" That was left to whispers. The vocal comments went from, "Nice spell of weather, isn't it?" to "Oh, I never miss our annual art shows. I come to all of them!"

At the folding table set up by the gym doors, Ted and Sherry were up and broadcasting. Tidbits of national news were followed by the weekly farm report and then live interviews with people in the crowd. Between them, Ted and Sherry knew just about everyone in town; so as they recognized people, they hollered to them to come over to the table, where a microphone was then shoved in their face.

Right now, they were talking to Ms. Ruby Stafford.

"So, Miss Ruby, how is Miss Bitty doing?"

Sherry explained Ted's question before Miss Ruby could answer. "In case some of our listeners don't know, Miss Bitty is Ruby's dog…a Chihuahua, I believe?"

"Oh yes, Sherry, a Chihuahua, but she thinks she's a human… sleeps in the bed with me. Has her own pillow!"

Ted laughed. "We have a Doberman at our house. If he got in bed with my wife and I, one of us would have to abandon ship!"

"You've had Miss Bitty...well, it seems like forever!"

"Yes, Sherry. In dog years, she's almost as old as I am—and don't you dare ask me how old I am, Ted Bumquist!"

"Now, Miss Ruby, I wasn't going to do that. My mama told me that there were three things you never ask a lady"—he paused for dramatic effect—"their age, their weight, and how much they paid for the dress they're wearing!"

Sherry and Miss Ruby laughed, as did the small group of people surrounding the table and listening to the live broadcast up close.

Elsewhere in the crowd, Hannah Bugleman and Annie Whittier were trying to make their way closer to the gym doors. Hannah was determined to be one of the first ones in. "Stay close, Annie. Just follow me!"

"But, Hannah—excuse me, sir—you're just pushing your way through—excuse me, madame—I can't—excuse me—I can't do that!"

Hannah stopped, turned, and pulled Annie the last two feet. "This is close enough anyway! Now, where is that nephew of mine? He was with me when we started!"

Herman had stopped to talk to someone he knew from school, a computer wiz like himself. The two had once designed their own video game of aliens and astronauts. But months of planning had gone down the drain when the other fellow had discovered girls and lost all interest in anything cold and mechanical.

Herman, we might add, was just now on the verge of discovering girls. His misadventures with Sarah Louise had awakened some part of his brain that had been dormant, and he had begun to notice the opposite sex. Right now, he was admiring, not his friend's wife but her sister as they stood outside the exhibition.

It was close to nine-thirty, and the crowd was growing with each passing minute. No one wanted to miss the big reveal.

Young and old were there, rich and poor, black and white, male and female—curiosity knows no limits.

Clarence Lipowitz sat in his wife's green Corvette in the parking lot. He didn't mingle with the masses if he could help it. He would wait till the doors opened and the riffraff had pushed their way in. He played with Avis's radio, trying to find a station he could enjoy. He had rather have been in his big SUV, but Avis needed it to take the kids to that birthday party.

Outside the town limits, a panel truck was barreling down the road toward Sulphur Springs. The town was nowhere near an interstate or even a four-lane highway. It was in one of those gray areas that got left behind when such thoroughfares were being laid out. That was one reason it had remained a small town. It wasn't close to anything big or important. It had always been a town that was just down the road a ways and always would be.

Because of its location, off the beaten track, pretty much all traffic came in one road and left by another. If you went in any other direction, you were doomed to miles and miles of twisting roads where you were as likely to encounter a tractor or a wayward cow as another car.

The panel truck—with "Channel WKAZ" in big letters on the side and "Live Broadcast Remote Cam" in smaller letters—was going as fast as it could. "Hurry, Pete...that last sign said we're still ten miles away from Sulphur Springs!"

"Sorry, Sissie...I've never been here before. I had no idea it was two-lane all the way!"

"All this for a lousy art show!" Sissie was angry. Shoved off to the boonies for an art show was, she felt, an insult. To make matters worse, a morning fire at a Nashville apartment complex had been given to someone else because she was already en route to this haven for hicks.

Sissie opened her purse and touched up her lipstick.

If only, she thought, *there was something more.* But what Sulphur Springs could offer besides a little controversy over a painting at an art show was beyond her. Sissie closed her eyes and begged the gods of airplay and time on screen, *Please, give me something I can work with, something big, please...*

But, as we all know, the gods of the media are as fickle as the viewing public.

69

Clara Dorphman checked her wristwatch for the third time in almost as many minutes. She was trying so hard not to forget. Nine-thirty! That was the time Michael had repeated to her. There is an old joke in which the doctor tells his aged patient that he has bad news and good news. He then proceeds to tell the old fellow that he has Alzheimer's; that's the bad news. The good news, he then adds, is that, "By the time you leave my office, you will have forgotten it!"

If only life were that simple.

Clara knew the moments of "where am I going?" and "what am I supposed to be doing right now?" People talked to her of things that she knew nothing about—but should.

But they hadn't taken her car keys away!

"As long as I can find my way home," she said to herself. She checked her watch again. Nine-thirty on the dot!

Clara picked up her purse and headed out the kitchen door to her old Chevy Malibu, the only one still running on the streets of Sulphur Springs, thanks to Hubcap Reynolds.

The Tenth Annual Spring Fling Art Show and Antique Auction to Benefit the Art Guild's Town-Beautification Project had been on her mind for weeks. She was in no real danger of forgetting it. If distracted, she might momentarily forget it, just as she had forgotten that her grandson had told her to be at the gym at nine-thirty, not to leave the house at nine-thirty!

She put the old car in reverse, backed up a few feet, and changing gears, she headed down the drive.

In town, people were at their usual Saturday morning routines. Men were getting spark plugs at the car-parts place for their lawn mowers. Kids of many shapes and sizes were at the park to play Little League. Teenagers were at the car wash. Women were at the grocery store or at the beauty shop. Throw in the added traffic headed to the old Sulphur Springs High School gym, and it made for a busy day and more than usual traffic.

Larry was directing some of that traffic at the old school's parking lot. When Cecil Womack and Stubby checked on him and his volunteer crew earlier, Larry had commented that the battery in his bullhorn was dead.

"No problem, Larry!" Cecil had said. "Stubby, grab Larry's bullhorn from his truck there, and let's you 'n' me head down to the department and get a new battery. We should have two or three of 'em down there."

"That's a big ten-four, Captain," Stubby had replied, and the two of them had headed off.

As they had driven out of the parking lot, they passed Clarence Lipowitz, still fooling with the radio dial in his wife's car. Not able to find anything other than country music, he turned the radio off and got out of the car to stretch his legs. He walked twice around the small vehicle then took up some more time by lowering the canvas top. The drive home would be nicer with the top down.

In the growing crowd, Coach Hatton was gritting his teeth over the painting by Sarah Louise. He had never taken a teacher before the school board on a morals charge. He kept thinking of that painting Sarah Louise had shown him and board chairman Simpson, the one of a naked woman walking down a flight of stairs—if only Sarah Louise's painting was a mess of unrecognizable shapes!

Back with Ted and Sherry, Brother Armstrong was entertaining the radio audience with one of his favorite pastoral jokes, the one about the eloquent preacher who extolled the virtues of the departed so well that the deceased man's wife got up to see if it was still her husband in the coffin.

Herman Bugleman had stopped talking to the young lady, the attractive sister of his friend's wife, to look for his Aunt Hannah. Woe to Herman if he was not where she wanted him to be. He scanned the crowd, first one way and then the next. His eyes caught the reflection of the sun off the shiny green chassis of Avis Lipowitz's Corvette.

Corvette!

Herman had a weakness for sports cars, which was stronger than his recently acquired weakness toward the opposite sex. He walked a few steps from the crowd to get a better look. The shiny chrome, the top down, the smooth lines of the hood, the—there was that man again!

Clarence saw Herman at about the same time Herman saw him. Their eyes met, and in one of those quirks of memory, it suddenly dawned on each of them who the other was!

"That fool at the art teacher's house the night I nearly got shot!" Clarence almost said it out loud.

"That fellow I leapfrogged over at Sarah Louise's house, the one she asked me about when Winslow got me back to her studio, the one who left his shirt and shoes!" Herman took a few more steps from the crowd so he could see better.

Clarence, not sure what to do or say if Herman came any closer, took the easy way out. He slid back into the driver's seat of the green sports car and turned the ignition. In a matter of seconds, he was out of the parking lot.

Herman put his hand to his chin with a perplexed look on his face. Then with a shrug of his shoulders, he turned back to the crowd. Now where was his Aunt Hannah?

As Herman turned his back to the parking lot, another car drove up and took the vacant space left by Clarence. Larry had tried to direct the car to the other end of the lot because this end was full, but Calpurnia and Lucy Pendergrass were not to be dissuaded. Lucy needed to unload her cookie jars, and Calpurnia had people she was to meet—all those reporters from out of town. So Larry waved her on, mumbling under his breath. A drunk driver he could handle, but two old ladies he was outmaneuvered by.

Clarence's vacant spot had appeared to Calpurnia as if by divine intervention.

"Look at the crowd, Calpurnia! Do you think we've got enough cookies?" Lucy almost screamed.

Calpurnia wasn't worried about cookies. She was stretching her neck, looking for the camera crews and reporters from Nashville, Bowling Green, and Louisville, all of whom were supposed to be there by now.

The missing WKAZ panel truck was still barreling down the only highway into Sulphur Springs. Although Sissie Lassiter and her driver-cameraman, Pete, were not aware of it, the reporters from Bowling Green and Hopkinsville were only minutes behind them. Like her, they had been delayed by one of the old two-lane highways leading into town.

All three of the news crews were about to turn into West Main Street, the town's main thoroughfare. Everything, it seemed ran into or turned off West Main Street. The intersection of West Main and Dorphman Avenue was the busiest in town, seconded by the intersection of West Main and the bypass where the super-Walmart had been built.

Clarence Lipowitz was approaching the same intersection. His perpetual state of halfway between "mad at the world" and "don't bother me" was leaning more toward "mad at the world." Having been spotted by Herman, Clarence was now trying to decide the best way to kill time till the tenth annual Spring Fling art show opened and the crowd died down. He decided to circle back toward La Vista Country Club and the 19th Hole Lounge, a few Bloody Marys might help him pass the time.

Coming from the other direction was Clara Dorphman. She had left home in plenty of time to be at the gym by now, but when she had driven out of the driveway, a patch of yellow jonquils at the gate had caught her eye. Jonquils—some people call them buttercups—were favorites of her late husband. Then it happened, one of those distractions that took over her thoughts. Clara had driven right past Dorphman Avenue and the way to the old school, and gone by the cemetery across town.

She hadn't gotten out of her car. She just drove into the cemetery entrance and made the loop that carried her by the Dorphman family plot. Yes, the soft yellow jonquils with the white centers, the ones she had planted the first anniversary of her husband's death, were there and in bloom. Pleased, Clara exited the cemetery and turned the old Malibu toward home.

70

"Park there, Winslow…by that red truck…I knew we should have left earlier. Look at this crowd!"

Winslow followed his wife's bidding.

"Hurry, you two!" Claudette clamored as she got out of the family car.

Winslow hauled himself out and politely opened the door to the backseat, where his daughter sat. But Sarah Louise sat still.

Claudette stuck her head into the car. "Sarah Louise…aren't you coming?"

"I don't think I can get out."

"What do you mean, Sarah Louise? Is something wrong? Are you sick?"

Sarah Louise looked at her mother. "Look at that crowd, Mother. I had no idea!"

Claudette slipped into the backseat and scooted over to her daughter. "Sarah Louise, I know this is difficult for you…but we both know your painting is fine…you have to go in there sooner or later…you can't just sit here…oh, it's all my fault!"

Claudette's eyes started to tear up.

"Oh, Mom…stop that…if you start crying, you'll have me crying too!"

"What are you two doing in there?"

"Shut up, Winslow...can't you see that Sarah Louise is nervous!" Claudette berated him. Then she slipped one hand into the clasped hands of her daughter. "It will all be over in a few minutes, dear...we can wait here if that's what you want...your father can go in and—"

"No...I guess I better go in myself. If I don't go, it will only make me look worse...as if I'm ashamed...which I'm not! Oh, Mom...I'm just afraid of what some people might say!"

"You know what I think? I think if someone doesn't like the way I do things, that's their problem! I'm not going to let it ruin my day!"

Claudette and Sarah Louise turned in their seats to see where this comment had come from. There—standing by the open door, next to Winslow—was Michael Dorphman, grinning from ear to ear. "Come on, ladies," he said. "Let's show those people some real class and march in there like Grant took Richmond!"

Across town, Clara Dorphman was smiling as she drove down West Main Street toward home. It had pleased her immensely to see the jonquils blooming on her husband's grave. It was a beautiful old cemetery. Over the years, families like hers, those with family plots, had planted redbud and dogwood trees and peonies and jonquils in corners and by the entrance. The ancient burial ground needed a little grooming, she thought. Maybe the Sulphur Springs Burial Association, which maintained the cemetery, would like to have some help in sprucing up the old place. Sprucing up the old cemetery!

Clara lingered on that thought for a block or two. "A good beautification project," she said half out loud. "Yes, that could be next year's annual project for the Art Guild."

The Art Guild! The art show!

Clara realized where she was supposed to be heading, and she realized it twenty feet from the intersection of Dorphman Avenue and West Main Street. Clara didn't slow down for the hard left turn she needed to make. All she did was grab the steering wheel with both hands and made the sharpest left-hand turn the Malibu had seen in its lifetime. Her tires squealed, and she gunned the engine to complete the turn. The rear end of the Malibu fishtailed, but the vehicle straightened and headed south. a NASCAR driver couldn't have done any better.

Of course, a NASCAR driver would have been in the turn lane and would have looked to see if the light was green, red, or that third color—yellow!

It's a good thing she didn't change lanes and get into the turn lane because sitting in that lane, waiting for the arrow, was Clarence Lipowitz. If Clara had gotten into the correct lane to turn, she would have ended up in his lap.

Clarence was leading a charmed life—at least for the ten seconds between Clara's tire-squealing turn and the screech of tires from the six-ton flatbed truck driven by Travis Morgan. The six-ton truck with "River Bend Poultry Ranch" written on the doors. The flatbed truck with five hundred chickens onboard. The flatbed truck coming from the opposite direction, trying to get through the intersection before the yellow light changed. The same flatbed truck that hit its brakes and swerved to keep from running over a little gray-haired lady in an old Chevy Malibu.

The six-ton truck swung to the right, inches from the front fender of the green Corvette.

Clarence's life, as dismal as it was, passed before his eyes.

Travis held on to his steering wheel with all the strength he could muster, his right foot on the brake so hard that he was almost standing on it. Sweat broke across his forehead as the cab of the truck obeyed, and he made the turn successfully!

The same can't be said for the five hundred crates of chickens.

The strain of the sudden turn caused a strap to break, and with that one strap broken, the others were quick to follow. *Pop, pop, pop*—the broken straps sounded like gunshots. The load on the back of the truck shifted.

Suddenly, live hundred chicken coops, each with a feathered leghorn hen, lurched forward—right on top of the little green Corvette.

Clarence threw his arms up to shield himself, but in a matter of seconds, he was entombed by the coops.

Travis Morgan brought his truck to a halt, and he leaped from the cab. He ran around the front of his truck and looked for the tiny green car he had seen only moments earlier. Other cars stopped, and other drivers jumped out.

The intersection was a mammoth pile of chicken coops, feathers, squawking birds, and busted containers—and somewhere at the bottom of the pile was a man in a little green automobile.

71

"What now?" Sissie Lassiter said, both frantically and in disgust. "Aren't we late enough already?"

"Looks like someone's just had an accident, ahead, at the next intersection!" Pete leaned forward in his seat to get a better view. His eyes grew big, and he turned to face the agitated newswoman. "I think I just saw a chicken go flying through the air!"

Sissie dropped her compact back into her purse and turned to face forward just as Pete spoke again, "Yep...a chicken...and there goes another one...no, two...make that three!"

Sissie's jaw took a serious turn. *That's great*, she thought, *an accident of some sort ahead, a traffic jam, a bunch of loose chickens...*

Then she heard it—music to her ears! A siren! "Do you hear that, Pete? A siren!"

Roaring down Dorphman Avenue, from the direction of the Civil Defense and Emergency Management Building, was the Sulphur Springs Rescue Squad and Emergency Response vehicle number one. Cecil Womack had hit every siren button the vehicle had.

He too had heard something that was music to his ears. A call had come in to the 911 station with the words *personal injuries, possible fatality, man trapped*. Any one of those terse phrases would have sent Cecil Womack into hyperdrive, but all three at the same accident, and he was in rescue heaven. This was what he was trained for—it was what he lived for: busted cars, broken windshields, the smell of gas and oil on the road, the screams of panic and pain, and the blood! Yes, the blood! Cecil would be disappointed if there was no blood.

Cecil hit the horn on the rescue vehicle, the one that sounded like a foghorn. What cars that hadn't pulled over after hearing the siren were literally blown off the road by this new noise.

Dotie Fisher and her husband, Moose, on their way to the art show, were in that line of traffic. When Cecil hit the foghorn, Dotie jumped two feet out of her seat. "Good Lord, Moose!" she screamed. "What was that?"

"It's just Cecil and Stubby…musta been an accident…bad one too, the way he's driving…up ahead…looks like maybe at the intersection of West Main and Dorphman."

And Cecil hit the foghorn again.

Sissie was all ears. She turned to her companion. "Set up the antenna, Pete, and hand me the microphone. I'm going down there to see what's happened. As soon as you get the antenna set up and you have transmission, grab the mobile cam and join me!"

"Yes, ma'am!" Pete answered, and he swung into action.

Sissie took one last look in the dashboard mirror, and she was out the door and running down the street, past stopped cars and people sticking their heads out their windows. Sirens meant injuries! Injuries meant news! It might be what she was hoping for, something big—or at least something she could make big! You never knew what opportunities lay around the next corner for the news reporter with a little imagination!

Cecil couldn't believe his eyes.

There in front of him was a ten-foot-high pile of busted chicken coops that stretched almost thirty feet wide. Feathers were everywhere, and the noise was deafening. Panicked chickens squawked and clucked in every direction.

He hopped out of the rescue vehicle, Stubby right behind him. They ran to a small group of people clustered around a man down on his knees. The man was Travis Morgan.

"Oh my God," Travis was wailing, "I've killed him!"

"Who?" shouted Cecil.

"The man in the green car!" Travis shouted back.

Cecil looked around. All he saw was chickens and more chickens and chicken coops and chicken feathers.

One of the people standing beside Travis spoke up, "He says there is a man in a green sports car under the pile of coops. I didn't see it. I ran up when I saw the wreck, but I was in the other lane. I couldn't see over here…but he swears there's a man trapped…"

Trapped?

That was what Cecil wanted to hear again. "Stubby, get the bullhorn! You fellows get this man to the side of the road, and then I'm gonna need some help. And, Stubby, call the station and tell them I need the Jaws of Life."

Sissie arrived at just that moment. She heard the lovely syllables, *Jaws of Life*. Her heart raced. She took in the scene in milliseconds, not to see what the damage was but to find the best camera angle.

In the next five minutes, Travis Morgan was moved to the side of the road, where several people tried to calm him. Cecil had the bullhorn and was barking orders, "Stay back, people! We have a possible fatality here! Stay back!"

People were catching loose chickens. Another rescue vehicle was on the way with the Jaws of Life. Sissie was going live with the arrival of Pete and the camera. And buried in the pile of debris— unable to move his face, hands, or feet—Clarence Lipowitz was pinned, covered with chicken feathers, waiting for the world to just go ahead and end.

72

They coordinated their movements the way a stage director does when the male lead enters the stage from one side and the female lead exits from the other side, doomed to not see each other till the last act.

In this case, precisely as Huey Pugh opened the double doors to the entrance of the gym of the old Sulphur Springs High School, Isadora Biederman was opening the back door of the old coaches' office to let Montricia Ifama, Ronnie Jean Gump, and Hamilton Goodpasture out.

Isadora had learned years earlier to get the judges out of the way before the public saw the ribbons. In small towns where vanity, pride, and family names clash with the nouveau riche, the social climber, and the talented wannabes, such a trivial thing as who got a ribbon and who didn't can stoke emotions to the breaking point. The breaking point was, unfortunately, the innocent judge's nose or neck or head or whatever body part was most convenient.

It was a well-known fact that the sheriff escorted the high school beauty-pageant judges out of town every year—not out of courtesy but out of fear for their lives!

Granted, the crowd this year was double in size due to the notoriety of Sarah Louise Upshaw's scandalous painting, *A Room*

Full of Naked Men, but the regular crowd was there to see who did and who did not get a ribbon.

Talent had nothing to do with it.

If one member of the Fourth District Home Demonstration Club got a ribbon for her patchwork quilt and no one from the Third District got so much as an honorable mention, bragging rights for a year were secure. Patchwork quilts, needlepoint pillows, cross-stitch samplers, and appliqué aprons were veritable battlegrounds where a woman's reputation lived or died with the color of her ribbon.

The fine arts, with its charcoal still lives, watercolor ocean scenes, and oil paintings of lighthouses were of little interest to most people. Except this year, of course, where everybody and their Aunt Lulu wanted to see the painting by the high school art teacher whose reputation was now on the line.

And there was the rub.

When the doors opened, the surge of people went straight to the center of the gym, where paintings, both acrylic and oil, were hung. As Huey had laid the folding panels and folding tables out, the way to the center was clear and unencumbered. Yet the painting that actually hung in the center of the gym, where all roads seemed to lead, was not a room full of men in their birthday suits but the life-size African queen *Shakila* by Lucy Pendergrass.

There she stood in all her ebony glory, with her skimpy leather skirt, feathers, and beads fooling the eye. Her statuesque physique—that is, her rather large bosom—was there for all to see. And see they did!

As soon as the flow of people began to glimpse the regal black beauty, they rushed to get a closer look. They stood there mesmerized, a respectable distance away, mind you. Indeed, she was impressive. Lucy's skills as a painter were limited, but she was adequate. It wasn't her skill in using the paintbrush that mattered here anyway. Her subject matter—the way the queen stood, the boldness of her bare chest—demanded the people's attention.

So *Shakila* stood there and, thanks a great deal to Huey's eye touch-up, captured the crowds of curious people and held them.

As if that wasn't enough, Lucy Pendergrass stood there and began handing out cookies!

No one even noticed Sarah Louise's painting. The rush of people had walked right past it. Only Coach Hatton had stopped to gaze. He had on his reading glasses to make sure he could read the little index card taped beside each picture, the card that told the medium, the artist, and the title of the work of art. Coach had only lingered a moment at *A Room Full of Naked Men* because someone had grabbed him by the elbow and said, "Hey, Coach, you gotta see this...Lucy Pendergrass got Best of Show with a naked lady!"

For all his bravado about marching in like Grant took Richmond, when Michael Dorphman escorted Claudette and Sarah Louise into the gym, no one took notice. The mass of people had already entered by the time the three of them and Winslow had gotten from the parking lot to the gym doors.

Even Huey, who was catching Malvenna up to date on things, didn't see them. Malvenna had been forced to wait outside like the others, and when the doors opened, she had sought out Huey first. Now Huey was spilling his guts to her; and Malvenna, between pops of her ever-present gum, was saying, "Huey...you didn't!"

But Huey did, and he was proud of it.

The only other person at the entrance was Calpurnia Pendergrass, who was anxiously waiting for the media to arrive.

Michael and his small entourage, arm in arm, headed into the depths of the gym. They were following the crowd, believing it led to Sarah Louise's painting. What else could all the commotion be about? It came as a surprise when they walked past Sarah Louise's painting, and Winslow hollered, "Wait up, you guys! Stop!"

Claudette turned to see what her husband needed, forcing Michael and Sarah Louise to stop as well.

"It's here! It's right here, Lou! Your painting!"

And there it hung. No one, no one except them, was paying any attention to it.

Michael and Sarah Louise looked at each other in surprise.

Claudette looked to her daughter and then to Winslow. Her face was one of shock. "What are all those people looking at? The people there...there in the center of the gym...what's going on? I don't understand!"

"I don't know what those people are looking at, but I know Sarah Louise's painting when I see it, and this is it!" Winslow retorted.

Claudette, still confused, looked from her daughter's painting to the middle of the gym, where people were milling about and gawking. "Winslow...go down there and see what's going on... right now! You two"—she directed her attention to the young couple, still arm in arm—"you two stand right here...right in front of this painting...I'm going to find Hannah and Annie... something odd is going on!"

Claudette had an ulterior motive for having her daughter and Michael stand in front of the painting. It had to do with the two subtle changes she had bribed Huey into doing.

Winslow ambled toward the crowd of people, and Claudette pretended to be looking for Hannah and Annie.

Suddenly conscious that he still had Sarah Louise's arm in his arm, Michael carefully slid his arm free; and per Claudette's instructions, he went and stood in front of *A Room Full of Naked Men.*

Sarah Louise, both relieved to see no one glaring at her painting and a little aggravated that no one was even looking at it, moved to stand beside him. She didn't need to see the painting again; she had seen it a thousand times. Her eyes darted here and there over the painting. She didn't see anything she hadn't already seen, and she turned her face to the direction her father had taken.

She felt a tap on her shoulder.

"When did you do that?" It was Michael's voice.

She faced him. "Do what?"

"My eyes...your eyes."

Sarah Louise stared at Michael's face. It had taken a funny glow, and a silly smile formed across his lips. Before she could say anything, he turned to face the painting again. "I like it," he said.

Sarah Louise faced her painting. *What's he talking about?* she asked herself. She followed his stare. Then she saw it.

Her eyes were no longer staring into the open book in her hands, the book with *Much Ado About Nothing* on the spine. They had somehow moved to the side, as if she were looking out of the corners of her eyes—looking at the man seated next to her on the sofa. But just as mysteriously, the eyes of the man seated beside her, the figure Michael had posed for, had gone from looking absently straight ahead to looking out of the corners of his eyes at her!

She was speechless. How did that happen?

Sarah Louise turned to face Michael and to say something to the effect of, *I didn't do that, and I don't know how that happened.* But before she could get the words out of her mouth, she felt his lips on hers, and she was—well, speechless again!

The press of lips was followed by an arm around her waist as Michael Dorphman pulled her closer, and Sarah Louise realized she was happy to be there, in his arms, and—dare she say it— in love.

Ten feet away, her head poked from around the corner of a folding screen of pen and ink drawings, Claudette smiled, as all scheming mothers do when things go their way.

73

Alma Peterman changed the channel on her TV. There was so little worth watching these days. Her time spent in front of the television went from the game show channel to Fox News. One channel was safe from sex and drugs and violence; the other constantly reminded her that the world was going somewhere in a handbasket.

With *The Price Is Right* rerun over, Alma decided to check a local channel for an update in the weather. She clicked the remote.

"In this battle between life and death, we remind you that this is Sissie Lassiter, station WKAZ, coming to you live from Sulphur Springs..."

Alma couldn't believe her ears! She hit the volume button on the remote and kicked it up ten notches. The walls of the kitchen began to vibrate, but she heard it again.

"In the debris from this potentially tragic accident on the main intersection of Sulphur Springs, we have an individual trapped...yes, trapped beneath tons of twisted metal cages is a helpless victim...and we are here to witness his rescue or his..."

Alma squinted her eyes. She recognized the intersection: West Main and Dorphman. She could see Danny's Donut Den in the background, and standing there with a bullhorn was

Cecil Womack. She knew him. He was a third cousin to her late husband, and he was right there on her TV!

Cecil shouted through the bullhorn, "Hacksaws, we need hacksaws! You two, bring the Jaws of Life over here—where's that ambulance? Stand back, people, stand back!"

Rescue efforts were hampered by the way the chicken coops had been loaded onto the flatbed truck. They weren't individually stacked; rather, they hooked together in rows of five. It made it easier to load and unload when you were doing large quantities like five hundred. Cecil and his crew of emergency personnel couldn't just start grabbing and tossing coops of wild-eyed chickens to the side. It would take two people to move each bulky section; and now, because of the wreck, most of them were snagged and locked onto other sections. If you tried to move one, you had to pull it free from the one next to it.

Blowtorches had crossed Cecil's mind, but it would mean a lot of fried chicken before it was over, and he didn't want the SPCA to be on his neck. And to be honest, he didn't know for sure that there was a person trapped beneath the pile of busted coops. Only a few people, the hysterical Travis Morgan being the main one, had claimed to see a man in a green sports car there. *Poor fellow*, Cecil thought. *If you are there, it must be a living hell.*

It was.

Clarence Lipowitz was trapped. He could do little more than breathe, and each breath sucked in chicken feathers. He kept spitting the loose feathers out with one breath and breathing them back in with the next.

The same configuration of coops that was delaying his rescue was also the same configuration that had saved his life. By being in sections, the mass of coops had formed an arch over him that, while keeping him pinned, kept the weight of the five hundred chickens off him. Not that he appreciated his predicament.

Clarence had used every expletive he knew and then had made up several. Clarence knew how to swear in three languages and four religions, and if foul language—no pun intended—could have rescued him, he would have been out of there thirty minutes ago!

Sissie Lassiter held her microphone firmly in hand and alternately commented on the "desperate" situation and interviewed innocent bystanders. She played fast and loose with the facts, telling viewers that "at least" one man was trapped beneath the debris but there "could be others."

"Minutes and seconds counted," she reminded her listening audience, "so stay tuned."

When WKAZ took a commercial break, she quizzed her contacts at the station about hooking up with a national news channel, like they do in California with live car chases.

The other two news crews, the ones from Bowling Green and Hopkinsville, were caught in the traffic jam from the wreck. Helpless to move forward or backward, until they got wise to the situation, they offered her no competition.

The stage belonged to Sissie.

"They are removing the first of the chicken coops from the pile on top there...Pete, do a close-up for our viewers. The hacksaws have arrived. Each desperate second counts now...the pain and agony the trapped victim...or victims...must be feeling now, words can't express...but now we switch back to our main station for this important commercial break. I'm Sissie Lassiter, WKAZ, and I'll be here when we return to this live broadcast."

The eyes of Sulphur Springs were glued to their TV sets. As soon as WKAZ had interrupted its regular Saturday morning cartoon schedule to feature the scene of the wreck and Sissie Lassiter, phone lines across town had lit up. "Quick, turn on your TV and click on WKAZ—we're on the news!" was relayed from house to house.

Down at Pearl's Beauty Shoppe, the beat-up old portable TV was the center of attention. Pearl and Charlene both stood there, blow-dryers in midair, their eyes glued to the screen. Two women, their hair in curlers, were equally enthralled.

At Hubcap's place, Duffy's cell phone had alerted him to the situation, and the small TV in Hubcap's office was broadcasting to a circle of men in overalls and blue jeans.

Bonnie Crookshank, her purse still by her side, was only minutes away from the door when her daughter, Elizabeth, called and yelled into the receiver, "Turn to WKAZ, Mama. You won't believe what's happening!"

Afraid another global terrorist attack had leveled a major American city, Bonnie turned to the channel as instructed. She was relieved it was only a car wreck, but it looked like she wouldn't be going to the art show anytime soon. From the TV, she could see the traffic backed up in four directions.

One of those people backed up was Lucinda Hardin-Powell. She was boxed in by the cars ahead and behind her, so she had to just sit there. She was impatient at the delay and at the fact she couldn't be at the art show to see for herself Sarah Louise's painting. The longer she sat, the more she fumed!

At the super-Walmart, just off the bypass, the row of TVs on sale—at least fifty of them lined up and turned on—had been changed to WKAZ. Every shopper and most of the sales staff were standing in the electronics section, three and four deep, watching the live broadcast.

Across town, at the birthday party, Avis and the other moms were watching on a big screen and sipping coffee while the children in the next room overdosed on sugar from birthday cake and punch. The women chatted casually, none of them aware that Avis's husband was the subject of the rescue.

Back at the Sulphur Springs gym, cell phones had begun to alert people of the unfolding drama, and people were leaving to rush home and turn on their TV sets. The traffic jam was no obstacle to most of them because all residents knew at least ten different ways to get from here to their homes.

Sarah Louise was oblivious to what was happening. People were passing by her right and left, but she was sitting calmly on the first row of the bleachers at the rear of the old gym. She was quietly resting there, softly humming to herself, "We've Only Just Begun." She had heard it recently at a wedding, and although it was an oldie, it was a goodie. Funny it should come to mind now.

Michael had left to return to work. We would be remiss if we neglected to say he gave Sarah Louise a parting kiss as he reminded her that she and her parents were to be his guests for supper, before he took them and his grandmother to that evening's antique auction, the second part of the weekend's Spring Fling.

Winslow and Claudette had made the rounds of the art show. Winslow had plotted their tour so that they kept passing Lucy Pendergrass and her cookies. He had tried four different kinds now.

People had seen Sarah Louise's painting for sure. After the shock of seeing the half-naked Shakila, there was nothing in Sarah Louise's canvas to raise a single eyebrow. The talk of the day would be Lucy's portrait of the African queen, although the winning cross-stitch had raised the ire of several ladies who were convinced the blue-ribbon-winning piece was made in China, not by Gertrude Stillman from the Fifth District. Those cheap imports were everywhere nowadays, and it would be like Gertrude to try and pass it off as her own.

At the gym entrance, Isadora Biederman posed for photos with Huey, Malvenna, and Clara Dorphman. Poor Clara. She had no idea she had caused the wreck down at West Main. She was just happy to be there. No one commented on her late arrival. Louise Smith, the project chairman, took the photos using her digital camera because the reporter from the *Sulphur Springs Sentinel* had failed to appear.

Of course, that reporter was Clarence; and right now, Clarence was indisposed.

Nationwide, it had been a slow Saturday morning. Congress was not in session, and the president was at Camp David, so nothing to report on there. There were no big sporting events going on. Even terrorists, it seemed, had taken the weekend off. And to top it off, Mother Nature had kept herself quiet. Volcanoes, earthquakes, hurricanes, and tornadoes—nothing happening, not even a good tidal wave to report.

So it was the dull day that played into Sissie Lassiter's and Cecil Womack's hands.

The station manager back in Nashville called FOX. They were hesitant at first, but there was something quirky about a person buried alive by chickens that was strangely appealing; and when nothing else came in on the wire services, they relented. The eyes at CNN, as soon as their monitors caught FOX with the story, jumped in as well. CNBC was next, and on down the line of 24-7 news channels. For a few minutes, the nation watched the rescue unfold in Sulphur Springs—through the eyes and voice of Sissie Lassiter.

"At least a hundred chicken coops have been removed from the pile and still no sign of life as rescuers frantically try to uncover the trapped man ... and, ladies and gentlemen, we can only pray that the man's family was not in the vehicle with him..." Sissie paused and looked contemplative as if she were viewing a row of bodies laid out on the road beside the carnage of chickens and busted coops. Then another loose chicken flew past her head, and she revived. "Let's see if we can get a comment from Civil Defense and Rescue Squad director Cecil Womack as he directs his team of selfless volunteers. Mr. Womack, may we speak to you?"

Cecil stepped from his perch atop two busted chicken coops and leaned over to Sissie's microphone. If he appeared distracted and anxious to return to the rescue, it was good acting on his part because the two of them had arranged for this little interview during the last commercial break. Cecil relished the camera as much as Sissie!

"Mr. Womack, if we may for just a moment speak to you, for the benefit of our viewers, can you tell us what you know about the individual trapped beneath this mass of twisted metal and frenzied chickens?"

"Ms. Lassiter, we have witnesses that saw the accident. The driver of the truck, that's the truck with all of them chickens onboard, he swerved to keep from hitting a little old lady in a Chevy Malibu, and when he did, his load shifted and landed on a vehicle stopped at the light waiting to turn."

"And what can you tell us about that vehicle?"

"All we know for sure is that the witnesses say a man was driving."

"They saw the man clearly?"

"Oh yes, Ms. Lassiter…it was a convertible, so they got a good look. It was a little green convertible…"

Avis Lipowitz stood up from her seat on the couch and screamed, "Clarence! That's my husband!"

At Dorphman's Hardware and Appliance, Michael Dorphman sat down in shock. The other employees looked from the TV in the For Sale rack to their boss and knew why he was placing his hands beside his head. There was only one Chevy Malibu in town, and they all knew who the driver was.

74

How many times can a person replay an imagined event in their minds? Brides picture a future wedding over and over in their heads, each time the flowers more beautiful and the groom a tad handsomer. Candidates for office visualize themselves making great speeches—acceptance speeches, that is—and the crowds get larger and more enthusiastic. Athletes see the winning goal, home run, basket, or finish line; beauty queens, the crown; or gardeners, the winning tomato or monster pumpkin.

So it was that Clarence Lipowitz visualized his funeral. It was at least the tenth time he had rehearsed it in his head, and it was a somber affair, somber because—he hated to admit it—the only person crying at his grave was Avis. And he knew too well that the time would come when she realized she was better off without him.

Clarence would have wept at the thought, but he had to spit another chicken feather out of his mouth.

Not that the five hundred chickens in their coops were in any better mood. They clucked and squawked at the slightest provocation. As each coop was pulled loose from the top of the pile, it had a ripple effect on the remaining chickens, and they flapped wings and squawked in response. Waves and waves of frenzied clucking surrounded Clarence. He halfway wished he was dead just to have some peace and quiet.

Across town, Avis was in anguish. The other mothers were busy keeping the kids entertained and away from the TV while trying to keep Avis from going into hysterics.

In her head, poor Avis played and replayed a scene where her husband's dead body was pulled from the wreckage.

Other people were visiting their brains.

Michael Dorphman, his head still in his hands, was replaying the trial—the reckless driving and accidental homicide trial of his ninety-year-old grandmother. Would his brawl at the kickoff party make it look like a conspiracy to kill Clarence?

But on a lighter note, we have Sissie Lassiter and Cecil Womack. While Cecil pictured himself with the local Rotary Club's Man of the Year certificate and its accompanying faux bronze medallion, Sissie was picturing herself sitting at the anchor desk for NBC's nightly national newscast!

But reality brings us all back to earth sooner or later.

Stubby stood carefully on the pile of chicken coops, handing one at a time to the volunteer rescue-squad members, as well as a slew of men and boys who pulled off the street to help in the crisis. Besides the confusion of the handing off of the damaged coops and their restacking on the sidewalk, there were loose chickens everywhere. Boys were running up and down the rows of stopped cars, trying to catch the traumatized birds.

People caught in the traffic jam had left their cars to get a close-up look for themselves. In fact, Danny's Donut Den had never seen such good business. Cam Tang was pulling everything he had out of the cooler and into the grease!

Back at the gym of the old Sulphur Springs high school, the crowd had all but disappeared. A few people continued to arrive and view the exhibits, but 90 percent of the population of Sulphur Springs was either at the scene of the accident or in front of their TVs.

Even Ted and Sherry were tapped into the audio feed from WKAZ so that the two of them could sit and listen to someone else do the talking. That left them free to visit with Herman Bugleman. His aunt and Annie had left the art show to rush home and see the unfolding event on TV, leaving him behind. Herman had an interest in anything electronic, so he was quizzing them about their equipment. He also took time to tell Sherry that the lure of a career as a professional model and possible media star was to be short-lived as he found it too hectic for him.

Inside the doors of the gym, some folding chairs had been pulled up, and several people sat there while Huey kept them up to date, via his cell phone and its Internet capabilities, on the rescue efforts a few blocks away. His signal was spotty, so he had to hold the phone at arm's length and to his right at a forty-five-degree angle. He looked like a general about to lead his men into battle.

Malvenna was explaining to Sarah Louise the color scheme she had finally chosen for her living room. It had fuchsia throw pillows so the topic was appropriate.

"When I saw your painting, Sarah Louise, I said to myself...I said, 'Malvenna, that's just the shade of fuchsia you need for your throw pillows!'"

"It was my third attempt at that color, Malvenna...it seems like so long ago now. I had picked up a pot of flowers at the flower shop, and they were that shade...but it wasn't an easy color to mix...do you remember that night, Mom...the night I painted those fuchsia flowers?"

Claudette turned from Isadora. The two had been discussing caterers. She looked at her daughter. It was a changed Sarah Louise from the one she had been living with the past two weeks. That worried look was gone. The new Sarah Louise looked at peace; she even had a glow about her face. There was more. Sarah Louise had taken to calling Claudette *mom* again. But most interesting, possibly disturbing, Claudette thought—Sarah Louise was sounding more and more like her.

"What did you say, Sarah Louise?"

"The flowers...the fuchsia flowers...remember the night I painted them, and you came by the studio about something...the same night the cat got loose..."

"Commercial break!" Huey hollered. He lowered his arm to let it rest.

"Where's Calpurnia?" Isadora asked, noticing that the Chamber of Commerce director had left her chair.

"I think she gave up on her newspeople...but Sulphur Springs is in the news, so she's not too disappointed," Winslow offered.

"She's gone back to speak to Lucy, I imagine. Lucy has certainly had a big day," Louise Smith commented.

"I think I'll follow. I need to get Lucy's recipe for those chocolate peanutbutter cookies! They are fantastic." Winslow got up and started in that direction.

Claudette hollered after him, "You should know, Winslow... you've had at least four!"

The group laughed, even Clara Dorphman, who sat in the center of the little group. She so enjoyed being in the conversation, although she had a feeling someone was not telling her something. It was that blank look she was occasionally getting from them.

"I do hope they rescue that poor man under all of those chickens. Do we know what caused that accident and who that man is?"

Huey rolled his eyes.

He knew, as did the others, from the conversation Sissie and Cecil had broadcast across the nation, across every TV in Sulphur Springs, across the loud speakers in front of Ted and Sherry, and across the tiny screen in Huey's hand—"he swerved to keep from hitting a little old lady in a Chevy Malibu and..."

Only Clara hadn't heard it. She had been walking up and down the aisles of the art show when that tidbit of information was dropped. The group had each one individually decided not to mention the cause of the accident, so Clara was spared, as least for the moment, the embarrassment of knowing.

"Check your phone again, Huey," Louise urged, not wanting to miss anything.

Huey stuck his arm out and up over his head. He squinted at the screen. "I think they've got to him!" Huey hollered. He turned the volume up on his cell phone.

The voice of Sissie Lassiter hit their ears.

"Cecil Womack has just motioned to two of his rescue-squad members to join him on the top of the pile—Pete, use your zoom—they are moving a section of coops that are crucial...I see him...a man's head is visible...it appears to be moving...yes...I see the man's face—he is...he is spitting feathers from his mouth ...he's alive!"

In the living room of the birthday party, Avis Lipowitz gave a huge sigh of relief and closed her eyes. Her dear Clarence was alive. The other women in the room looked to one another in a mixture of relief and dismay. Clarence was alive—was that good news or bad?

Michael Dorphman sat down and let out his breath as well. At least his grandmother wouldn't be brought up on murder charges! He grabbed his cell phone to call his uncles. They would need to meet and decide who would be the one to take their mother's car keys away from her. But he paused. Then he decided to call Sarah Louise first.

When her cell phone rang, Sarah Louise hardly noticed. There was so much commotion around Huey and his own phone. She reached into her purse and looked to see who was calling. She and Michael had only exchanged cell phone numbers yesterday.

Knowing Huey's trouble with his signal, she stepped outside the gym and walked over to the edge of the parking lot. "Michael?"

"Sarah Louise! Do you know about the big wreck in town, at West Main and Dorphman?"

"Yes, it's all that everyone here has been talking about."

"Do you know who was trapped?"

"We were all sitting here guessing that it was Clarence Lipowitz. I wouldn't know him if I saw him, but isn't he the one you punched at the kickoff party?"

"That's the one...and ...did you hear who caused the wreck?"

"Your grandmother, I'm afraid!"

"Yes, my grandmother! Have you seen her? Is she there?"

"Yes, Michael...she's here, and she's fine. No one's told her that she caused the accident...she's sitting here with a bunch of us trying to keep up with what's happening by listening to Huey's cell phone...this Clarence fellow...is he going to be all right?"

"It looks like it. I'm watching a TV right now, and they're pulling him from the wreck...he looks a little addled, but he doesn't appear to be hurt. He's got a lot of chicken feathers and chicken poop on him...couldn't have happened to a more deserving guy!"

"Oh, Michael!"

"Would you do me a favor, Sarah Louise? Would you keep Gramma there till I can come over and get her...I'll be there as quick as I can!"

"Sure, Michael!"

Michael paused for a moment. "Are you okay?"

"Me?"

"Yes. Are you okay with the art show and how it turned out? I know you said you were when I left you earlier...but are you... really, I mean? You weren't just saying that?"

"No...I am really...thanks for asking...I am...and I owe some of that to you!"

"Me?"

"You're being here for me this morning...all you've done for me the last week...I don't know how to thank you..."

"I bet I can think of a way. How about having supper together not just tonight...but tomorrow night...and the next night...and the next night..."

75

"The Eleventh Annual Spring Fling Art Show and Antique Auction to Benefit the Art Guild's Town-Beautification Project will be held the second weekend of April this year, Art Guild vice president Huey Eugene Pugh has announced."

"This year's beautification project will be the old cemetery on Greenbrier Pike."

"That is the oldest cemetery in the county...am I correct, Sherry?"

"That's right, Ted, and Art Guild members hope to raise enough money to restore the old rock wall at the entrance to the cemetery and repair some of the older monuments and tombstones."

"We all recall the attention that last year's art show received. I wonder if this year's show will—"

Claudette reached across her kitchen sink and turned off the shiny red radio that sat there on a shelf above the faucets. She didn't need to be reminded of last year's art show. Then again, all things considered, it hadn't been so bad. Claudette turned around and surveyed her kitchen, her new kitchen!

She had talked Winslow, after forty years of tangerine, into redoing their kitchen. This time, the color scheme was red and white. It was quite attractive, if she did say so herself. Winslow had done all the painting and papering. The trim was all white, and the wallpaper above her new chair rail had lovely red flowers to match the painting of red geraniums done by her daughter Sarah Louise.

Claudette was especially proud of her new cabinets, the handiwork of her new son-in-law, Michael.

Yes, she mused, *it had turned out rather well.*

Her revelry of thought was broken by a loud voice. "Claudette!"

"Yes?"

"Claudette…are you going to bring that pot of tea, or will one of us have to come in there and get it ourselves?"

"Be right there, Hannah!"

Claudette grabbed the pot of tea from her lovely red stovetop and rushed into the dining room where the girls waited—the girls being Hannah, Bonnie, and Annie.

"I went ahead and dealt the cards, Claudette, while you were in the kitchen. I hope you trust us to not have looked at your hand!"

"Of course, she trusts us, Annie! She lets us have tea with her grandmother's bone china, and these cups are irreplaceable! I know! My nephew, Herman, was telling me just yesterday what some of my old cups and saucers are worth, and it's shocking! Your bid, Bonnie!"

"Speaking of Herman…are he and that girl, the one he met at last year's Spring Fling, are they still seeing each other?" Annie asked.

"I don't want to talk about it, Annie!"

Annie's face looked surprised at Hannah's retort.

Bonnie explained, "Hannah's convinced the girl is a gold digger, Annie, that she just wants to marry Herman for his money."

"Money! Herman doesn't have any money! She wants to marry him for *my* money! She knows I'm leaving everything to him!"

The three women stared at Hannah.

"But I've got a surprise in store for them!" Hannah continued. "I'm going to live to be a hundred! They may get everything I have—but they'll have to wait for it!"

The three other women couldn't keep from laughing.

"Oh, Hannah…you might be surprised…I sure have enjoyed having a new member in our family…and my kitchen is just one example… Michael is so handy…you should see how he and Sarah Louise are decorating the nursery."

"Oh, tell us, Claudette!" Bonnie blurted out, so excited she laid her cards down.

"Pick your cards back up, Bonnie! It's your bid! We can hear about the nursery later!" Hannah barked.

"It'll just take a second, Hannah. They picked the bedroom next to theirs…it's the one Michael grew up in…and Sarah Louise has picked the sweetest wallpaper…blue and pink stripes…," Claudette said.

"Isn't that nice!" Bonnie gushed. "Blue for the boy and pink for the girl! Twins—how exciting! Have they picked names yet?"

"Sarah Louise says they have narrowed the list down to four names for the boy and seven for the girl…but they won't tell me any of them…she just says, 'Mom, you'll have to wait till they're born to find out…just like everybody else!'"

Annie spoke up, "I bet they name the girl *Clara*. Like his grandmother! How's she doing?"

"How does anyone do in a nursing home, Annie!" Hannah offered up, her voice still showing aggravation from the delay in the game.

"Sarah Louise says she's happy at Monthaven…Michael goes to see her every day…and Ester Mae goes by twice a week to sit with her…"

"You'll never get me in Monthaven, Claudette!"

"Oh, Hannah, it's nice there," Bonnie interrupted. "My Dewey's aunt lived there the last three years of her life…besides, it's better than jail!"

They all agreed with Bonnie by shaking their heads. Clara Dorphman had avoided jail by agreeing to give up her car keys. It was the family's decision to move her to Monthaven.

They returned to the card game. Later, over dessert, they would discuss Clara and babies and Herman and whoever else came to mind. The real allure of the weekly card games was to catch up on who knew what about who and when it happened.

There were others whose lives had been changed by the Tenth Annual Spring Fling Art Show and Antique Auction to Benefit the Art Guild's Town-Beautification Project.

Isadora Biederman was now the president of the Art Guild. That left a vacancy, and after much discussion, it had fallen to Huey Eugene Pugh.

And what about Lucinda Hardin-Powell? She had dropped out of the Art Guild. Her new part-time job as society-page editor for the *Sulphur Springs Sentinel* kept her too busy. It was a job she could sink her teeth into, and she did just that. She and Avis had bonded over the course of last year's Spring Fling. Avis was so bendable to Lucinda's suggestions that Lucinda almost enjoyed their time together.

And Clarence?

We can't say that Clarence found Jesus under the five hundred chicken coops that kept him pinned for over an hour, but we can say that he was a changed man. Five hundred frenzied feathered fowl had their effect, besides the way he now jumped whenever he heard the squeal of tires. Clarence, having come so close to losing his life, had a new appreciation for it. He was nicer to Avis, even if it was just to make sure she would actually miss him should he not survive another such calamity. He had also begun to appreciate his kids.

He took Sophia to her gymnastics class and Arnold to the golf course with him. The boy was showing promise. With his son along, Clarence couldn't stop at the 19th Hole Lounge as often, but he found out he didn't really miss it. Besides, he and his new friend BJ could down a few beers together when the two couples visited each other, which had become a weekly ritual.

Oh, Clarence was still Clarence…but he was an easier Clarence to be around.

Cecil Womack got his Rotary Club's Man of the Year certificate, and he had been asked by several people to run for mayor in the next election. But Cecil's goals didn't run that high. He would never tire of the siren and the sight of broken windshields and crushed bumpers.

The wreck at the corner of West Main and Dorphman had been good to Sissie Lassiter as well. She didn't make it to the national news, but she was now an anchor on the six-o'clock news—in Duluth, Minnesota! The cold of Minnesota was, to her, just a temporary stopping-off place. She still had her red dress and her tube of lipstick, and the goal of national prime time still beckoned.

And then there was Lucy Pendergrass!

The attention of the public at last year's art show had been overwhelming. So much so that she gave up painting. She could never paint another masterpiece like that, she had told her sister—and anyone else in hearing. The African queen was now hanging in the office of Montricia Ifama at the state university an hour down the road, where it was still an attention-getter. That was good news to everyone in Sulphur Springs, who had been afraid Lucy would give the painting to one of them.

Lucy Pendergrass wasn't sitting home doing nothing, mind you. Her interests now ran to sculpture, and she had blocks of plaster and marble sitting in her backyard, where every day she took mallet and chisel in hand. Her current project was a large—well, we'll let your imagination fill that in for you.

The town of Sulphur Springs went on about its daily routine. A stop at Danny's Donut Den was still a morning ritual for most folks. Ruby Stafford, like the other regulars, still got her hair done at Pearl's Beauty Shoppe—with two *p*'s. Men still hung out at Hubcap's place. Ronnie Junior still patrolled the streets, with the occasional help of Alma Peterman, who still kept up her neighborhood watch. Coach Hatton continued to hand his paperwork over to the school secretary, keeping his desk spotless. And Dotie Fisher was baking desserts with her home-ec class.

And in the old Dorphman home, Sarah Louise and Michael were decorating and remodeling and buying baby furniture, and—need we say it?—they were happy. Spring was just around the corner. Life was good in Sulphur Springs.

CPSIA information can be obtained
at www.ICGtesting.com
Printed in the USA
FFOW01n0944190916
27725FF